## SWEET TEMPTATION

"Look at me, Katie. Don't you feel what happens when we get near each other? Doesn't it drive you to distraction as it does me? Something as rare and precious as this can't be ignored. I've never felt this way before."

"Oh, Zack, how can I believe that?" she cried. Her heart was racing wildly, hammering beneath her ribs. She backed away from him, retreating from the fearsome excitement already blossoming inside her. He stood before her, dark, male, dangerous, and she could only stare in mesmerized fascination.

"No more running, Kate. Now is the moment of truth." He pulled her hard against him and captured her lips in a kiss that, for all its gentleness, was relentless and demanding. She struggled against his imprisoning arms, against the insidious current of desire that was snaking its way so temptingly through her body. If she let down her resistance, she was lost.

She gripped his shoulders, giving a small cry deep in her throat, as she was pierced by a stabbing shock of need. She couldn't pinpoint the moment when she surrendered, but she found herself clinging to him, demanding that his mouth return again and again to hers . . .

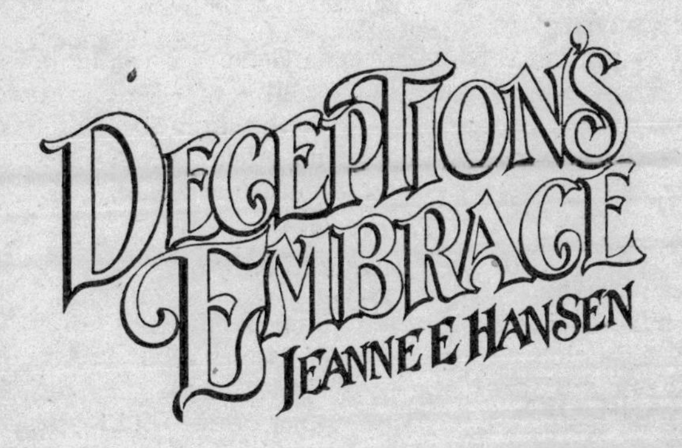

**ZEBRA BOOKS**
**KENSINGTON PUBLISHING CORP.**

*To my family*
*for their love and support.*
*Thanks.*

ZEBRA BOOKS

are published by

Kensington Publishing Corp.
475 Park Avenue South
New York, NY 10016



First printing: July, 1989

Printed in the United States of America

# Chapter 1

She had no time to lose. Into her one valise Katrina Montgomery stuffed as many of her belongings as she could, and then only very basic and sturdy garments. She gave the row of elegant gowns hanging in her dressing room no mind at all as she hastily donned a plain gray skirt and simple pink blouse. She was leaving everything behind. Everything except what was in the valise and in her memory. She wanted nothing of Sam Bennett's. Not now.

The grandfather clock in the downstairs hall chimed in soft clear tones three times. Taking one last look at what had always been her room, she draped her cape around her shoulders, picked up her case, and tiptoed into the dark corridor. By morning she hoped to be far enough ahead of them to escape.

Escape. How good that sounded, but it would not be an easy task. To give herself every advantage, she had one more stop to make. Taking her time and keeping against the wall where the old stairs wouldn't creak and groan so much in the silence of the night, she crept down to the library. Behind the portrait of her beautiful stepsister Corinne was a wall safe, one she knew how to open, though she'd kept that knowledge to herself.

Inside the safe was a black lacquered box, inlaid with mother-of-pearl, and inside that were her mother's jewels. Katrina tamped down the thought that she was stealing. Maybe she was, technically, but her mother had always intended for her to have the jewelry when she died. That her stepfather, Sam Bennett, had taken it for himself and his daughter when no written will existed stating her mother's wishes, didn't change that fact.

And Katrina needed the jewels. She also needed money. She lifted a stack of bills from the safe and tucked it, with the jewelry box, into a secret compartment in the bottom of her valise. She wasn't normally the sort of person who would take money from a man's safe, but she was desperate, and after what she'd overheard earlier that night, she reckoned they owed it to her.

Holding close everything she had to start over with, she let herself out the back door of the house and fled for her life. She had a long way to walk to reach Memphis, but she also had almost three hours before dawn, and if she was lucky, another three or four before anyone at the Manor went to her room looking for her. She had last night's ball to thank for that. Junie, one of the young maids, and Katrina's only real friend at the Manor, wouldn't come to wake her before nine or ten. No one else would think of her.

But when Sam Bennett and his partner, Peter Standish, learned that she was gone, they'd be after her in the blink of an eye. They would guess that she knew, and they wouldn't dare let her get away. She cringed to think what they'd do if they caught her.

Her arms began to ache from the weight of the case, and her feet, though she wore good leather shoes, began to feel every pebble. Though her body was weary from hours of walking, on top of hours of dancing, her mind still whirled crazily, going over and over what she had heard, trying to make sense of it, remembering what her life had been like in the three years since her mother's death, seeing it all through very different eyes. Eyes that had been rudely opened.

No wonder they hated her. No wonder Corinne, who had been so excited over her father's marriage to the wealthy Lawrence Montgomery's widowed daughter-in-law, had suddenly turned bitter and spiteful. If what she suspected was true, then old Lawrence Montgomery had second-guessed them all. A hint of a grin curved her lips, but vanished just as quickly when she thought of all the heartaches and headaches she'd had to endure at their hands. And all the time . . .

"I'm sorry I doubted you, Grandfather," she said to the star-studded sky, remembering the white-haired gentleman who had been her best friend as she was growing up. Lawrence Montgomery had taken her to his heart, more so when his only son had been killed in the war soon after her birth. He had taught her to swim, to ride, to fish, he even taught her to handle a gun, most of it against her mother's wishes. He taught her how to judge horses, he taught her business and how to balance the accounts for the plantation, he taught her fairness in dealing with people, he taught her independence and self-confidence. She understood now. Now that it was too late.

What would they do? All three of them, Sam Bennett, Corinne, and Peter Standish, were uncompromisingly selfish, highly motivated by greed. They'd be enraged that she'd foiled their plans, doubly so when they learned that she'd had the audacity to take the jewels and the money in doing so. They'd use every means at their disposal to bring her back. Their desire for revenge, if not their own fear of reprisal, would demand it.

She thought again of poor Jeremy Hart. Her latest suitor had outlasted her other gentlemen friends, but he still hadn't been wise enough or strong enough to avoid the pitfalls set by her stepsister and stepfather. Well, maybe Sam Bennett would be too busy looking for her to bother Jeremy now. She hoped so, but she knew better. Even with a party going on around them the night before, Sam had taken his anger out on Jeremy. Sam Bennett wouldn't be satisfied until he crushed Jeremy for defying him.

Katrina found a log along the side of the road and sat down, removing her shoes and shaking out the grit. She rubbed her sore feet, resting her head on her updrawn knees. What she would give for a few hours of sleep. But she had to keep moving. She had to put as much distance as possible between herself and Sam Bennett. Wearily she slid her feet into her shoes and stood. How much farther could it be?

She'd walked for hours. She was even too tired to be scared anymore. She was alone, making her way to an unknown destination. She'd lived a solitary life in the past three years, but she had always had Junie, several others who worked at the farm, a few friends. Never had she been this alone. She should have been terrified, but she was too numb to feel.

The last hours of the previous evening, the ones that had sent her running, played back in her mind.

She'd put down her brush and gone to stand at the window overlooking the garden. The sweet scent of early blooms had wafted up to her on the evening breeze. Everything was as it should be, neat, orderly, even though not two hours earlier the Manor had been swarmed with guests for the annual spring gala. But as beautiful as the Manor still was, it had lost its charm for her.

"Oh, Grandfather," she had whispered, "they've ruined it all. Everything you worked so hard to build. Nothing's the same anymore."

Her stomach had grumbled, reminding her that she hadn't eaten since noon. Despondently, she turned away and pulled on her dressing gown. Sam had instructed their cook not to pander to Miss Katrina's erratic appetite, but she knew the older woman wouldn't say anything if she helped herself to something to eat.

As quietly as possible she left her room and tiptoed down the back stairs to the kitchen, and by the light of the moon fixed herself a sandwich and a glass of cool milk. How ironic, she had thought, that she had to sneak around in her own home to get something to eat. She was about to return to her room when she heard footsteps on the main staircase. Frightened that she would be found out, yet curious as to who else was awake at after two in the morning, she'd pressed herself to the wall by the open door and listened.

"I thought you might still be up," Peter said, turning up the wall lamps in the foyer.

"And I thought you'd be sound asleep. What's got you restless at this hour?" Sam asked from his study.

"I couldn't help worrying about our little problem."

Katrina's heart began to pound, but she didn't move away. Something kept her rooted to the spot, and she blessed whatever sixth sense had prevented her from scurrying back to her room. As the men's voices faded farther into the library, she inched closer to the heavy double doors.

"What problem? There will be no problem. Katrina will do exactly as she's told. I've already broken her spirit. She won't fight us."

"I wonder," Peter said. "Sometimes I think you're right, at other times, like tonight, I have my doubts. Don't make the mistake of underestimating her."

"Nonsense."

"Have it your way," Peter said. "But have you ever wondered just exactly what she knows? I don't think she's broken at all, I think she's biding her time. You may yet find yourself out on your backside."

"That's ridiculous. She hasn't the spine for that."

"Maybe. Or maybe she wants you to think her weak and harmless. I've seen her fight. She has spirit. And if she knows, she'll use that spirit to fight you."

"She doesn't know, I tell you. There's no way she can know."

Katrina moved closer still, her heart beating so heavily that she was having trouble hearing. Know what? Biding her time for what?

"She can't do that if my plan works."

"What plan? She'll be twenty in four months."

"It won't matter. Four months is a long time. Anything could happen. Anything at all. Just like with her mother's accident."

"What does that mean?" Peter had demanded. "Look, Sam, I bought into this place in good faith, little knowing I was purchasing a deed to nothing. I won't be cheated, Bennett. But neither will I be party to murder, if that's what you're suggesting."

"Come now, Standish. Let's not be faint of heart here. Our whole way of life is at stake."

"You'll never get away with it, and I don't relish a long prison term as an accomplice."

"Don't be so pessimistic. Besides, what would you suggest? I can't keep running her men friends off. Jeremy Hart will be more difficult than most to stop; he thinks he loves her. I'll have to shut him down completely, force him to leave town. But one day someone will show up who won't be so easily deterred. We can't chance that."

"But murder?" Peter had said, dismayed. "Is there no other way?"

"Sure. You could marry her, and within the year be wishing you'd taken my first suggestion. And I'm sure you know how my daughter would feel about that."

"Sam, Sam. You have to know how much I resent this. I'm tempted to expose this whole thing. You took my money in a fraudulent deal, now you're suggesting I implicate myself in your criminal activities."

"You've done that already, simply by keeping quiet. What judge would take your complaint seriously now? You've been living the life of a king on Katrina's money."

"No. On my money. On what you took from me."

"You didn't ask too many questions when I offered you the partnership. Pull out, if you like, but you'll lose everything just the same as I will. Go along with me, and you'll have what I promised you. You'll have half the Manor. It's your choice."

"Some choice," Peter grumbled, but Katrina could hear him weakening. How could she have been so blind? How could she have shown so little faith in her grandfather? He had always been a fair man, a very wise and respected man. And if what she gathered from the conversation she had just overheard was true, it explained everything.

She had heard enough. Weak-kneed and light-headed from shock, she made her way carefully back to her room and sat down. Her mother's accident? Anything could happen? Murder? She jumped up and pulled her valise from under her bed. She had no intention of waiting around to be Bennett's next victim.

Katrina tripped on an exposed root and fell to the ground, bruising her hip on the sharp corner of the valise. Tears came to her eyes. All around the black shadows threatened to engulf her. Why did darkness seem so total before dawn? Her tears came faster.

She wished Junie were with her. Junie would have come with her, she was sure of it, even though it would have meant leaving Cy, the big, kind stablehand she was in love with. Katrina couldn't ask that of her. And Cyrus was sure to suffer if Junie was found missing along with Katrina.

No. She had to do this on her own. And self-pity wasn't getting it done. She pushed herself to her feet and trudged on. She knew how to take care of herself. And just because she'd never been required to do so before didn't mean she couldn't. She'd show them what being a Montgomery meant.

Her mother had been blindly foolish where Bennett had been concerned, always believing in him. Or maybe she simply couldn't admit to herself that she'd made a terrible mistake. She'd had such pride. But then she wasn't a Montgomery, really. Only by marriage. And she hadn't had the benefit of a wise grandfather to teach her the dangers of false pride, of turning a blind eye to whatever one didn't wish to see because it was more comfortable that way.

Fresh tears erupted for her mother. She might have been foolhardy, but she hadn't deserved to die. An accident? A stroke of bad luck? Katrina knew then beyond any trace of doubt that her mother's death had been very carefully planned and executed. And now she knew why.

It wasn't going to happen to her. She tucked her carryall under her arm and hastened her pace. With renewed determination she strode toward Memphis.

Dawn was breaking across the eastern sky when the familiar outskirts of the city came into view. She chose a road into town that was infrequently used, one where a neighbor or acquaintance enroute to market was less likely to come upon her. She pulled her hood around her face and hid her valise under her cape as she traversed the last mile into the city.

The streets were still quiet, only a few early risers up and about. If any of them noticed the lone woman crossing town, making her way toward the mighty Mississippi, they paid her little mind, probably thinking her a servant in search of the day's bargains at the early morning open market.

She crossed through alleyways where no woman should go, where malodorous refuse had been dumped, where derelicts slept off the night's drinking, where mongrel dogs, baring discolored teeth, growled and snapped at her heels.

Suddenly the enormity of what she was doing hit her. Where was she going? She'd made no plans beyond her immediate race to escape the Manor. Should she buy a ticket upriver or down? Would Bennett be able to trace her through the ticket agent? Maybe she should buy a horse instead, or take the coach or train. She looked around as if the answer might be etched into the old boards of the dilapidated buildings.

She realized then what a truly horrid part of town she was in. But she could smell the river. She had no idea where she was, but if she got to the river and the waterfront, the docks couldn't be far away. She didn't know till then that she'd made her decision. She'd take the boat north to St. Louis. St. Louis was big enough to hide her until she made further plans. One step at a time, her grandfather used to say.

With that thought foremost in her mind she trudged onward until the buildings stopped and the road ended. Nothing lay ahead but the brushy high ridge of earth and rock that kept floodwaters from the city. A footpath ran the length of the floodwall. She headed north toward the main part of town.

Not far ahead she saw a man approaching on horseback. So far she'd run into no one, but she couldn't expect that to last. Daylight was upon her. She pulled her hood forward, hoping that, as the others had done, this man would ignore her.

He rode directly at her, and when he was in front of her, he pulled his horse to a stop. She chanced a quick upward glance. He was a burly man, rough-looking and ill-dressed, but his manner was not at all threatening.

She hesitated momentarily as his big horse sidestepped in front of her, but as soon as the animal was again under control, she continued on.

"Ma'am," the man said from behind her. "Ma'am, you shouldn't ought to go that way. Ain't safe down there. Ma'am?"

She didn't answer, just hurried her pace. It was funny that no matter from which direction anyone came, the docks were always "down there." She heard the man mumbling something and wondered if he'd come after her, but he didn't. She breathed a sigh of relief, only then realizing that she'd been holding her breath. Her palms were moist, her heart pounding in her throat, and the man had been harmless, concerned only for her safety. What would happen to her if she met someone truly dangerous?

Truly dangerous? She laughed, and the sound seemed to calm her. Who could be any more dangerous to her than Sam Bennett and Peter Standish? With anyone else she'd at least have a chance. Most people were reasonable and decent. If she treated them with respect and open friendliness, they'd do likewise with her. Feeling a bit calmer, she continued on.

The docks, when she reached them, surprised her, though she didn't know what she had expected. The warehouses were old and run-down, the wharf itself was roughly uneven with nails that protruded in places. Men were already at work at the far end, loading bales of cotton or tobacco and crates of other merchandise onto a barge. Assuming the riverboats also docked where the men were, she proceeded in their direction.

She was halfway down the long boardwalk when two men stepped out from between the buildings and blocked her way.

"What have we here?" one of them asked, smirking at the other.

Boys, she thought. They weren't men at all. Just mischievous boys. "Please excuse me," she said quietly, trying to remember the resolution she'd made only minutes before.

"Please excuse me," mocked the taller of the two. "Ain't she highfalutin'."

"Yeah. And pretty, too." The small wiry one snatched off her hood, pulling her hair sharply as he did. Long black tresses tumbled down her shoulders.

"What do you think you're doing?" she snapped, backing away. "Have you no manners at all?"

"She wants manners, Clyde," said the tall one.

"We can show her manners, can't we? All the manners she needs."

"Sure can. Come on, sugar, we have this room in back . . ."

"No! Let me go. Get your hands off me."

"You don't really mean that, now, do you?"

"Nah, she wouldn't be down here if she really meant that. How much do you want, sugar?"

"Want?" she shrieked in outrage. "I'm not what you think.

Now go away."

"Real ladies don't go strolling by theirselves along the river, neither."

"Aw, let her go," Clyde said. "She's too scared to be a whore."

"Sure, sure. But let's see what she got in the bag first."

Katrina tried to hold on, but the tall one wrenched the grip from her fingers.

"Give that to me. You have no right. Help!" she cried.

But the taller boy only laughed and shoved her to the rough boards of the wharf.

# Chapter 2

Tears of anger and frustration burned her eyes as she watched the boys run off with all she possessed in the world, or at least, all she could hope to claim. What was she to do now? Let them go without a fight? Her old Montgomery spirit rose to the surface, and she got to her feet and ran after them.

She saw them skitter into an opening between two buildings, and she bolted after them. With any luck, they'd dump out her clothes and never find the secret compartment with all her money and jewels.

She rounded the corner at a run and, surprised, saw they had already stopped and were rummaging through her bag. Had they thought she'd give up so easily, that she'd be afraid to follow them?

"Put that down," she yelled, racing to retrieve her possessions from their hands.

The boys looked up, startled by her attack. The tall one with the bag shoved her roughly aside, pulling the valise from her reach. He pushed his friend ahead of him, and the two of them ran out of the narrow alley, back onto the boardwalk. She was on her feet quickly, following. But when she reached the dock, another surprise awaited her. Her two assailants were fighting with another boy. A boy in a dirty red cap.

"You ought a be horsewhipped."

"This ain't your business, Red. Shove off."

"Like hell. I'll take the lady's bag."

"Let 'im have it, Jeb," Clyde wailed. "It's only got clothes in it, anyway."

"Maybe, but Red here's been getting too bossy lately. I don't happen to want to give this back. My sister can use some clothes. I'm takin' this bag, and you ain't stoppin' me."

"I'm warnin' you, Jeb. I don't want to have to take it from you."

"Oh yeah? Well, let's see you try. Come on, curly-locks," he taunted. "Let's see if you's as good as you say."

The boy named Red needed no more encouragement than that. He flew at his opponent with both fists flying, and landed several good punches. Clyde stared wide-eyed at them both, then snatched up the bag and ran.

Katrina didn't wait to watch, she ran after Clyde and her valise. She grabbed a fistful of his shirt and jerked, swinging Clyde off balance. He fell hard. As fast as she could, she picked up the valise and ran, but Clyde was right behind her reaching for her hair. Every fighting instinct she ever possessed surfaced. She would not lose what belonged to her again.

Her cape tightened around her throat momentarily, choking off her breath, but the fastener tore away, freeing her and leaving Clyde holding an empty cloak.

"Jeb," Clyde yelled, "she's getting away." But Jeb was too busy fighting off a whirlwind of fists and feet to help his friend.

"Help!" Katrina screamed at the men at the far end of the dock. She saw them turn and look their way, she thought they started to walk toward her, but she was never certain. She was hit from behind as Clyde threw himself at her. She watched in total shock as her valise flew out of her arms and as the wharf came up to meet her.

As small as Clyde was, he knocked the wind out of her when he landed on top of her. Her head hit rough boards and exploded in a spray of light. She'd always thought that "seeing stars" was just a silly phrase. It wasn't.

Behind her she heard a cry of pain, followed by a high keening moan. Then a splash. She was free of the heavy weight that had held her to the rough boards. Bones crunched against bones, and another cry went up, followed by footsteps pounding down the boardwalk.

"Come on, girlie," the boy in the red cap said, dragging her to her unsteady feet. "I don't know what the blue blazes you're doin' down here, but you better hightail it back where you came from."

Red grabbed up the carryall and the cape, took Katrina's arm and steered her away. "Move, missy. You think Jeb's gonna stay in the river all day? He'll come outta there spittin' fire, and I already got beat up enough on your account. And those men headin' this way, some of 'em ain't no better."

Katrina shook herself back to a semblance of consciousness and obeyed, making her feet follow where Red dragged her, which was down another dark alleyway.

She felt a trickle of warmth run down the side of her face, and instinctively brushed at it. Her hand came away with blood on it, making her gasp and falter.

Red turned and looked at her. "Hell's fire, you're bleedin'." He turned Katrina's head to see her face and whistled. "That's some goose egg you're growin'. Smack your head pretty hard, did ya?"

"I feel funny." Katrina managed through numb lips.

"Don't you go keelin' over on me. Aw, shucks," he added resignedly, seeing Katrina's face whiten. "Come on, then. I'll take you to my place."

"I need to sit down," Katrina said.

"Not yet. Hang on for a minute. It ain't far."

Katrina didn't know how she got to the little room where she woke up. The cubicle was dark, with no windows, and only one stub of a candle burning, but it smelled clean enough, and the cot was soft and comforting beneath her. And she was safe.

She lifted her aching head and looked for Red, but he wasn't with her. Had he deserted her? She looked frantically for her valise. It was sitting on a crate across the small room. With a sigh of relief she lay back down.

Minutes, or maybe it was hours, later a hand shook her awake. Katrina opened her eyes to see an elfin face amidst a flaming cloud of long, curly red hair.

She pushed herself onto her elbows inspite of her headache. "Who are you?"

"That's gratitude. Who do you think I am?" the girl answered in a very familiar voice.

"You're Red? I thought you were a boy."
"Well, I ain't."
"But you fought . . ."
She snorted. "Course I fought. Whipped 'em, too," she bragged.
"But why?"
"You needed help. Clyde and Jeb, they been a pain in . . . a general pain for months now. They don't want me workin' the docks."
"You work here?"
"Sure. It pays good enough. Oh, I can't do the heavy work, but I do what the other men hate doin', like sweepin' out, and delivering messages, making coffee."
"They don't . . . bother you?"
"Not with Ol' Jake around. He watches out for me. Besides, they ain't guessed the truth yet."
"Ol' Jake," Katrina repeated, lying back down. "Where was he today?"
"He had to go downriver."
Katrina's eyes blinked open. "On horseback? A big man, with a big voice?"
"That's Jake."
"I saw him. He was nice. He warned me not to come here."
"Ya should'a listened."
"I had to come. By the way, thank you."
"Aaah," she shrugged. "I stopped at Miss Hazel's. I told her I had a patient with a bad head. She gave me some powders for ya. She also said not to let you sleep too long. That's why I woke ya. You want some now?"
"Oh, yes, please."
"I couldn't get no ice, so the water's not cold, but it's wet. Here."
"Thank you again. You're very kind."
"S'nothin'." She shrugged her slender shoulders again. "You're nice, too, for a highborn lady. At least you got some spunk."
"Highborn lady?" Katrina asked, grinning.
"Yeah. You know what I mean. And you are, ain't ya? I heard 'em talkin' in town. Sam Bennett's got an army out

lookin' for a runaway ward of his. Old Man Montgomery's granddaughter, in fact."

Katrina's face paled. "Already?"

"You must have some good reason to run away from a grand place like the Manor."

"The best." Katrina didn't know the young girl sitting across from her, but for some reason, maybe the same sixth sense that held her to the library doors, she trusted her. "Bennett killed my mother."

"Lordy, I thought she died in a riding accident."

"That's what everyone thinks. But Bennett murdered her. I heard him talking to Peter Standish about it. And he wants me dead, too. Either that or I have to marry Standish. I'd rather be dead."

"Ooo-eee. You sure about that? I mean, they're real gents."

"They're no gentlemen, I assure you."

Red searched her face, her eyes. What she saw there must have convinced her. "Okay, then. You better lay low for a day or two."

"But I have to get away."

"We'll work that out when you're stronger."

"We?"

"Well, someone has to look after you."

"You'll help me?"

"On one condition."

"Whatever you want," Katrina accepted willingly.

"Take me with you. I got some money saved back."

"I don't need your money. But I do need a companion. I'll hire you to travel with me. I can afford it."

"I know that, too. Bennett's put the word out that you stole his money and some very costly jewels."

"I did. They're in my bag. That's why I couldn't let those boys have it."

"There's a warrant out for your arrest. And a reward."

Katrina sighed. "I knew he'd do something like that."

Red's head shook disbelievingly. "They seem so upstandin' and fine. It's hard to believe . . ."

"They put up a good front, but underneath they're mean."

"I just can't cotton you're here and they're out there lookin' for ya. Wasn't last night your big do out at your house? I seen some of the ladies and gents that was headin' that way."

"Yes, but it was not *my* do. I'd just as soon curl up with a book as go through that again."

"All those people can't be horrible."

Katrina sighed. "No, of course not. I'm just not comfortable with them anymore. Sometimes I catch odd looks in their eyes. Pity. Curiosity. Disdain. That's the worst. I'm a disappointment to them."

"Why?"

"I don't know. More of Corinne's ugly lies, no doubt. Who knows what she says about me."

"You don't like her?"

"A natural reaction to someone who despises you."

"Why does she hate you? If not for your mama, she wouldn't be livin' in that big house."

"She doesn't see it that way. She thinks that because of my mother, she has to put up with *me* living there still. She'd rather see me anywhere but at the Manor. And frankly . . ."

"Careful what you hope for. You might get it."

"Besides, it's not my home anymore. Last night in the middle of the party, Sam Bennett kicked out my latest suitor and my only guest because he dared to speak up to Corinne and tell her what he thought of her. Granted, he wasn't very nice about it, but she had it coming."

"How so? What did he say to her?" Red was alive with curiosity.

"He called her a Jezebel. Well, you see, Corinne seduced Jeremy. That's his name. Oh, I know he's as much to blame for that as she is, and I did blame him. I told him I didn't want to see him anymore after last night. He was upset that I'd found out. And ashamed."

"How did you find out?"

"Corinne told me this morning."

"She admitted it?" Red was incredulous.

"But it doesn't matter, you see. If she hadn't been successful, Jeremy would have suffered just the same because he'd spurned her." Katrina's hands flipped outward in futility. "Once Jeremy took an interest in me instead of Corinne, his fate was sealed. Corinne accused him in front of all the guests of swindling Mrs. Tyree out of her last few dollars."

"You mean Jeremy Hart? Of the General Store Harts?"

Katrina nodded. "Sam Bennett practically owns Mrs. Tyree. He rents her that little house, and rumor is that he's supporting her, if you know what I mean. She won't risk being tossed out by countering what Sam Bennett says. Not with two children and no means of support."

"Can you do anything for him? His business will fall apart with a rumor like that spreading around."

"That would only make it worse. Any reaction whatsoever on my part spurs the Bennetts to be meaner than they already are. And if I did anything for Jeremy now, Sam Bennett would find me."

"What's Peter Standish like? I heard tell he's very handsome."

"Yes, and he knows it. Peter spends enough of his nights in Corinne's bedroom to make them married. During the days he tries to seduce me. Last night Sam made me dance with him. Peter told me I was foolish for ever getting in Corinne's way. He knows how vindictive she is. With his next breath he's crooning sugary compliments in my ear and suggesting he come to my room that night. Have you a guess what Corinne would do if he did? They're all crazy, I swear it."

"So, you want to hire me to help you get away from them, do ya? I really do have some money. Not much, mind you."

Katrina turned her head to look at the girl who'd saved her from disaster. "I'm the one who needs the help. Let me pay you to travel with me."

"I don't want no pay. Just whatever it costs to get by. Is it a deal, then?"

"I don't even know where I'm going."

"That don't matter."

"Where would you like to go?"

Red thought a minute. "Oh, I suppose if I had a choice, I'd go to California."

"California? Why?"

Red's eyes drifted off in thought. "It's sunny. Doesn't rain much. It's new."

"It's so far away."

"That's another good reason."

Katrina laughed. "How old are you, Red? Is Red your real name?"

"Nah. Jake started that. My name's Annie. Annie Spooner. And I'm seventeen, almost eighteen."

"I'm Katrina."

"I know. You'd better be Kate from now on. And you better drop the Montgomery, too."

"I guess so. How about Lawrence? It was my grandfather's name. Lawrence Montgomery."

"Kate Lawrence. Sounds good to me."

"Do you have any family, Annie?"

"No. Not anymore."

It was said with such finality that Katrina knew it was true, and that Annie's past was a topic not open for discussion.

"Well, my new friend, I'd welcome you as my companion and partner. Being on my own isn't working out so well for me."

Annie laughed, and her laughter was very girlish. "We'll do just fine together. You wait and see." Annie was so jubilant that Katrina couldn't help laughing with her.

"Have you found her?" Corinne demanded when Peter and her father returned to the Manor.

"No. But we will," Sam said resolutely.

"It's been two days now. She could be anywhere," Corinne wailed.

"Let's discuss this in the library, please," Peter chided them, handing his gloves and hat over to Junie, who eyes slid away from his own.

"We'll have tea now, Junie," Sam said, leading the other two into his personal domain.

"Yes, sir. I'll tell cook, sir."

Peter closed the doors as he followed the Bennetts into the book-lined room. He'd been having some thoughts of his own over the past two days. What did he need the Bennetts for if he could find Katrina and convince her to marry him? He wouldn't mind having Katrina for a wife. She would be a good mother, a faithful partner, probably easily controlled. Far more so than Corinne. And he wouldn't have to share the Manor with Bennett; he could get his own back for the underhanded trick Bennett had pulled on him. He would be the one to oust Bennett and his daughter. The thought held a great deal of appeal for him.

"Well, what have you learned?" Corinne asked impatiently.

"First of all," Peter answered her, "we know she didn't go by conventional transportation. We checked the depots and ticket agents. No one has seen her."

"So you think she's still in town?"

"Possibly. But she could have bought a horse or hired a boat."

"Can't you find out?"

"We have men investigating that now. We'll know soon," Sam answered. "Personally, I think she's hiding somewhere. And we'll find her."

"What if we don't?"

"Then you'll lose everything," Peter couldn't resist.

"And so will you," Sam reminded him curtly. "No. We'll discover a ransom note on the doorstep. And after a few weeks, if she doesn't return, we'll receive a letter proving her dead."

"Oh, that's good," Corinne said snidely. "And what happens when she does come back? After she's turned twenty?"

"She won't."

"How can you be sure?"

"I'll make sure."

"You should have made sure she never had the chance to leave in the first place. I've been telling you that all along. What if she marries someone? Have you checked on Jeremy?"

"Jeremy Hart is still in town," Peter replied. "And we have a man watching him."

"That doesn't mean she won't marry someone else."

"Who would she marry? Katrina's not the type to get married just to spite us."

"More than spite is involved here," Peter reminded the older man. "Corinne has a valid point."

"We'll just have to make certain that doesn't happen, then."

"This is disastrous," Corinne moaned. "How could you have been so careless as to let her, or anyone, overhear you?"

"We had no idea she was prowling around. We didn't know until we learned from cook that someone had left dishes in the sink that night."

"You should have made certain you were alone."

"Look, Corinne, that's neither here nor there, now," Peter snapped. "It does no good to harp on it."

"It does me good," Corinne retorted. "It was a stupid mistake. We can't afford mistakes."

"It certainly wasn't my first. My first mistake was in trusting the two of you in the beginning. You're out on a limb now, and I have the feeling you're trying to get me to climb out there with you just to keep me quiet."

"Enough, the both of you. Do your scrapping later. Right now we have to do some planning."

"What's there to do?" Corinne sulked, dropping into the leather chair by the desk.

"First of all, the sheriff wants a list and description of the jewelry Katrina took. That's your task, Corinne, since you know more about that than either of us.

"Peter you take that painting of Katrina and her mother in the upstairs hall to Eli Matthews and have him do an ink drawing of Katrina so we can make up some handbills to send out. I want her face on every post office wall possible, and I want the reward high enough to tempt any man's conscience."

"And what will you be doing?" Peter asked gruffly.

"I have an appointment this afternoon with a representative of the Pinkerton Detective Agency."

Kate prowled restlessly around the small room. She'd straightened and cleaned all she could. Nothing remained to be done except wait for Annie to return.

What a true friend Annie had become in a few short days, seeing to Kate's injury, bringing her food, water, and more importantly, information. Everyone at the docks had been questioned, especially Jeb and Clyde, who were forced to admit publically that they had tried to rob a young woman, but that Red had bested them both. Annie, too, had been questioned at length about the young woman she had helped at the riverfront, but from years of practice at getting herself out of scrapes with the law, she convinced everyone that she'd showed the girl in question back to the main street of town and sent her on her way. What would she want with some snippy upper crust miss, anyway? She did confess to taking a reward from the girl, and proudly flashed a new crisp bill from the pocket of her overalls to prove it. They believed her. How else would a ragtag have come across such a sum of money?

"Did you see which way she went when you left her?" Mr. Bennett had pressed. "It's important that we find her."

"Yeah? Why?" she'd asked for the benefit of all the people listening curiously. "What'd you do to make her run away?"

"Just answer the question, young man," the sheriff had reprimanded.

Annie had stared them down, so she claimed, and told them it wasn't her business where the lady decided to go as long as she stayed away from the river.

And now Annie was out gleaning more information about the search for the missing Miss Montgomery, and Kate was waiting impatiently for her return. As anxious as Katrina was to be far away from Memphis, she was thankful that Annie had insisted she stay put for a day or two. She would surely have stumbled into Bennett's network of men if she'd been on her own. She was beginning to realize how unworldly-wise she was.

She jumped when the door swung open and Annie burst in. "Hi," the redhead bubbled. "I got us some food."

"And scared me to death," Katrina said, still clutching her stomach. "What did you learn? Is Bennett still in town?"

"Here. Eat. And yes, your stepfather is still nosing around. Him and a dozen hired men. Word is he's even called in the Pinkerton men."

"Oh, no," Kate groaned. "We'll never get away."

"Are you doubting me? Have I let you down yet? Remember I got friends."

"Do you mean that someone knows I'm here?"

"Jake. I had to have his help."

"What if he tells? I mean, the reward . . ."

"Jake? Good heavens, you can trust Jake. When I told him what you told me, he said he could believe it. He also said he owed your grandpappy. It seems Lawrence Montgomery once done him a good turn, got him out of some trouble or other. He wouldn't say what, only that until now he never got the chance to repay him. He has a plan to get us on this evening's boat to St. Louis."

"This evening," Katrina choked, attacked by a wave of anxiety. "But Bennett . . ."

"We have to make a move sometime. The longer we wait, the more time Bennett has to get his men spread out. We've waited too long as it is."

Katrina let out a shaky breath. "I suppose you're right. I'm scared."

"Hey, don't be. You got me here, remember?"

Kate tried to grin. "Yes, I know. But Mr. Bennett and Peter Standish aren't Clyde and Jeb."

"They're men, aren't they?" Annie said scornfully.

"Well, yes, but—"

"Then don't worry. They won't believe that they could be duped by a young girl. This will be an easy snap. You'll see. Now eat. And tell me again what we're gonna do when we get to California."

"You mean *if* we get there."

"You leave gettin' there to me. That's my part."

"Why haven't you gone long ago?" Kate asked.

"I guess because I was afraid. Here I have a few friends, and Jake. Out there . . ."

She let her explanation fall away, and Kate could see that the prospect of being on her own was as unsettling to Annie as it was to her. But they had each other now. Together they could manage. Together they could draw on each other's strengths.

"We'll begin a new life," Kate said confidently, building up Annie's dream. "With the money I have and what I can get for my mother's jewelry, we'll buy a small business."

"A business?" Annie exclaimed. "I don't know nothin' about business."

"I do. We'll find a small shop, we'll sell ladies' finery, or general merchandise. I'll keep the books, you convince the customers to buy whatever we sell. Then again, a restaurant might be nice, except that I can't cook."

"I can cook," Annie said enthusiastically.

"Then you can cook and I'll do the serving. There, we already have two possibilities."

"This is fun. Do you think you'll ever come back here?" Annie asked.

Kate's lips twisted sardonically. "To what? If the time ever comes when I can return, nothing will remain to return for. Somehow Bennett will manage to take it all for himself."

"Doesn't that make you furious? Shouldn't some of it be yours? Your grandfather built it in the first place."

Annie was angry enough for the both of them. Kate shook her head. She didn't want to reveal the full extent of Bennett's perfidy. She didn't want to think of all she was losing and had already lost. It was a betrayal of all her grandfather had done for her to give up, but she could see no way to fight Sam Bennett and Peter Standish without risking death. They would never let her win, and they were too powerful for a lone woman to fight.

"I took a chunk of their fortune. I got my mother's jewelry back. I'll have to be satisfied with that. Of all they took from me, that was the one loss I regretted most. Would you like to see it?"

"Oh, yes. You don't mind?"

"I'd like to show you," Kate answered, anxious herself to once more see the glittering brilliance of her mother's legacy. She unlocked the false bottom of the valise and dumped its contents on the bed.

"Lordy-lord, look at that money. It's a fortune," Annie exclaimed, filling her hands with stacks of bills.

"Don't get excited. It will barely get us started. It's not all that much."

"It would last me a lifetime."

"Only if you intend to live like this for the rest of your life. I have better than this in mind for us. We'll have to work hard, but one day we'll have a nice home, pretty dresses again, we'll . . ."

"Again? I ain't *never* had a pretty dress."

"You'll have dozens of them," Kate said dismissively. "Look at this." She opened the black lacquered box, and one by one, laid the jewels on the old gray blanket.

Annie's eyes grew enormous, and her mouth gaped speechlessly as she stared at the winking jewels. Kate chuckled fondly at her friend's reaction.

"My mother used to come to my room when I was terrified by a bad storm and show me these. I'd forget all about the thunder and lightning outside."

"Are these real pearls?"

"Very real. These are sapphires. They were her favorite. They matched her eyes."

"Yours, too."

"Yes, I guess they do. These are emeralds."

"These are diamonds. Even I know that. And rubies?"

"Actually they're garnets. Not as valuable, maybe, except that they're very old. They came from Spain. They belonged to a contessa."

"What is this?"

"An opal. My grandmother had it made into a brooch. It's said to have fire in it."

"It does. Look," she said, turning and twisting the pin to catch the candlelight.

"She put diamonds around it so their light would fire the opal. Mother used to wear it on a blue velvet ribbon around her neck."

"It's beautiful. You shouldn't sell it."

"Of all this, the opal is the one I'd really like to keep. But I may not have a choice. We'll have to see."

"It's a shame to sell any of it," Annie bemoaned, slipping ring after ring onto her slender fingers.

"Most of it is too ostentatious for my taste. I like simplicity. I like the pearls and the brooch, and this." She held up a single fine gold chain with a teardrop diamond suspended from it.

"Oh, yeah. That's beautiful. It would suit you much better than this," she agreed, draping the wide antique chain of filigreed discs and deep red garnets around her own throat.

"That always reminded me of drops of blood."

"Yeech," Annie grimaced, putting aside the garish necklace. "But some gaudy matron will grab it up. Mark my words."

"No doubt." Kate put the pieces back into the case and snapped the latch.

"Aren't you afraid I'll steal all this and run?" Annie asked, watching Kate return the money and jewels to the bottom of the valise.

"You could have done that a dozen times already, but you haven't. You must have thought about it?"

"Yeah, I thought about it. But then I'd be on my own again. I like being with you. Besides I ain't no thief."

"Do you think I am? I mean, I did steal this."

"Rubbish. You can't steal what's already yours. It is yours, ain't it? That's why Bennett wants you dead. You're gonna inherit everything. Right?"

"Now why would you say a thing like that?" Kate asked, dismayed. She hadn't wanted to hear it put into words, even though it was quite probably true.

"Just put the facts together the way I see 'em, not how Bennett's tellin' it. It's true, ain't it?"

"I think so. They were very concerned about my twentieth birthday. Or about any man I took a fancy to. They've been running off all my friends for years. I thought it was because my stepsister was jealous of me."

"But they were just keeping their sticky hands on your inheritance?"

"It looks that way, but I can't be certain. I've never seen any will."

"Which don't mean it doesn't exist. It must, or they wouldn't care if you left."

"They could have burned it, then it wouldn't exist. That's what puzzles me. Everyone thinks Bennett and Standish own the Manor anyway."

"So maybe there's a second copy somewhere, and they know it. Maybe they just don't know where it is or who has it."

"I wonder. That sounds like something my grandfather would do. You're very clever, Annie. You know, I didn't want you involved in this. I thought you'd be in less danger if you didn't know."

"I've been in danger before. I'm not afraid. So," she said, jumping to her feet. "Let's get our things together. Jake'll be by after a bit. The boat leaves at seven."

Kate packed her bag and sat brushing out her long hair in front of the piece of broken mirror propped against the wall. A dozen questions came to her lips, none of which Annie would answer. "Wait and see," was all she could get out of the girl. That and a sly grin. And by that grin Kate knew that whatever Annie and Jake had plotted would be supremely sneaky.

"Do you want me to do your hair?" she asked Annie when she'd finished fastening her own into a neat twist at the back of her head.

"What for? I'll tuck it in my cap as usual."

"Are you going to wear that?" Kate asked, eyeing Annie's old shirt and baggy overalls.

"It's all I got. Besides, I'm travellin' as your kid brother. Jake said it'd be safer for both of us that way. So call me Red," she finished impishly. "I'm used to it," she added when Kate was about to object.

"But even in these clothes I don't look so poor that I'd let my little brother go about in rags. Take some of the money and get some decent clothes."

"I will when we get to St. Louis. I won't need any till then."

Whatever that meant, she was not to know, because they were interrupted by a sharp rap at the door. Annie jumped up, a broad smile on her face, and opened the door.

"Hi, Jake. Come on in. We're ready."

Jake stepped into the tiny room, dwarfing it even more by the sheer bulk of his size. Kate stood, too, and smiled shyly at the big man.

"So, you came to no harm after all, I see," he said to her.

"Only because of Annie. You remember me?"

"Not many has eyes as bright as yours. Red told me why you're runnin' off. If I'd known then who you was, I'd have saved you that nasty bruise on your forehead. I had great respect for your grandpappy. He was a good man who believed in fairness. If you're anything like him, then I guess I can trust my little Red here to you."

"I was rather hoping Annie would take care of me," Kate replied wryly. "And I'd like very much to apologize to you for being rude that day."

Jake laughed a booming laugh. "Ain't no need. Any girl in her right mind would be scared of the likes of me. It's me needs apologizin'. I shouldn't have roared at you like I done."

"I deserved it. Please . . ."

"Enough said. I don't know what you two are plannin' to do with yourselves after you leave here, but I guess you got the right to decide that without me. I ain't never seen Red so excited about anything as she is about this scheme of yours, so I'm helpin' ya. You just be sure to steer clear of trouble. Stay out of rough parts of town, don't believe everything you hear, especially from men, keep a hand on your money, and keep your eyes open and your ears to the ground."

"Yes sir," Kate responded at the same time that Annie laughed.

"Sorry," Annie said, not at all contrite. "I was picturin' what we'd look like if we did all that."

Jake turned to her. "Don't get sassy, girl. You remember everything I taught you, now. Keep your guard up."

"And my back to the wall, and my ear to the ground, only on the right side of town," Annie finished, nodding but still grinning.

"I give up," Jake growled. "Come along if you're ready. We ain't got all night."

"Mr.—ah, Jake," Kate said, laying a detaining hand on his muscular arm. "I do want to thank you for helping us. And I will do my best to make wise decisions for both of us. And you have my word that I'll keep Annie with me. I won't desert her."

Jake's dark eyes bore into hers. Then he nodded as if satisfied. "Try to teach her some ladylike manners."

"Aw, Jake," Annie grumbled.

Jake laughed and flicked his fingers through her mop of red curls. "Let's go, mite. Tuck that hair in your cap."

Kate followed them outside, peering both ways in the alley to assure herself that no one was lurking in the shadows. Only a broken-down horse hitched to an equally broken-down cart stood outside the door. On the cart were two open crates. Her eyes went from one of them to the other, then swung to Jake and Annie.

"You don't mean . . . we're not . . ." she sputtered, flapping her hand between herself and Annie and the two crates.

"Sure, Kate. It's perfect," Annie enthused. "We'll be on board the barge before you know it, and right under the noses of Bennett's men."

"Barge?"

"Well, don't you think they'll search the riverboats? We'd be caught in a minute. But no one will expect us to go by barge."

"No. I can agree with that."

"Don't worry, Miss Kate," Jake said, fighting to keep a straight face. "I put some food and water in each crate, and a blanket. As soon as night falls, you can get out and sit under the stars. You'll enjoy it."

"It sounds . . . interesting," she said doubtfully. Yet the more she thought about it, the more she liked the idea. She could just imagine Bennett's face when he learned she had escaped right from under his nose. On a barge. She grinned. "Okay, let's do it."

"Atta girl," Jake said, beaming a broad grin.

"Told you she had spunk," Annie crowed.

# Chapter 3

"We must hurry," Dan urged when Zack Standish finally emerged from the barbershop. "The train is due to depart in less than an hour."

"Relax. I have been assured, with the help of a little cash, that our requirements will receive personal attention, both here and in Kansas City. We aren't that far from the depot that we can't take our time. I need to stretch my legs before another day of sitting on a train."

Dan, always a worrier, wasn't convinced, but he gave in to Zack's logic, as usual, with a brief, "If you're sure."

"Besides, how many trains have you taken that departed on schedule?"

Dan acknowledged that with a brief grin. "I see your point, but it's not as though we can simply catch the next one. Our recent acquisitions would be days ahead of us. Who would see to them in Kansas City or Omaha? Or in Sacramento, for that matter."

"So we'll walk briskly."

"Peter," a soprano voice called from behind them. "Peter Standish."

Zack's stride faltered at the name. A name he hadn't heard or thought of in months.

"Peter," it came again as his arm was taken from behind.

Zack stopped and turned to see who had spoken the name. A vivacious brunette looked up, a wide smile on her pretty face.

"Peter, you naughty man. You're in St. Louis and you

haven't been to see me. It's been ever so long," she rushed, stopping only when she looked more closely at his face.

"I'm sorry, miss," Zack said curtly, "but my name is not Peter. You have made a mistake."

The woman colored fiercely. "Oh, yes. I see I have. I apologize, sir. But you do look very much like—someone I know."

Zack took pity on her discomfiture. "I'm sorry, too. It isn't every day a beautiful woman stops me on the street."

She blushed again, but she laughed. "I do apologize. And you're kind to try to make me feel better."

"Not at all," Zack said, "and I'd stay to make your acquaintance, except that we are late for our train, and my friend here will worry until we are safely boarded."

"Oh, you're travelling then?" she said wistfully.

"I'm afraid so."

"Well, safe journey. I won't take more of your time. Again, I'm sorry."

"It was a pleasure. Good day."

"Peter Standish?" Dan asked when they were again striding toward the depot.

Zack shrugged, not caring to be reminded of someone he'd tried to forget.

"Curious that you and this man should resemble each other and share the same last name. Could he be a relative?"

"Thousands of people share the Standish name," he said diffidently. "Pure coincidence." And coincidence it was that he should run into that name now, now that his mother had died. Now that the need to find him for her was gone. He had never understood his mother's deep-seated desire to be reunited with the elder son who had left them stranded in an alien land, penniless and with no one to turn to for help. Zack had resented her preoccupation with her firstborn, but he had sincerely tried to grant her wishes. He always had done that for her. But now, his irresponsible, uncaring brother could stay lost. He hoped never to hear his name again.

"Hmm," Dan responded, glancing first at his friend's closed face, then back over his shoulder. The woman had disappeared. Another mystery. And unless Zack had a rare bout of talkativeness, it would remain a mystery. But that was Zack. No one knew what went on inside Zack's head.

"Ah, Mr. Standish, Mr. Siebert. We have your accommodations prepared, and your personal transport cars are coupled at the rear of the train. Your horses have been tended already. My own boy saw to them, and he's good with animals."

"I appreciate that. The other car, with our freight?"

"I checked it myself this morning. It's locked tight."

"Fine, fine. And were you able to contact Kansas City?"

"My cousin says he'll see to you personally. You relax now and have a good journey."

"What a little money can do, eh?" Dan said humorously when they had been escorted to their private car.

"Doesn't hurt," Zack said, "but still wish I'd checked the horses myself. I would hate for any of them to be injured. We've a great deal of money invested in those animals. And in this car," he said, running a hand over the plush velvet upholstery of the lounge chairs.

"We'll turn a tidy profit on the car. I already have a buyer for it in California. Everyone is train mad these days. Our buyer wants to use the car to ferry wealthy investors across the country for some big land deal he's putting together."

A knock sounded, and Dan opened the door to find the porter bearing a basket of fruit, cheese, rolls, and a bottle of wine. "Compliments of a young lady, sir, by the name of Miss Amelia Waring. She described you both to the last hair, though she did not know your names."

"You didn't tell her, did you?" Zack asked watchfully.

"Oh, no, sir. She fluttered those long lashes at me, but I wouldn't tell her. It wouldn't be the thing to do without askin' first. I mean . . . well, there's no tellin' who she might be or what she might be after." He winked knowingly, and Zack relaxed.

"Thank you, Thomas, you're quite right."

"She did say she was apologizing."

Dan laughed. "Don't give it another thought, Thomas. It happens all the time. Every woman he meets sets her cap for Zack. But we'll accept her gracious gift, and her apology."

"Oh, and I'm sorry to say we'll be a few minutes late in

departing. The police are searching all the trains for a missing woman."

Zack threw Dan a look that plainly said, I told you so. "Will they be long?" he asked Thomas. "I could check the horses."

"I wouldn't, sir. They're almost finished, and your animals are fine, really."

"Why are they searching for this woman?" Dan asked, not so much concerned with the woman as with getting Zack's mind off his horses.

"She's a thief, I guess. Too bad, really. She looks a pretty thing. Here." He pulled a folded paper from his pocket and handed it to Zack. "There's a reward for her."

Zack unfolded the handbill and looked at the face drawn there. His brows drew together. "She looks young," he observed, handing the picture to Dan.

"Keep that," Thomas said. "I have plenty more. There's the whistle. We'll be leaving now. Sorry for the delay."

Annie crumpled the paper and tossed it at her feet. "At least they could have drawn a decent picture of you. They make you look like a child. A sneaky child."

"Shh. I am a thief," Kate whispered sardonically. "I'm supposed to look sneaky. Oh, we're moving."

"Thank the good Lord. Now we can get out of here. I thought for a minute there they were gonna search in here, too."

"The door's locked, in case it slipped your mind. Anyhow, what woman in her right mind would deliberately ride in a car with five horses?"

"You don't like horses?" Annie asked, untangling her legs and shoving back the leather flap that concealed the luggage compartment of the black carriage.

Kate followed her out, stumbling as the motion of the train threw off her balance. "I love horses."

Her eyes toured the colorless car. Four small windows were set along each side. She slid one open for some fresh air. Most of the car had been fashioned into separate narrow stalls for the horses. Only the forward end was open, and that was nearly taken up by the carriage that was secured to the walls by heavy ropes. Bales of sweet, fresh straw were stacked along the stalls with sacks of feed and a barrel of water. Several large crates, which probably held tack, were stacked beside the carriage under one window.

"Wee-oww, this is some rig in the daylight," Annie exclaimed, examining the carriage. "You suppose it belongs to a prince from some exotic country, or a senator, or the President?"

Kate eyed the shiny black paint and the gold and red trim. "Probably someone just like Bennett," she said scathingly. "He has one exactly like it. Who else would hire an entire railroad car to transport his carriage and horses? But whoever owns these horses has never hitched them to any carriage."

"Whoever he is, he has my thanks. The seats made a decent bed last night. These are nice horses."

"Nice?" Kate repeated. "They're magnificent."

A sudden jolt as the train rounded a corner and picked up speed unsettled the high-strung animals, and they stomped and whinnied nervously.

"Easy there," Kate soothed, choosing the ebony stallion to minister to. If he were calm, the mares would settle as well.

The great black beast tossed his head and snorted, but finally submitted to Kate's gentle stroking. One small white diamond stood out in the blackness of his face. She wondered what he was called.

"There, you see? You've nothing to fret about. You'll get your sea legs soon enough."

"Sea legs?" Annie scoffed.

"He knows what I mean, don't you, fella?"

"This must be his first time on a train. I thought—I guess the owner must be from around here after all."

"What do you mean by 'after all'?"

"The carriage was built in New York. It says so on the brass plate. See? Doesn't it?"

"Can't you read?"

"I get by."

The horses did indeed calm down once they became accustomed to the motion of the train and the vibrations beneath their hooves. Kate in turn gave each of the animals a reassuring pat and moved back toward the carriage to further explore her surroundings, all the while considering what Annie had disclosed, however unwittingly.

She should have recognized the truth earlier, but Annie was clever. She'd given Jake's note of introduction to her to keep, then asked her, after they were safely enroute to St. Louis, to read it to her.

Kate sat down next to her friend. "Annie, didn't you go to school?"

Annie jumped up, agitated, and turned away. "We lived too far away. But my ma taught me when she could. When my pa was gone. He thought it was a waste of time for a woman to get book-learnin'."

"Your mother? Is she . . ."

"She died when I was twelve," Annie said flatly. "She was beautiful. I didn't learn much cause I'd sit and stare at her and let myself drift away on the sweet sound of her voice."

"You loved her very much."

"She was a lady, too, like you, before my dad got to her. Not rich or nothin', but a lady. She had pictures."

"Is your father alive?"

Annie climbed a crate and slid open another of the windows, filling the car with fresh air and the clacking of the wheels on the rails. "I don't know," she answered bitterly.

"Did you ever learn to read?" Kate asked again after a silent interlude.

"I get by."

"Is that a yes or no?"

Annie twisted around, glaring at Kate. "You are a nosy thing. I don't like people pryin' into my past. I said I get by. I get by."

Frowning, Annie jumped down and made herself a seat against the wall. She said nothing, and Kate began to fear she'd badly offended her. She hadn't meant to do that. Annie had helped her when she most needed help; Kate only wanted to return the favor.

"I didn't mean to pry," she said so quietly that her voice was almost lost in the sounds of the train. "You spoke so fondly of your mother and of her being a lady. You could be a lady, too."

"That's not likely," Annie said softly, a little sadly. "I am what I am."

"You are what you make of yourself."

Annie turned cynical eyes to Katrina. "Do you really believe that?"

"I think it can be true, yes."

"And you think I can snap my fingers and be like you?"

"I didn't mention magic at all, nor did I say it would be effortless. But if you really want something within reason, and if you're willing to work for it, I think you can achieve it."

Annie gave a disbelieving snort and turned away. "You realize, don't you, that I'm using you," she said with blunt honesty.

Katrina hadn't really thought about it, but she supposed that, in their own ways, they were using each other, and she said as much.

"I'm using you to get out of there," Annie confessed. "What are you getting from me? I ain't got nothin' to give."

Kate chuckled. "You have knowledge I could never have, and courage and confidence that put me to shame. That's what I'm getting from you."

"You mean because I can swing my fists? That was a matter of survival for me. It ain't what I wanted."

"You wanted to be like your mother."

"Except that I don't intend to let no man do to me what my dad did to her. He made an old woman of her while he drank himself stupid all day. I hated him."

"Is that why you left him?"

"Nah, but that's another story, and I don't want to talk about it."

"Fine. But remember my offer. I may have hired you, but I want to help you, too."

Nothing more was said, but Kate had a feeling that the odd tension which had sprung up between them since stowing away on the barge had been eased. Annie was uneducated and uncultured, but she had her pride. She made her way on her own, and taking advantage of someone else didn't sit well with her. Annie was relieved to hear that they were helping each other. Kate let her mind drift off, remembering how much she'd depended on Annie in the past two days. She was very glad to have Annie with her.

"Is there a door at the far end like this one?" Annie asked suddenly.

Kate looked up and craned her neck to see around the stalls. "Yes." She stood and, out of curiosity, tried the door that would have given them access to the rest of the train. It was locked. Was there no way out? "I never considered it before, but what if this train crashes? How do we get out?"

Annie came to stand by her side. "You could always try the key," she said, reaching up to slip a key from its nail beside the door.

"Oh, I didn't see it, but then I didn't expect to, either. Why would anyone lock the door and then leave a key?"

"So you can get out, but not in?" Annie guessed.

"Give it a try," Kate suggested eagerly.

The door slid open easily to admit more of the racket of the wheels on the track and a gust of cool air. Annie closed it again and pocketed the key.

"Now we can get off at the next stop and look around."

"We can't do that. What if we get caught?"

"You worry too much." Annie paused. "I've been thinking about what you said. About teaching me to read and the like. And if you're still of a mind to, I reckon I could try. I don't wanna be no dunce all my life."

Kate laughed gently. "Good. Then here's your first lesson. You mustn't say 'don't' and 'no' in the same sentence. They're both negative words, they cancel each other out. You are then saying you want to be a dunce."

"Huh? What am I supposed to say?"

"You say, 'I don't want to be a dunce.'"

"I don't want to be a dunce," Annie repeated, copying Kate's precise diction.

"Right," Kate laughed. "Now stand up—no—take your hands out of your pockets . . . don't slouch. Stand tall with your shoulders back and your head up, as if your balancing a book on it. Now walk. No, not like that. Walk softly, and glide. Watch me."

"You make it look easy."

"Not easy, just natural. You need practice, that's all."

Kate leaned back against the carriage wheel and watched as her friend moved from one end of the car to the other, all the while reciting, "I don't want to be a dunce."

During the day the train stopped frequently to board or let off passengers, to take on water and replenish fuel. The first few stops were brief, not long enough to allow the passengers time to disembark. At noon, however, the train pulled into a station, and the conductor strode up and down the platform, announcing in his booming voice that the train would be stationed for one hour, and anyone not back by one o'clock would be left.

"We're gettin' off here whether you like it or not," Annie declared, tucking her hair haphazardly under her red cap. "I'm about to bust a seam inside. Can you make yourself look—poorer?" She pulled the key from her pocket and opened the door.

Kate was uncomfortable enough to agree. She tied Annie's blue bandana around her hair the way she'd often watched Junie do, and she draped a dark shawl around her shoulders. "How's this?"

"Come on," Annie whispered urgently from the open doorway. "Someone's coming this way."

Kate obeyed, sliding the door shut behind her and waiting for Annie to relock it. They climbed down from the train on the side opposite the platform and hid until the two men had passed by. They could hear their low voices and a door being shoved aside. Their eyes met, both realizing that the men who had walked the long length of the train had done so to check on the horses.

"Let's hightail it," Annie said, "before they come out."

"Don't run, Annie. You'll draw attention to us. Stroll slowly and look as if you belong here."

"Do you remember if we left anything laying out? Tarnation, your satchel's still in the back of the carriage. What if they find it?"

Kate stopped and looked back briefly. "They won't. Why would they check the carriage?"

They walked to the front of the train, skirting the steaming, hissing locomotive. Workers were all about, but no one paid any attention to the two stragglers who crossed the tracks and ambled toward town. The men were busy shooing off the youngsters who wanted to climb aboard for a look.

"Did you see some of them cars?" Annie whispered.

"I wasn't looking at the cars. Let's find a washroom."

The platform was crowded with travellers, all being directed by the stationmaster to one eatery or another, as their purses could afford. The hotel two blocks up the street offered a small dining room, the larger cafe served a substantial meal at a lower cost, and the several venders on the platform sold cold sandwiches and coffee. There was also a market where passengers could refill their hampers.

Kate heard none of it. She stood transfixed, staring at her own face on a flier pinned to the billboard by the train schedule.

"Damn and damn," Annie swore, seeing what had captured Kate's attention. "Well, don't just stand there waiting for someone to recognize you."

Kate let herself be towed away. She had begun to believe they had really escaped. With each mile they'd travelled her fear had abated. But to come face to face with a wanted poster with her name and picture, and one that offered a reward of more cash than she had taken from the safe . . .

"They're never going to let me go," she said despairingly, gasping for breath as she ran with Annie toward a less populated part of town. "They're going to kill me."

"Not if I can help it. Take heart, they haven't got us yet. Look, there's an outhouse, and nobody's around."

"How can you be so calm about it?"

"No sense gettin' in a tizzy. You gotta keep your mind clear so you can think your way out of trouble." She helped herself to the facilities. "Fear can be a good thing," she called from behind the door. "It gets your blood going. But, if you let it, it can clot your brain, and then you ain't got a chance of thinking straight. So, you look at those posters, and you remember who put them there, and why, and then let that fear turn to anger. Then you do whatever you have to do to survive."

She stepped out of the cubicle, still tucking her shirt into her trousers. "Your turn. And don't forget one important fact," she went on as they changed places. "Bennett and Standish are counting on you to act the way you always do. From the little you told me, they take you for granted. You've always been pampered, and you've been little Miss Proper. You got all that money, they'll expect you to use it to escape. They'll be checking the hotels, restaurants, looking for you to buy a ticket to somewhere. They'll check the dress shops, they'll check the jewelers in case you try to sell them jewels. They'll expect you to give yourself away somehow. They've fooled you so long that they think you're simpleminded."

"I was simpleminded, I didn't see any of it, but I was clever enough to get away when I did," Kate called back.

"Maybe so, but they won't expect you to escape. My guess is they're still searching the area around your home, or more likely, up and down the river. But these people out here in the countryside, they're caught up in their own lives. They don't pay no mind to posters. Not unless you make 'em."

"So what you're saying," Kate said, joining her friend, "is that I shouldn't react when I see my own face on those papers?"

"Yeah. Just go about your business. You okay now? Think of it as a game."

"Some game, with my life at stake."

"Yours and mine. They'll have to go through me to get to you."

"I still can't understand why you would do that."

"Because people like Bennett make me furious. Who do they think they are? Did you bring any money?"

Kate searched her pockets. "Forty cents. I didn't think—"

"That's plenty. We'll get some food at the grocer's. By then those men will be finished with their horses."

Zack unlocked the door and slid it open, jumping nimbly into the car. Dan hefted himself up behind Zack, dusting off his trousers as he stood.

"Don't be too long, we'll miss our lunch."

"I'll eat better if I know these animals are fed and watered. Give them each a tin of oats, I'll get the water. We'll have to see they get some exercise when we reach Omaha."

"We? I'm no jockey. You won't get me on any of these beasts."

Zack laughed. "You can walk them, can't you?"

"I'd rather not. Flash some more of that money around. There are some who'll be glad to risk life and limb for two bits."

"They look good. I expected them to be more—distraught. Reynolds said they'd never been off his ranch."

"They're fine. Let's get to the restaurant. I don't like to rush my meals."

"All right, all right. Let me just check the doors."

Dan shook his head in exasperation. "Why do you pay people to do these chores, then insist on redoing them yourself?"

"Habit, I guess," Zack said, grinning. He tried the front door as he had the back.

"There, see. Needless effort." Dan jumped down to the ground. "Thirty minutes."

Zack turned at Dan's impatient prompting. "I'm coming." His eyes were drawn to the nail that should have held the key. He paused, then looked briefly behind the two crates stacked against the wall. He couldn't see a key anywhere, but then it could have been jostled under the boxes. He'd check later. After giving the carriage a tug to assure himself that it was still firmly secured, he joined Dan.

"What were you looking for?" Dan asked as Zack closed and locked the side door.

"Nothing. The key slid off the nail. I'll get it later. Where are we going?"

"The hotel, I think. We'll get faster service."

Kate and Annie returned to the train with a paper sack of food. For the most part, the folks in the town ignored the young woman and the boy who were part of the throng of travellers who invaded their town daily. The two women walked calmly down the platform. When Annie was sure no one was looking, she pulled Kate between the two cars, climbed up and unlocked the door, then pulled Kate up and into the car.

"Nothin' to it," she bragged, relocking the door and tossing the key into the air.

"Don't get overconfident. We have a long way to go," Kate warned.

Annie hung up the key and opened another window. "It smells like a barn in here. The least those men could'a did is clean this place out."

"Could have done, and why should they? Their horses don't care. Or do you reckon they should be thinking of our comfort?"

Annie made a face. "Let's eat. And save me one of those sugar lumps."

"We have plenty. Go ahead and eat." Kate went first to the big black stallion. "I wish I knew your name. I brought you a treat." She held out a lump of sugar. Liquid dark eyes stared curiously at her, and warm puffs of air enveloped her flat hand before velvet lips and a rasping tongue took the proffered sweet from her palm.

He was a beautiful animal, not young, but still lean, sleek, strong. "My grandfather would have loved to own you," she said in low crooning tones. "Such handsome foals you'll sire."

One by one she talked to the horses, giving each a taste of sugar, admiring each of them in turn.

Shortly thereafter people started to return to the train. Most of them remained outside, chatting with each other, walking around, enjoying the fresh air and sunshine before enclosing themselves in the confines of the cars again. From atop one of the boxes the girls watched them.

Kate tried not to think that she should be travelling in comfort, that she could have afforded a compartment of her own. She dared not let herself reflect on what could have been if Bennett had not come into her life. That life was over and she must go on from here, and if that meant she travelled in a cattlecar, then she would. But she vowed to herself that she would have better again someday. She would make a new life, and a good one. She would use every skill her grandfather ever taught her. She would succeed, and nothing or no one would stand in her way.

The whistle sounded. "All aboard," the conductor called, announcing also that this was the last stop until Kansas City. Annie gave up watching the people outside and jumped down from the window. Kate turned also, but at the last second was caught by the sight of a tall man. He was vaguely familiar to her, and her heart skipped a beat. She looked more closely at him, but she didn't know him. Still she couldn't turn away. He walked with a casual grace but held himself aloof from the rest of the crowd waiting to reboard the train. He turned his head as the man beside him spoke, then he threw back his head and laughed. Something very odd happened to her stomach, and she snatched her eyes away and jumped down.

With no fear of being disturbed, both girls napped during the afternoon, and didn't rouse from their sleep until the train slowed and pulled into the outskirts of Kansas City.

"We'll have to wait until dark to leave. There's a hundred people out there," Annie said, peering out the high window again. "And policemen. They're checking everyone who gets off the train. Double damn. I think they're looking for you. They're showing those posters around."

"I knew this was too easy," Kate said, shaking her head. "You could go on your own, they won't stop you."

"Quit babbling," Annie retorted, "and get in the carriage. We'll hide like we done before, and wait them out. Even if we have to stay here all night."

They hurriedly gathered together their belongings and folded themselves into the luggage boot, fastening the leather cover in place to conceal their presence.

"Wait," Kate whispered. "I forgot my washcloth."

"Never mind that. Someone's coming. Now be still or the whole carriage'll wiggle with you."

Kate closed her eyes and made herself as small as possible. Barely breathing, she laid her head on her tightly drawn-up knees and waited. Sam Bennett's cruel twisted grin and mocking eyes flashed into her mind. How he would enjoy seeing her caught and publicly humiliated. And Peter Standish's eyes would narrow and his lips would tighten in scorn, as if to say, "You foolish girl. Haven't you learned anything?" And Corinne would laugh that bitter, spiteful laugh. Katrina's eyes snapped wide open and met Annie's steady gaze as the lock clanked and the side door slid open.

"It's no trouble, Officer Windley," a deep, resonant voice said. "We would be checking the horses in any event."

"We appreciate your cooperation, sir. I know this must be annoying as hell; it is to us, but we gotta do it. Someone with powerful friends wants her caught. The governor himself ordered all the trains searched."

"That's rather drastic just for a young girl who stole something, isn't it? Murderers don't get this much attention. What exactly did she steal?" The second voice was younger sounding, but just as cultured as the first.

"Reports to us say she stole a large sum of money and a packet of very valuable jewels worth thousands. Personally, I think she's long gone. We're wasting our time."

Kate closed her eyes and prayed that the rest of the world would believe that, too. She wished she could disappear from the face of the earth.

Dan decided to remain outside, but Zack pushed himself up into the car and gave the officer a hand up "Look around to suit yourself while I water the horses," he said.

"Are these other doors locked?" the officer asked, trying the forward handle.

Zack turned. "Yes, they're both locked from the inside." His eyes went to the empty nail where the missing key should be. The hand bearing a tin of water stopped midway between the barrel and the stallion's water pan. The key was back.

Officer Windley stepped over the carriage tongue and joined Zack. "Beautiful animals. They must have cost dear." He checked all the stalls then looked over the bales of straw and the boxes.

"Worth every cent," Zack said, resuming his chores as if he hadn't just received a shocking jolt. Someone had been in here, a fact further verified by the water still standing in the trough. The horses had been watered. He emptied the tin and turned casually back to the barrel. The water level was definitely lower than it should have been.

"I'll finish this later," he said. He saw a square of flannel draped over the edge of the barrel. He picked it up and dampened it, bringing it to his face. He inhaled the flowery scent of soap. He finished wiping his face and hands and laid the cloth aside.

"I'm finished here," the officer said, stepping away from the carriage after checking under the seats.

"Fine. Shall we go then?"

Officer Windley jumped down and joined Dan on the platform. Zack looked from the key to the washcloth. His eyes swung to rest speculatively on the carriage. Before he left, he silently slipped both keys from their nails and put them in his pocket. Grinning smugly, he slid the side door shut and snapped the padlock in place.

For nearly half an hour Kate and Annie stayed in the stuffy confines of the carriage boot, expecting the return of the two men.

"They're not coming back," Kate whispered. "I'm getting out of here. I can't breathe."

"All right, but let me check first."

Kate sat on the carriage step and fanned herself. "I'd give anything to take this corset off."

"You're wearing that thing again? Why?"

"A proper lady must be—"

"Properly attired," Annie mimicked. "Who's here to know if you're cinched in or not? Go on, take it off."

Annie paced the aisle by the stalls while Kate removed the offending garment. "I don't feel good about staying here tonight. Kansas City's a big town. Maybe we could find a room for tonight, maybe for a couple of days, then catch another train."

"You mean because they said they'd come back later?" Kate asked, adjusting her clothes. She folded her corset and tucked it into her valise. "That's better." She brushed past Annie and picked up her washcloth to bathe her face and arms. She gasped and dropped it as if it had stung her.

"What?"

"It's wet. My washcloth is wet."

"Ain't it—isn't it supposed to be?"

"No. And it wasn't where I left it. He used it. Oh, Annie, he knows we've been here."

"Are you positive? I mean about the washcloth?"

"Yes," she sighed. "I'll bet he noticed the water I gave the horses, too. I'm sorry, Annie, I didn't consider that."

"Well, it's done. Let me think. We could chance leaving now, but after that search, we'll be on everyone's mind."

"I will, anyway. But we can't stay here. We have to take that chance. Those men might already be on their way back with the authorities," Kate said.

Annie turned away and began to pace again, her eyes darting here and there in thought. "If he suspected someone was here, he'd have said so when the officer was here. Why didn't he? I'll tell you why. Cause he didn't notice anything. He was in a hurry. And anyway . . . Kate?"

Kate looked up at Annie's oddly quiet tone of voice. "What is it?"

"The key. Did you take it?"

"I thought you had it." Her eyes followed Annie's to the naked nail. "You do, don't you?"

"I hung it up, I'm sure of it. The other one?"

Kate dashed to the back of the car and looked everywhere a key might have been placed, hidden, or lost. "It's not here. Are you certain it isn't in your pocket?"

"Yeah. Well, that explains that. The conniving devil locked us in. No wonder he isn't in a hurry to get back to his horses. He's making us sweat it out."

"I don't believe it," Kate said, trying first one door then racing to the other. "He can't do this. Why would he do this?"

# Chapter 4

Zack checked his pocket watch as he waited for Dan to finish his coffee. His long, lean fingers drummed on the linen covered table.

"Are you in a hurry?" Dan asked, setting his cup slowly onto the saucer. "We don't have to be back at the station for an hour yet. We're already checked into the hotel. Why are you so anxious?"

Zack took a long drink of his water. "I want to get back to the horses before those boys arrive to clean the car. Unless I miss my guess, we'll find an intruder in with the horses."

"An intruder?"

Zack placed the keys on the table. "Someone was in there. I think she still is."

"She? What are you talking about?"

"Someone who washes with French milled soap that smells of wildflowers."

"Where was she when you searched the car? Zack, be reasonable."

"Officer Windley searched all but one place. The luggage compartment. Remember when I mentioned that the key to one of the doors was gone? It was back."

"And you took it, both of the keys, so this—intruder couldn't get out again?"

Zack grinned mirthlessly and nodded. "And I intend to find out who she is." He took a folded paper from his breast pocket and opened it, pressing it flat to the table.

"You think this person is the woman? The thief the police are searching for? You'll have to notify the authorities, Zack. Why didn't you mention your suspicions to Windley?"

Zack stared at the sketch on the table. "I don't know. Look at her. She's so young. Would you like to see her imprisoned? Imagine what she'd look like when she got out, if she got out."

"But Zack, if she's a thief . . ."

"I've jumped to conclusions too many times in my life already. If she turns out to be this Montgomery girl, and if she really stole all that Windley claims, and if she doesn't have a damn good reason for doing it, then I guess I'll have to deliver her into the hands of justice. But what if she didn't? I could cause her unforgivable pain and embarrassment."

"So you're going out there yourself to play detective. What if 'she' has a gun? What if she's not alone? What if she has a 'he' in that car with her?"

"We can handle it."

"We," Dan grunted in resignation, pushing his coffee cup aside.

"Mr. Standish," the stationmaster exclaimed. "Didn't expect to see you back this evening. Your cars have already been detached. They're on track nine. Can I help you with anything?"

"I've made arrangements for two young lads to clean out the stablecar. And I've another horse coming. I forgot to leave the key with you. Could you let them in and lock up after them? I am going now to check the animals before I enjoy an evening on your town."

"Yes, of course."

"Oh, and this," Zack said, withdrawing an envelope, "is for the young men. And for your trouble." He handed another bill to the stationmaster.

"I'll see to it. Have a pleasant evening, sir."

"I can think of more pleasant ways to spend an evening than playing sleuth," Dan grumbled as they crossed the tracks to where their three cars were waiting to be coupled to the morning train. "Do you really trust him with that key?"

"I'll have to. I don't want to come back later."

When they reached the three cars on track nine, they

stopped to listen for any sound of voices inside. Knowing they'd never be able to enter the car undetected, Zack jumped up and reached a hand to Dan. He boldly inserted the key, allowing whoever was inside time to take cover.

"After we finish here," he said conversationally, "we might investigate the theatres. We could enjoy a play or perhaps a concert recital before a late dinner."

"Now that idea appeals to me," Dan said dryly. "Infinitely more than this . . ." Zack's raised hand stopped his tirade. "Than feeding horses," Dan finished stiltedly.

Zack took the precaution of locking the door after they had entered the hot stuffy car, winking conspiratorially at Dan's raised brows. Zack did indeed feed and water the horses, taking time to talk to each of them as he did, prolonging the suspense for the intruder.

"In another year or two we'll have built a reputation for raising the finest horses in the west. And you, my friend, will have to learn to ride."

"That will be a desperate day, I'll tell you."

Zack laughed and raised the washcloth for Dan to see before wetting it to wash his hands.

"I think we're almost done here," he said. He tossed the flannel square aside and moved toward the carriage. Slowly and very deliberately he walked to the back and unhooked the fasteners. In one fluid motion he flipped the leather up and reached inside.

The arm he grabbed was slight but firm, and attached to a hundred pounds of the meanest wildcat he'd ever met. He was a boy, a young boy, and he wasn't about to give up without a good fight.

"All right, you, get out here," Zack said, hauling the lad over the backside effortlessly.

"No," came a strangled cry from inside.

Zack's head snapped back around, but he had time for only a glimpse of big blue eyes before the thing he was holding began to bite and kick.

"Bastard! Don't you go near her," it yelled, struggling to break Zack's grip, kicking at his shins, reaching for his face.

"Dan, take this kid."

Zack wasted no time. He shoved the boy at Dan and turned to see who owned those blue eyes.

The girl came out of the boot with much less resistance until she saw the boy fighting with Dan, then she, too, began to struggle. Surprised at her strength and speed, Zack swung her around and clamped her back to his chest to protect his face from her fists and nails.

"Can't you leave us alone? We aren't hurting anything," she cried. She fought against his restraint and followed the boy's example by kicking his shins.

"Zack, I can't handle this one," Dan yelled as Annie broke loose and lit into Zack to help Kate.

She landed a solid blow before Zack pushed her forcefully away, sending her sprawling on the floor.

"Brute," the woman in his arms cried, increasing her efforts to escape.

"Sit on him," Zack ordered his friend. "Don't let him get up again."

Kate couldn't let them treat Annie that way. She was pinned to the tall stranger, his arms binding hers to her sides. He had all but lifted her off her feet anyway, so she clamped her hands over his arms and swung her legs up, planting her feet in the smaller man's side and kicking him away from Annie.

Annie sprang to her feet and jumped on her assailant. Kate felt the arms around her slacken, and then she and her captor were falling to the floor.

"Damn you, woman," she heard, before his weight fell on top of her.

Zack had no trouble subduing her. He pinned her wrists above her head and clamped his legs around hers.

"You vile snake," she hissed, twisting and thrashing against his superior strength and weight. She would have continued fighting had she not made the mistake of looking at him. And she wouldn't have looked had he not gone strangely still above her.

Grunting and groaning came from the couple beside them, and a few cuss words Zack wouldn't have expected a young boy to know, but he didn't care at that moment. His attention was caught by the face below his. If she was the girl in the picture, the artist had done her a grave injustice. But then no ordinary artist could have captured the velvet texture of her skin, the perfection of her delicate features, the extraordinary color of her eyes, made the more vibrant by her thick black lashes and finely arched brows.

He watched her as she continued to fight him, and then she stilled and looked straight into his eyes. His heart slammed almost painfully in his chest and began to pump hot blood through his veins.

Katrina couldn't have moved had she been free to do so. She had expected black eyes, dark and dangerous and sinister. Instead his were a warm, pale blue, like the sky on a hot summer afternoon. As she watched, the band of blue turned a deeper hue, the dark pupils enlarged. She felt his body stir unmistakably against her own.

In one far off corner of her mind she heard Annie cry out her name, and she panicked. Annie needed help. She pulled her hands free and raised them to rake her nails down his handsome face. He didn't try to stop her. He just watched her with the most astounded expression on his face.

Her fingertips came in contact with his face and her hands tightened, but she couldn't do it. She couldn't hurt him like that, deliberately and with no provocation, not when he was looking at her with those eyes.

She clenched her hands into small fists and beat them ineffectually against his broad shoulders, as tears of frustration and defeat squeezed from the corners of her tightly closed eyes.

"Don't. Don't weep," he said softly, and his lips touched the corner of one eye, following the salty trail to her ear. "I won't hurt you. I promise."

He could see she was thoroughly bewildered by that; he was too, and before his senses could right themselves, Zack touched his lips to hers. She struggled against him, pushing at his shoulders, but only halfheartedly. If she felt just a fraction of the swirling sensations he felt at the moment, she couldn't resist them either.

Her lips softened, her hands relaxed. Zack was suspended in heaven. And then she stiffened. He didn't want to fight her, and he didn't want her frightened of him, so with one last brush of his lips he lifted his head.

"My God," Zack heard. "She's a girl."

Zack's head turned, in time to see Dan drop the red cap and lower the fist he had raised, in time to see a wild mane of flaming hair tumble free and a vindictive female fist connect with Dan's left eye.

Dan would never raise a hand to a woman, so Zack was on his feet in a second, pulling the redhead off his friend. "That's enough. Stop this instant, or I'll deal with you myself."

"I'm not scared of you. Go ahead and try it," she rounded on him.

Zack held her at arms length. "Get a rope out of the last stall, Dan. We'll tie her up until she's willing to be reasonable."

"Reasonable?" the hellion spat. "You're the one who started this. Damn Yankee."

"Don't hurt her, please," Kate begged, laying a hand on Zack's arm. "Please. She won't fight anymore."

Zack took one look at her pleading sapphire eyes and his heart turned over. This might be worse than he first thought. Already he couldn't deny her.

"Can I count on that?" he asked the red-maned virago. "You can't escape. The doors are locked."

"Oh, turn loose of me," Annie snapped, jerking her arms free, turning to glare at Dan. "Just keep him away from me."

"I don't want to be anywhere near you, believe me," Dan retorted, brushing off his clothes.

"All right. Let's have a few answers," Zack said calmly. "First of all, who are you?"

When neither answered, Dan's temper snapped. "I'm getting the police."

"No," Kate cried. "Please," she said more quietly. "I'm—Kate Lawrence. And this is my—cousin, Annie. Annie Spooner. We didn't harm any of your possessions. I swear it."

"I can see that for myself. You were even thoughtful enough to water the horses."

"They'd a been kickin' the walls out if Kate hadn't a calmed them down," Annie added for good measure.

"For that you have my gratitude," Zack said to Kate. "Now why are you here, and more importantly, how did you get in here?"

Kate lowered her eyes. "I'm sorry, but I can't tell you that. We only wanted to get to . . ."

"We wanted to find a new town to live in," Annie interrupted, "and we didn't have no money—any money."

"So you helped yourself to my stock car?"

"Yes," Kate said boldly, returning her gaze to his. "That's what we did. And if you hadn't locked us in, we'd have gone long ago."

"Why must you find a new town? What was wrong with your own town?" He leaned back against the carriage wheel, his arms crossed, and openly studied the slender curves of her body.

Her breasts tingled, and she felt naked. She blushed and looked down. "We couldn't stay there."

Annie watched Zack's inspection of Kate's face and figure. He didn't fool her. He was a man on the prowl, and he had a fancy for Kate. "It was her husband," she invented impulsively.

"Husband?" Zack demanded, his eyes suddenly cold and hard.

Kate looked at Annie and frowned. Husband? She didn't want a husband. Not now. "He died," she found herself blurting.

"He died," Zack repeated quietly. "You don't sound very heartbroken."

Annie groaned inwardly. Talk about dunces. She tried again. "Of course she is. The guy was a rat. He treated her awful, then left her penniless. She was humiliated. We couldn't stay there, not when all his friends started to make a nuisance of their—themselves."

"I see. And how do you fit into this sad story, Miss Spooner? It is Miss, isn't it? Or do you have a dead husband somewhere?"

"I ain't got no husband, and I don't want none," she bit out, forgetting her lessons.

"Eloquently stated," Dan mocked.

"You hoity-toity lout. I oughta blacken your other damn eye."

"Settle down," Zack interceded. "That is no way for a young lady to act. Or speak."

"I ain't no . . ."

"Enough! We are gentlemen, and since you are with us, you will both henceforth deport yourselves as ladies."

"What do you mean by henceforth?" Kate asked warily.

"I mean we have a problem here. Can you prove who you are? A marriage certificate, a diploma, anything?"

Kate looked away. "No."

"I thought not. So we have only your word that you are who you claim to be. On the other hand," he went on, pulling a paper from his pocket, "we have this."

He flipped the poster open in front of the two women. Kate controlled her expression admirably, but even she could not prevent the color from draining out of her cheeks.

"We already seen it," Annie grumbled.

"And don't you think it bears a striking resemblance to Mrs. Lawrence?"

"Maybe," Annie shrugged. "So? I've seen hundreds of women who look as much like that as Kate does."

"A hundred, hm? And you, Katrina Montgomery, what do you think?"

She raised her chin stubbornly. If one had to tell a lie, one had better stick to it through the bitter end. "My name is Kate Lawrence. Mrs. Kate Lawrence. You have made a mistake, sir."

"Then you won't mind accompanying us back to our hotel for dinner?"

"Zack, are you serious?" Dan asked, appalled. "They'll not be permitted in the dining room."

"Then we shall have to remedy that."

"No," Kate cried. "We can't. We have no money. Couldn't you let us go? Please?"

"I'm afraid I can't do that. You see, I'm not convinced yet. I would hate to think I let a criminal go free. You have until we finish our coffee this evening to convince me you are telling the truth."

"What proof do we have that you won't hurt us?" Annie scorned. "I know what men are like."

"I see. In that case, my word that no harm will come to you will mean very little."

"You're right. It means nothing."

"We don't even know who you are," Kate argued mildly, unable to meet the sardonic glint in his eyes.

"I'm Zack, this is Dan. Now you know."

"Just Zack and Dan?"

"For now," he nodded. "Have you any belongings with you?"

"Yes. One valise. I'll get it."

"Stay here. I'll get it for you."

"Do you know what you're doing, Zack?" Dan asked, shaking his head disparagingly. "Have you given any thought to what—"

"Not now, Dan," Zack dismissed, pulling the valise and the bag of leftover food from the luggage compartment. He dropped the food in the corner to be disposed of. "Is this all?"

"Yes."

"Do I have your word that you won't try to run away?"

"And where would we go?" Kate replied resentfully, eyeing her case.

"And you?" he asked Annie.

Annie crossed her fingers and smiled benignly. "You have my word."

Zack's eyes met Dan's over the girls' heads. "If you run, we'll catch you and turn you over to the first policeman we meet."

Dan jumped down from the front of the car and reached up to help Annie, but she slapped his hands away and climbed down on her own. Kate was not so inclined. When Zack lifted his arms, she went to him. She braced her hands on his shoulders and let him swing her into the air. It was foolish, crazy, to want him to touch her again. Her heart was fluttering wildly. She looked into his eyes and felt his hands tighten at her waist. He lowered her slowly, never taking his eyes from hers.

"Give me the key. I'll lock the door," Dan said irritably.

Annie submitted resentfully to Dan's hand around her elbow as they walked. Kate, finding it unnatural and uncomfortable, preferred to tuck her hand around Zack's elbow. He had strong arms, firmly muscled, unusual in a man who obviously didn't need to earn his living by strenuous labor.

She remembered how firm his legs had felt, too, and his abdomen. And she remembered how, even when fighting with her, he'd controlled that strength so that he hadn't hurt her. He'd said he wouldn't hurt her. Instead he had kissed her. It hadn't been her first kiss by far, but it had been the first to leave her so shaken.

She found she wanted to kiss him again, and that made her wary. Why should one kiss lead to another when it never had before? Because she wanted to see if she'd feel the same wild leap of pulse, the same burning fire in her veins, the same sweet yearning in her breast. She didn't want to think that it was true, that for the first time in her life she had felt that overpowering feminine response her mother had once told her about. He was a stranger. With luck they'd never see each other after tonight.

She should hate him for that, for causing her to feel something when nothing could come of it. But why couldn't it? Wasn't a man exactly what she needed? Not just a man, but a husband. She mentally shook herself. Don't be fanciful. You don't know anything about him—except that he's handsome, wealthy, and conscientious. Otherwise he would have turned them in for the reward and not given them another thought. He obviously didn't believe their story.

Zack's mind was working, too. He wished he had not been carrying her valise. He wanted to cover her hand with his own, feel her soft skin again, and the satiny shape of her well-tended nails. As it was, he could only press her hand to his side.

Kate glanced up, startled at the brief pressure on her wrist. She was caught again by the blue warmth of his gaze. She felt a smile tug at her lips. Zack smiled back, then looked away.

"How long were you married, Mrs. Lawrence?"

Her foolish heart, buoyed by his smile, plummeted again.

"Ah—a year."

"How did your husband die?"

"I'd rather not talk about it, if you don't mind."

"Still too painful?" he asked with mock sympathy.

"Yes, that's right." She glanced up and saw his mouth tighten.

They crossed the tracks and walked several blocks. Dan, taking Annie by the arm, approached a waiting hansom cab and spoke to the driver in low tones. Kate kept walking, but turned her head to watch them. Was Dan leaving with Annie?

"You mustn't grieve for too long, you know. You're still young and quite lovely. It would be a waste."

She looked up, but he was gazing straight ahead. "What does that mean?" She glanced back at Dan and Annie.

"You were married. It should be easy enough to follow my meaning."

"Oh," she said, blushing first in embarrassment, then in anger. "I'm a waste if I'm not in some man's bed, is that it?" He grinned, which made her angrier, and very uncharacteristically, she lost control of her tongue. "In my opinion, that's the biggest waste of time there is." She tugged at her hand, but he increased the pressure of his arm against her wrist, keeping her locked at his side.

"Oh, I don't know. Some of my best memories are . . ."

"I don't want to talk about this either," she snapped irritably, to mask her disappointment. So much for fairy-tale princes.

"Very well," he said amicably, but she knew he was inwardly laughing at her. "Where are you from?" he asked instead.

"The East," she lied, glancing backward again. Dan and Annie were following again.

"You sound southern."

"The Southeast, then."

"No names? What city? County? I'll settle for what state."

"Why are you interrogating me?"

"Was I doing that? I thought I was being civilized. My questions were general enough. I could have asked you what different ways you and your husband made love, but I didn't," he hastened to add when she stiffened. "All I asked was the name of your hometown. A harmless conversational opener."

"I don't wish to converse at all."

"You appear well-educated. You have a graceful carriage, perfect grammar and elocution, discounting your delightful accent. Your manners are a little rusty at the moment, though."

"My manners are a far sight better than yours, sir. Are we nearly there? We've gone blocks and blocks."

"We thought it best to go by way of a dress shop. Dan was kind enough to inquire on your behalf where we might find one at this late hour. I hope you'll be appropriately grateful."

"I can't permit you to buy clothes for us," she said adamantly. "It's indecent."

"No more indecent than taking you to dine in the garments you are wearing."

"I have perfectly adequate clothing with me, thank you."

"And your cousin?"

"Well, no, but she won't take any. She's very self-sufficient."

Annie defected completely when Dan led them to a dress shop a few blocks away and stood her in front of racks of ready-made gowns in every color of the rainbow.

"These, I believe, will fit you, miss," the proprietress said, eyeing Annie's petite size.

"They're all so pretty," Annie said, her face beaming. "What do you think, Kate?"

Kate caught the smug grin on Zack's face and threw him a quelling glare. "I like the green dress with your hair, or the tan and gold."

"We'll take them both," Zack said, "plus the appropriate undergarments. And a pair of shoes if you can fit her."

"Yes, sir. I'm certain we can. And for the other young lady?"

Kate balked. "Nothing for me, thank you."

"Then I won't take none either," Annie said, fingering the fine material of the green dress one last time.

"The blue gown would look lovely on you," Zack said close to her ear. "Annie means it. She won't take anything if you don't. Look at her. She really wants that dress. Can you deprive her just for the sake of stubborn pride?"

Kate saw the disappointment in Annie's eyes even though she tried to hide it. Could she do that to a friend, a friend who had never owned one good dress in all her short and unhappy life? Kate thought of all the elegant dresses she herself had left behind at the Manor.

"You don't play fair," she whispered to Zack. "Well, I might try the blue gown, just to see how it fits," she said aloud.

"Oh, do," Annie squealed. "And this bonnet with it."

"All right. Come with me."

The shopkeeper returned with several more items, which she handed to Zack for approval.

"Yes, these will do nicely. See the young lady wears them. And those wretched clothes she has on, burn them."

"Yes, sir. May I also offer them the use of the washroom upstairs to freshen themselves?"

"We'll wait outside." Zack handed the woman several large denomination bills to cover the cost of the clothing and to compensate the owner for her time and personal attention.

"I'll return shortly with two lovely young ladies."

"You realize what she thought, don't you?" Dan asked when the door closed behind them.

"It doesn't matter. She'll be discreet."

"I suppose you saw to that."

"I did. She doesn't know who we are. She can do no harm."

"What do you think, about who they are?"

"They're lying, I know that much."

"Do you think she's the Montgomery girl?"

"I'm almost certain she is. But I can't believe she's a thief. She doesn't look or act like a thief. She's too sensitive. She was truly offended at the thought of a man buying her clothes."

"Hmm. Maybe they did it together. I can believe it of Miss Spooner."

"We'll have to wait and see."

"For how long? We leave early in the morning."

"For as long as it takes. They're coming with us."

"Now wait just a minute. If you think I'm spending the rest of this trip in the company of that harridan, you can think again. I'll take another train."

Zack's brows rose a notch at Daniel's vehemence. Rarely did Dan speak his mind, let alone so adamantly.

"I'll make a deal with you. If you feel the same way in the morning, I'll send them on their way."

"Fine, but I can tell you now I won't change my mind."

"Fair enough."

Annie turned this way and that in front of the long mirror. "I can't believe I'm real. Kate, look at me. I look like a real lady."

"Of course you do," Mrs. Weaver said, stopping Annie's gyrations to pin a dainty green bonnet to her clean and styled hair.

Mrs. Weaver, seeing that Kate was able to tend to her own needs and did indeed have some lovely undergarments with her to change into after her quick bath, gave her full attention to the fiesty redhead who was beside herself with the excitement of owning her first real dress.

"You do look beautiful," Kate said warmly. "I told you you would."

"I know, but I never thought . . ."

"I only wish I could have paid for the clothes. I don't like owing a man."

"Nonsense," Mrs. Weaver said, coming to help Kate with her hair. "It's true some men will take advantage of women every chance they get, and I've known some of 'em, but those two down there, they seem like proper gentlemen. They'll take 'no' for an answer if that's what you want. Let them pay, they can afford it."

Kate wanted to explain that they'd only known Zack and Dan for a little over an hour, but how could she? Who would believe it, unless she explained everything, and that she couldn't do. So she nodded and said nothing.

"Now you best hurry on down. You've kept your gentlemen waiting long enough. I'll bring your packages."

Kate opened the door and stood aside for Annie to walk through. She crossed her fingers and hoped the men wouldn't disappoint her. They didn't.

"Well, well," Zack said first. "That's quite a change. You look lovely, Miss Annie. It will be an honor to dine in your company this evening."

Annie stammered her thanks and turned to look at Dan. The look on her face mirrored her conflicting emotions, daring him to contradict Zack's opinion, as if she expected him to do just that, but pleading with him not to spoil her moment.

"You certainly do *look* a perfect picture," he said smoothly, and Annie relaxed and gave him a genuine smile. Her first.

Kate's eyes met Zack's. Had Annie not heard the back-handed compliment in Dan's words? Zack grinned and held a hand out to her. "And you are as beautiful as I knew you would be."

Kate automatically slipped her gloved hand into his and didn't object when he tucked her hand around his elbow again. He picked up Kate's valise and turned to Mrs. Weaver.

"You came highly recommended. I see we were not misled. My compliments to you."

Mrs. Weaver looked from one man to the other. "My pleasure. Just remember one thing. In spite of what they looked like when they arrived, these are decent young ladies. You mind your manners." She handed the package of Annie's new garments to Dan with a stern look of warning.

Dan's reaction was one of astonishment. Whether he couldn't believe they were decent, or ladies, or whether the thought of taking liberties with Annie was too much to contemplate, Kate couldn't discern. Zack merely nodded solemnly and assured Mrs. Weaver that the ladies would receive their utmost respect.

Grand hotels were not a novelty to Kate, but Annie's mouth fell open when Dan escorted her into the flashy opulence of the lobby.

"La-di-da," she exclaimed. "Look at all the gold, and them mirrors."

"Don't gape, Miss Spooner," Dan said. "You're drawing curious eyes."

Kate laid a calming hand on Annie's arm to stem the tide of anger she saw swelling in her bright hazel eyes. "Ignore him," she whispered, "and enjoy yourself. We may be back to stale bread and cheese tomorrow. Act as if you're bored."

"Bored?" Annie whispered. "How could I be . . . But he's

right. I don't know how to act here. I'll make a hash of it."

"Just follow my lead. Do as I do."

"This way, ladies," Zack said indulgently. He led them to a restaurant off the main lobby, bypassing red velvet lounges on Persian carpets, marble statues, elegantly clad ladies and gentlemen strolling under the crystal chandeliers.

"Good evening, Mr. Standish," the maitre'd greeted them. "We held your table for you. Follow me, please."

Kate was struck dumb. She stopped in her tracks and stared at the man beside her. Standish? Mr. Standish? The room began to spin sickeningly. She reached out to Annie and felt herself falling.

# Chapter 5

Zack moved forward to follow the maitre'd. Kate's hand fell away from his arm. He thought nothing of it until he heard Annie's soft gasp. He swung around and caught Kate just as she was sinking to the floor.

"Good heavens, young lady, you're white as a ghost. What's wrong?"

"It's nothing," Annie said quickly, covering for Kate's shock. She put a supporting arm around Kate's waist. "We haven't had much to eat today. The smell of the food—it must have made her light-headed. Let's get her to the table. Kate?"

"Yes, yes. I need to sit down. I'll be fine in a moment."

"Would the mademoiselle like a glass of water?"

"Yes," Annie answered, "and something stronger. Can we get her a chair?"

"This way, then."

"It's that blamed corset you're wearin', if you ask me," Annie grumbled, bringing a reluctant grin to Zack's lips and a little color to Kate's cheeks.

"Really, Miss Spooner, you have the most outrageous tongue," Dan declared disparagingly from behind them.

"And you're a swell-headed upstart. Leave me alone."

The maitre'd gave all four of them a wary frown as he saw them seated. "Will a sherry be suitable?" he asked, looking down his long nose. At her brief nod, he moved away swiftly, as if he couldn't wait to separate himself from them.

"He must think we're all a bit mad," Dan groused.

"Why do you care what he thinks," Annie asked derisively. "Who is he, anyway? You'll probably never see him again. Are you better, Kate?"

"Yes," she said, but the blue eyes that met Annie's said differently.

Annie squeezed her hand and nodded her understanding. Standish. An innocent coincidence, a nasty trick of fate, or what? Had the men in St. Louis known who owned that particular railroad car? Had they been working for Bennett? Annie didn't know the answers. How much more confused Kate must be feeling.

Their waiter arrived bearing a small crystal glass of sherry and a goblet of water on a silver tray. "I'll return later for your order."

"Drink this," Zack coaxed, pressing the glass into Kate's trembling hands.

She took it without looking at him and sipped the warming drink. She was disgusted with herself. How could she have felt what she had for a Standish? How could she have let herself like him? Had he planned to deceive her? Had he known all along she was on the train? Was he following her? And why? How could she not have seen the resemblance?

"I think her head is clearing now," Annie said, giving Kate's hand a warning pat. "Don't be afraid. We'll have a nice relaxing meal. You'll feel fightin' fit in no time. You'll see I'm right."

Kate looked at her friend and found comfort there. The coldness began to ebb away. Annie understood. There was encouragement in her words, and a promise. Somehow Annie would get them out of this predicament, but she had to help. She began to relax and get herself under control. Zack must not suspect that they knew.

"Has she been ill?" Zack asked Annie.

"You don't suppose it's something else," Dan suggested, meeting Zack's baleful glare squarely. The suggestion was not so outrageous, whether she was the Montgomery girl or not. She claimed to be a widow, after all, but, if not, being with child, perhaps by someone not free to marry her, would also be a motive for theft and flight. As he held Zack's gaze, he saw his friend reach the same conclusions.

Zack found he hated the idea. His gaze swung to Kate and narrowed as he saw that her face had lost color again. "You'd better finish that sherry," he said curtly.

Kate longed to disappear. Dan's suggestion was scandalous, and Zack's accusing eyes condemned without a hearing. But Annie had given her hand another squeeze, and so she kept quiet. Annie was definitely in a better frame of mind to handle this.

"I'm sure you're both dead wrong. She's had an unmerciful bad time lately. She's exhausted, and she's hungry. But if she is carrying a babe, it's nothin' to scowl at."

"No, of course not. We'll order dinner now. You don't mind if I order for you both?"

"Not at all," Annie replied primly, secretly relieved that she wouldn't have to struggle with unfamiliar words on a menu.

"I would prefer chicken to beef, please," Kate said, gathering herself together, letting her anger fortify her as Annie had suggested. "Something in a light sauce, I think. Would that suit you, Annie? And fresh fruit, melon perhaps, for starters."

"That would be lovely," Annie said carefully.

Kate turned blank eyes to Zack. She knew she appeared composed, a defensive tactic she'd mastered at the Manor. "Would that be possible?"

Zack's fingers drummed on the table as he listened to Kate's little speech. What was happening with her? Where was the spirited vixen who'd almost scratched his eyes out, where was the vulnerable creature who'd almost collapsed in his arms? Where were the luminous eyes that mirrored the turbulent emotions underneath? He had been drawn to that volatile creature so ready to fight or cry or flee. This face, these eyes, were of a different person. She had closed herself off, and he was shut out. What had caused it?

"Mr. Standish?" Kate said, the taste of that name bitter on her lips.

"Yes, I'll see that you have what you want." And just what was that? What did she want from him? Freedom? Help? He didn't know how to help her yet, but he knew he couldn't give her the freedom she wanted, not even if Dan decided to follow through with his threat. Not until he found again the girl he'd kissed. Not until he had learned what had sent her into flight. Not until he knew for a fact that he couldn't have her. Only then would he let her go.

Kate felt her skin grow chill at the intent manner in which he studied her, but not by so much as a blink did she show it. The waiter arrived to take their order, giving her a few additional minutes to steady herself.

"Tell me, Mr. Standish, do you have a family?" she asked when the waiter had gone.

"A family?"

"Yes. A mother, father, wife, children?" She felt Annie tense beside her and knew she probably wanted to kick her shin under the table, but Kate needed to know how Zack would respond.

"No, I don't have any family, Kate."

"None? Not even a cousin?"

"My mother died three months ago. She was all the family I had. She was all I needed."

"I'm sorry about that." She looked at his face, seeing the same wide brows, the same firm chin, the same bone structure at his cheeks and nose. On Peter the features had added up to a handsomeness that was nearly pretty, and Peter's light hair and gray eyes added to the illusion of gentlemanly perfection. Peter played those looks to get what he wanted.

On Zack the same features, the nose a bit bolder, the chin firmer, shaped a man more dangerously male. His black hair and his piercing blue eyes added to his aura of power. Zack was a remarkably handsome man, but had he been ugly, he would still have possessed that certain commanding presence.

Yet, however much they differed in character, they were too much alike in person to ignore. He had to be lying to her, but why lie about a thing like that unless he'd been instructed to? Her grandfather had always said that what was on the outside could never completely mask what was on the inside, but sometimes it was hard to believe. She wouldn't have taken Zack for a liar, but then she wasn't a liar either, and she'd lied. How she hated lies and deceit.

"Kate?" Annie said for the second time.

"Oh, I'm sorry. What did you say? My mind was miles away."

"Dan asked if you had any family."

Kate remembered her mother, who would still be alive but for Bennett. "No. Not anymore," she answered. "My parents were both single children."

"You said Annie was your cousin," Zack reminded her.

She shook her head. "That wasn't the truth."

"No?"

"No."

"I see."

"We're friends," Annie said, defending Kate. "We've been friends for a long time. We're more like sisters than cousins."

Zack turned to Kate. "And your husband? Did he have family?"

"She don't wanna talk about that scum," Annie answered blisteringly.

"No, I'd rather not," Kate concurred, studying her flatware.

"Very well. Have you any idea where your new home will be?"

"Annie wants sunshine and not too much rain."

"But not the desert." Annie clarified. "Someplace green."

"Do you like mountains? How about snow?" Dan asked. "I hear Colorado is beautiful."

"You go there then. I've been through enough cold winters. Is New York cold? That's where you're from, isn't it?"

"Why would you guess New York?" Daniel asked, suspecting she'd heard of the Sieberts of New York. "Do you recognize my name?"

"I don't know your name. How could I? I saw where your carriage was built. What is your name, besides Dan?"

Dan looked at Zack as if seeking his permission. At Zack's slight nod he told her. "I thought perhaps you'd heard of it."

"Why should I?" she shrugged. "I don't move in them high and mighty circles. Are ya famous?"

Dan didn't know how to answer that. The men of the Siebert family had often been quoted and noted in newspapers and journals for their business acumen, so had he and Zack, for that matter. "No, not famous," he decided.

"Everyone else here is a loner. Do you have any family?" Annie asked Dan.

"I have more family than I sometimes care to claim. They're scattered all over the east coast."

"That must be nice. I always wanted—"

"What did you want, Miss Spooner?" Dan queried suspiciously.

She shook her head. "Nothin'."

"And you, Mrs. Lawrence?" Zack asked, his eyes intent on Kate's face. "If you could have one wish, what would it be?"

"One wish?" To have her mother back, her grandfather, to have possession of the Manor as was always intended? No. As much as she missed her family and her home, they had been gone from her life for too long to ever imagine they'd be real again. With sudden clarity she knew what she could wish—that Zack had a different name, that he hadn't just doused that faint glimmer of hope that had sprung to life within her. She had dared to reach out toward that beckoning light, to hold it in her hands for a little while, and for a couple hours her life had lost that loneliness that had engulfed it for years. She should have known better.

Zack saw the sheen of tears in her eyes before she blinked them back. Her quiet words pricked his heart.

"Wishes are weapons for the whimsies of Fate to use against you."

"Yes, all right, I will concede that they don't act like criminals," Dan argued later that night. "But I still maintain that Kate is the Montgomery girl."

"Which is exactly why they're locked in the next room."

"My room," Dan grumbled.

"Your room only had one bed. If I could have secured a third room, I would have, but . . ." He poured another finger of brandy and swirled it in his snifter. "Have you changed your mind about tomorrow?" he asked, glancing furtively from his glass to Dan. "If you still feel we should contact the police, then we can do so first thing in the morning. I see no reason to deprive the ladies of a comfortable night. It will be the last they'll have for a long time."

"Don't try your games with me, Zack. I've watched you work your wiles before."

Zack grinned unrepentently. "At least we gave them a good meal. For a little thing Miss Spooner can pack away the food."

"She can pack a wallop, too," Dan said, fingering the bruise below his eye.

"She's a tornado, all right. I wonder where she and Kate found each other. They're an unlikely pair."

"Do you hear yourself, Zack? You know she's Katrina Montgomery or you wouldn't be questioning the long-standing friendship she and Annie claim."

"Did I say that? Perhaps I did. It is evident that Kate was raised with the finer things in life. She took for granted the surroundings tonight, the service, the food. Annie was lost. She'd never been anywhere near a place like this. She watched every move Kate made before she copied it. Her eyes never stopped moving, taking it all in, and she was enthralled by everything and everyone she saw."

"Like a child on Christmas morning," Dan agreed. "She handled herself fairly well, if one can overlook her misuse of the language."

"Even in her speech she was trying to imitate Kate."

"Did you see her after dinner when we passed the mirrors in the lobby? She couldn't take her eyes off her own image. And when the elevator started up, she gave a little gasp and took hold of my arm. This is a new world for her. You probably didn't notice any of that. You couldn't tear your eyes away from Kate."

Zack sat down and leaned back into the thickly stuffed settee, stretching his long legs out in front of him. "I've never seen eyes the color of hers before. And never outlined with lashes so thick and black. She is without a doubt the most naturally beautiful woman I've ever met. She intrigues me, Dan. Her eyes . . . One minute they're dancing with life and laughter, the next they're veiled, shutting her off from the world."

"Like watching your own, hmm?" Dan said, slanting him a

mocking grin.

"Mine? I don't do that. Do I do that?"

Dan didn't answer, just loosened his tie and walked to the open window to look down on the city. It had begun to rain, and the lights were magnified and reflected from the slick pavement and glossy tops of the hansom cabs. The air was cool and fresh. Thunder rumbled, low and long and near. He enjoyed storms, but he'd always been able to watch their sometimes violent nature from a place of comfort and safety.

Where would Annie and Kate have been tonight when the storm finally hit, had they not been in the next room? Would they have remained on the train, or would they have gone in search of someplace else to hide, someplace cheap and rat-infested? Did they have any idea what could happen to them if they fell into unfriendly hands? They still could unless . . . Dan didn't like the thought that he'd be harboring a fugitive, but he liked even less the thought of those two helpless girls being attacked, raped, killed. And though he could well imagine the grit Annie would have if they were thrown into a jail cell with common criminals, exposed to the filth and stench of those before them, made to endure shame and degradation, he knew Kate would be devastated.

Kate had spirit, but it was obvious she was used to being protected. The seamy side of life had never touched her. Annie was different. She'd never seen the better side of life. If the two of them were friends, then they had been friends for a very short time.

And then there was Zack. Dan had never seen Zack so interested in a woman before, nor had he ever seen a woman, or a man, evade Zack's probing eyes and demanding questions as Kate had done. Zack could level a building when his eyes turned silver-blue. The best of con men crumbled under his intensity, the most ruthless of business men backed off to reconsider their propositions. But not Kate. She stared right back with unflustered calm and stuck to her story.

It might be worth enduring Annie's sharp and untutored tongue to see if Zack could break down Kate's lies. He turned his head to look at his partner, a man he knew well. Zack had met a challenge, and Zack loved a challenge. Even now Dan could see the wheels turning in his head, the light of battle in his eyes.

"I've made a decision," Dan said, not that it mattered. Zack had already decided. "I'm willing to give them a chance, but if we see that they're not the innocents they appear to be, we dump them at the next town. I don't want to see them in jail, but neither do *I* wish to end up behind bars."

Zack stood, looking pleased and relieved. "You have my word. And thanks. So, what would you say to a drink before bed? There's a tavern across the street."

The storm broke an hour later, unleashing its power over Kansas City. Snug under the downy comforter, Kate couldn't help remembering the storm that hit while they were on a barge on the Mississippi River.

"This is certainly cozier than sleeping under a tarp."

"This is pure heaven," Annie agreed.

"I keep thinking about Raleigh and Jasmine." Raleigh was the tough, negro dock manager who had found Kate and Annie hiding in the crates in St. Louis. At his intimidating stance Annie had been quick to explain and to show him Jake's letter. The man named Raleigh had read it then passed it to his friend, a wiry little old man he called Davey. The two men exchanged a strange look, and then Raleigh had rapped out a series of orders to his co-workers to forget they'd seen any lady on the dock, and sent the two stowaways off to his home with Davey.

"Why do you suppose they took us in like that?"

"Because Jake said to, I guess."

"I think it was more than that. I felt . . . I don't know how to explain it. I was pampered. You noticed it, too."

"They took a shine to you, that's all."

"For pity's sake, Annie. Jasmine washed and ironed my clothes, she carried all that water for our baths, she gave me their bed to nap on, she cooked that feast for us. And all their friends who stopped in, they gave me such odd looks. And Raleigh's prayer, thanking God for the chance to finally repay a kindness. I don't understand any of it. We were strangers, yet they did everything possible to help us and to get us out of St.

Louis safely."

Annie shrugged in the dark. "So, you heard the story of the good Samaritan. Don't make such a thing of it."

"What really frustrates me is that I think you know why."

"Go to sleep," Annie said and turned her back to Kate. She pulled the covers closer as a particularly bright flash of lightening rent the night with a thundering din. "Jeez, you're right. I'm glad we're here and not on the river."

"I hope the horses aren't upset by this," Kate said from her side of the big bed.

"I can't work up too much concern for the horses. I'm enjoying this luxury too much. Anyway, if they're from the Mississippi valley like Zack said, they're used to storms."

"What do you make of them, Annie?"

"Zack and Dan? I don't know. Zack was determined to trip you up. I was ready to dump my dinner over his head for a while there, until I saw how ya handled him. But then to go and give us this room . . . I just don't know. How could ya be so calm?"

"You, Annie, not ya."

"Yeah—yes. You nearly unravelled when you saw your picture on the billboard, you almost fainted when you heard his name, yet you faced him down when even I was losing my nerve."

"I've had years of practice. Dodging Zack's questions was no different from matching wits with Sam and Corinne, easier, perhaps, since I didn't feel the malevolence with Zack that I did with the other two. With Zack it was a contest, with Sam and Corinne it was a duel. I never realized until last night just how serious a battle it was."

"Do you think Zack's related to Peter Standish?"

"Yes. They look too much alike. I've been trying to figure out why he'd lie about it. My first thought, of course, was that he's in on it with Peter."

"You don't reckon that anymore?"

"I don't know what to think. I don't want to believe it. He's not like Peter, really, except in some of his mannerisms, and his looks. He's stronger than Peter. I can't see Zack taking orders from Bennett. Zack would be giving the orders. And

Bennett and Peter and Corinne are compulsively greedy and selfish. They burn inside with envy for anyone wealthier than they. You can actually see it in their eyes. Zack wasn't impressed at all when those people seated at the table next to us were made such a fuss over. Zack is content with himself. My grandfather told me once that contentment came through achievement, reaching a hard won goal. I don't think Zack and Dan have attained their wealth at someone else's expense."

"But you still think he's lying?"

"Yes, and it worries me."

Annie huffed. "If Peter were my relative, I wouldn't claim him neither. He sounds like a horse's ass."

"Annie, dear," Kate said, chuckling, "you must curb your impulsive tongue. Ladies do not use such language."

"What would you call him?"

"An arrogant swine, a conceited jackel, an—equine posterior."

Annie gave a bark of laughter. "A what?"

"A horse's butt."

Annie laughed and clucked her tongue. "I need to give you lessons, sweetie. When you say it, it sounds like a compliment. I heard you when Zack hauled you out of the buggy. 'Why you bi-i-g bru-u-te,'" she mimicked.

"I didn't say that."

"Near enough. You might just as well have fluttered your lashes at him."

"I did okay with Clyde and Jeb."

"Yeah," Annie admitted, "and with Zack, too. We didn't stand a fig of a chance with two grown men. We'll have to be more careful from now on. Two women alone in the west . . . We'll have to go out of our way to avoid trouble—like Jake said. I guess he knew."

"What's going to happen tomorrow?" Kate asked. "Will they turn us in?"

"They said they would, and we have to believe it, so we won't give them the chance. We'll leave before they're up."

"I wish we didn't have to," Kate murmured, knowing Annie was right.

"You like him, don't you."

"Don't be ridiculous," she denied. "I only meant that we haven't solved the mystery of who he is."

"Um-hmm."

"I'll always wonder."

"Yeah."

"It could be a coincidence."

"It could."

"Oh, don't be so agreeable. You don't believe a thing I've said."

"Neither do you."

# Chapter 6

In the exclusive lounge of a neighboring hotel the two men sat in conversation, enjoying a late evening drink. Zackery Standish was preoccupied with the horse he was to purchase early the next morning, not really concentrating on the page of figures that his partner Dan Siebert was explaining, figures showing their investments, their ready capital, what had been designated for the purchase of their newest enterprise, what would be needed for expansion, what was left.

"So you see, we've this amount remaining, quite sizable, even allowing for anything I may have overlooked. But I can't think what that could be. I've given considerable thought to this and can't believe I've missed anything."

"Nor can I," Zack said drolly, knowing Dan's genius with finances.

"What I'd like to propose then," Dan said hesitantly, "is to use this amount to start a winery. The area is conducive to vineyards, as demonstrated by those already existing."

"A vineyard, a winery?" Zack murmured thoughtfully.

"And we have the land and an option on more."

"When did this idea jump into your head?" Zack asked, curious, but not really surprised. Dan could spot opportunities faster than a hawk could spot a field mouse.

"I've been mulling it over for a while. Since we decided to move west, actually."

"You realize I have no expertise in that field, none at all," Zack pointed out.

In the past the ideas and the financial arrangements had been Dan's, the implementation of those plans had been Zack's. Where Daniel had a brilliance for ferreting out the next golden egg, he was too shy and retiring to promote it and reap the profits. Zack, on the other hand, was a manager of people. At least a half a head taller than Dan's five foot, nine inches, and dark where Dan was fair, with sharp, alert silver-blue eyes where Dan's were a soft hazel and often focused on some inner thought or calculation, Zack exuded a confidence and control that commanded attention, respect, and trust, in the business world. Men looked up to Zack when they often didn't see Dan at all. Zack felt uneasy about that and tried to draw Dan into the more public side of business, but Dan wouldn't budge. He was satisfied to remain behind the scenes. Together theirs had been an unbeatable partnership, he said, and why change it.

"I thought perhaps I could take this on myself," Dan went on. "I've studied grapes, climates, soils, I know wines. I even spent a summer in France when I was fifteen. My great-uncle was a vintner. Since that summer, I've been fascinated by wines."

"You should have said so earlier. We could have tried it back east."

"We had enough to keep us busy there. Now, with only a horse ranch to contend with, which you'll manage, I thought . . ."

"By all means."

"Not that I want to handle it entirely on my own, you understand, unless you don't want to get involved. The land acquisition, the marketing, labor, well you know how I am with that. I want to oversee the technical side, the vines, the grapes, the irrigation, the fermentation, bottling, and so on. I'll understand if you say no. We won't have a quick return on our money as we've had in the past. I must warn you about that."

"Do we need it? It seems to me, by what you've just explained, that we could retire to a life of leisure today."

Dan grinned. "Yes, I'm certain we could. I only wanted you to be aware—"

"Dan, my good friend, this ranch has been my goal for years. You never once objected to my going after it, even when it meant leaving Philadelphia. Why should I object to you're doing what you want? Actually, I was feeling guilty about that very thing. We've both worked hard for ten years, but I was the only one realizing my dream. This idea of yours is perfect. You've no need to convince me."

"I never objected to leaving Philadelphia for a very good reason. I needed to get away. You do remember Lorraine?"

"Blonde? Short and curvy?"

"And insistent? Yes, that's the one. She's been making herself at home with my family, so much so that my father asked me when the wedding was to take place."

"Ahh," Zack responded, leaning back and grinning at his partner.

"You wouldn't be amused if Ellen Bentley were twisting your arm to marry her," Dan retorted.

"Lord, spare me the Ellen Bentleys of the world," Zack laughed.

"And the Lady Duckworthys and Miss Ashleys. How do you always manage to become entangled with that particular type?"

Zack grunted. "Not because I choose to. Their brothers or daddies orchestrate the initial meetings. The lovely ladies take it from there. I tell you, Dan, it's a relief for me to be away from all that scheming. In fact, if you want to know the absolute truth, that's why California appealed to me."

"And to me," Dan agreed. "It was like a promise of freedom when you suggested it."

Zack laughed, drawing an unusual burst of laughter from Dan as well.

"We are cowards, aren't we?" Dan admitted.

"I never did know how to handle a woman's tantrums or phony tears with any tact. Sometimes the best defense is retreat. How did your parents react when you told them our plans?"

"With a dozen objections," Dan answered. "How could we even think of selling a lucrative business like ours? How could we give up proven success for the unknown? Are we out of our minds? Whose harebrained scheme was this, going off on some lark, and why did I fall for it? Hadn't Dad taught me better? It was a shock for him, for all of them, the suddenness of it all. Dad still likes to take credit for my successes. Now that I'm gone, he'll have to admit to himself that I can manage without his constant advice. He won't like that. And Mother cried, as I expected. How can she see me suitably married when I'm across the country from her? I'm sure to be snared by some unscrupulous female who will reduce my life to ruins."

"And Lorraine?"

"You mean Lorraine's mother, don't you? She couldn't believe I was throwing it all away, and that I wasn't going to marry her sweet daughter. Such a wonderful match, that. She was even willing to consider allowing Lorraine to move away as long as my ring was on her finger. That would have lasted a month, at most, before Lorraine demanded to return to Philadelphia. I'm not staunch enough to stand up to Lorraine or a mother-in-law like Mrs. Smythe. I'm beginning to wonder if I should marry at all."

"Why worry about it? From what I've seen, marriage is overrated."

"Cynic," Dan accused.

"I suppose. I might change my mind if I ever find a woman who thinks more of me than my money. What are the possibilities of that?"

"Ay, there's the rub," Daniel quoted dryly. "But then hasn't it always been?"

"Need I remind you of my less than affluent beginning? I was dirt poor when we first met."

"You weren't poor," Dan rebuked. "You had a beautiful, loving mother, who was willing to stand beside you in whatever you decided to do. And you had a stepfather who was very generous."

Zack's face softened. "Yes, I did have that." He sipped his brandy and remembered. For the first time he began to talk about his past. "I was too proud by half. I was an ingrate. I never did like the man she married until it was too late to right things with him. I wish I had. Mother sensed the tension between us, though we both tried to hide it, and it still hurts when I think that I caused her pain."

"You were young, and she understood," Dan said, just as he

had understood the tension between the two men who had loved Margaret Standish. "Simon was good to you in spite of it."

"I can't deny that, but he reminded me too much of my father for me to relax around him. My father was very possessive, too, although my father wanted Mother's total adoration along with that of his various mistresses. I was always in the way."

"Simon didn't think so. He respected you enormously for the way you gave up a life of your own to support your mother. That's why he paid for your tutors and sent you off to college."

"With my mind I knew that. In my heart I always felt he was getting me out of Mother's life so he could take over. I resented it like hell. That's why I feel so guilty now. Simon loved my mother, and what he did for me, he did for her sake as well as mine."

"Don't be so hard on yourself. You were only seventeen."

"Hmm. But old enough. Simon certainly didn't have to bother with me. It wasn't until his accident that I finally realized that. Do you know what he said to me when he was dying? He said, 'I've had her for five wonderful years, my boy, but I'm going to have to give her back now. She has enough money to live in comfort, but you must see that she spends it wisely. I'm counting on you.' Can you believe that?"

"Of course. To whom else would he entrust her care?"

"That's just the point. All along he'd had faith in me, while I'd inwardly accused him of all manner of selfishness. I was the selfish one, and I was too ashamed to admit it. How could I explain how I'd felt? I was resentful and jealous that he could give Mother what I couldn't. But he knew that. While I stood there battling for words, he told me he'd known all along that he hadn't many years to live. He'd never mentioned it until then, but he had cancer. He said his accident, though it robbed him of time with my mother, saved him from a long and painful death. He didn't send me away to be rid of me, he sent me away to prepare me to take care of the woman we both loved. Because he knew he wouldn't be here to do it himself."

"He'd have been proud of you," Dan said solemnly.

"I . . . How did we get on this subject? I must have had one too many drinks. I'm getting maudlin."

"Just clearing away the cobwebs. Your mother's only been gone for three months. Everyone goes through a period of introspection after losing a loved one."

Zack's lip twisted ruefully. "I've been doing my share, that's a fact. Sorry to put you through it with me."

"Does good to talk. You've always kept your feelings too much to yourself."

"So you keep telling me." Zack stood and stretched his tall body. "I think I'll get some sleep."

"Sure. If you don't mind, I'm going to work on a few more calculations before I retire. I'll try not to disturb you. And thanks, Zack. This opportunity means everything to me."

"No thanks required."

"I disagree. Our success has been primarily due to you. I didn't want to impose my—"

"Hey, wait just a second. I wish you wouldn't keep intimating that you are superfluous. If that's what your father has been telling you, he's wrong. Separately we could not have reached this point as quickly or as easily. I may not always show it, but I depend on you heavily. I'd be lost without you."

Dan's eyes skittered away from Zack's, back to his notebook. "If you say so. But thanks again, just the same."

Zack grinned crookedly and shook his head. Dan just couldn't admit his own value. The flip side of the coin from his father. It would do Daniel a world of good to be away from Logan Siebert's cutting tongue. This move was precisely what both of them needed.

Morning brought with it sunshine and clear skies, but also more frustration. Annie tried the door for the fifth time, then gave it a sound kick.

"This is twice they've locked us in," she said in a red temper. "They're not getting away with this."

"Sit down, Annie. Your temper tantrums won't get the door open."

"I could kick myself for not checking this last night when we had time to do something about it."

"Apart from tearing down the door altogether, what would you have done?"

"That's it. We'll take the door off the hinges."

"Are you mad? Have you the slightest idea how to take a door down?"

"Not yet, but how hard can it be?"

They were not to find out, because the lock clicked and a knock sounded on the carved wood panel.

Annie yanked open the door, fury mounting with every move she made. "You contemptible swine."

Zack swept by her, ignoring her completely. "Good morning, Kate."

"She's Mrs. Lawrence to you, you blasted—*man*. How dare you lock us in?" Annie's tirade continued. "What right do you have?"

Dan waltzed into the room, oblivious to what awaited him. "The porter will see our luggage to the depot. Good mor—uuf." He staggered back, clutching his stomach.

A stunned silence followed. Deep color seeped into Dan's face, and his gentle brown eyes came alive with anger. Annie stepped back.

"Why the devil did you do that, you ungrateful wretch?"

"I hate being locked in. I hate it, do you hear?"

"Did you ever think we may have been locking everyone else out?" Dan retorted, nose to nose with her.

"I can turn the damn key from my own side of the door."

"What's got into you? Weren't you able to run away as you'd planned?" he taunted. "All this nonsense about hating locks. You never knew you were locked in until this morning, you spiteful brat. And if you slug me again, so help me, I'll turn you over my knee and spank the daylights out of you. And any more cussing and I'll wash out your mouth with lye soap. Have I made myself understood?"

Dan straightened and tugged down his vest. Annie was dumbstruck and could only stare at him. Kate's gaze moved warily between the two of them, Zack's brows were drawn up in surprise.

Dan cleared his throat. "Now, if we're to make the train," he said, in his usual constrained manner, "I suggest we get down to breakfast now." He picked up Kate's valise, took Annie's arm in a steely grip, and strode toward the door. Annie turned bewildered eyes to Kate, but Dan was already pulling her out the door and down the hall.

Kate turned to Zack. He was still watching the empty doorway, a curious grin tugging at the corners of his lips. He met Kate's gaze.

"Shall we go?" With a mocking bow, he held out his arm.

"What are you up to?" she asked, ignoring his arm. "You're planning something."

"No. It's beyond the planning stage. Come, we'll be late."

"What are you talking about? Have you already contacted the police?"

"On the contrary, my dear. You wanted a new place to live. We have arranged for you to have it."

"I don't understand."

"You see, I've had all night to think about this, and the only logical move is to take you with us to California."

"California," she whispered, stunned. "You'll take us to California?"

He took her arm and guided her out the door. "There are conditions."

Her face paled, then filled with hectic color when his words registered. She jerked to a halt. "No. No. Let me go. You are vile, sir." She frowned at how little that sounded like an insult.

He pulled her forward and rang for the lift. "Don't get hysterical, my darling Kate. A woman in your position can't afford to turn down a perfect escape on mere principles' sake."

"Yes, sir, I most certainly can," she fired back.

"Ahh, all that money. I forgot."

His expression, the tilt of his head, his whole manner were mocking her. She withdrew. "All what money? All the money in the world wouldn't induce me to become your mistress. I'll get where I want to go on my own."

"Mistress? What a nasty little mind you have." The elevator arrived and the attendant began sliding the cage doors open. "I meant nothing so sordid as mistress," he whispered at her. "You shall come with me as my wife. Don't make a scene now, people are watching. Be a good girl and take my arm."

Kate was grateful for the presence of others in the small elevator even though it meant she was pressed to Zack's side. She had a few minutes to pull herself together after what he had announced. Wife, indeed. She looked straight ahead and breathed as normally as possible, but inside she felt scattered. One could hide only so much turmoil. She made the muscles of her face go limp and released the tension in her arms.

Of course he wasn't serious. He was trying to get her off balance so he could trick her into revealing some damning piece of evidence. And he was far better at throwing her than Peter or Sam Bennett had been. Sam had eventually stopped trying to goad her into a show of emotion. He was content now to insult and belittle. Peter and Corinne loved to pick at her. Peter was more persistent, he stayed at it long after Corinne stormed off in a huff when she was denied her fun. More than once Peter had laughed and given her a slight nod of appreciation. If no one else at the Manor knew what she was doing, Peter did.

And Zack knew, too. But where Peter's frequent crude suggestions left her cold, Zack's sent her heart and her stomach dancing around each other. The suggestion that she be Zack's mistress, though she would never have done it, had sent heat racing through her veins and left her oddly breathless. And the idea of marriage to him, she found, was far from repugnant.

Even so, he was a Standish, and until she could prove to herself that he was not associated with Bennett or Peter, she must be wary. Marrying now could solve all her problems; marrying a Standish could well prove fatal.

Zack led her wordlessly out of the hotel and across the street to a small cafe where Dan and a mutinous Annie sat at a corner table. When their breakfast had been ordered, Zack turned and, for the first time since they left the hotel, addressed Kate.

"Have you reached a decision?"

"Yes, I have," she said impassively.

"And?"

"No."

"May I ask why?" He was laughing at her again, she could feel it.

"No."

"I am a wealthy man, Mrs. Lawrence. Doesn't that entice you?"

"No."

"Then I'm led to believe you have money of your own."

"You may believe exactly what you wish. I will not marry you."

"Marry?" Annie and Dan exclaimed in chorus, turning several heads their direction.

"Give me one reason," Zack demanded, ignoring the curious onlookers.

"Were I to marry you, Mr. Standish, I would be placing myself in the very predicament from which I only recently escaped."

"A strange term to use—escaped. Wouldn't you say?"

"Not at all. There are many kinds of escape. Death is but one of them."

"And retreat is another?"

"Certainly."

"You are saying that because your first marriage was distressing for you, ours would be, as well?"

"If you have a great need, Mr. Standish, to rephrase everything I say to better suit your wishes, than I can't prevent you. Those are not, however, my words."

The waitress arrived with their food, and Zack leaned back in his chair, grinning, waiting.

Dan shook his head. What was Zack doing? He hated women who came after him because of his money. Here he was using it as an incentive, dangling it as bait in front of Kate Lawrence or Katrina Montgomery, whoever she was.

"Perhaps you'd be good enough to explain this current aberration of yours, Zackery," Dan said, once the waitress had returned to the kitchen.

Zack laughed at Kate's scowl. "I believe Mrs. Lawrence takes exception to my proposal being termed an aberration. Perhaps, however, it was." He turned to Kate, his eyes glinting mischievously. "I beg your forgiveness, madam. I withdraw the proposal. I spoke out of turn."

"Yes, I'm sure you did," Kate said cynically.

"Which leaves us in a rather precarious position, since we'll all be travelling together."

"Travelling together?" Kate said, letting her shock show.

"You will be going with us to California. You'll be travelling in our private car, so perhaps it won't matter so much that we are not wed. Who will know?"

"That's indecent. It's out of the question."

"I see. And hiding in my stock car and cheating the railroad out of your fares to Kansas City is decent?"

"You're twisting my words. You must see the difference."

"I've tried very hard to believe in you and your story, Mrs. Lawrence, but frankly, I'm having a problem with it. I can't, in good conscience, turn you loose on an unsuspecting society. God alone knows what you'd get up to next."

She laid her fork down and turned her blank face to him. "You draw a bleak picture of my character, Mr. Standish."

He reached over and took her wrist, tightening his fingers until she winced. "Has anyone ever told you how infuriating that cold little face is?"

"I beg your pardon? Please release me."

With a long sigh he did. Pushing her wouldn't get him anywhere. She'd retreat further. He would have to draw her toward him, break through that prickly guard to garner her trust, convince her that he had her welfare at heart. Then maybe he could get past her secrets to the woman beneath.

"Are you feeling all right?" Dan asked. "You've been acting oddly this morning."

Remembering Dan's explosion, he grinned and shook his head. "It seems to be a morning for unusual behavior, eh? I'm perfectly fine. And if I may make a suggestion, why don't we all start anew? We're four sensible adults, right? Dan and I have an entire car to ourselves—"

"An entire car?" Annie interrupted, agog.

"It was an investment. Anyway, as I was saying, we have room to take you with us if you'll agree to come. California may be exactly what you're looking for, climate-wise."

"Oh, it is," Annie agreed enthusiastically.

"Annie," Kate growled.

"You've already told us you want to find a place where you

can begin a new life. Dan and I both understand that, and we are offering to help you."

"And your conditions?" Kate reminded him.

"No conditions, except that you relax and enjoy the trip, and the company. It'll be quite different than riding with the horses."

"I don't know. It doesn't seem right."

"What's right? None of this is right," Annie said, "but desperate situations call for desperate measures. You said that yourself. We have no money, we'd have to sneak on some other train if we want to go any farther."

"We could find work," Kate argued, glaring at Annie, trying to bring her to her senses. Annie was oblivious. She'd changed camps, leaving Kate to argue alone.

"We'd have to work forever," Annie complained in an unnaturally harsh voice, "and by then some of your—husband's people could find you."

Zack's gaze bore into her. "I thought you didn't have family."

"They aren't my family," Kate blurted, unnerved. "I want nothing to do with them. If they find me, they'll make me go back there. I'll be a prisoner."

Something in her expression held Zack speechless. For once her guard was down. She may be lying about everything else, but she was telling the truth about that. That and something much worse that she wasn't revealing, something that terrified her.

"Then don't argue. You're coming with us, and damn propriety. Now eat."

Kate managed to get Annie alone by insisting they make a trip to the washroom before leaving the restaurant.

"What are you doing, Annie? Have you forgotten he's a Standish?"

"He said he doesn't have any family."

"So did I. And all this talk of marriage. What was that?"

"Maybe he fancies you."

"And maybe he wants title to the Manor. Maybe once he has it, I'll become extraneous, just like my mother."

"He don't strike me as the type to murder a woman. He's

rich. Why would he need the Manor?"

"We only have his word that he's rich. He might be a very clever con man."

"I don't believe that. Dan would never be involved in anything dishonest."

"Dan? I thought we were talking about Zack."

"You can't talk about one without the other. Dan's as starchy and stuffy as they come. It's only because of Zack that he hasn't turned us in already."

"Which proves what a good trickster can do."

"Alright, supposin' you're right. If you don't marry the man, what can he do? If he wanted the reward, he could have it by now. The least we get out of this is time and distance. In a few months you'll be twenty."

"What good does being twenty do me? I have no proof, no will, I have no legal claim. Don't you see, yet? The only good I am to Bennett is dead, and he has months to kill me. He holds all the cards. I can't go back, I can't go to the authorities without proof, all I can do is wait."

"I'd rather wait in California," Annie said. "Kate, this is perfect. Without them, we're two women alone, easy prey. Men will stare, they'll make advances, they might recognize you. This way, we have protection and comfort. And you don't have to spend any of your money."

"And when we get to California? Do you imagine they'll let us walk away?"

"How can they stop us?"

"Annie, don't make the mistake of thinking you're in control here. Zack planned every move he made. He said nothing that wasn't carefully thought out. And I have this sinking feeling that we've fallen nicely into his plans."

"Well, what do you suggest? Do you want to make a run for it?"

Kate laughed grimly. "He has my valise."

Zack was leaning indolently against the wall when the girls left the washroom. He gave them a mocking bow and extended his arms for them to take. "Shall we go?"

"Where's Mr. Siebert?" Annie asked.

"He's gone on to the train to prepare for our arrival. You,

Mrs. Lawrence, are my widowed sister, who had kindly consented to accompany me to California and set up my household for me. And you, Miss Spooner, are Mrs. Lawrence's niece by marriage. All very proper."

"Hmm," Kate grunted. "Well, it appears it is all set then. How can I object?"

"Very gracious of you," Zack chided.

"For some reason, I don't feel gracious. I feel like a little fish facing the alligator." Zack threw back his head and laughed.

"What's so funny?" Annie demanded to know.

"How cheerfully he seems to grin," Zack quoted. "How neatly spreads his claws, and welcomes little fishes in with gently smiling jaws."

"From *Alice in Wonderland,*" Kate explained.

"Except it was a crocodile," Zack said, showing perfect white teeth in a devilish cheshire grin. "You think I'm your fate? I prefer to think of myself as your destiny."

"We shall see."

"La-di-da," Annie gaped when she saw where Zack was leading them. "This is your car?"

"For the trip west only. We'll sell it in California." They joined Dan, who was unlocking the side door.

"Wow, you must be rollin' in money. Wish I was."

"Really, Miss Spooner. Control yourself," Dan said scathingly.

"Oh, get off your high horse, your majesty. A girl can dream, can't she?"

Zack helped the girls in. "Try to be patient with her, my friend," he said when Dan preceded him up the steps. Dan rolled his eyes.

"What do you think of it?" Zack asked, closing the door and moving through the car to open the windows.

"I never seen anything like it," Annie cried, trying out one of the plush chairs. "It's a palace on wheels."

"It's lovely," Kate said, looking around at the elegance of the decor. Nothing had been spared. The domed ceiling, lacquered in red and trimmed with black and gold, was inset with stained glass fan windows. The same red was picked up in the patterned carpet. Brass lanterns with fluted tulip globes were attached to the panelled walls, gold velvet curtains with flounced valances hung at the windows. Two overstuffed chairs in tufted gold velvet with red tasselled skirts and two matching chaises flanked the large windows at the front of the car. Behind them, another smaller chair and a settee faced a wood-burning fireplace. A wall, holding a large antiqued Venetian mirror and sporting a miniature bar, separated the salon from the sleeping compartments. At the rear of the car were two narrow rooms, each with two bunks and a private washroom. "You ladies may have this compartment," Zack said, dropping Kate's valise onto one of the bunks. "I'll move my belongings into Dan's compartment later."

Kate turned to thank him only to find that she and Zack were alone. He looked very big in the small compartment, and she began to feel threatened, but in an oddly exciting way. She lifted her chin and looked away. "You're fortunate to be able to travel in such splendor."

Zack took hold of her stubborn chin and turned her face to his. "I lied when I said there were no conditions. There is one."

She shrank away from him, but he held on to her, sliding his other hand to the back of her neck, forcing her to look at him.

"I won't be your mistress," she said in a strangled whisper.

"No. You won't be," he replied gently. "What I want is for you to leave behind that cold little mask you wear when you're trying to hide your feelings."

"I don't . . . know . . ."

"Yes, you do."

She shook her head, trapped by the power of his captivating blue eyes. She tried to look away, but he wouldn't let her. "It's a habit," she said in a whispery voice.

"You have no need of it now. I told you I want to help you."

"I've learned not to believe everything I'm told."

"You can believe me, Kate."

She was transfixed by the movement of his lips. She felt hot and dizzy, and she found breathing a difficult chore. To steady herself she reached out blindly, finding her hands braced against the firm wall of his chest. Under her fingers she felt his heart beating.

"You're trembling. Katie?"

She looked up. "I'm scared," she whispered, but she knew that it was not her past that frightened her, but her own reactions when Zack came near her.

His head lowered slowly, giving her time to retreat, but she couldn't move away, so caught was she in the powerful aura surrounding him. She remembered the last time his lips touched hers, and the wildfire that had pounded through her veins. It was the same now, and he hadn't kissed her yet.

"Zack," she murmured pleadingly.

He pulled her into his arms and covered her lips with his own. There was hunger in his kiss, as if he'd been starving and was now offered a feast. She had no will to deny him.

His lips coaxed hers open and his tongue ventured forth tentatively to explore the softness of her lips, the straight line of her teeth. Then in the grip of some wilder impulse, he molded her against his tall body and plunged his tongue deep within the warmth of her mouth.

A shudder ran through her, a shock, and a soft moaning sound came from the back of her throat. Never had a man dared to kiss her in such a way. Never had a man forced her to open herself to him, never had she wanted to, until now.

She was turning to warm honey in his arms, melting and flowing into him. Her strength deserted her. Her breasts felt alive, her body ached with a soaring urgency that cried out to be fulfilled.

A voice broke into her euphoric state. Annie's. ". . . man to see you, Mr. Standish. Mr. Standish?" she heard.

Standish. The name itself was enough to chill her ardor. The fact that she'd permitted him such a liberty filled her with shame and panic. She jerked herself out of his arms and, trembling, sat on the edge of the bunk. She pulled her valise to her side and began unpacking her belongings.

"Mr. Standish?"

"Yes, Annie?"

"There's a policeman at the door. He wants to see you."

Kate's huge fearful eyes snapped up, connecting with Zack's. Zack looked away and ran a hand around the back of his neck.

"Tell him I'll be right there, Miss Spooner."

Kate felt his eyes boring into her bent head, willing her to look at him. She couldn't. With a sigh of frustration, he turned and left. Kate pulled out her pink blouse and folded it neatly in her lap, fingering the rows of delicate lace. Then she flung it across the room.

# Chapter 7

The whistle blew and the conductor called for final boarding on the train to St. Joseph and Omaha. The train slowly began to move. Kate put on a calm face and joined the others.

"What did the policeman want?" she asked.

"To show us the poster on Katrina Montgomery," Annie explained. "The stationmaster told him that Zack took on two new passengers."

"He didn't ask to see me?"

"Annie told him you were suffering a bout of weeping after losing your husband and leaving your home," Zack said dryly. "She offered to bring you out if he required it, but he took a good look around the car and apparently decided the woman he was searching for couldn't be with us."

"I gave a good performance," Annie bragged. "I acted as hoity-toity as any of those ladies last night."

"She was quite convincing," Dan said, giving one of his rare grins. "I even felt sorry for you. She had just the right amount of reluctance in her voice, but enough willingness to cooperate to put the man's mind at ease."

"Thank you, all of you, but I would rather face their questions myself than have you lie for me."

"It was only a white lie," Zack said watchfully. "Unless you are Katrina Montgomery."

"You're not still beatin' that dead horse, are ya?" Annie asked disdainfully.

Zack chuckled. "No, we'll leave it for the time being." He

stood and ambled to a storage locker between the bar and the first stateroom. "I'll put out the table, and we can play a game of cards."

"Bridge?" Dan suggested, helping Zack set up the drop leaf table and organize the chairs around it.

Kate accepted readily, taking the place indicated by Zack. Annie held back.

"I don't know how to play," she murmured. "All I know is poker and solitaire, and a couple of kid's games."

"Poker?" Dan exclaimed, incredulous.

"I had more important things to do than playing cards," she snapped indignantly.

"Never mind," Kate said. "We'll teach you. Come, sit down across from me. You can be my partner."

"Do you think that's wise?" Zack asked. "Either Dan or I would be happy to—"

"You don't think Annie and I will be enough competition for you? Is that it?" Kate challenged.

The men exchanged glances. "Not at all," Dan said. "But we usually play for stakes. More interesting that way."

"What kind of stakes?" Kate demanded warily.

"Nothing earthshaking. No money, since you have none."

"This sounds more and more like poker," Annie mused.

"What stakes?" Kate asked again.

Zack grinned and shuffled the cards. "How about this? The winner gets the honest answer to one question."

Kate looked at Annie, who returned her look of suspicion. One question. She knew what Zack would ask if he won. Who *was* she? But if she refused his challenge, he'd know she was trying to hide something. If she won, though, she'd have the privilege of that one question. Did she dare ask it? Would he answer her? And if he didn't know Peter Standish, would he try to discover who Peter was? Would he eventually make the connection between Peter and Bennett and her? It was just as dangerous to ask her question as to answer his.

"That's hardly fair when Kate is at a disadvantage with me," Annie argued.

"It's only a question," Dan said dismissively.

"You said stakes. What are you risking?"

"What are you risking?" Zack turned the question back to Annie, his mind swift to pick up on any little slip. "If you've told us the truth, there is no more risk to you or Kate than to us."

His grin was too smug by far. "Before we go further with this," Kate said quietly, "I will warn you that my question, should I win, will require that you tell me about all the members of your family, alive or not."

His grin disappeared. "I've already told you I have no family."

"Yes, I know that's what you said. That will, however, be my question, to which I shall expect a forthright answer."

"I'm sorry, I don't discuss my past."

"But you must, if I win. You chose the stakes. I accept."

He studied her unreadable features. "You were irritated last evening when I wouldn't answer your questions. Are you so interested in my background?"

"Neither of us wishes to discuss our past. I am simply insuring that you are as motivated to win as I am."

"And you will answer truthfully?" he asked skeptically.

"I will. And you?"

"Yes. So it is agreed then. Now, Miss Spooner, let us see how quick a student you are."

He sat alone in a dingy restaurant in Kansas City, watching the train depart, taking his time over a breakfast that was greasy and unpalatable. He finished his bitter coffee and threw down his napkin. He was disgusted. He wanted better for himself than cheap food, cheap hotels, cheap women.

He was not a tall man, nor short, he was neither dark nor fair, he was not particularly handsome, but not homely either. He was undistinguished, nothing like the tall, striking man he'd seen escorting the beautiful woman to his private railroad car earlier that morning. Dissatisfaction burned within him at his lot in life, like a hot pebble in his stomach.

He had a decent vocation with a reputable firm, opportunities to travel, enough money to live outside of poverty. He even had excitement and challenge in his life as a detective.

Still he was not content. Only his immediate superior knew when he had been successful. No one else knew him, he had nothing to show for his twenty-six years. And never had a stunning black-haired beauty looked at him the way Katrina Montgomery had looked at her escort.

He slipped the paper from his pocket and unfolded it, ironing it flat with his hand. He traced the features he'd memorized over the last couple of days. He couldn't be absolutely certain, but he had a hunch. Hunches were his stock and trade.

He supposed he ought to tell his boss about his suspicions, but he didn't want to do that this time. He'd be taken off the case and put on something else to get him out of the way. Katrina Montgomery meant a large fee as well as the reward money. If he could bring her back himself, he'd be famous, he'd get his name in the paper, people would remember him. He'd be promoted, then his father wouldn't be able to criticize him anymore. His father, the big judge in a no-account town in Ohio.

He slowly refolded the picture and replaced it in his coat pocket. He paid for his meal, handing his money to a pretty girl who didn't look beyond the change in his hand. The smile died on his face. She didn't see him either. No one ever really saw him. Soon they would.

He left the restaurant filled with new determination. His steps quickened as he turned the corner and strode toward the depot. It would be a small matter for him to learn the destination of the fancy red and gold private car called the Pacific Palace.

"Oh no," Annie wailed, throwing down her cards in defeat after Zack trumped her and gained the lead. "I was sure you had that card," she lamented to Kate.

"The rest are mine," Zack gloated.

"Such a humble winner," Kate said sarcastically, but the reluctant grin that tugged at her lips took the sting out of her words.

"And are you a good loser?" he countered.

She shrugged. "I don't go back on my word, if that's what

you're expecting."

"Kate, I'm sorry," Annie bemoaned, her eyes pleading for pardon.

"You've no need to be."

"Certainly not," Dan agreed. "You played remarkably well for the first time."

"Once I knew it was like Whist," she explained.

"Ah, you've played Whist. I wonder if you would have admitted that had you won. Or would you have let us believe we were defeated by a novice?"

"It would have done your soul good, having the wind taken out of your sails."

"Probably so," he agreed, gathering up the cards and shuffling them into a neat pack.

"So now for the payoff," Zack said. "One truthful answer, I believe, was the bet."

Kate's eyes connected with his and held. She didn't have to see into his soul to know what he would ask. No more tricks to draw her out, and no more evasions on her part. She would answer him as she'd promised. A heavy sadness settled on her pounding heart, and she looked down at her clenched fingers. She would have liked a little more time with him, but it was not to be. And, considering all, it was for the best. He was beginning to mean too much to her. She would only be hurt and disillusioned again if she let it continue.

She felt sorry for all four of them. Dan had come to accept them, if grudgingly. He'd be badly torn between his duty and chivalry. He'd blame himself for suggesting the wager in the first place. Annie would be terribly disappointed. She was enjoying her brief taste of the finer things of life. She'd blame herself for losing the game. And Zack. Zack wanted to win. He would learn the truth, just as he'd been trying to do for the past twenty-four hours. Would that be enough for him when she and Annie were gone again? She thought not. For reasons known only to him, Zack saw himself as their protector. He, too, would feel the weight of remorse. And no one was to blame but her. She had let him outmaneuver her.

Once they knew who she was, she would have to leave them. This time she would give Annie a choice, to come with her or to stay. If Annie chose to stay, she would give her enough money to get by with until she could build a new life for herself. And Zack and Dan had dreams to fulfill in California. They deserved to realize them.

Lying to the law, when they didn't know they were lying, was pardonable, but they could be arrested and jailed for knowingly protecting a fugitive from justice, however innocent she claimed to be. She couldn't put them in the position of having to perjure themselves for her, of compromising their principles. She couldn't destroy their hopes and risk their freedom.

She looked up at the three intent faces around the table, then took a deep breath. "One truthful answer," she agreed solemnly, her words falling heavily into the expectant silence.

Zack met Dan's gaze, trying to read his partner's thoughts. Annie looked away. She was tense, as if waiting for doom to fall. Kate's chin was tilted valiantly, but her gaze was somewhere else, inside herself where she was alone and afraid and trying to be brave.

"How old are you?" he heard himself ask.

Kate's eyes snapped into focus, and found his. Dan let out a long sigh, Annie's taut shoulders relaxed. That was his question?

"I'm nineteen, almost twenty," she said feebly, her shimmering eyes conveying heartfelt relief. "Excuse me, please," she managed and hurried to her stateroom.

"I'll see to her," Annie said quietly, following her friend.

"Why?" Dan asked from across the table. "I was sure you'd—go for the kill."

"She's not one of my business rivals," Zack answered, understanding Dan's reference. Zack had a reputation for being ruthless, especially if he suspected someone of lying or attempting to flimflam him in a deal. He would keep at him with his own brand of interrogation until the truth came out. Dan had often said that he would have made a remarkable lawyer.

"You wanted the truth," Dan reminded him.

Zack massaged the back of his neck and rose from the table.

He braced an arm against the ornately carved walnut bar and stared out the picture window at the passing scenery.

"I was afraid to ask." He swung around to face Dan. "Strange, isn't it? You didn't want me to ask either."

"It would have meant the end of it," Dan replied obliquely.

"Of what? The lies? What stopped me from asking?"

"You knew they would have run away."

"Yes, I did feel that, but why? What more could they want than this?" Zack asked, sweeping over the elegance of the car with a long arm.

"Miss Spooner? Nothing. She's loving this. But she'd have gone with Kate. It's Kate who would have left. This luxury means nothing to her."

"She'd leave just because we know? We can help her, hide her, keep her safe."

"Exactly. As long as we're unsure of who she is, we aren't breaking the law in taking her with us. The minute we know and don't turn her in, we become accomplices. You know that, I know it, so does she. She won't drag us down with her. She'll just disappear."

"Which means she is Katrina."

"Do you have proof?" Dan asked. "Can you swear in court that she's Katrina Montgomery?"

Zack's lips tightened. "No."

"That's how it has to remain if you want her to stay."

"If that's the case, why involve Annie?"

"I suspect that what Annie is running from is worse in her eyes than anything that could happen with Kate."

"And you? You don't object to their being here anymore?"

Dan shrugged. "With four we can play bridge."

Omaha, at first glance, was a sea of tracks and fences. Muddy cattle yards, packed with herds destined for slaughterhouses in the East, stretched endlessly beside the secondary tracks. Battered cattle cars stood in straight rows, some being loaded, some unloaded. Some would be coupled to trains going to other cities, some would go back for more cattle.

"I've never seen so many animals in one place," Kate said

in awe.

"They come from all over the Middle West," Zack said, "Wyoming, predominently, some from Colorado and Nebraska. Most go on to Chicago for slaughter. Omaha can't handle this volume."

"The cattle industry is big business these days," Dan agreed, putting aside the book he was reading. "We'll go through Wyoming, you'll see the herds."

"Will we stop anywhere?" Annie asked. "Look at the size of those horns."

"Once we connect with the Coastal Flier," Dan explained, "we won't stop until we reach Sacramento, except for fuel and water and mail, and the odd passenger, perhaps. No excursions, I'm afraid."

"But we have the remainder of today," Zack said. "We aren't scheduled to leave Omaha until early morning. We'll sleep in town tonight."

"Where is the train coming from?" Annie asked.

"It's a transcontinental run, New York to San Francisco, direct. It is not the same train the whole way. The passengers change tomorrow morning to the Union Pacific in Council Bluffs. It stops only in major cities for passengers with reservations, and to restock. It's a deluxe train, complete with sleeping cars and dining facilities. The latest in elegant travel. I had to pay extra to keep the horses and our freight with us."

"You mean that third car is yours, too?"

"Yes, as is the stock car. Actually the stock car is an old mail car we had rebuilt."

"What will you do with them?"

"Sell them. California is growing. Someone will need a freight car. It is cheaper and more convenient for a manufacturer to buy his own cars than to pay freight costs on what he exports to other cities, especially if he deals in large quantities."

"Why did you—I mean—well, you're not a manufacturer, are you?"

"We were. Our company owned six cars at one time, all of them busy. We kept these two when we sold our business."

"What did you make?"

"Oh, look, here's the depot," Annie cried postponing Zack's answer. "I'm glad it's not in the middle of all those cattle."

"Why don't you ladies tidy your hair or whatever you have to do, and then we'll take a tour of the town before dinner. We might find some unusual entertainment tonight."

Kate closed the door to their compartment and began unbuttoning her blue dress. "Why don't you wear the gold dress tonight? I'm going to change into my lavender suit."

"You're having fun, aren't you?" Annie asked, seeing the sparkle in Kate's eyes.

"I shouldn't be, but yes, I am. I still feel guilty, but I also feel safe with Zack, which is funny since he's a Standish. Am I terribly bad, Annie? I should tell him."

"No, you're not bad at all. Turn around, I'll help you."

They were soon attired in fresh garments, Annie in the pale yellow and gold gown that set off her upswept red hair and amber eyes, Kate in a two piece deep lavender dress that nipped in snuggly at the waist, emphasizing the high, firm curves of her bosom.

"Can I wear my hat with this dress?" Annie asked.

"Let's not wear hats. I don't think we'll cause a major upheaval in Omaha if we go hatless."

Omaha didn't care, but Dan did. At the first opportunity he ushered them into a millinery shop and personally selected brimmed hats to compliment their costumes. "You must guard your skin against the sun," he said to Annie. "People with your coloring have sensitive skin."

"I like the sun," she argued for argument's sake. "Are you poking fun at my freckles," she flared, seeing him smirk as he looked pointedly at her petite nose. "Look, you snob, I know I'm not like the prissy females where you come from, but my survival doesn't depend on daddy's good favor. I have to work for my keep. Sometimes, most of the time, that means being in the sun. So if you—"

"Whoa," Dan laughed. "Did I say I didn't like your freckles? They're very cute, as are you."

"Cute," she scoffed, turning up her nose.

"Is this the thanks I get for buying you a bonnet?"

"Well, if you think buying me a hat gives you the right . . ."

"Shh," he said, nodding a smile to a robust woman just entering the shop. "I mean no insult, you prickly thing. Now let me help you with the hat, and do keep your voice down."

Her hat, like Kate's, was of soft straw, with a shallow flat top and a brim that turned down in front and up in back. Both were trimmed in ribbons and silk flowers to match their dresses. When Dan adjusted Annie's hat and secured it with long hairpins to her thick hair, he turned her to see her reflection in the mirror.

Her eyes lit up and she laughed. "Oh, Dan, you're very good at this—I mean Mr. Siebert. Thank you."

He nodded. "You're welcome. I have two sisters and three sisters-in-law. They all need help from time to time."

"Five sisters," Annie intoned.

"And three older brothers. I'm youngest."

"Are they all married?"

"Oh, yes, with large families of their own. I'm the black sheep." He pulled her away from the mirror and out of the store.

"Because you aren't married yet?"

"That and other reasons."

"Why haven't you married?"

"I have no need of a wife who will harp at me day and night to get her own way. So don't entertain any notions about becoming the next Mrs. Siebert."

"Me? I told you I don't want a husband. Least of all one like you."

"You could do worse," he argued, piqued by her flat denunciation.

"It won't do no good to try and convince me. I'm not marrying you," she countered heatedly.

"I wasn't trying to convince you."

"Sounded like it to me."

"You are the most infuriating woman. And do get your grammar right."

They walked wordlessly, both annoyed, in the wake of their friends. Not one to stay angry or quiet for long, Annie broke the silence.

"Do you think Mr. Standish is interested in Kate? I mean romantically interested?"

He slanted her an impatient glance. "You'll have to ask him."

"They make a handsome couple, don't they?"

Dan looked ahead at Zack and Kate strolling arm in arm, Zack's dark head bent to Kate's lively face. He looked besotted. She looked angelic. "Looks can be deceiving."

Annie thought about Zack Standish. Was he deceiving them? Had he been sent by Bennett? Was Dan trying in a roundabout way to warn her about him?

"Does Mr. Standish really have no family?" she asked.

"None that I know of," Dan said, frowning slightly at the memory of the dark-haired lady in St. Louis who had addressed Zack as Peter. Zack had never mentioned anyone by that name, but then Zack didn't speak of his past at all. "Why would you question that?"

"I'm not," she replied quickly. "How long have you and Mr. Standish known each other?"

"I met him at college. We've been together since then. Eleven years now."

"You knew his mother then?"

He nodded. "Margaret was a lovely woman. No matter what life threw at her, she faced it with grace and dignity."

"Mr. Standish must have been heartbroken when he lost her. How did she die?"

"Her heart was weak. She caught influenza. On top of that she got pneumonia. It happened very rapidly. No one could help her."

"How awful."

"Yes, it was awful. It's taken Zack months to get over her death. It's still difficult for him to talk about her."

"I know how that is. My mother died almost six years ago. It's still hard to think of her being dead."

"Your father, too?"

"No. As far as I know, he's still alive. Somewhere."

"You don't care about him?"

"When your own father tries to peddle your body to the local boys for drinking money, your feelings tend to rot. I'm sorry, I don't know why I told you that. I've never told anyone. Not even Kate."

"I won't repeat it. So what did you do?"

"I left home. I was fine, and still am. I can take care of myself."

"Yes, I don't doubt that," he said, touching his forefinger to his bruised cheekbone.

"I'm sorry about that," she said with a crooked grin. "We were only trying to protect ourselves. We had no way of knowing . . ."

"You don't have to explain," Dan chuckled.

"It's just that I have this—temper. When I saw Mr. Standish attacking Kate—"

"Zack wouldn't attack Kate, or any woman."

"No, but I thought he was. He kissed her," she said indignantly.

"There are kisses and—kisses."

She snorted. "Are you saying he kissed her because he fell instantly in love with her?"

"I wouldn't go that far, but she did knock him off his feet." Dan turned his thoughtful gaze forward to the couple ahead of them. "He's acting peculiarly for a man who's always been painstakingly sensible."

"I guess that means you and I are going to have to spend our time together, at least until we reach California."

"That does appear to be the case, but I can endure it if you can," he bantered.

"Well, don't strain a gut."

He clucked his tongue. "Your language, Miss Spooner, is deplorable."

She jerked her arm from his grasp and stormed off, leaving him behind. He watched her stiff-backed stride, her unladylike gait. He shook his head and chuckled, then trotted ahead to catch up with her.

His stage arrived late that evening, and after a restless night on a lumpy mattress, he secured a seat on the morning train to California, although the fare was considerably more than what was the norm, even for second class. But the Pacific Palace, where she would be, was coupled to the rear of the train, so he was forced to pay the extra in order to stay with her.

He found a seat by a window and stowed his bag in the small rack attached to the wall overhead. People crowded in around him, taking up the few open spaces remaining, making the elegant car look cramped and untidy. Someday, he swore to himself, he would be able to travel first class, with a sleeping berth of his own, privileges in the observation car where uniformed waiters would serve him tea from real silver pots or champagne in crystal goblets. Someday he'd be able to travel in style, like the man who was with Katrina. His stomach burned with envy.

The train left Omaha on schedule. The man shut out the excited voices of the passengers who had boarded with him, and turned his thoughts to the woman. Katrina Montgomery. He wanted her badly. The thought of all the reward money he would get for her return sent his pulse racing. He'd have to work for years to earn that kind of money.

And then there was the money she was reported to have stolen. And the jewels. If he could find them, he'd be that much richer. The reward said nothing about the return of the valuables, only the girl. His insides churned in anticipation. Never had he wanted anything so much in his life. Luck had been with him when he'd spotted her. This was his chance. It would never come again.

While the men settled themselves into their armchairs with the morning newspaper, Kate and Annie had time to inspect their plush surroundings. They had left the table and chairs out the day before and the table was now covered with a snowy linen cloth. In the center stood a vase of daffodils, a gift from Zack to Kate.

It was a wonderful reminder of the evening they had spent together. They had found a boarding house where their hostess had fixed them a delightful meal of baked quail, they had gone into town to see a play presented by a troupe of travelling performers, they had strolled the sidewalks, listening to the bawdy music coming from the barrooms and taverns.

Kate had talked freely to Zack of her love of gardening, her years spent studying music, her grandfather and the poetry he used to read to her, although she was careful not to mention his name. She spoke a little of her mother, and her childhood, told him of her first pony, the day she learned to swim. She told him of the wicked headmistress at the school she attended, and how her grandfather had marched into town and had her removed because she had dared to strike his granddaughter for an infraction she'd had nothing to do with. She said nothing, however, of her recent past, but he hadn't pressed her. He was satisfied to hear whatever she had to say.

They laughed together over silly jokes, they tried to sing along with the drunks in one of the saloons, they stopped to share a long and deeply moving kiss under a stately cottonwood tree. Zack bought the flowers from their hostess the next morning.

Zack had opened the transom windows for fresh air when they boarded, and the blinds had been drawn up. The morning sun poured into the car, gleaming off the brass fixtures and trim and dancing off the facets of the bevelled mirrors.

Annie led the way through the car, poking her curious nose into the storage lockers, a third washroom with its porcelain hand basin and hopper, the small galley in the front that would go unused on this trip, but that had a berth in it for the convenience of a cook. She peeked into the china closet behind the bar, whistling when she saw the Tiffany china and silver, she poked through the bookcase, ran her hand over the inlaid tea tables. Kate followed, taking pleasure in Annie's exuberance. She was impressed, herself.

"How many people will this car take at one time?" she asked, returning to the parlor.

"It can accommodate thirteen, counting the cook," Zack answered. "Each of the compartments sleeps four. Above the lower beds are two additional bunks that lower from the ceiling. When the dining table is stowed, the bar opens and another double bunk can be unfolded. The two chaises fold down to sleep two more."

"Can we see the rest of the train?" Annie asked eagerly.

"I'll see if it can be arranged. We're at the tail end because ours are private cars, so we'll have to pass through several cars to reach the dining car anyway. I'll check with the conductor."

"Dining car? You mean a travelling restaurant? We're actually going to eat there?"

"We won't be stopping for meals. We'll eat lunch there. A porter will serve our dinner here this evening."

"Glory! I can't take all this in. It still seems like a dream to me."

"An expensive dream," Dan said laconically, looking up from his paper.

Annie bristled. "Are you reminding us of your generosity? Of how much we are indebted you? We didn't ask to be here."

"I was doing nothing of the sort," Dan said, defensively. "You are a tetchy snippet."

"I . . . Oh, never mind. Why are you always reading?"

"Because I like to keep abreast of current events."

"What makes you think whoever wrote that knows what he's talking about?"

Dan patiently folded the paper and laid it aside, knowing in her present garrulous mood, she wasn't going to permit him to read. "I use my own intelligence to sort fact from opinion. You ought to try it."

"I can tell fact from fancy," she retorted.

"I meant reading." He rose and went to the secretary in the corner, running quickly over the titles. "Have you read *Jane Eyre?*"

"No," she said sullenly.

He handed the volume to her. "I believe you'll find it scintillating. It's a love story."

She took it hesitantly. "What's wrong with a love story, and why give it to me and then make me sound like an idiot for reading it?"

He gave a long-suffering sigh and picked up his paper. "My sisters loved it. I thought you might. Read it or not, as you wish."

Zack stood up and stretched. "I'm going back to check on the horses. Come with me, Kate?"

"Yes, all right."

He led her through the back door onto the platform, holding her arm firmly as the train was moving at a good speed.

"Oh, this is dizzying."

"Don't look down. Now watch your skirts as you jump across."

He unlocked the stock car and pushed the door open. She stepped through swiftly, engulfed by the familiar sight and odors. The horses snuffed and snorted at their arrival, bobbing their heads over their stall doors.

Sensitive to Zack's nearness, Kate stepped away and walked to the black stallion, holding out her hand to reacquaint him with her scent.

"Why couldn't you come back here anytime you wanted on the other train?" she asked.

"They put two refrigerator cars between us and the horses."

"Did you miss me, you handsome devil?" she crooned to the stallion.

Zack came to stand behind her, close enough for her to feel the warmth of his body. His hand came around her waist, brushing her ribs.

"I have some sugar for them," he said at her ear, his warm breath caressing her exposed neck.

A shiver of pleasure ran through her. She shouldn't be here alone with him, not with a Standish, but she hadn't been able to deny him or herself when he'd asked her to come with him. He was too exciting by far, and even though she knew he was dangerous to her, she wanted to be with him.

His hand opened under her breast, displaying the sugar cubes. "Go ahead, feed them."

Her fingers shook when she removed the sugar from his palm. He stood aside as she treated each of the animals and talked to them. She took the few minutes apart from him to try and gather her scattered wits, but she could think of nothing but his nearness and the fact that they were alone.

Zack took out his linen handkerchief and dampened it in the water barrel for her to use to wipe her hands. "It doesn't smell like your washcloth."

"I knew you'd found that."

"It smelled of wildflowers."

She cleaned her hands and laid the handkerchief aside, moving nervously away. "It's a shame to keep the animals confined for so long."

"They were exercised last evening."

"Oh," she said, turning to look at him. "That's good. Do they have names?"

"Yes, and very noteworthy titles they are. This one you called a devil is appropriately named Prince of Darkness. He won last year's—"

"I know who he is," she exclaimed. "How did you get him?"

"His owner needed the money. Prince came up lame in his last race. He won't race again. So . . ."

"And the others?" She turned away.

"All fine runners, but no winners. They have outstanding bloodlines, however."

"Breeding stock," she said, nodding her understanding. "Good breeding stock." She swallowed dryly.

"Just so." He turned her to face him. "Some day we'll have the best horses in the West. That's my dream, Katie."

"You'll make it come true. I think you could do anything."

"Do you?" He stepped closer, and his hands came to her shoulders, cupping them gently. "Do you have dreams? There's still so much about you that I don't know. I wish I could make everything right for you. I wish I could make your dreams come true."

"Zack, I . . ."

"Shh."

His hands drifted inward across her shoulders to her neck and upward to cup her jaw. His thumbs traced her cheeks and feathered over her parted lips.

"Beautiful. So beautiful," he murmured, lowering his head to hers.

She stood transfixed by his face, his eyes, his deep voice, hypnotized by the feel of his hands on her face, his thumbs touching her lips.

She closed her eyes. This was why she'd come with him. She knew he would kiss her. She wanted to be in his arms again, and all her earlier denials couldn't erase that fact. Where another Standish left her cold and repulsed, this Standish compelled her to him and set her aflame.

Being with Zack was like falling down a dark hole. There were handholds all around her as she dropped, she could easily reach out and catch herself, but she didn't want to. The sensation of falling was too sweet, too delicious, too erotic. She'd never felt anything like it, and she couldn't stay away from it.

His lips brushed hers, and her heart set up such a clamor in her chest that she was certain he must be able to hear it. Back and forth his mouth brushed hers, barely touching, until she couldn't breath for the mounting suspense.

She reached up blindly, her hands clutching his wrists. Her entire being strained toward him, silently pleading.

He groaned and covered her seeking lips with his own, one hand going around her neck to support her head, the other pulling her into his embrace.

She went weak from the overwhelming assault on her senses. Her hands lifted and clung to his shoulders as his kiss went on and on, until her mind was spinning away from her and she was left a boneless mass of sensations.

Reluctantly he lifted his head, parting his mouth from hers. He pulled her head to his heart and rested his lips on her fragrant hair. She felt melded to his body, a part of him, and he tightened his arms to keep her there. He wanted to do so much more than kiss her, but he knew if he went any further, he'd frighten her. She claimed to be a widow, but she had been no man's wife. That knowledge gave him enormous satisfaction. He wanted her to himself, he wanted her to belong to him alone.

She turned her face up and opened passion-dazed eyes. "Zack," she whispered thickly.

His name on her kiss-swollen lips was too much for him. He tossed sensibilities to the wind and kissed her again.

# Chapter 8

After a long passionate moment when Zack began to visualize them lying together in a bed of straw, he got himself under control and eased Kate away from him. "We'd better go back," he said firmly.

Kate was dazed. "The horses," was all she could think to say.

"I didn't want to see the horses," he confessed, smiling at her disoriented state. "I couldn't look at you anymore without kissing you. Does that offend you?"

"No, how could it?" she replied shyly. Guilt came swiftly, because she shouldn't have encouraged him. She shouldn't have enjoyed his kisses, yet she had.

"Because you kissed me back, is that it?" he teased.

"Now you're being impertinent," she scolded, giving him her back.

He chuckled at her. "You did want me to kiss you. Admit it."

Her heart was still racing. She turned, unable to lie. "I did, but I'm sorry I did. You don't understand," she said earnestly. "So many obstacles . . ."

"I never let obstacles stand in my way, Katie, not when I want something. If you haven't learned that by now, you will."

"And what is it you want? What do you want of *me?*" Her voice was frantic in her confusion.

He shook his head, searching her eyes. "That had better be my secret for the time being."

"I hate secrets, I hate lies, I hate all of this." She swung around and stepped away from him.

"But you're caught in it, aren't you? Whatever it is. And so am I. I won't pry, Katie, but neither will I let you leave me. So keep your secrets if you must, lie to me if you must, or tell me what troubles you. But know this, I'm here to stay, and I intend to make you admit you want me as much as I want you."

"Oh, but you can't. If you knew . . ."

He turned her, his hands resting on her shoulders. "I know all I need to know."

"And what is that?" she asked, staring at the buttons of his waistcoat.

He tipped her chin upward. "That I affect you the same way you affect me. That what is between us can't be ignored. That I intend to discover exactly what that is and where it will take us. So, be warned, Katie, my girl."

Be warned. The threat stayed with her all during the foursome's lunch in the Pullman dining car. She found her eyes straying to Zack's face too often for her own peace of mind, especially when she found him watching her in return. Where would their attraction lead them? Would she fall in love with him, if she hadn't already done so? Would he turn away from her when he learned who she was? Would they even have a chance to find out what might develop between them? Or would Bennett find her first?

She realized then that she believed in Zack. Zack couldn't be the man he was and be involved with the likes of Bennett. In spite of sharing a name, Zack couldn't possibly have anything to do with Peter Standish.

She realized something else, too. She wanted to know what being in love and being loved in return was like. She might not have much time left—a week, a month, a year—for Bennett *would* find her, but she had the present. Zack had shown her a little of what could exist between a man and a woman. Would it be so wrong to let him love her, to love him? Would it be wrong to take what she wanted before time ran out?

Her conscience pricked her. Of course it would be wrong. How could she think otherwise? She'd lived too long around uncaring men not to know that Zack was very different. Love, loyalty, compassion, patience, generosity, these were not the attributes of the very selfish. If Zack fell in love with her and lost her, he would be deeply hurt, as she knew she would be. How could she even consider deliberately hurting him?

"Aren't you hungry?" Zack asked, watching her absently toying with the food on her plate. He lay his fingers over her wrist to stop her.

She looked up, laying her fork down and slipping her hand from his. "No, I—ah—I guess I'm not."

"Try to eat a little more, you'll be hungry before dinner this evening."

"No, I . . ."

"Katie, relax," he said, refilling her wine glass. She looked into his eyes, her own full of confusion. "Eat. I won't rush you."

She deliberately misunderstood. "No. Others are waiting for the table. I've had enough, really."

"Not by half," he murmured, but he didn't press her. "If you're ready then, we'll continue with our tour."

They paused in the small luggage compartment at the rear of the next car, looking down the long aisle between the rows of seats. The car was full, not a space remained.

"How uncomfortable they must be," Kate commented sympathetically.

They passed through two similar cars beyond that one. Kate was aware of the curious eyes on them as they walked up the aisles, eyes of people who must know they came from the first class section of the train. It was a strange feeling, and not altogether comfortable, knowing she was the object of their curiosity, envy, even resentment.

The mail car followed, its lone occupant keen to show them around, to share their company for a few minutes.

"The westbound mailbags are thrown aboard as we pass through the towns. It's my responsibility to sort the mail into these bags along the wall." He directed their attention to a map above the sorting counter. "To explain, all the mail addressed to post offices in a certain area, such as this area around Cheyenne, goes into the Cheyenne mail bag. As we pass Cheyenne, that bag goes out the door for the Cheyenne Post Office to distribute, and westbound mail from those post offices comes in. The same happens at Laramie and every town down the line."

"That's very efficient," Kate observed.

"You must be busy all day," Annie said. "How do you manage it?"

"After twelve years I'm used to it, ma'am."

"Are there other cars of interest up ahead?" Dan asked.

"Just the commissary—the supply car. This is a fairly standard express, except for the one private varnish at the back."

"That's us," Annie enthused.

"Is it now? Well, ain't you the lucky ones."

"Oh, yes. It's marvelous."

"Last year we had a train, let me tell you. We were full up with the big wigs from the railroads. They had three palace cars, three sleeping cars, a lounge car where they drank and played cards. They even had a piano in there. They had a car just for fixin' the ladies' hair and barberin' the gents. They had their own dining car and their own chef, and a separate car for their servants. I never seen the likes before. The Coastal Flier is an A-rated train, mind you, but then you've seen it, to get up this far."

"Yes, it appears to be quite comfortable. We'll leave you to your work now. Thanks for your time."

"We enjoyed talking with you," Kate said sincerely. "If you have time this evening and you'd like to see our car, we'd be pleased to offer you a glass of brandy."

"That's very generous of you, ma'am. I've never been invited back before, and I appreciate it. Them that own the private varnish are usually offish to the rest of us mere mortals. I have to decline, though. Policy, you know. Thanks, just the same."

"We'll say good-day," Zack said, ushering Kate out. "You're a gracious lady, offering my spirits. Will we have the brakeman and engineer in next?" he teased. "And when they're all drunk on my brandy, who will run the train?"

Kate grinned at her own impetuousness. "I'm sorry, it's not my place to issue invitations, but he seemed lonely."

"Don't worry about him. I dare say he has a poker game to sit in on his free time. Are you feeling more at ease now, Katie?"

"Yes, I suppose so, but you can be a very unsettling man."

"And you are a surprisingly softhearted woman who definitely needs a keeper."

"I can keep myself, thank you," she retorted with a scowl, but as usual, her words lacked the sharpness she had tried for.

They passed back through the second class cars, the dining car, to the Wagner sleeping cars that followed, cars built of fine walnut and leaded glass, draped with deep green privacy curtains that matched the brocade upholstery on the deeply cushioned benches. Each private cubicle contained two facing seats that converted to a bunk, plus an upper berth that was raised during the day and concealed by an ornate panel of burled walnut inlaid with long bevelled mirrors.

"In the evening," Zack explained, "the porters come through and make up the bunks. When the passengers are tucked in, they come back through and fasten the curtains in place so the people don't tumble out. But once you're in, it's almost impossible to get out until morning."

The observation car followed, where ladies and gentlemen were assembled in conversation over tea and coffee or spirits. Large picture windows lined the sides, offering an unobstructed view of the vast prairie outside. A card game was in progress in one smoky corner.

"Zackery Standish," a tall gray-bearded gent called, rising from his chair and making his way to them. "Zack, my good man. You're the last person I expected to see on this train. Are you touring?"

"Hello, Malcolm," Zack said distantly. "As a matter of fact, we are relocating permanently. You remember my partner, Mr. Siebert."

"Daniel, yes. Good to see you, my man. You are moving to the west coast, did you say?" he asked, his eyes avid with curiosity. "What of your business?"

"Sold, to Masters."

"Masters?" he scowled. "I wish you'd contacted me. You knew I'd be interested."

"Masters offered us a generous price. We saw no need to look further. Excuse us, please."

Malcolm's eyes turned cold and hard and shifted to the women with prurient interest. "Are you still engaged to be married to Miss Bentley?" he asked boisterously.

Zack stopped and turned. He had never liked Malcolm Bray, he liked him less now. His muscles tensed at Malcolm's sneering and vindictive implied accusation, and it wasn't until Kate touched his hand that he realized he was squeezing her arm.

Dan came to the rescue, sensing Zack's hostility and fearing what form of retaliation he might take. Malcolm Bray must be insane if he thought he could cross swords with Zack Standish and come away in one piece.

"I don't recall an engagement between Zack and your niece, much as she schemed to attain such an alliance, Mr. Bray."

"The better for her, if this is an example of his philandering tendencies."

Annie took offence, and before Dan could restrain her, she jumped into the fray. "For your information, you pompous lout, whoever you are," she fired, oblivious to the bug-eyed eavesdroppers around them, "Mr. Standish is married to my cousin, so kindly keep your dim-witted comments to yourself."

"Malcolm, do sit down," Mrs. Bray said crossly, coming to his side. "Don't be a meddling fool." She turned to Zack apologetically. "Congratulations, Mr. Standish."

"Married?" Malcolm sputtered, stunned. "We heard nothing about a wedding."

"Why should you?" Annie asked imperiously. "It was a private affair." Her glare defied him to comment. He didn't.

"Come along, Malcolm. Please accept our apologies, Mrs. Standish. My husband has a tendency to speak before he thinks. Have a pleasant trip."

"Why in the world did you say that?" Kate demanded the minute they reached their car.

Annie shrugged. "He made me mad. You heard him, you know what he was insinuating in front of all those people."

"Oh, Annie," she sighed. She looked at Zack. "What do we do now?"

He shrugged, beginning to see the humor of it. "Why do anything? If Annie hadn't said it, I would have."

"What?"

"Don't worry about it, Mrs. Standish," Dan teased. "Malcolm Bray is a gold digger. He wanted Zack to marry his niece because he thought Zack would give him the money he wants to expand his floundering business. Good money after bad, I'd say. Did you hear him, Zack? He wanted to buy our business." Dan snorted.

"Showing off for his in-laws. He hasn't got two extra nickels to rub together."

"How can he afford this trip then?" Annie asked.

"Mrs. Bray's parents take a trip each year, and Malcolm tags along. He married into money and he's still looking for the easy buck. Forget him."

"Can he make trouble for us?" Kate asked.

"If he tries, I'll quietly remind him of one or two of his past indiscretions. That ought to stop him."

"You wouldn't," Dan said, incredulous.

"Oh, yes. In this case I would, I assure you. I'm going to get out of this suit since we'll be in for the rest of the day. Perhaps we could have another game of bridge?"

Kate changed, too, into her gray skirt and pink blouse, leaving behind her bustled petticoat. She washed her hands and face at the porcelain handbasin and straightened her hair.

"You're not really angry with me, are you?" Annie asked sheepishly.

"I should be. Whatever got into you? Zack has ideas of his own aplenty, without you adding to them."

"So he does have a fancy for you," she crowed.

"Hush yourself," Kate rasped. "You behave this afternoon. I have too much on my mind without having to worry what you'll say next. Just, please, don't give me anymore husbands."

Kate lay in her bunk later that night listening to the muted sounds of the wheels on the tracks. That and the gentle rocking of the train should have lulled her to sleep hours ago, as it had Annie, but she was wide awake. It seemed eons had passed since she laid her head on her pillow.

Irritated with herself, she got up, draped her light blanket over her nightdress, and let herself quietly out of the stateroom. She curled up on one of the chaises and stared out the window at the moon-drenched prairie whizzing past at forty miles per hour. Or was it the other way around? She had never imagined the vastness of the prairie, or its endless emptiness.

Coming from the Mississippi Valley, where hills and valleys, rocks and rills, trees and flowers abounded, this land seemed stark and barren. The few trees she did see were a delight to her. She'd read about the emigrants who had trekked west, who were still doing so, she had seen pictures of their homes and their living conditions, but none of it had seemed real to her until she had seen for herself how utterly alone they were, how isolated from a society they had once known.

Yet how much more alone could they be than she was? She flopped her head back and closed her eyes. Life was most ironic. Here she was, running away from wealth and comfort, riding into the unknown in resplendent style with a small fortune tucked away in her compartment, yet she felt poorer than those families out there on the bare prairie, living in sod houses, eking out a living from nothing but the land.

She was feeling sorry for herself, and she knew why. She was disconnected for the first time from all that was familiar and stable. Life at the Manor, for all the unhappiness it held, was at least comfortably predictable. Nothing was predictable now. She was living from minute to minute among strangers she knew virtually nothing about. But time would bring familiarity. She must give herself time.

She berated herself for entertaining the slightest self-pity. They were strong people out there on the prairie, she was strong, too. They had made new lives for themselves, she would, too. She was a pioneer soul, she was a Montgomery.

In her place, her grandfather would have turned his escape into a great adventure. He would have faced his problems, taken whatever steps were necessary to solve them, and got on with living. But never at the expense of others. And neither would she. The answer to her dilemma came to her in her half-dreaming state. She would go to California with Zack, because Annie wanted to go there, but she would find a different city to live in. Perhaps in southern California. There would be other times for love if she were lucky. Her new plan would give Annie what she wanted and protect all of them. Zack wouldn't like it, but he'd get over it. He was physically attracted to her, that was all. At least she wouldn't break his heart.

She thought she might be able to sleep now. In the morning she would have a serious talk with Annie and make her see the rightness of her decision.

Zack stood in the doorway and watched her. God, she was beautiful. Her head was back, her eyes closed, her soft, full lips parted enticingly. Her hair, thick and black, fell like a curtain around her pale, moonlit face. The blanket had fallen from her shoulders, and he could see the shape of her high firm breasts. His body burned with desire. Never had he wanted or needed a woman as he needed her, not just for a night or a brief time, but for every other night of his life.

"Couldn't sleep?"

Kate jumped, clutching the blanket to her chest. "Oh, you startled me."

"Sorry." Zack strolled into the parlor, fastening the lower buttons of the shirt he'd hastily donned. "I thought I heard someone moving about."

"Couldn't you sleep either?"

"I did for an hour or so. I kept thinking about a certain raven-haired woman . . ."

"Don't, Zack."

He sat down on the edge of the chaise. "Don't? Do you think I have any choice in the matter?" He reached out and lifted a fall of her long hair, letting it slide through his fingers. "You're bewitching with your hair down."

Her breath caught. With one touch he could set her heart jumping in her breast. He would kiss her again, she couldn't let that happen. She made to move off the other side of the chaise, but Zack blocked her escape with his arms.

"Running away again, Katie?"

"Zack, please. I've been thinking."

"I suspected as much. You've been quiet all day. Ever since this morning. I didn't mean to frighten you."

She sighed and sat back again. She had to make him understand. "Zack, listen to me. I am frightened, you do frighten me, but that's not all of it. This is difficult to explain and probably harder to understand, but I'm not free to pursue a relationship with anyone, not the sort I think you want."

"Not free? You're not married?" he said, going still.

"No."

"Engaged?"

"No, but . . ."

"Then what's the problem? I don't care about your past, Katie. We can go from here."

"But my past isn't over. I'm not free of it, and until I am, I can't involve anyone else. If I thought we could just be friends . . ."

"Friends?" he repeated, bewildered. "What nonsense is this?"

His outstretched arms caused his shirt to fall open. His chest was as bronzed as his arms, broad and firmly muscled, dusted with fine dark hair. She swallowed convulsively and tore her eyes away.

"Zack, I don't want you to be hurt. Don't let yourself—don't let me—become special."

"You mean don't fall in love with you." He straightened, pulling his hands from the armrests.

"Please, Zack, . . ."

"And you? Can you order your feelings to please you?"

She nodded her head. "I have to."

"How convenient, but I don't believe you," he said angrily. "And I intend to prove it to you."

"No, don't," she cried as he closed the space between them. He pulled her roughly into his arms and buried his face in the crook of her neck and shoulder. Shivers of sensual delight danced through her at the touch of his lips on her sensitive flesh. Her thinly clad breasts brushed against his warm, bare chest, driving shocking spirals of desire into the core of her being. Frantic, lest she lose her resolve, lest she lose herself, she pushed against him. "Don't do this."

He lifted his head and cut off her words with a hard, punishing kiss. She struggled, but his determination was stronger than hers. One of his hands left her body and groped with something at the side of the chaise. The latch clicked, the back of the chaise lowered, and then they were lying side by side. Zack's legs intertwined with hers, his hips pressed her into the chaise, his hands held her head to his.

"You can lie through your teeth about everything else, Katie, but you're not going to lie to me or to yourself about this. I won't let you."

He captured her resisting hands and pinioned them above her head as his mouth plundered hers. His kiss was hard, rough, full of frustration and anger, so unlike the kisses he'd given her that morning. Here was a Zack she didn't know, the man behind the steely blue eyes, whose unwavering tenacity shoved aside all impediments to what he wanted, including her own feeble attempts to spare him.

She turned her head, tearing her mouth free. "Zack, please don't. Not like this."

"Don't fight me, Katie," he said hoarsely against her cheek. "It's too late. You know it is."

"No. It can't be," she murmured before his mouth covered hers again. What she'd said must have penetrated his anger, for this time his kiss was gentle, coaxing, demanding a response that her traitorous body gave willingly.

"No," she murmured one last time before her mouth opened, welcoming his questing tongue. Her willpower was no match for his, not when her weak flesh refused to help her.

Her hands were still imprisoned in one of Zack's, but instead of feeling like a manacle, his fingers were a warm caress. She gripped his hand and held on as her mind began to float away.

His other hand moved down her arm, her side, his thumb grazing the swell of her breast. He found her slender waist and the small of her back and lifted her into his body, letting her feel the proof of his desire for her.

She should have been shocked. A proper girl would have quailed from such an intimacy, only Kate didn't. She was flooded with such a delerious wave of weakness and wantonness she felt she was drowning. She gasped his name against his mouth and arched into him, surrendering to her desires.

"Katie, you're so sweet. So sweet. I need you so much," he said. His lips trailed kisses across her jaw to the sensitive column of her neck.

He moved his hand upward and covered her breast, holding its weight in the palm of his hand, urging the peak to rigid tautness. All day he had wanted to touch her. He tore at the buttons of her nightgown, struggling with all his strength to control his fingers. She was so responsive. He wanted to feel her flesh against his own. She couldn't know what she was doing to him.

The cool air against her breasts shocked Kate back to reality. Appalled at what she was doing, what she was letting him do, she pulled a hand free and grabbed his wrist. "No, Zack. Please, stop."

"I can't. Marry me, Katie."

A sick dread washed over her. Marry him? Why was he in such a hurry, why so insistent? She could find only one answer, and she hated it.

"Let me up." Managing to get her other hand free, she pushed against him and twisted away. "Zack."

He pulled her back into his arms. "Katie, don't. Trust me, sweetheart."

"No, I don't trust you. I can't. Please, get up."

"Listen to me first," he pleaded, trying to calm her. His mind was clear now, too, and he realized he'd terrified her. "Stop it. Sweetheart, I'm not going to hurt you. Calm down."

"Let me go."

"Let her go, Zack."

Zack's head snapped around. Dan stood in the doorway, blocking Annie from entering the parlor. Dan had spoken quietly, but he was poised to interfere if he thought it necessary. Annie looked like thunder, even standing there in her nightdress with her hair mussed. Zack swore and got up, turning away from all of them.

Annie hurried to Kate's side and bundled her up in the blanket. "Jake said men weren't to be trusted. He was right again. Come on, you get into bed now. Mr. Siebert, could you get her a glass of sherry?"

When Dan returned to the parlor from his errand, Zack was pouring himself a whiskey. He poured a second for Dan.

"It wasn't what it must have looked like."

"Thank God."

Zack sat down in the nearest armchair and laid his head back. "I found her out here. She was half asleep. I would have left her to herself, but, damn, she was so beautiful."

"A moth to the flame," Dan said dryly.

"She started spouting all this rubbish about being friends. Friends, for chrissake! Can't she see how I feel about her?"

"So you proceeded to show her."

"I kissed her, yes. She didn't fight me till I asked her to marry me. Then she panicked. I was trying to calm her when you came in."

"You really are serious about her."

"She has me tied in knots. I want her so damn bad, and I feel as if she's slipping away, or trying to, and . . ."

"And you panicked."

"Yeah. I guess I did. She's so frustrating."

"Zack, are you certain you want to take this on? You could end up in big trouble."

"I can't think about that. My head is full of visions of her in prison. I break out in a cold sweat when I think of what some drunk jailer would do with a woman like Kate. God damn. If she were my wife, I could prevent that. I'm not without influence of my own."

"Drink your whiskey, and calm down. You're letting your emotions run away with you."

Zack sighed and looked levelly at his friend. "You're the one with all the cool logic. What would you do?"

Dan gave it some thought, pacing the narrow width of the car. "Since you're well and truly in this situation, I recommend you find out exactly what that situation is. Why not write to Phillips and have him do a little research on this Montgomery thing. If we knew what she was running from . . . It's a pity she won't simply tell us, but you've scotched that tonight."

"Why won't she marry me? What's wrong with *me?*"

"Not a thing."

"I'm not ugly."

"On the contrary."

"I have money."

"More than you'll ever use."

"Dozens, hundreds of women would jump to marry me."

"Thousands." Dan turned away to hide his grin. Zack had wanted someone who wouldn't fall at his feet and grovel for his favor, or his money. Seems he got one. Now he didn't like it. Dan was amused, watching Zack, the boy wonder, the prince of panache, actually struggle for something he wanted.

"So why won't she?" Zack persisted.

Dan laughed, unable to contain his mirth. The Zack he knew had fallen off the train somewhere. Here was a crazy man.

"For starters, you tackled her in a railroad car, you locked her in an hotel room, you abducted her across the country, then you attacked her in her sleep. She might be a tad wary yet."

"I'm rushing her, huh?"

Dan laughed. "I'm going to bed. You're a smart man, you can take it from here. But I will give you one warning. Whatever you decide, don't get crosswise of Annie Spooner."

"Who is this Jake Annie mentioned?"

He shrugged. "Truth will come to light," he quoted, turning to leave.

A chill raced up Zack's spine as the rest of that quote presented itself to him. *Murder cannot be hid long*. No. He wasn't dealing with a murderer, but that brief thought served to drive Dan's advice home. He needed to know what he was dealing with. Until then he could do nothing. He found writing paper and pen and ink in the drawer at the bottom of the bookcase. John Phillips had often worked for them when they were considering a sale or acquisition. He was an excellent and trustworthy investigator.

Dan escorted Kate and Annie to breakfast the next morning, giving Zack's apologies for being late. Kate relaxed. She'd acted disgracefully the night before and she wasn't ready to face Zack. He must think her a terrible tease, encouraging him one minute, rejecting him the next. Her cheeks burned at the memory.

She needn't have worried, for Zack didn't come to breakfast, and he was still in his stateroom when they returned to their ear. When he did emerge, except for a brief pause beside Kate when he apologized and asked if she would still consider numbering him among her friends, he greeted them as if nothing at all had occurred the previous night.

She was relieved that he wasn't angry, but oddly disappointed that he was now eager to accept friendship in place of . . . In place of what? Oh, she was hopeless. Her mind couldn't sort out what she wanted. Love wasn't such a great emotion if it turned a normally sensible mind to mush.

She was still confused by late afternoon, when they were nearing Rock Springs, Wyoming. Zack had busied himself with the horses or kept his nose in a book. He was uncommonly quiet, and when he did speak, he addressed either Dan or Annie. She might not have been with them.

Dan was left to entertain them with tales of the railroad, of ruthless Indian attacks, holdups, howling blizzards, floods, mudslides, of prairie fires that engulfed the trains as they roared through the walls of flame, leaving the passengers baked and broiled and suffocating from smoke. He spoke of the perils of the brakemen who often lost fingers and hands from misjudging speed and distance when coupling cars, of the dangers to them when they sprinted across the tops of the cars to apply the handbrakes before the train derailed, especially when the cars were sheeted in ice. He talked of trestles collapsing, of trains buckling and toppling into ravines, of couplings snapping in two, leaving the stray cars to their own fate.

"Of course, that was all years ago. One would hope we've made progress beyond all that."

"You mean that could still happen?" Annie asked, aghast.

Dan shrugged. "Life is a gamble."

"Oh, I wish you hadn't said all that," she groused. "You did it deliberately to frighten us. You are mean."

The conductor arrived to inform them that, because they were early, they would have to lay up for an hour to wait for an eastbound cattle train from Odgen, Utah, to pass.

"We're making good time then?" Dan asked.

"So far," the conductor agreed, "but you have the Sierra Mountains to cross yet, and that can be slow going. You might want to take the sun when we get into Rock Springs. Stretch your legs some. It's been a pleasure having you aboard."

"Do you get off in Rock Springs?" Annie asked.

"A little farther on, in Odgen. The Central Pacific takes you from there. The UP turns around and goes back to Iowa."

"Is the Central Pacific a good train?" Annie asked. "It will get us there safely?"

"We like to think the Union Pacific is better, but, yes," he answered, glancing curiously at Dan and Zack.

Zack got up, setting aside his book. "Don't mind her. My friend here has been filling her head with tales of horror."

The conductor's eyes twinkled. "Ah, well, set your mind at ease. Of course, there is that storm sitting over the mountains now, but that should be no problem. Unless it freezes. Well, good-day to you." He left with a wide grin on his face.

Annie wasn't to be placated. "I've half a mind to get off the train. Men! You're enjoying this, aren't you?"

"Relax. Go tidy your hair. We won't have to wait for you in Rock Springs. Go on, now."

"You've been quiet today," Dan said to Zack when the girls had gone.

"I've had some thinking to do," he said offhandedly. "I also have an urgent errand to see to in Rock Springs. You keep those young ladies with you at all times. I don't want them running off."

"What are you going to do?"

"Find the post office. I'm taking your advice. Dan, something has come up, and I don't know how you'll take it. But I want you to go along with me."

"All right. What is it?"

"I found proof that Kate is Katrina Montgomery."

"What—how?"

"I went through her things this morning while you were at breakfast. I had to know."

"Not very gentlemanly, but I understand. So?"

"I found the money and the jewels."

"Ah, damn. I had hoped . . ."

"I'm not ready to give up on her, but I'm taking matters into my own hands. She's *not* going to be convicted of theft, because I'm sending the money and jewels back to whomever they belong to. I've asked Phillips to do a complete investigation and to see that the stolen goods are returned, in exchange for an affidavit clearing Kate of the charges. I've made up my mind, so don't look so censorious."

Dan shook his head. "It's your neck, pal."

"Look, I don't feel great about this, but I have to do it. I don't know why she stole it in the first place, but it's going back."

"And what's she going to do without means in California? Have you given that any thought?"

"I'll take care of her."

"Zack, she didn't want to take a dress from you. What makes you think she'll let you keep her? She's not the mistress type. She'll scratch your eyes out for suggesting it."

"I'll risk it. Just don't tell her about this. Give me your promise."

"You've got it. I don't want my eyes scratched out either. But—"

"Not now."

"Are we there yet?" Annie asked, bounding out with her straw hat in her hand. "This is fun. I love seeing new towns. Mr. Siebert, could you help me with my hat? Kate's still dressing."

Kate joined them as they slowed and rolled into the lay-by at Rock Springs. She was dressed in the blue gown Zack had bought her, and her blue hat sat at a jaunty angle on her head, drawing out the vivid color of her eyes. Her face was alight with anticipation.

She turned her sparkling eyes to Zack, looking for some sign that he was ready to forgive her, to talk to her again. He returned her gaze with no expression at all. Her heart plummeted.

She bit her lip and turned to Annie. "I'll straighten your hat for you."

Annie looked at Dan, shrugged, then turned to Kate. "Sure. Thanks."

The flowers blurred as Kate rearranged the bonnet and pinned it in place. She blinked hard, arranging a few curls to wrap around the side of the upturned brim. "There. You have beautiful hair."

She felt a fool for crying. Had she learned nothing over the past years? She got herself in hand and turned back to the men, giving them a vacant smile. "Are we going anywhere in particular?"

"Dan will show you around town today. I'm going to check on the horses. I'll join you later, if I can find you."

He watched her face, her eyes, for some reaction, but was met with nothing at all. He played the same game.

She didn't breathe easily until they had left Zack far behind. Only then did she let the pain show.

"Does he hate me so much now?" she asked Dan.

"He doesn't hate you at all."

"It wasn't his fault last night."

"He explained what happened."

She blushed. "He hasn't said a word to me all day. Is he punishing me?"

"Zack isn't a vindictive man. He had some business to tend to."

"In Rock Springs?"

"No. Something he needed to clear up in Philadelphia. Unfinished business. You're worrying for nothing."

He hated this. Zack ought to be answering these questions. If lies were to be told, Zack should be telling them. Dan didn't like what Zack was doing, even though he understood his motives. He liked less the position in which he was placing the ladies.

They had claimed to be penniless before, but Dan knew, as Zack must have realized, that had the girls not been discovered, Kate would have been capable of providing for them wherever they went. But Zack had interfered, coerced, threatened until they had had no choice but to go along with him. Now he had taken their means of support. Now they were truly stranded and penniless. Kate would not view that as an act of love.

# Chapter 9

They traversed the Bear Creek divide soon after their departure for Utah, giving them a taste of the perils Dan had spoken of, sharp curves snaking downhill and up, black tunnels that took them into the dark earth, trestles that left them suspended on spindly-looking wooden frames, hundreds of feet from the rocks below.

While the passengers were being transferred from the Union Pacific to the Central Pacific in Ogden, and while their own cars were being coupled to the rear of the train, they found a clean hotel which was serving early meals for the travellers.

Zack was in better spirits, which lifted Kate's heart, though why his moods should have such control over her own disposition, she didn't know. He'd been arrogant, domineering, downright tricky, and he'd ignored her all day, except for periods when his narrowed scrutiny bore witness to a latent anger directed toward her. By rights, she should have been fuming at him, instead, she attempted to mend their shattered rapport.

"Did you manage to resolve your problem in Rock Springs?" she asked, hoping to break through his distant withdrawal.

"I did," he answered. "I regret that I had to leave you, but the matter was a pressing one. It is settled now to my satisfaction."

"Good, I'm glad."

Her smile was tentative as if she feared it would not be

accepted, and his heart slammed against his ribs. He had heard of love happening this way, swift and sure, like a bolt of lightning rending a tree trunk asunder, but he had scoffed at the notion. He was not scoffing now. Emotions rose within him that had never stirred before with such intensity—possessiveness, protectiveness, joy, fear.

He had felt all of them for his mother in one sense or another, but never with this desperation. He was beginning to understand how men in some countries could forbid their women to be seen in public. He had caught several men staring at Kate and had discovered a savage streak inside himself that wanted to tear their eyes out for the offense and scrape the vision of her from their memories forever.

The fear that constantly resurrected itself was the most astonishing and the most foreign to Zack. He was unaccustomed to being out of control in any set of circumstances. He ruled his life with an iron hand, and fear had no part in it. But this emotion had become a constant since meeting Kate. The fact that she was afraid of something in her past, something he knew nothing about and could not control, frightened him. The fact that she was so young and naive frightened him, not for his sake, but for hers. The fact that she resisted him, that he had sensed in her a compulsion to flee from him, sent terror through him.

Kate stirred uncomfortably under the concentrated probe of his silver-blue eyes. He was a most difficult man to understand. One minute he could be laughing with her, teasing, testing her mettle, the next minute looking as if the demons of Hell were gnawing at his soul. Would she ever know what to make of him?

In a sudden burst of energy, Zack shoved aside his plate, excused himself momentarily, and left the restaurant. Annie looked thoughtfully at his tall form as he walked away.

"He still looks distracted. Can you help him with his problem?" she asked, turning to Dan.

"Not this one. But he's done all he can for the time being. Don't worry, Zack is resourceful. He'll manage to head off trouble."

Zack returned a few minutes later and took his seat, offering the girls a brief smile, throwing Dan a direct look that Dan immediately understood. Dan rose to his feet.

"Miss Spooner and I are going to walk back to the depot by way of that clever park we saw. She would like to ride the swing. Don't be too long, you've only about another hour till departure."

"Yes. Fine. We'll follow shortly."

"You chased them off," Kate accused.

"Would you like more coffee?"

"I'm having tea," she reminded him, qualmish about what he was up to. "I'll have another cup, thank you."

Zack was quick to see she had it. "You have the most incredible eyes," he said solemnly, his long forefinger running over the pale flawless skin and the shiny manicured nails of the hand she had rested on the table. He turned her hand over in his, rubbing his thumb over the base of her thumb, up to her wrists. "Your skin has the texture of finest silk. A thoroughly pampered daughter, I should think."

Her lashes dropped, shielding the thoughts running haphazardly through her head—joy at his compliments, bitter resentment at the memories he evoked. Thoroughly pampered? Perhaps, in one way she was. But she was no man's beloved daughter. His hand tightened around hers, but still she could not raise her eyes to his. She feared he'd see too much in their depths. With him, when he was like this, she lost the ability to guard her feelings.

"Don't look away," he ordered velvetly.

She was overwhelmed by Zack. He could get beneath her skin so that she was unable to get control of her responses. She'd never had to deal with that weakness in herself before, she'd always been able to shut herself off from others. She looked up, and her deep blue gaze connected and held with the soft blue of his. He watched her intently, his eyes unwavering, full of purpose, and she felt as if she were about to tread on jagged shards of glass.

"Why did you send them away?" she asked, trying to diffuse the tension drawing her nerves into taut hot wires.

"One can have too much togetherness. I can see into your soul. Right now you're frightened of me, but you've no need to be. You're safe with me, Katie."

She pulled her hands away and lifted her cup to her lips. She didn't feel safe. She felt as if she were walking in the dark toward the edge of a cliff, as if at any moment she would take the step she dreaded and plunge to her doom. Her cup rattled against its saucer when she replaced it.

"There was a woman in Philadelphia a few years ago who wanted very much to marry me," he said quietly. "She was a lovely girl, too, one a man could be proud to call his wife."

He had her attention again. "Why didn't you marry her?" And why was she so glad he hadn't? Why was the thought of him with another woman so disturbing?

"I seriously considered it. I liked her, I respected her, maybe I loved her a little. Something my mother said changed my mind. She liked Bethany, but she said Bethany was not the girl for me. She said I was too composed, too self-controlled around her. You see, my mother knew me. She said when I met the right girl . . ."

"Don't, don't go on. I don't want to hear this."

"Look at me, Katie. Don't you feel what happens when we get near each other? Doesn't it drive you to distraction as it does me? Something as rare and precious as this can't be ignored. This is the first I've found it since I came into manhood."

"Oh, Zack, how can I believe that?"

"Because it's true. Don't you believe that two people can be meant for each other?"

Panicked again, she stood. "Zack, please, let's go back."

He rose and escorted her from the restaurant, but instead of guiding her out the door, he led her firmly past the registration desk and up the stairs.

"Zack, where are you taking me?"

"Hush. I have to be alone with you."

"No. You can't—we—I'm not going." She dug in her heels and stopped.

Swinging her up in his arms, he climbed the remaining steps and strode purposefully down the dim hallway with her. She caught only a fleeting glimpse of curious eyes turned their direction from below.

"Put me down," she hissed, struggling against his grip. "What are you doing?"

"I'm fed up with having no privacy. If this is the only way I can be alone with you, then so be it." He opened the door to room 2B and carried her inside. He lowered her to her feet and turned to lock the door.

"Have you lost your mind?" she demanded in a hoarse whisper. Her heart was racing wildly, hammering beneath her ribs. She backed away, retreating from him, retreating from the fearsome excitement already blossoming inside her. He stood before her, dark, male, dangerous, and she could only stare in mesmerized fascination. The memory of his hard body pressed to her hips, his leg between her thighs, his strong hand on her breast was still vivid in her mind, still had the power to make her blood pound thick and hot through her veins.

"Among other things," he answered, stalking her.

She took another step backward in the small room and found her legs against the bed. She looked back at its broad expanse and knew a real moment of fear. He could not mean to . . . Shocked eyes, large and dark, turned to his.

"No more running, Kate. No more hiding, no more denials. Now is the moment of truth. Now we will know this force between us. Now we will put a name to it."

"Please, no . . ." She dodged away from him, intent on getting to the door, but he blocked her way and pulled her hard against him.

His head swooped down and his mouth captured hers in a kiss that, for all its gentleness, was relentless and demanding. She struggled against his imprisoning arms, against the insidious current of desire that was snaking its way so temptingly through her body. If she let down her resistance, she'd be lost.

But like that of a small creature caught in the closing talons of an eagle, being borne up and away to an unknown destiny, her resistance was futile. To be free of the talons was to fall to a worse death. Sometimes Fate gave no options.

He lifted her to him until her feet barely touched the floor, the hard column of his aroused male body clamped to her hips, her breasts, tingling and taut, crushed against his chest. She began to feel her body giving in to his sensual onslaught. Halfheartedly she struggled, a token protest, but he stole away her feeble defenses by plunging his tongue deeply into her mouth, plundering, taking.

She gripped his shoulders, giving a small cry deep in her throat, as she was pierced by a stabbing shock of need. She couldn't pinpoint the moment when she stopped resisting and surrendered, but she found herself clinging to him, demanding that his mouth return again and again to hers.

In her innocence she was unprepared to handle the madness that claimed her senses. Zack's skilled and masterful assault kept her mind and body in a white-hot turmoil of desire. His mouth and his hands never ceased their magic as, piece by piece, their clothing fell to the floor.

Stripping back the covers, he lowered her to the bed and covered her nakedness with his own, fevered flesh to fevered flesh. His hands and lips were everywhere, seeking and finding secret places that caused her to writhe against him in mindless wantonness.

His hot mouth seared a trail downward, drawing near the yearning breast he cupped in his hand. His tongue flicked over the deep rose crest, making her stomach muscles quiver. Again and again he teased her until her head was rolling from side to side in mute denial of the sweet agony.

Restless hands that sought to know her lover clutched at his head, urging him to cease his sweet torture. In a savage move his mouth closed over her engorged nipple, drawing it into his warmth, nipping it gently, laving it with his tongue.

"Zack," she cried out. "Please, Zack." She was on fire for him, burning, needing, aching, for what she did not yet know.

His body surged against hers at her wimpering cries of passion. She was so perfect, so wild in her response, so much more than he had ever dared hope for. He loved her unequivocally, and he longed to become a part of her very essence, to absorb, to be absorbed.

Overwhelmed by the powerful and drugging reactions of her body to Zack's inexorable lovemaking, Kate rode one madly rocking wave of sensations after another, waiting for and longing for more with shameless greed. When she thought nothing could be more beautiful than what he was making her feel, he proved how utterly wrong she was.

His hand shaped itself to her ribs, her waist, the flare of her hips. Slowly he eased his way toward the hot moist center of her womanhood, coaxing her thighs apart, exploring the long slender lines of her legs, tempting her desire to yet new heights.

His hand, sliding slowly up the inside of her thigh, caused her a momentary stab of alarm. Her eyes opened to find Zack watching her. His hand never slowed its upward journey as his dark gaze probed her soul. Silently he compelled her to look at him, even as he moved to touch where no man had touched before, even as her young body convulsed at the suddenness of his claim upon her.

He positioned himself over her, slowly, deliberately, making a place for himself between her soft thighs, all the while watching her eyes. His body met hers, retreated, met again.

"Zack," she murmured, fear dying a swift death in the face of her rising passion. Her body clamored in restless agitation for his possession. "Oh, Zack."

Her surrender stripped away his rigid self-control. He gathered her in his arms in a hard embrace and plundered her mouth. His control snapped. One sure and swift stroke breached the thin barrier to the inner heat of her woman's body.

Brief pain gave way to a greater pleasure as the yearning, aching void of her body was wonderfully filled.

He groaned her name as if in pain. She realized that he was as vulnerable in his need for her as she was for him, and her heart soared on wings of love. She wrapped her legs around his hips and enfolded him in her arms, holding him close to her heart. He was so much bigger, so much stronger, so very male against her slight feminine form, yet they fit perfectly. The very thought of them joined in the most intimate act sent new waves of passion through the innermost parts of her body. Slowly he rocked within her until her uninitiated body accustomed itself to his invasion. Pleasure and hunger of a vastly different nature began to grow and center inside her until she was moving with him in an urgent quest for fulfillment.

Zack felt her respond to him as her need grew, and his body quickened. Slowly he tutored her, with patience he led her into a world of experience, until he bore her up with him to the shimmering heights of ecstasy where their bodies exploded together in wondrous completeness.

Exhausted they lay, side by side, wrapped in the warm aftermath of their passion. He held her close as their ragged breathing evened, as their thudding hearts calmed.

Kate snuggled closer, floating slowly down from the euphoric heights of splendor. She felt closer to Zack than she'd ever felt to anyone in her whole life. He had not devastated her, he had not plunged her to her death. He had lifted her to his world, given her wings, and taught her to fly.

She ran her fingers adoringly over the corded muscles of his arm. She loved the shape of his arms. She loved how they felt around her. She turned her head and glanced at his relaxed face.

"That's a very smug grin," she teased languorously.

His smile widened. "That was a very precious gift you gave me, Mrs. Lawrence."

She shot up and stared down at him in dismay. How could she have been so thoughtless? How could she have forgotten she was supposed to be a widow?

He watched her eyes fill with uncertainty. She struggled to find a way to explain. "Come back here," he ordered, pulling her into his arms. "Don't say anything if you can't tell me the truth. Tsk, tsk," he clucked. "Such a pack of lies."

"It was Annie's fault," she confessed. Her lips twisted exasperatedly. "She has this uncontrollable urge to marry me off all the time."

"So do I. To me. You'll have to marry me now, Katie, love. I've compromised you."

She stiffened and pulled away, suddenly self-conscious in her nakedness. She reached for her clothes and held them in front of her. "Don't pressure me, Zack. I've told you I can't marry you."

"Nonsense. We belong together. You may already be carrying my child. Have you thought of that?" He watched her pull her clothes on with stiff, jerky motions. He sat up and began to sort out his own clothes from the pile on the floor.

"Did you bring me here for that reason?" she asked woodenly. "To get me pregnant? To force me to marry you?"

"No. Of course not."

"Because I won't."

"Why are you so damned stubborn?" he rapped out, jerking his own clothes over his limbs.

"Stubborn? You're the one who won't let go of this insane idea?"

"Insane? Marriage to me is insane?"

She heaved a sigh. "No, not you, just marriage. I don't want to talk about this, I want to leave."

"Fine!"

They dressed in obstinate silence, Kate struggling with hooks, Zack whipping his coat on and straightening his cuffs and collar in short aggravated movements. He ran his hand through his hair to bring it to order. Kate was still fighting with her corset.

He looked impatiently at his pocket watch then back to the rigid lines of Kate's back. "Leave the blasted thing off."

"I can't do that."

"Then turn around here." Kate held her breath when Zack's knuckles brushed against her sensitized breasts as he dealt with tricky fasteners. She glanced up furtively to find his lips drawn into an angry white line. Wordlessly, in emotion-fraught silence, he helped her into her dress, found her a comb, and picked up her hair pins from the floor.

"This isn't enough," she said.

"Damn right, it isn't."

"I meant the pins," she said, twisting her hair up and jabbing at it with the few pins he gave her.

"Let's get out of here." He took her arm and propelled her along beside him as he strode down the stairs and out the front door.

People stopped and stared at them. She averted her eyes. She must look an absolute mess. "This is awful. Slow down. They probably think that . . ."

"What? That I took you up there for a quick tumble?"

"That's disgusting."

"Isn't that what you wanted—a moment of carnal pleasure with no commitment?"

She wrenched free of him and pivoted away, storming off in the other direction in a rage of hurt and shame, heaping every foul name she could remember on his damnable head.

His hand clamped around her upper arm, and he spun her around. "Tut, tut. No temper tantrums now."

"You bastard. Let me go."

"You're going the wrong way."

"No, I am not."

"The train is the other way."

Her fury whipped itself into a fine fit. "Then go that way. You don't want to miss your train. And be good enough to tell Annie that I'm staying here. She can bring our luggage."

"All right, all right," he gave in, fearing her implacable pride might force her to carry out her threat. "I'm sorry. It was a rotten thing to say. I apologize. Now, let's go."

"Are you apologizing just so I'll go with you?" she taunted.

"Yes," he retorted, suddenly equally angry. "But if I may say so, suggesting I made love to you in order to impregnate you so you'd have to marry me was just as despicable and just as unforgivable. I am not that desperate a man."

His chilling silver eyes sent her back a step, fearing his retribution. "Then why do you always bring up marriage?" she cried in anguished tones.

His anger melted and vanished. "Wishful thinking?" he suggested hollowly.

Ignominious tears welled up and spilled over. She swiped at them furiously. Zack cursed under his breath and, taking out his linen handkerchief, tilted her head up and wiped the tears from her face. "Come back,'" he said gently.

She nodded defeatedly and followed as he took her hand and led her toward the train. "Zack," she said, "have you no patience?"

"I like to think I do. Why?"

"You say you love me, that I can trust you, but it isn't easy for me to believe in words. I've only known you a matter of days. In that time, you've been anything but consistent.

You've been tough and unrelenting and threatening; you've also been kind and generous—and loving. I don't know what to believe of you.

"I don't want to talk of my past, but I will say this much. Since my grandfather's death, my life has been ordered by lies and deceit. I can't forget all that in a few days. I learned just recently how easily I can be fooled, and how little some of the people I had known for years could be trusted."

"You want me to prove myself?"

"No. Not at all. I'm simply asking for time. I have no confidence in my own judgment anymore. I've been insulated in lies and I never recognized it. I have to learn to see the world with less idealism and more realism. I have to have time to grow up, Zack, and to be able to believe in myself. Until then . . ."

"Do you trust Annie?"

Her brow creased thoughtfully. "Yes, but . . ."

"But she's not a man," he finished for her.

"Zack, I just don't know," she replied emotively.

"And during this time," he asked expressionlessly, "are we to remain merely *friends?*" He looked straight ahead, waiting for the answer he dreaded.

She stopped walking and waited until he looked at her. He had that obdurate jut about his jaw again. He was as convinced in his mind that he was right as she was. If they could find a compromise . . .

"All 'board," came a faint cry from the distance, along with a shrill combinations of toots and blasts from the train whistle.

"The train," she cried. "Oh, no. We'll never make it."

He laughed. "Can you run?"

They did make it, but with only seconds to spare, Zack towing Kate in his wake, laughing at her flushed face as he swung her up into the car ahead of him.

"You gave us a fright," Annie reproached.

"She thought she was doomed to be alone with me," Dan mocked.

"Enough to scare the devil," she retorted.

"We lost track of time," Zack explained. "Sorry to worry you."

Kate laughed merrily. "We must have looked a sight, dashing through the town like two children. Look at my hair, I've lost half my hairpins." She tossed her hat aside and removed the rest of the pins. Her heavy hair tumbled down. She looked up and caught the arrested expression on Zack's face.

"You should laugh more," he said, watching her mobile mouth. She blushed self-consciously, and her smile slipped sideways.

"I had better fix my hair."

Zack watched her go, then turned to Annie. "How often *does* she laugh?"

"When her funnybone gets tickled," Annie said, jumping to Kate's defense, then added more sedately, "Not often."

"I'd like to get my hands on the person who took that from her." He shook his head as if to dispel the whole wretched thought. "I'm going to freshen up."

When Kate left her stateroom, she could hear Annie and Dan talking in the parlor. She saw that Zack's door was closed, and knocked softly, wanting a moment alone with him.

"Come in," he called. She opened the door and stepped in before she realized that he wasn't fully dressed. He had his trousers on, but his fresh shirt was still in his hand.

"Katie," he said. "I thought you were Dan."

"I—I'm . . . ," she faltered. His shoulders were broad, muscular, tanned, his chest, whorled with dark hair, tapered to a taut, flat abdomen. His arms, the arms that had held her, were so very male. She hadn't had time nor the inclination to observe his body earlier. She did now. She looked down at her own slender arms, her own very different shape and remembered.

"Kate," he said almost soundlessly.

She had come to answer his question. Could they remain merely friends? She had planned to tell him that was exactly what she wanted, but was it? To be treated with casual courtesy, never to be held in those arms again, never to feel his hands on her body, or to touch his. To live knowing he would never kiss her again, never make love to her.

"Katie, did you want something?" He dropped his shirt on the bunk and came to stand before her.

Her breasts rose and fell with her shallow and labored breathing. She tore her eyes from his naked torso and looked at his face, so dark, so handsome, so achingly familiar. His blue eyes, bright and intent, watched her, waiting for her to speak. But what could she say? That she wanted friendship when she longed to be in his arms again, that she'd be satisfied with brotherly affection when she . . .

When she had fallen in love with him.

"Well, well," he said, his lips twisting upward in a crooked grin. He gripped her jaw, tilting her face to his. "Shall we have no more talk of friendship now? You and I, my darling, can never be less than lovers. I will allow you the time you need, but only so much, and then, Katie, you will belong to me forever."

She was held motionless by his vehemence. Mixed with the remnants of anxiety and fear within her that urged her to go from him was an even stronger need, compelling her to surrender.

In one motion he swept her into his embrace and covered her mouth with his. She didn't fight or resist, she let him have his way, because she hadn't the will power to do otherwise. She opened her mouth to his possession, she met his searching tongue with her own, her hands ran up the sinewy length of his arms to his shoulders and into the soft thickness of his hair.

Her body, sapped of its strength, was infused with a fiery liquid heat. She was floating in his arms and being borne away on a wild and craven desire to be consumed by him again, to join and become part of him one more time.

Leaning her backward over his arm, he pressed her waist and hips to his strong body. His hard thigh forced its way between her legs, arousing her, intensifying the ache that grew there. He tore his lips from hers and closed them again over the frantically beating pulse at her throat. A small cry escaped her, and her head fell back, giving him the access he sought.

He murmured incoherent phrases against her neck, then

lifted her head and took her mouth in another deep and hungry kiss.

The train lurched sideways on irregular tracks, throwing them off balance. Kate never felt it, she was lost in Zack's kiss; but Zack steadied himself and lifted his lips from hers. She gave a throaty plea for him to return.

"Katie, honey," he said in hushed tones. He leaned her gently away. "Katie, we have to stop."

"No."

"Katie. This isn't the time or place."

"What?" Her knees felt like water. She clung to his arms.

Zack smiled down into her face, holding her until she regained her senses. "You see now? How can we ignore this? All I have to do is see you and I want you. And when you're in my arms, nothing else exists."

"Oh, Zack," she sighed, moving back to sit down. She took a deep shaky breath and blinked to clear her head. "What are we to do?"

He knelt in front of her and took her hands in his. "Don't worry. Take your time and learn to trust me, and yourself. I'll wait."

"I didn't want this to happen. I tried to prevent it."

"It was too late for that the moment I saw you. I did warn you."

"I didn't want to believe you. This makes everything so much more complicated." She got shakily to her feet and went to the window. "Oh, why did you have to interfere? You don't know what you've gotten involved in."

Zack picked up his shirt and shrugged into it. "Why don't you explain, then?" he said hopefully.

To her consternation she felt her throat tighten and tears threaten her eyes again. She took a deep breath and blinked rapidly. "I wish I could. But I can't. I just can't."

"Never mind. When the time is right, you will." He tucked the tails of his clean shirt into his dark slacks and rolled back his sleeves to his elbows. "Why don't we see if Annie and Dan would like a game of Ludo. I believe I saw that in the game closet. Or dominoes. Or we could humor Annie and play poker."

Kate turned and nodded, trying to smile. Zack had doubted one or two of the decisions he'd made during his life, but he was more convinced than ever, seeing her poignant expression, that returning the stolen money and jewels had been right. She was free of that crime, even though she didn't know it. Apart from that, he could handle whatever else her past held. He had only to look at her to know he'd fight the dragons of death for her.

He bent down and gave her a mocking gloomy face. "Can't we have a better smile than that?"

A feeble grin was the best she could do.

"Don't overdo it."

Annie was up early the next morning, too excited to sleep. She bustled around the compartment, straightening her bunk, washing and dressing, whistling a silly tune, making as much noise as she could without being blatantly obvious.

Kate pulled the pillow off her head and scowled. "For pity's sake, it's barely dawn."

"Oh, Kate, get up. The men are awake, I heard them talking."

"Probably drawing straws to see which of them would come in here and strangle you."

"Come on. We've already left Reno. We're in California."

"We've hours to go yet," Kate groused.

"California, Kate. We made it. If we hurry, we can find a table at the first seating for breakfast. Oh, do get up."

Kate supposed there was nothing for it but to go along with her. Annie'd be relentless in her chatter until she did.

"All right. Go out to the parlor and do your dancing around so I can wake up in peace."

"Now who's the grump!"

Kate stretched and got out of bed. She had slept unusually well, in spite of the fact that all her earlier turmoil over Zack and all her plans to escape him had been for naught. Yesterday she had found the truth in herself. She loved Zack, and to be separated from him would cause her more misery than she could bear.

She dressed quickly in her lavender two-piece dress, taking extra time with her hair so that it was just right. After straightening the bunk and setting the compartment in order, she took one last look at herself in the mirror. She smoothed the bodice of her dress, thinking how nice her mother's brooch would look where the scooped collar came together in the front. She shouldn't wear any of the jewelry, but it *was* hers, and she was at the end of the world from Bennett. Just this once she would. She wanted to look her best for Zack.

She pulled her valise out of the locker and sat on the bed. Listening to assure herself that the others were still in the parlor, she released the secret latches and opened the false bottom.

It was empty.

# Chapter 10

Kate had no idea how she came to be sitting in the dining car, but somehow her body must have been able to take her there. She held a cup of tea, which she didn't remember ordering. It helped to warm her numb fingers, but the rest of her felt frozen through to her bones.

Had Zack left the car unlocked? Had someone broken in and robbed her? Why would a thief take her possessions and leave behind the valuable silver tea service on the bar? And if not a thief, then who?

Annie? No, Annie was as loyal as any friend could be. Besides, she'd already had a perfect chance before to take the money and jewels. Then again, she might have seen no need to hurry when she had found a perfect chance to get out of Memphis. Oh, how could she let herself even think such a despicable thing about Annie, Annie was her friend.

That left Dan or Zack. Dan was too honorable to stoop to theft. Dan was—Dan was Zack's friend. And Zack was . . .

Zack was a Standish.

Zack had had ample opportunity to search her compartment. She remembered the morning he didn't breakfast with them, and the time in Rock Springs when he claimed he had an urgent matter to tend to. Exactly what was it that had caused such urgency? And in Philadelphia? It was improbable that two businessmen as astute as Dan and Zack would leave unfinished business behind, even a trivial matter.

The longer she thought about it, the more it fell into place, and the more her fury mounted. Zack had ignored her the entire morning before Rock Springs, but after Rock Springs he had turned about face, charming her, wooing her, winning her over. How he must have gloated. And how debased she felt.

She hadn't even put up a fight. *Naive, stupid, idiot girl,* she railed at herself. He knew exactly how to disarm her, how to charm her, and seduce her. Well, she wouldn't make that mistake again, not with any man. She had said she needed time to grow up. Well, she'd had her first lesson.

"You're not eating again," Zack said. "Are you feeling nervous?"

Nervous? Because she didn't have two nickels to rub together? Inscrutable eyes met inscrutable eyes.

"Perhaps I am a bit apprehensive about our arrival," she allowed.

"We haven't spoken of your plans, Katie. What are you hoping to do in California?"

"We're going to start a business of our own," Annie bubbled. "Kate is real good with figures, and with you and Dan there to give us advice, we can't fail. We're really going to make this work, aren't we, Kate. I'm so excited. The difference between us is that I get hungry when I'm excited. Can I—may I have your breakfast, if you don't want it?"

Kate managed a weak smile. "Sure. Help yourself."

"Kate has it all figured out," Annie went on thoughtlessly. "We'll look around first and find out what the town needs, then we'll rent a shop and go into business."

"And what will you use for money?" Zack asked.

"Oh we have . . ."

"We have plans to find employment when we decide where we'll settle," Kate said with deadly calm. "When we have saved what we need, we'll take the next necessary step."

Annie looked at Kate and recognized the passive face, the blank eyes, the stillness of her features. Something was wrong. "Yes, that's right," she concurred.

"When you decide where you'll settle? What does that mean?" Zack demanded, taken aback. "You'll stay in Sacramento."

"No. I think not. A smaller town, maybe." If he thought that by taking her money then making love to her he'd be able to force her to fall in with his plans, he was due for a surprise.

His mouth tightened to a straight line and his nostrils flared with annoyance. "And where will that be?"

"I haven't decided. Perhaps south on the coast. At any rate, it needn't concern you. You've been more than generous with us already. We won't impose on you any further."

"Annie," Dan said uncomfortably, "shall we have coffee in the observation car?"

"I . . ."

"Come." Dan took the fork out of her hand, laid it down, and escorted her with gentlemanly force out of the dining car.

"Now what is this, Katie? I thought we'd reached an understanding last night."

So charming and sincere. "Understanding? What do you mean?"

"What game are you playing now?"

"You'll have to be more specific, I'm afraid."

"I'm talking about this nonsense of leaving Sacramento. You can't do that."

She raised a challenging brow.

"Did yesterday mean nothing to you? What we shared, that was special."

"I *thought* it was," she agreed cynically.

He ignored her sarcasm. "Then why?"

"You and Dan have plans for yourselves in Sacramento. Annie and I have our own plans."

"We can arrange our plans to include you. I want you in Sacramento."

"Why?"

"How can you ask that?"

She sighed and leaned back in her chair. "All right. I'll be direct. We don't have an understanding," she said, although she was sure she understood him perfectly. "We may be attracted to each other on a purely physical level, but we . . ."

His hand moved convulsively, knocking over the salt shaker. He jumped to his feet, anger spitting from his eyes. "Will you precede me to our car in a civilized fashion, or shall I throw you over my shoulder and carry you there?"

"Goodness," she goaded. "There is no need to embarrass us both unnecessarily with a show of masculine brutality."

"Bru . . . By God," he swore under his breath as she brushed haughtily past him.

She was aware of him towering behind her all the way through the train. Dan and Annie rose as they passed them in the observation car, and Kate prayed that they'd follow, but one look at Zack had them sitting back down.

"I want your promise that you won't leave Sacramento," he ordered when they stood in the parlor. Clamping his hands around her shoulders, he swung her to face him. "Promise me."

"Be reasonable, Mr. Standish," she retorted acidly. "We shall have to go where we can find work. We don't have unlimited wealth at our disposal."

"But you knew that all along. Why make an issue of it now?"

Very clever, but she wasn't fooled. "I haven't. You have."

His hands dropped to his sides, and he turned away. She was driving him insane. What had gotten into her? Was she always so fickle? Or, he thought, going cold, had she discovered what he'd done? Dan had told him he'd have Hell to pay. He'd have to convince her all over again that he had her welfare at heart. And after all that talk of trust.

"Look," he said, spinning around, "I'm concerned about you. I can't bear the thought of you struggling in some strange city to put food in your mouth or a roof over your head."

"Really? As I said before, my experience has taught me that overly benevolent concern for my well-being, especially from a man, usually shields an ulterior motive. I wonder if I can guess what yours is."

"You're very cynical for one so young. Why must I have an ulterior motive? Can't I simply care about you?"

"Can you? That's my point. There is no way I can know that."

"Do you make a habit of this?" he asked scathingly. "Yesterday you were in my arms, you were pliant, willing, responsive. You were a real woman with real feelings. Now you're a cold little miss who holds herself above all men, expecting the worst, demanding we prove ourselves before you grant us your acceptance. Well, keep your acceptance. I've done my damnedest to help you, but all I get is suspicion and rejection. I've finished with you, do you hear me? Just don't come crawling to me when you find out that real life is too tough for you."

Her chin tilted defiantly. How was it that she was the wronged party, yet she felt lashed by his chastisement? He had taken her money and her virginity in the same day, and now he stood there daring her to ask help of him so he could refuse her. She'd die first.

"Life has never been a problem for me until unscrupulous men have taken a mind to interfere."

"Unscrup . . ." His eyes blazed at her, and his hands clenched, and for a second she thought he might actually strangle her; but he pivoted instead and slammed his way out of the car.

She sank onto the chaise, trembling from head to toe. It couldn't be avoided, she told herself. Everytime they were together, emotions of one sort or another got out of control. It was better this way. She no longer had any money, but he was no longer in danger. Her nightmares of Zack drowning in a creek like her mother, pinned under an overturned buggy, would stop.

What would he do with her jewels? Save them for his wife? Sell them? Turn them in to the sheriff? That thought sent a chill through her. If he gave them to the sheriff, they would be returned to Bennett. Bennett would be able to trace her.

The door opened, and she started, but it was Annie who entered, not Zack.

"What happened? Zack was like a madman."

Kate's bravado crumbled. "Oh, Annie," she cried into her hands as her tears of hurt and anger came. "I hate him. I truly hate him."

"Hey," Annie soothed, sitting beside Kate and wrapping a comforting arm around her shoulders. "It's all right. We still have each other."

"You don't understand. We're broke. He took it. It's gone, all of it."

Annie went perfectly still. "What's gone?"

"The money, the jewels. Everything. We have nothing."

"Zack took it? He admitted that?"

"Be serious. He wouldn't admit to theft. But he did it. I know he did. In Rock Springs, when he was so busy he couldn't come with us."

"Why would he steal from you?" Annie asked, trying to make sense of Kate's ranting. "He doesn't need money. That doesn't sound like Zack. Did you confront him?"

Kate gave a weary snort. "If I did that, I'd be admitting who I really am." Her mouth tightened. "But he knows. And he knows I can't claim he robbed me without giving myself away. I can't do anything about it."

Annie was stunned into silence. She could comprehend the wisdom in that. Who better to rob than a robber. But Zack? And where did that leave Dan?

"It could have been someone else—the porter . . ." she offered, grasping at straws. She was as unconvinced as she sounded. "Okay, let's suppose Zack did it. To what purpose?"

"He wants me, Annie. He told me I would belong to him. How better to prevent me from leaving than to make me dependent on him?"

Annie shook her head disbelievingly.

"He's a Standish, for God's sake," Kate burst out. "Add it up. We get caught in his railroad car. We thought we were being helped, but we were being handed over to the enemy." She got up and paced agitatedly as she thought. "He had no reason to be on that train, he could have had his horses shipped to Omaha. Yes! Don't you see? They arranged it all."

"No, I don't see."

"And when he found us, he immediately began pressing me to marry him. What man would do that but one who *knows* what he has to gain."

"If he meant you harm, why not just turn you in or take you back to Bennett?"

"Because you were there, an unexpected witness, and they had to know what I'd told you. How much have you told Dan?"

"Nothing, I swear it. He hasn't asked."

"No, Zack had become convinced there was no need," she

speculated wildly. "He thought he'd already won. But when I refused to marry him the night you found us out here, he used another means to bring me to heel." Two, if she considered his crafty seduction.

"Oh, Kate, what if you're wrong about him?"

"What if I'm right? And let's not forget who always manages to get you away from me, or us away from Zack when he had plans to carry out."

"You mean Dan," Annie said, disheartened. "Well, what are we going to do now?"

"I don't know. I really don't know."

Zack downed his whole glass of whiskey before he was under control enough to speak to his partner.

"Must have been some row," Dan remarked, observing the high color in his partner's face. "What was it this time?"

"She said she was not staying in Sacramento. God, that woman has two personalities. I swear, one minute she's in love with me, the next she hates me. I think she knows about the money and jewelry."

"I warned you. Did she accuse you of taking her ill-gotten gain?"

"To do that, she'd have to confess."

"So she suspects you robbed her, but can't question you; you suspect she knows, but won't admit it to her. In the meantime she's frantic about how she'll live, disillusioned about the man who's been trying to seduce her for days, and may have succeeded, for all I know, a man she was beginning to trust. Now she's determined to have nothing more to do with you, a wise move on her part, and you, if I know you, probably became so frustrated you gave her the sharp side of your tongue, which confirmed for her what a loathsome worm you are. Have I about summed it up?"

"God, you can be infuriating," Zack growled.

"What did you expect, Zack? That she'd fall weeping into your arms, begging you to come to her rescue?"

"It had crossed my mind."

Dan shook his head disparagingly. "Love fells the most brilliant of men. Kate is a fighter, a survivor, or she'd never have done what she did. That was a desperate act. And now you are the enemy as well. You'll have to back off until she calms down."

"I can't just leave her to fend for herself."

"I'll see to the girls when we get into Sacramento. You go on ahead by yourself and make some arrangements for their accommodations. We'll meet at the Western Union in two hours after our arrival. I'll stop there to wire my family. Will that give you enough time?"

"Yeah. Thanks, Dan. I'm going to stay here and think for a while. You go on back. These mountains will frighten your Miss Spooner."

"They might at that," he said, looking outside at the sheer drop beside the tracks.

Several hours passed and Zack didn't return, hours in which Kate tried to bring order to her chaotic thoughts and emotions. She declined Dan's offer of tea and a stroll through their new train later that morning, and remained in her compartment. She felt cornered, not only by her own circumstances or what Zack had done, but by her own feelings. She hated Zack, but she loved him. She felt a deep sense of loss that he would no longer be part of her life. She had thought that she wanted him gone, but she hadn't known it would be so painful.

She kicked off her shoes, removed her dress and petticoats, and lay down on her bunk. The blanket she pulled over her was little consolation against the cold she felt. She covered her burning eyes with her forearms. She felt completely defeated and so very tired.

Her restless mind went back over the time since that fateful ball, searching for anything she might have overlooked in forming her conclusions. If she could find only one detail that would point to Zack's innocence, she'd grab it and hold on to it. What if he was unrelated to Peter, much as they possessed the same characteristic features?

She went to the beginning of it all, to the argument she'd overheard between Peter and Sam Bennett. Had there been the mention of a third partner? Of anyone else who knew their secret aside from Corinne?

And what of their argument? Could she have misunderstood that? No. Every word they spoke was indelibly imprinted on her mind. They had killed her mother, had rigged the accident that robbed her of her life, and they were contemplating the same fate for her. Or one even worse.

She wished she knew exactly what her grandfather had written in his will. Sam had said he and Peter would lose everything on her twentieth birthday, or if she married. But how could they keep something like that a secret? Surely their lawyer knew.

A numbing chill raced through her. Sam had hired his own lawyer after her mother's death. Her grandfather's lawyer, Mr. Beauchamps, had died. She wracked her brain to remember how. Mrs. Tyree, who'd been his housekeeper, said he'd been ill for weeks before he succumbed to heart failure. And Mrs. Tyree now lived in a house bought for her by Sam Bennett, and Mrs. Tyree, who had struggled to support her two children after her husband ran off, no longer had to work at all. Everyone, including Kate, suspected she was Sam's mistress. Perhaps what lay between them was far more sinister than that.

With her grandfather dead, her mother out of the way, and Beauchamps silenced, why the need to kill her? Unless Annie was right, and another copy of the will existed somewhere else. Somewhere where they couldn't get their hands on it. But where? Who else knew? Who would her grandfather have trusted with such a document?

She had no idea how long she lay there before she realized she was not alone. Her bunk sagged, but she was too spent to move.

"That was a fast cup of tea," she said, wishing Annie would go back to Dan. She wasn't up to Annie's chatter.

"I wasn't drinking anything as innocuous as tea," came Zack's deep reply.

She shot up, grabbing the blanket to cover herself. "You!"

"Don't be alarmed, I didn't come here to yell at you again."

"What *do* you want?"

"I want to apologize. I didn't mean what I said earlier."

"Yes you did, but it's okay. As I said before, this whole situation is impossible. It's best this way, believe me."

"I can't accept that. I won't accept that. Let me help you. I'll never be able to live with myself thinking I'd turned you out into the unknown with no money. God, have you any idea what could happen out here to a woman alone? This isn't the East. These men are governed by different rules, or no rules at all."

"You should have thought about that before . . ."

"Before what?"

"Before you got involved with us," she said, covering her near slip.

"But that's *why* I made you come with us. I felt the same way then. Ah, sweetheart, can't you be honest with me? I'm not an ogre. Some even consider me a very nice man. You really can trust me. Everything I've done since we met, I've done for you."

Sardonic skepticism glinted from her eyes. She sagged back against the seat and pulled her knees up, huddling under her blanket. He didn't touch her, he made no move to come closer. He just talked. But with every word she felt her resistance ebbing away.

"I know it doesn't appear that way to you, and I don't blame you for doubting me. I've lost my temper, insulted you, rushed you into a relationship you aren't ready for. I must look like the worst cad in the world. But Katie," he said earnestly, taking a deep breath, "I love you."

"Zack, . . ."

"I don't want you to say anything. I know you're suspicious of words, but I wanted you to know. And I intend to show you, too, to prove myself, if you'll let me. Give me that chance, sweetheart. Don't shut me out of your life."

"I don't want—"

"Don't say anything yet," he interrupted, jumping up.

He was afraid, she realized, and she took heart. His eyes skittered around as if searching for inspiration, some means to convince her. His breathing was harsh, hectic color stained his neck. He ran his hands distractedly through his hair and sighed deeply, as if from the depths of his soul.

"Zack, come here and sit down."

"Kate, please."

This was the man who had shown her what love was, who had cradled her against his body and opened a new world to her. This man had been closer to her than anyone in her life, he'd shown her true intimacy between two bodies and two spirits. He couldn't have faked the emotion that passed between them. What she saw in his eyes now couldn't be manufactured at will.

Zack wasn't the sort of man to beg or plead, but that was exactly what he was doing. She was probably a fool above fools, but her heart relented. She held out a hand.

"I'd like you to put your arms around me," she said simply.

She was in his embrace in a second, her head cradled against his pounding heart. She closed her eyes and breathed deeply of his clean, spicy scent. *Don't betray me,* she pleaded silently.

"I'm afraid, Zack. I'm torn two ways. If I stay with you, you could be hurt or killed. If I go, I lose you anyway. I didn't know how much that would hurt until you said you were through with me."

"I didn't mean it. And I can take care of myself." His lips planted kisses in her hair and down the side of her face. "Please stay in Sacramento. I know you won't stay with me, but let me help you find a place. Let me know you're safe."

"You'll let me pay you back when I have the money?"

"Anything you want. I'll try not to interfere anymore. I won't bully you, I promise. If you'll let me call on you."

She laughed and leaned away. "Oh, Zack, even your promises have strings. What am I to do with you? You are a thoroughly spoiled man. What a wretched child you must have been. Have you always had your own way?"

"I told you before. When I want something, I don't stop until I have it."

"I want my way, too. I won't be a kept woman. I've seen what happens when a woman lets a man buy her. I'll have to work, and I have Annie to consider. I'm not going to marry you or anyone until I can stand on my own two feet again. I won't have it said I married you for your money."

"Such fierce independence," he teased fondly.

"I'm serious, Zack."

"That may be a long time. I can see you intend to make me pay for . . ."

"For what?" she asked archly, knowing he'd almost made

the same slip of the tongue she had.

"For being so spoiled. Do you forgive me?"

"I guess so," she drawled with mock forbearance.

"And you won't run away from me?"

"I'll try not to. You might try gentle persuasion instead of arrogant dictates."

"Oh, now she wants sweet talk, does she?" he said, tumbling her backward onto the bunk so that she lay beneath him. "Usually women take me as I am. It's been a while since I had to resort to such silly romantic fancies, but I'll try."

"You are a conceited cad."

"That's not very sweet," he reproved, tapping her impudent lips. "Now, let me see if I can remember."

"Don't bother if it puts such a strain on your powers of recall." She twisted to get away.

He pulled her back, chuckling. "Not so fast. We made an agreement. I think we should seal our bargain with a kiss. Your lips are a temptation I can no longer resist."

"One kiss," she stipulated, "then you must let me get dressed. This is indecent."

"Nothing about you could ever be indecent. You are delectable, even with clothes on."

"What a thing to say," she complained laughingly, but Zack could see she indeed was affected by compliments, even given in fun. "Zack," she said more seriously. "Don't wait too much longer to kiss me."

"Are you enjoying this, too?" He moved his hips seductively against hers. "I haven't been able to forget making love to you, Katie, and every time I remember, I want you more."

Had he been sarcastic again or aggressive, she might have been able to resist him, but he was neither. His hands were patient and gentle on her bare arms. His fingers paused at her sensitive throat on his way to the thickness of her hair. One by one he removed her pins, and with tender slowness he spread her black curtain of hair over the pillow.

His eyes burned into hers with fierce love and longing. She could no longer doubt his feelings, no matter what he did in the name of love. She'd gladly give him everything she owned if he'd only look at her that way for the rest of her life. Her own love filled her with a deep instinctive desire to hold him close to ease his worry, to give him the pleasure he was giving her.

Zack's senses soared. She was his dream, all he'd been searching for in a woman. She was strong, independent, delightfully and infuriatingly temperamental, yet vulnerable and innocent and sweet. And she was so beautiful his insides twisted painfully at the sight of her. Never in all his years had a woman stirred him to the depths of desire he felt for Katie. She had become a fever, a fire in his blood, a wild conflagration that couldn't be doused with the coldest and hardest of logic and argument. He had given up trying.

He smoothed her hair back from her face, falling in love all over again with the flawless silken texture of her creamy skin, the jet black of her delicate brows and her long thick lashes, her eyes the color of the clearest, purest, most exquisite sapphires. Eyes that were glittering like stars in the night as they looked into his.

"You are perfect," he said solemnly. "You're the loveliest woman I've ever known. And I want you beyond sanity. If I succumb to that craziness from time to time, you must make allowances for me."

"Please stop talking and kiss me."

His breath hissed from his lungs. "I can't." If he did, he'd never be able to stop.

"Then I'll kiss you," she responded, holding his head and lifting her lips to his.

A shudder ran through him, and his good intentions flew to the far corners of the earth. He crushed her to him, molding her body to his, and captured her lips in a kiss that cast their senses spinning and careening into another plane of existence.

"My dearest Zack, you turn me inside out. I want you so."

Their lovemaking had an almost frantic quality to it, each giving all to the other in fevered haste to reach the final union, where they became one. It was as if, deep in the back recesses of their minds, they knew the whole train trip was a moment stolen, that once they reached their destination, reality would raise its ugly head and tear asunder the fragile link that held them together.

Even after their bodies were exhausted, sated on the ecstasy of fulfillment, they clung desperately to each other.

*If only time could be suspended,* Katie thought, *if only this could be eternity.*

The muted keening cry of the train's whistle severed their embrace. Reluctantly, Zack released her and sat up, swinging his long legs to the floor. He picked up his discarded shirt and slid his arms into the sleeves.

"Dan is waiting for us to return for them. He and Annie will be at each other's throats by now."

"You go on ahead. I need a few minutes," she said quietly.

"Are you all right?"

"I love you, Zack."

# Chapter 11

Kate looked out onto Second Street from the window of her second-story room in the Hotel de France. Gaslights lit the wide brick street and boarded sidewalks and glowed from the windows of the establishments across from the hotel. Sacramento. Already, in a brief time, it felt like home.

Annie came in from the bathroom and flopped onto her bed. Immediately she jumped up again and took off her bathrobe, then pulled back the covers.

"I hate to mess this one up," she sighed, but she hopped in anyway. "I'm sorely tired of making beds. How are you holding up after a week of washing dishes?"

Annie had been given the task of cleaning the hotel rooms each day while Kate worked in the kitchen of the hotel restaurant. Both girls deemed themselves fortunate to have work of any kind, let alone in the same hotel, and to have so pleasant a room to live in. But working for a living, Kate found, was taxing the limits of her energy. Had she not been so pampered, she'd have more endurance, she'd be tougher.

She looked disgustedly at her miserable red hands and shook her head. "Would you like to trade work for a day or two?"

Annie was quick to jump up again and bring Kate her jar of hand cream. "Oh, Kate," she said in dismay, "they're worse. You can't go on doing that kind of work. Have you shown Mrs. Williams?"

"I can't. She'd make me stop. She'd tell Zack."

"He'll see for himself tomorrow. They're coming for dinner."

"They'll be better by then," she said hopefully.

"Not if you stick them in that hot water one more time."

"It isn't the water, it's the soap," Kate said wearily.

"Do you know what I found in the back of the basement storeroom today?" Annie asked mysteriously, hoping to raise Kate's spirits. Kate, who had never worked a day in her life, had labored from dawn each day until the restaurant closed each evening. If she wasn't washing dishes and scrubbing pots and pans, she was cleaning tho floors between meals, resetting tables, polishing brass and silver, arranging fresh flowers. Annie had tried to convince her to slow down, but Kate was determined to earn enough money to repay Zack for the first month's rent and their new wardrobes.

"What did you find?" Kate asked, trying to inject some enthusiasm into her voice.

"A piano. It's covered with an old blanket, and boxes of junk are stacked on top of it, but I plunked a few keys and it plays. I don't know how good it is, but . . ."

"Really," Kate exclaimed, truly excited in spite of her exhaustion. "I've missed my music lately. Let's go see it."

"Now? It's nearly ten. You're dead on your feet. I'll take you after breakfast tomorrow. I promise."

Kate understood the next day why Annie hadn't wanted to go down there at night. The basement, though dry enough, was airless and dark, and, with its thick stone block walls, looked awfully like a dungeon. Old furniture and crates were stacked helter-skelter, covered with dust and cobwebs. A headless dress form stood against the wall like a sentinel watching over her dark domain. A mouse scurried into a corner. The alcove with the stored supplies was the only moderately clean place down there.

Annie led her to the dark corner farthest from the stairs and lifted the blanket, revealing a long row of stained ivory keys.

"Oh, it's beautiful."

"Beautiful? It's a wreck," Annie scoffed, but then Annie didn't understand what the sight of black and white keys could mean to someone whose only solace for years had been the piano.

"Well," Annie urged, "try it out."

Kate was almost jumping with eagerness. "I need a stool. Oh, it must be here."

"Is this it? Gad, it's dirty." She dusted it with her long pinafore apron and set it with a flourish before the keyboard. "Your audience of one awaits you."

Kate ran her fingers up and down a few arpeggios. The strings were out of tune, but not terribly. She lifted her fingers, took a deep breath, then launched into Chopin's *Prelude in F*.

Annie didn't move a muscle until the last chord sounded and died away. "Oh, Kate," she sighed. "You shouldn't be washing dishes with those hands. You should be making music."

"Indeed," came a voice from behind them.

Annie spun around to find their employer standing with her arms crossed over her ample waist. "Mrs. Williams, I can explain," she insisted guiltily. "It's my fault. You see, I was getting supplies yesterday and I couldn't help snooping a little. When I found the piano, well . . . I knew Kate played. I thought—oh, I didn't think at all. Please don't blame her."

Kate stood up and moved away from the keyboard. "It is my fault. I was the one playing, after all."

Mrs. Williams stepped forward and lifted one of Kate's hands. Her brow creased in concern when she saw the angry red patches and cracks that covered her once beautiful hands. "Why didn't you tell me?"

"I need the money, Mrs. Williams."

"Well, no more dishes for you, young lady."

"Kate could do the beds. Soap doesn't bother *me*. We could trade," Annie suggested hopefully.

Mrs. Williams' eyes narrowed thoughtfully. "No. I have others who can wash up. You may get back to your duties, Miss Spooner, but you, Mrs. Lawrence, are to march yourself over to Dr. Allen in the Morse Building and see to those hands."

Kate's face fell. "Am I dismissed?"

"And while you're gone," she went on as if Kate hadn't spoken, "I'll have the piano brought up to the dining room. I wonder if Clive Gunter still tunes pianos. I'll get in touch with him also. You do know how to read music, don't you? Of course, or you couldn't have learned that piece. Somewhere down here is a box of music. I'll look for it."

"Mrs. Williams, I don't understand," Kate said.

"We are reputed to have the finest restaurant in Sacramento, Mrs. Lawrence. Now we shall add music to dine by. What a marvelous idea!"

"Oh, yes," Annie piped up. "Who would go anywhere else to eat when they could come here and listen to Kate play?"

Mrs. Williams arched a brow. "I like to think my menu has some appeal."

"Oh, yes. I didn't mean to imply . . ."

"Of course not. We shall try this tonight, and if it works, then the position is yours. You shall have Sunday and Monday off. I'll arrange it so Miss Spooner is off then as well. But you must realize I'll need you in the afternoons to help set up for dinner." The last she directed to Kate who nodded that that was perfectly fine with her. "Now off with you both. This dust isn't good for my bronchitis. And Kate," she added as an afterthought, "tell Dr. Allen he is to have dinner here this evening, on the house, for attending to your hands."

Kate returned from the doctor just before lunch to find that Mrs. Williams, true to her word, had indeed had the piano moved to a corner of the dining room. Annie was applying a coat of furniture polish, buffing the neglected rosewood to a high gloss.

"It's beautiful," Kate exclaimed, running her fingers over the glowing rectangular cabinet.

"It belonged to my mother," Mrs. Williams said sentimentally. "I never learned to play myself. I found her music for you."

"How are your hands?" Annie asked.

"The doctor said they aren't infected. He gave me some salve. They feel better already, thanks. And thank you, Mrs. Williams."

"Can you play this evening?" Mrs. Williams asked. "Mr. Gunter will be here at three to tune the piano. That will give you a couple hours before we open for dinner to select your music."

"I—yes. Oh, this will be fun, not like work at all."

"I'd say you've already put in long hours of work at your music," Mrs. Williams remarked. "That's how it is with artists. Just remember, when you're in great demand, who gave you your start."

Kate hugged her impulsively. "I will, I promise. I wouldn't want to work anywhere but here."

"That's an impetuous promise which I won't hold you to. Now back to work. We've tables to set up."

Kate was a mass of jangling nerves by the time the first diners arrived that evening. The thought of playing for the usually large Saturday night crowd didn't bother her nearly as much as the thought that Zack would be listening to her. Even wearing the stylish new blue dress he had bought for her when she had finally been settled in the Hotel de France didn't raise her confidence as she had hoped it would.

"Time to begin," Mrs. Williams said, joining Kate in the back room used as the hotel office. "Are you nervous?"

"A little."

Kate sat down at the piano and began her first piece. Mr. Gunter had spent two hours cleaning and tuning the instrument. It was lovely sounding. As the strains of a familiar melody left her fingers and filled the space around her with music, she began to relax and enjoy herself, and if their frequent applause was any indication, the diners were delighted as well.

After an hour she went to the kitchen for a cup of tea, which was always ready for the staff, and which she drank thirstily. Annie was there, too, talking with the chef while she waited for Zack and Dan to arrive.

"You're a success," Annie praised, beaming. "Mrs. Williams has received buckets of compliments. Have you eaten?"

Kate nodded. "Before we opened the doors," she answered. "Are you dining with Zack and Dan?"

"Yes. Zack is expecting you to be working in the kitchen. Won't he be surprised?"

Kate poured a second cup of tea, wishing she could have Zack's company for the evening. But at least she'd be able to look at him instead of stacks of dirty dishes.

She excused herself to visit the washroom, and Annie

departed to the lobby to await the men. Kate was much restored since her lazy afternoon, but still she watched enviously as Annie moved sprightly down the hallway. Annie had boundless energy, she never seemed to tire. But, then, Kate reminded herself, Annie's duties were easy compared to what she'd done before.

Kate had apologized to Annie when she learned the work Zack had been able to procure for them. She had envisioned something more refined for her friend than cleaning rooms. But Annie had been exuberant.

"Nothin' to it," she'd said when Mrs. Williams explained her responsibilities. "I can do that easy. And the room you gave us is lovely. We can be together."

Mrs. Williams had flicked a glance at Zack, and Kate suspected then that both the room and the positions had been prearranged. That, above everything else, spurred Kate on to prove her worth. Kate, though she'd never washed dishes in her life, had accepted the assignment willingly. She'd had no choice, she hadn't even thought of her music. Now she had acquired this position on her own, and it gave her immense satisfaction and confidence to know she had a skill she could earn a living with.

Zack was seated at a table close to the piano with Annie and Dan when Kate returned to the dining room. His stunned expression, when, instead of coming to greet them, she sat at the piano, told her that Annie hadn't warned him.

She threw him a grin and a sassy wink, then began to play. She looked up frequently during the next hour, always to find Zack's eyes resting on her. He barely touched his meal.

Mrs. Williams came over to her and suggested another ten minute break. "He'll sit there all night if you don't go and talk to him, and I have guests waiting for a table."

"Oh, I'm sorry," Kate had apologized. "Shall I suggest they go?"

"No, no. I'm going to open the doors between the dining room and the lounge. We'll offer coffee and drinks in there after dinner so we can accommodate the guests who wish to listen to you while we feed the crowd in here. I told you this was a good idea. We didn't even have to advertise. The sound of your playing reached the street and drew them in. Wait till next week after the gossips are through this weekend. We'll be swamped with customers."

Kate laughed. "I'm making more work for you."

"And more money. Maybe I should open on Sunday and Monday, too. I'll have to give you a increase in pay. Now go to your man. He can't take his eyes off you."

Zack stood and held out the fourth chair for her. He said nothing, merely looked at her in wonder.

"Mrs. Williams would like us to move to the lounge for coffee, or brandy, if you gentlemen prefer. She's opening the doors now."

"Can we hear you from there?" Zack asked. He stood again and helped Kate to her feet, escorting her to the area already being organized for after dinner lingerers.

"You never said you played," he accused.

She shrugged. "I said I studied music."

"Annie told me about your hands," he said remorsefully. "I'm sorry, Katie."

"Why should you be? You weren't to know. Goodness, I never expected I'd have such a reaction."

"Still, I should never have considered such employment for you. At the time, I thought it would be easier than all the racing around the other position required."

"Oh, Zack, it isn't that I can't endure hard work. I'm just allergic to the soap. And anyway, the problem resolved itself nicely. We do appreciate what you've done for us."

She was grateful. After he'd taken her only security from her, she was grateful. The irony struck deep within him. Zack took her hands in his, running his thumbs gently over the irritation. He raised them to his lips and kissed them, then made a repugnant face at the scent that met his nose.

"What the . . ."

She laughed. "It's salve. Dr. Allen gave it to me. Awful, isn't it? But it helps."

"You've been to the doctor?"

"Mrs. Williams insisted as soon as she saw them."

Dan and Annie joined them. "We're going for a walk. Annie wants to see the boats on the river. Join us there when you're finished?"

"Yes, that's fine," Zack said abstractedly.

"Can I get you some coffee, Zack?" Kate asked.

"I'll get it later. You play like an angel. How did you learn?"

"My grandfather insisted I have lessons when he heard me picking out tunes on our piano. I was five. I studied with a very demanding teacher for thirteen years, a wonderful old man who had come to America from Germany. Then I was forced to quit. But I continued to practice."

"You could have your own students now."

"Yes, I suppose I could. I hadn't considered that. I must return to my piano. Mrs. Williams is signalling me. Are you going to stay?"

"I moved in here, but this is as far away as she's chasing me. I'll be here when you're done if I have to buy the hotel."

Kate laughingly conveyed Zack's sentiments to Mrs. Williams, who scowled and gave an inelegant snort.

"I suppose he'll become a darned nuisance if I don't get him a private table beside the piano. Oh, here's Dr. Allen. Excuse me, dear."

Kate let her fingers rove over the keys, playing by ear a selection of old folk tunes of the South. Mrs. Williams sat with Dr. Allen until his meal arrived. Was a romance in blossom between them? She smiled, liking the idea. She played a waltz.

Dr. Allen approached her after his meal, reluctant to disturb her concentration, but obviously wishing to speak with her.

"I can talk and play at the same time," she said, "as long as I'm not playing anything difficult."

"It all sounds difficult to me," he said warmly. "I've often taken meals here as payment for services to Mrs. Williams, but in this case I have been overpaid. I cannot remember such an enjoyable evening. Had I known I was treating such talented hands, I would have trembled."

"Oh, nonsense," she said and blushed. "I'm happy you enjoyed yourself."

"And your hands?"

"They feel much better, thank you, although they look a fright."

"And you will not plunge them in anymore dishwater! Come

see me in a few days."

"I will, thank you."

Dr. Allen was not her only visitor. Several couples stopped to thank her, and one man, who, although obviously apprehensive, introduced himself and seemed loathe to leave her.

"I wondered if I might buy you a cup of coffee after you finish," he asked clumsily.

"I'm sorry, Mr. Walter, I have a friend waiting for me."

"Oh. Perhaps another night?"

"Perhaps," she answered tactfully, wishing he'd take the hint and depart.

"I would really like to get to know you, Miss . . ."

"Mrs. Lawrence."

"You're married?"

"She's a widow," Zack said coldly, appearing at her side. "Are you nearly finished here, darling?" he said more gently to her.

She looked up and gave him a mocking grin. "Nearly. Would you order me a cup of tea, please?" She turned to her admirer. "It was nice meeting you, Mr. Walter. I hope you enjoyed your meal."

"I'll come back tomorrow. Would you permit me to call on you then, say two o'clock? We can take a Sunday stroll through the parks."

"I have . . ."

"She's busy," Zack said abruptly.

Two angry pairs of eyes locked over her head, and she could see in her mind's eye the rubble the restaurant would be reduced to if Zack's temper got away from him.

"I'm sorry, Mr. Walter, I am busy tomorrow."

"Please call me Ted."

Kate caught Mrs. Williams's eye and sent her a silent plea for help. Her employer dropped what she was doing and came over immediately.

"The last customers are leaving, Mrs. Lawrence. Why don't you and your gentleman run along? We'll be closing now, sir," she said to Ted Walter.

"I'll see you again, Mrs. Lawrence," Ted said, nodding a bow at her then pivoting and walking out.

Mrs. Williams watched him go. "That almost sounded like a threat. Who is he?"

"I never saw him before," Kate said, bewildered.

"He was on the train," Zack said laconically.

Kate's eyes skittered to Zack's taut features then back to the empty doorway. "Are you sure?" A dozen explanations flew through her head as to Walter's presence on that particularly exclusive train, but she didn't believe any of them. She was left to suspect the worst. Ted Walter was interested in her because of the reward. Had he guessed who she was? Had he seen one of those posters? How many other people had seen them?

"Well, I daresay you'll have more admirers in the future than you'll know what to do with," Mrs. Williams said, grinning at Zack's thunderous scowl. "Will you be dining with us on Tuesday evening, Mr. Standish?"

"I'll be here."

"I thought you might," she chortled, and shooed them both out of the dining room.

"Zack, you're jealous," Kate teased, pouring herself a cup of tea from the service on the tea table. It had cooled, but it felt good against her parched throat.

He glared at her.

"Are you blaming me? I didn't encourage him."

"You didn't have to. Every man in there tonight had eyes only for you."

"They were listening to the music."

"Hmph," he grumbled, and added an impolite word or two.

"If my playing bothers you, I could go back to washing dishes."

"Don't be asinine."

She drank her tea quickly. "I've been sitting for hours. Are you going to take me for a walk in the moonlight?" she asked, rising to her feet.

"Yes, if you're ready."

"I am, but leave the grouch behind."

Under the same night sky, half the continent away, John Phillips lit another cigarette and reread his report on Katrina Montgomery. He had uncovered some thought-provoking information, some that Zack might be very interested in hearing. John was not a man to ask questions, he simply carried out his assignments, but he couldn't help wondering how Zack had come to know Katrina Montgomery and if he knew how much trouble she was in.

John had made his usual inquiries when he had reached Memphis, and he had also visited the hall of records in the courthouse. Everything about Katrina Montgomery and her family fascinated him. The Montgomerys were one of the few Southern families who had held on to their plantation during the war, but then Lawrence Montgomery had been a crafty old fox. He'd played both sides of the board, selling horses to the Union Army to buy arms for the Confederates. He'd had powerful friends on both sides, but John couldn't help but suspect he was a Confederate through and through, especially after his son was killed. Although there was that one brief accusation of his being an abolitionist. Curious. He was probably one of those few men who didn't let the blood-red fever of war rule him. He probably saw the right on both sides, hating the injustice to the negroes, the aristocratic snobbery of the South, objecting to the idea of secession, but at the same time seeing the purpose of the North: to secure absolute political power and industrial expansion at the expense of the southern way of life, cloaked neatly under the humanistic fervor of freeing the slaves. He no doubt knew the South could not win, perhaps even believed they should not, but hated the Union, nevertheless, for taking their victory at the expense of his son.

After the war Lawrence Montgomery had built his plantation into one of the richest in the nation. He had been a man to be reckoned with, noted for his astute wisdom, his fairness, his endeavors to see the South rebuilt into a contributing and profitable part of the nation.

John folded his report and slid it into an envelope. So far as it went, it was interesting reading. The next day, though, would reveal more of what Zack wanted. John had an appointment with the Bennetts. He would at that time make the offer to return their property and get a first hand look at the Bennett household. He could learn a great deal by seeing how people lived, how they acted and reacted. He was noted for his perceptiveness. In that he would have an advantage over the Bennetts. They didn't know that about him.

He had uncovered one piece of information that was sure to startle Zack Standish. The man he had searched for, the man John himself had tried to find before Mrs. Standish had been taken ill, was living at the Manor, Bennett's home. Zack's brother. John had decided not to mention that in his brief until he had seen the man for himself. John was curious to know what kind of man Peter Standish was.

John had previously uncovered information that led him to believe Peter was in Memphis, and he'd sent several letters asking Peter to contact Zack on an urgent matter. The letters, one sent simply to Memphis, one to the sheriff, one to the mayor, had never been answered. That had been the week before Mrs. Standish died. After that Zack had dropped the idea of locating his brother and had taken John off the case. John was close, he knew he could find Peter Standish, but Zack no longer cared. John couldn't help wondering if Zack knew about Peter and was exacting some form of retribution against Peter at the expense of Montgomery's granddaughter. He found that thought quite disturbing in view of all he had learned about the Montgomerys. Without ever having met her, he felt great sympathy for the young girl who had been robbed of her home by an avaricious guardian.

Sunday dawned bright and clear, perfect weather for an outing, and both girls, looking forward to a day away from the hotel, were up and dressed early. Zack had promised to show them his ranch.

"Let's wait outside on the bench. I can't stand to be indoors on a day like this," Annie suggested.

"Don't forget your hat and gloves. Zack said we'd be going to church after breakfast."

"I haven't been to church much. Just at the old schoolhouse where I grew up. Will this be like that?"

Kate smiled. "I doubt it. Don't worry, you'll like it."

"I love this whole town," Annie said with a complacent sigh, looking up and down the picturesque street. They reached the bench and brushed it free of dust before sitting down. "Have you noticed that this is a brick town? All the buildings are made of brick, except for the wood trim and balconies. Isn't that unusual?"

"No, considering it was once a wood town that burned to the ground. Wouldn't you rebuild with less incendiary material after a disaster like that?"

"Dan said they used to have floods so high people used boats to get around. He said they raised the whole city twelve feet."

"Good morning, ladies."

Kate felt the hair bristle on her arms. It was Ted Walter. She turned and gave him a cool greeting. "Good morning."

"I see you aren't busy this morning," he said accusingly. "Let me buy you breakfast."

He took her arm and propelled her to her feet. "Excuse us, miss," he said over his shoulder to Annie.

Kate jerked free. "What do you think you're doing?" she snapped. "You have no right to lay hands on me or to assume I'll go anywhere with you."

"I told you last night that I'd see you again. I meant that."

Kate's temper boiled over. "In the first place, it's customary to ask, not to commandeer, and in the second place, the woman must agree. I do not. Now, kindly leave me alone."

He caught her arm again, and this time his grip hurt her. "I've waited days to see you. You're either working in that damned hotel or you're with that man." The last came out on a sneer. "You said you weren't married. Well, I'm making my intentions clear. I've come to court you. It's my turn. Don't refuse me, Mrs. Lawrence. I won't like that."

"Take your hands off her," Annie threatened, jumping to her feet.

"Stay out of this, if you know what's good for you," Ted threatened. "This ain't none of your business."

"I said take your hands off her!"

Ted Walter laughed and started to pull Kate away. Annie ran after them and grabbed the arm that held Kate prisoner. With all her might she bit him, right through his sleeve. He yelped and released Kate, then he pulled back his arm to strike Annie.

"I wouldn't, if I were you," came another masculine voice, "unless you want your teeth knocked down your throat."

Ted Walter turned and glared at the intruder "Get lost, mister. This is between me and my woman."

"She's not his woman," Annie cried. "He just walked up and took her."

The man looked at Annie then at Ted Walter. "You have ten seconds to get the hell out of here, then your chance is over."

"Yeah, and what are you going to do?" Walter sneered, looking down at the smaller man.

The newcomer pulled a pistol from his pocket and levelled it at Walter's chest. "I'll shoot you."

Walter backed away. "Hey, pal, you can't go around shooting people."

"I am not your pal, and I can if they're accosting decent women. No court in the land would convict me for that. Five seconds, four, three . . ."

"I'm goin'."

Kate turned in relief to their rescuer. "Thank you," she said simply.

"You couldn't have timed your arrival better," Annie said.

"Happy to help. Will you be all right now? Why don't you sit down? You both look a little pale."

"We were sitting until that man came," Annie grumbled. "Do you know who he is?"

He shook his head. "If you're sure you'll be okay, I'll leave you. I'm on my way to church."

"What's your name?" Annie called after him.

He shrugged. "It's not important."

Annie's gaze moved slowly from the man's departing back to Kate. "Well," she said on a note of amazement. "That's certainly *one* way to start the day."

# Chapter 12

Sam Bennett paced the library agitatedly, setting Corinne's nerves on edge. "Sit down, Papa. He'll be here any moment. Getting yourself in an uproar won't help anything."

"Were you able to learn anything of this John Phillips?" Bennett asked Peter, who was sipping a whiskey despite the early morning hour.

"Not a thing, other than what he told us himself. He's an investigator from Philadelphia."

"The same one who was trying to locate you earlier this year?" Corinne asked.

"The same."

"But that was before all this happened. What has he to do with Katrina?"

Peter shrugged uncaringly. "We'll soon find out, won't we?"

"But you said he was trying to find you for your brother. Doesn't it seem strange that the same investigator knows something of Katrina?"

"Corinne, I don't know any more than you do." Peter snapped, irritated.

"Could she have gone to this brother of yours?" Bennett asked.

"She didn't know about him."

"We thought she didn't know anything about us either, and look where that put us."

Peter laughed scornfully. "I told you all along you were

underestimating her."

"Well, what if she did go to your brother then?" Corinne asked. "Could he cause problems for us?"

"Anyone could do that, my dear," Peter drawled bitterly. "You have handled this whole affair like bungling amateurs. And now I find myself in the center of it, an unwilling participant."

"What did your brother want of you? You received numerous letters from him,'" Corinne persisted.

"Not from him. From this man who is coming to meet us. All he said was that Zack needed to speak to me. I wasn't interested. I have no intention of letting my poor relatives drain my bank account. I've worked too hard to get where I am."

"What if your brother and Katrina are in this together? What if . . ."

"Corinne," Peter barked. "Why don't you keep quiet until we know something concrete? Your speculations are not helping matters."

A carriage clattered outside on the gravel drive. Sam Bennett looked toward the door as the knocker sounded. "We are about to learn the reason for this visit. I hope you are both in control of your senses. I wouldn't want a stranger to see us at odds with each other. We are supposed to be a family distraught by the disappearance of a loved one."

John Phillips was shown into the library by a quiet negro girl, who, for some reason, looked at him with her large black eyes as if seeking some reassurance from him. He thanked her and patted her hand. He knew without having to be told that she had been a friend to Katrina Montgomery. As did most servants, she probably knew more than she let on. He should like very much to speak to her, but he doubted that he'd be afforded that chance.

The room into which he was shown was exactly as he'd pictured Lawrence Montgomery's library would be. A true gentleman's domain. The three people sitting in it were jarringly out of place.

Sam Bennett rose and came to greet him, introducing himself, his daughter Corinne, and his partner Peter Standish.

Sam Bennett tried to look the part of a Southern gentleman, his impeccable dress and manner all firmly speaking to that status. Only his cold eyes belied his true character. Miss Bennett, dressed and coiffed in the latest expensive style to accent her outward beauty, left him just as unmoved. It was to Peter Standish that he directed his most curious attention.

Peter was, not surprisingly, an older version of Zack, tall, handsome, with a commanding presence. He might even find that he could like the man, though he suspected that was because he had liked and respected Zack so much. Only the fact that Peter had ignored all Zack's requests to contact him gave him a reserve in his greeting.

"I appreciate the fact that you made time in your day to meet with me," he said affably, taking the chair offered to him by Sam Bennett.

"We were most curious, especially when you mentioned that your visit had to do with my daughter," Sam said.

*His daughter?* "Ah, your stepdaughter," John said, making it clear he knew of their relationship.

Sam's mouth tightened perceptibly. "Yes. We are most concerned for her. She has been gone some time now, without a word to us about where she is, or if she is well."

"Are you sure your concern is for her?"

"Of course it is," Miss Bennett asserted, looking positively anguished. John gave her a searching look which she could not hold.

"Before I get down to the matter at hand, I must ask why, if you are so concerned, you went to the extremes of having posters run accusing her of theft and offering a reward for her return."

"That was an aberration of the moment," Peter said, "an unfortunate choice of actions, since it did not bring her back as we had hoped. We have regretted it."

"Then you no longer accuse her of theft?"

"She did steal from us,"' Corinne said, "but we don't want to see her in jail because of it. We just want her home with us."

"Have you any idea why she left in the first place?" John pressed. They didn't like his questions, but they were being very patient in the hopes that he would reveal her whereabouts to them. He had no intention of doing that.

A discreet knock sounded at the door, and the maid, the same young girl who had answered the door to him, entered, carrying a heavy silver tray of tea and coffee. When none of the others made a move to help her, John stood and took the tray from her. He set it on the table in front of the sofa where Corinne was seated.

Junie set about opening the drapes, letting the pleasant morning light into the darkened room as Corinne poured tea for everyone.

"She has always been a whimsical girl, out of touch with reality," Sam said. "We have had difficulty on more than one occasion with her addle-headed flights of fancy."

"Then this is not the first time she has left home?"

"Oh, it is. I was referring to other irregular activities she has pursued."

"Such as?"

John glanced up to see the dark eyes of the maid widen in indignation. She looked as if she were about to protest.

"Why all the questions?" Corinne snapped. "That will be all Junie," she said sharply to the young girl, seeing John's interest in her.

John turned unscrutable eyes to Corinne. "Do my questions disturb you so greatly?"

"I just don't see the need to go into all this."

"Might not anything I learn of Katrina help me in locating her?"

"We thought you already knew where she was," Sam injected, ovbiously disgruntled.

"I might very well know where she is." John accepted a cup of tea, offering a brief nod of thanks.

"Then you must tell us."

"Am I to understand that the reward you offer still stands?"

"Yes. We are prepared to compensate you handsomely for the information we desire."

"What irregular activities?" he asked, returning to his original question.

Sam sighed in frustration. "She lives in her own world. She spends hours in her room reading, she can't hold a decent conversation. I don't think she's altogether in control of her faculties, if you know what I mean. She can't handle being on her own. She needs her family to protect her."

"You're saying she's mentally incompetent?"

"Let's just say she has no concept of the real world. Isn't that obvious when she has run off on her own to who knows where?"

John wasn't so sure. Leaving these three may have been the first sane thing she'd done since Bennett took over. But he had to be sure, for Zack's sake. "Can you be more specific?"

Peter spoke to that, obviously sensing, as Phillips had, that Sam Bennett's temper was fraying. "Katrina is a lovely girl, Mr. Phillips, but she is a child. When Sam said she was incompetent, he didn't mean she was demented, only that she is incapable of caring for herself. She has to be watched. We had to deny her the use of the horses because she rode them with no regard for safety, either to herself or to the horses. We had to discontinue her music studies because she did nothing but play the piano all day. We've even had to curb the time she was permitted to read, or she'd miss her meals. It isn't normal for a person to be so solitary. She lives in a different world."

"And that's it?"

"I am her guardian," Sam blustered. "It is my duty to see she is taught the finer social amenities. In my opinion, she is a willful, undisciplined child."

John rubbed his chin thoughtfully. "Am I mistaken, or was not her grandfather Lawrence Montgomery? Was he not one of the finest horsemen in the East? Could it not be that he taught his granddaughter to ride, so that what may seem careless to an untrained rider might be well within her abilities to handle?"

"Mr. Phillips, those horses are valuable," Corinne said. "She shouldn't have treated them with such disregard."

"In what way?"

"She'd jump fences on them."

"Hmm. She must be very good. I, myself, own a jumper. It is exhilarating to fly through the air on the back of a good horse. About her music, I can't understand your aversion to that either. I have a very good friend who is a concert pianist. He practices from eight to ten hours each day. For him, that behavior is very regular."

"What's your point?" Sam demanded, going red around his neck.

"I'm not trying to make a point, just to understand. So far, I have heard nothing about Katrina that tells me she is incompetent. Perhaps she just wanted to get away, especially as you've seen fit to remove all the pleasures in her life. You, Miss Bennett, do you have any hobbies?"

"Hobbies?"

"What do you do with your days? Do you play the piano, paint, read, ride, sew, walk in the lovely garden I saw outside?"

"Well, no, but . . ."

"How dreadfully dull your life must be."

"Now look here, Phillips," Peter Standish objected. "You've no cause to insult Miss Bennett."

"No, I do apologize," he said, bowing his head to Corinne. "You are an exquisitely lovely young woman, Miss Bennett, and your dress is beautiful. It is too bad you do not have something more becoming than that bauble you are wearing to compliment it."

Corinne's hand went to the simple pendant hanging at her neck. Her eyes burned into his at the added insult. She was obviously not accustomed to being singled out derogatorily. "As it happens," she said spitefully, showing just how much she was concerned for her stepsister "the jewelry Katrina stole was mine."

"Would you care to have it back?"

"Of course. You don't think I like wearing these cheap trinkets, do you?"

"I could arrange that, on one condition," John said smoothly.

"Then you do know where she is," Sam crowed. "Stop playing games, Mr. Phillips."

"I am empowered to offer you the return of your money and your jewels in exchange for your signature on an affadavit clearing Miss Montgomery of all charges of theft."

"What?" Sam thundered.

"Oh, Papa, get the jewels back for me."

"I don't care about the jewels. I want Katrina back."

"Whom are you working for?" Peter Standish demanded, coming to his feet.

"That's confidential."

"You are the same man who contacted me about my brother."

"Your brother?"

"My brother, Zack Standish. Don't be obtuse."

"Ah, yes. I wondered if you were the one. I never had the opportunity to follow up on that case, but I did suspect you were in Memphis, although you elected not to respond to my letters. May I ask why you didn't?"

"I don't have to answer that."

"Of course not. I didn't mean to pry, and anyway it no longer matters."

"You mean he's not still trying to find me?"

"He never wanted to find you in the first place. It was only at your mother's insistence that he commissioned me to try. She wanted desperately to see you one last time before she died. Something to do with forgiveness. I'm not sure," he said lightly, all the while watching Peter's reaction. "Anyway, after she died, Zack dropped the case."

"So my mother is dead."

"Yes."

"I suppose Zack wanted money, for doctors?"

"Zack? I hardly think so." He chuckled derisively. "Your mother, Mr. Standish, was a very wealthy woman."

Peter's interest was piqued at last. "Oh. How did that come to be?"

"I might well have guessed that you would be curious since you left them penniless when Zack was but a small boy. As it turned out, she married a generously wealthy man."

Peter resented that disclosure, seeing surprise and disgust in Corinne's eyes, and he retaliated. "Perhaps I should contact my brother after all. If my mother left a large inheritance, I stand to benefit, as the eldest son, you understand."

"Oh, I understand perfectly. But I'm afraid there is nothing for you; Zack inherited everything. It is a shame you didn't go to see her before she died."

"I could contest the will."

"No. You see, your mother's husband signed everything over to Zack before he died. It was all for your mother, but it was legally Zack's. Your mother's husband knew Zack would never consider leaving her penniless."

That hit too close to home for Bennett, not only since he had done just that to Katrina, but that she could conceivably turn around and do it to him. He jumped up and strode to the bar. He poured himself a whiskey and threw it to the back of his throat. He turned and glared at John Phillips. "Where is my daughter? Is she with Peter's brother?"

John looked astounded. "With Zack? I don't believe I ever intimated such a thing. I simply answered Peter's questions concerning the letters I drafted to him. The two cases are quite separate matters."

"Where is Katrina?"

"I cannot reveal that information. Are you prepared to accept the return of the money and the jewels under the conditions I spelled out?"

"Yes." That came from Corinne Bennett. "Papa, I want them back."

"I'm not sure. If we sign an affadavit like that, we have no hold over her. She may never return."

"So what?" Corinne snarled.

Bennett gave her a look that made her slump back into her chair. "Why is it so important that we sign this agreement? She is guilty."

"I should think, in light of all your professed concern, that you would be eager to protect her from prosecution. The money and jewels will be returned, so you will be losing nothing in the deal."

"Except my daughter."

"I believe you've lost her in any case."

"She and Peter were to be married."

"Oh?" John queried. "You never mentioned that, Mr. Standish."

"I see no need to spread my private business around," Peter said waspishly.

"Had this willful, undisciplined child agreed to this marriage?"

No one ventured to respond. John stood. "I believe I've outstayed my welcome. If you agree to my terms, you will all three be required to meet with me at noon tomorrow at the sheriff's office. I shall await your answer there."

"The sheriff," Corinne asked. "Why the sheriff?"

"It must be duly noted that you are dropping the charges. Plus I shall want an official witness to the signing of the petition. By all three of you."

"It's nothing to do with me," Peter grumbled.

"On the contrary. You are Mr. Bennett's partner. All assets and liabilities are in your name as well as his. And as his daughter and heir, Miss Bennett is also an important player in this drama. I will want no chance that any of you could change your minds at some later date."

"Papa," Corinne entreated.

"Very well, we shall be there."

"I shall look forward to it. Oh, and by the way, if you decide not to come, I shall turn the property over to the sheriff, where it will be held as evidence until Miss Montgomery is found, which may be never. In either case the law will know Katrina is not a thief. As will the newspapers."

"I don't know who you're working for, Mr. Phillips, but after tomorrow I hope never to see you in my county again," Sam threatened. "I promise you will not be welcomed."

"Your county? Interesting. You're very certain of all this power?"

"Just go. And you can tell my daughter for me that we want very much for her to come back to us."

"I'm afraid I can tell your stepdaughter nothing, as I have no contact with her. Nor would I be all that interested in encouraging her to return to this nest of vipers. I find you all insufferable, and if anyone is mentally deranged, it certainly is not Miss Montgomery. Good day to you all."

On their gasps of outrage, he strode from the house, relieved to breathe unfouled air again. What an oppressive trio.

The little maid came running around the side of the house as he was climbing into his rig. With several glances at the front door, she approached. John moved her to the side of the buggy where she wouldn't be seen from the house.

"Did you wish to speak to me, Miss Junie?"

She was surprised to hear her name on his lips. "You know me?"

"I heard Miss Bennett address you. What is it you want of me?"

She shuffled her feet, looking away nervously. "It's Miss Katrina, sir. I wanted to know if she is well."

"Do you know why she left, Junie?"

"No, sir. No one knows that. Oh, them three in there, they talk about her sometimes, but we don't hear much 'cause they chase us off. But what they said, about her being addled and fanciful, well, that ain't true. She was the kindest soul. She just stayed away from them 'cause they was mean to her, always naggin' at her, pickin' on her. She has a good heart and a sound mind, sir. Don't let them tell you different. That's all I got to say."

"Thank you, Junie. I'm glad you said it, but I had sorted that out for myself."

Miss Junie gave a shy grin. "About Miss Katrina?"

"I believe she is well, and I think it's safe to say she's being looked after in the nicest possible way."

Her dark chocolate eyes beamed. "Thank you, sir. That puts my mind at peace."

"Go on back to the house now, before you are missed."

The next day at precisely noon, the Bennetts and Peter Standish arrived at the sheriff's office. None of them were in any better spirits than they had been in the day before, John noticed. The sheriff, though he treated Sam Bennett with deference, did not smile at him. Neither did he give Miss Corinne much notice other than to hand her the list she had made out for him of the pieces of jewelry that were stolen.

"Please look this over and see that nothing is missing," he said curtly. "When you have done so to your satisfaction, sign your name at the bottom of the papers Mr. Phillips has. Your money is here, Mr. Bennett, if you wish to count it."

"It's short five dollars," Sam said, after some moments. John Phillips drew out his wallet and added the missing amount.

"We wouldn't want to think she got away with anything of

yours, now would we?" the sheriff said sarcastically.

"You've no call to speak to me in that tone of voice, George. May I remind you that it was my influence that got you into office?"

"You have not ceased to remind me for two years now. I've done some dirty things for you in the past, Bennett, but none has made me sicker than what I did to Miss Katrina. Sign the goddamned papers. You, too, Standish. Then get out of my office."

John watched them get in their fancy conveyance, then turned to the sheriff. "Will you retract the wanted posters on Miss Montgomery?"

"I'll get right on it. Thanks, Mr. Phillips. I don't know what's going on in that family, but I'm glad she's out of it. Wherever she is, tell her to stay there. Bennett hates the very air she breathes."

"Why?"

"I don't know. She's a charming girl. Probably because she's a constant reminder of what a carpetbagger he is."

"What do you know of Peter Standish?"

"Not much. He came here a couple years ago and bought in with Bennett. He's been living with them ever since. Rumor has it that he and Corinne are . . . you know."

"Bennett claimed Peter was going to marry Katrina."

"First I heard of it. Now that's as good a reason to run off as any I know."

"Thanks, Sheriff. Can you do me another favor? Keep an eye on them. I don't think they're going to be satisfied until they get her back under their dominance."

"You mean they're bored without someone to push around? Oh, yes," he said when he saw John's surprise. "I've seen it. Everyone has."

"It goes deeper. I can't tell you how I know that, but I know it. I've never met Katrina Montgomery, but I don't want her anywhere near the Bennetts."

# Chapter 13

Kate and Annie were both laughing about their strange encounter when the familiar carriage came to a stop beside them.

"What a delight to find two such happy faces," Zack said and placed a chaste kiss on Kate's cheek. "Shall we go? Oh, ladies, I'd like you to meet Rollins, our coachman and general caretaker. Miss Spooner and Mrs. Lawrence," he introduced them. "Rollins and his wife have been in my employ since I purchased the ranch. You'll meet Martha when we get home."

"Good morning, Mr. Rollins," Kate said.

"Just Rollins, ma'am, if you please. Nice to make your acquaintance, ladies."

Rollins took them east and south until they were approaching the outskirts of the city. They passed palatial mansions, the much praised Capitol building, new schools, churches, parks full of stately trees and flower gardens.

"I didn't expect Sacramento to be so cosmopolitan," Kate said. "It's been a delightful surprise for me."

"I know what you mean. I felt the same way when I first saw the city."

"And gas lighting, that was a pleasant surprise. Do you have it at your ranch?"

"In a self-contained system. We'll have electricity soon. And I've already made arrangements to have a line run for a telephone."

The city gave way to green, rolling countryside, and Kate sat back and breathed in the smell of earth and grass. She liked living where she was, in the heart of the city, with the comfort of friends around her, but she missed dreadfully the open spaces, the feeling of freedom.

"Is Mr. Siebert not joining us today?" Annie asked. "Sick of me, is he?"

"Annie," Zack reproached. "Not at all. He simply overslept. He'll be waiting for us. He said he has a surprise for you."

"A surprise? Now what?"

Rollins led the coach onto a narrow road amidst white-fenced pastures and paddocks, past an oval exercise track, up a long lane, and around a fountain under several aged oaks to a wide stone and brick stairway.

"Jehosophat!" Annie cried. "This your house?"

"Zack, it's beautiful," Kate said sincerely.

The house sat on a small rise surrounded by towering trees and sculptured shrubs and flowers of every color. At the top of the steps on either side of the walk was a manicured carpet of green that stretched across the front of the house.

The house itself, like most of Sacramento's structures, was built of red brick, but Zack's home, instead of being decorated with excessive gingerbread, resembled more the homes of the colonial South. Tall white pillars rose from the wide front porch to the upstairs balcony where a white railing ran the length of the house. The windows and the front door were all trimmed in white, the only concession to the Victorian style of Sacramento being the rectangular carved cornices above each.

"It was built in '62," Zack said. "It has six bedrooms upstairs, three on each side, and—well, come in and see for yourself."

Martha met them at the door. "You must be Mrs. Lawrence," she said warmly. "Mr. Standish mentions your name in every other sentence, but he calls you his Katie. I think I'd know you anywhere."

"This is Mrs. Rollins. She insists on being called Martha," Zack explained.

"I think folks is talking to my husband when I hear the name Rollins. Shall I take your hats for you? No need for them here."

"Thank you, Martha. And please call me Kate. This is my friend Annie Spooner."

"Well now, she's as cute as can be. Not a bit of a hellion do I see."

"Martha," Dan remonstrated from the center landing of the staircase. "I'm in enough trouble with her. Must you make more?"

"Then you shouldn't go around behind my back calling me names," Annie bit back, her eyes sparking fire at him.

"It was meant fondly," Martha assured Annie. "Breakfast is ready to serve anytime. And my husband says I'm to remind you that you must leave here at half past ten to make the service, so you'd better not linger too long over your meal."

Zack laughed. "See how she runs the place? We've been here a week, and we're already under her thumb."

Martha winked at Kate. "I always say men need a firm hand."

"Oh, so do I," Annie chortled.

"Good grief," Dan complained. "Don't tell them that. I've already received a black eye from Miss Spooner's firm hand."

"At least you didn't get bit," Kate said, laughing.

They were seated in the breakfast room off the kitchen, a cozy garden room bordered on two sides by windows that looked out over the back paddocks and on the third by a fireplace. Martha served them warmed plates filled with sausages and pancakes. A bowl of fluffy scrambled eggs was added to the table, along with biscuits and a tray of coffee and tea.

"If there's nothing more you need," Martha said, "Rollins and I will be headin' to church ourselves."

"We'll be fine; we're not helpless. Enjoy the rest of your day off," Zack instructed.

"Thank you for breakfast," Dan added.

"So," Zack said, turning curiously to Kate. "What's this about being bitten?"

She grinned. "Annie bit a man this morning."

"You are going to explain that, aren't you?"

"It was the man from the last night, Zack." She went on to tell them about being dragged away, and of Annie's intervention. "Then out of nowhere this second man came and ran the first man off at gunpoint." Her eyes and Annie's were alight at the memory.

Neither Zack nor Dan could see the humor in her tale. "Where were you sitting?' Zack demanded.

"On the bench beside the front door of the hotel."

"What man last night?" Dan inquired. "You didn't tell me about a man last night."

"Me neither," Annie said. "You knew him?"

"Kate picked up an admirer who was very persistent," Zack explained.

"I'll say," Annie retorted, "if the way he acted this morning is an example. He wanted her and he meant to take her with him. I had to stop him."

"You're becoming a real bodyguard," Dan teased, but his eyes kept going back to Zack.

"Should I have stayed out of it like he told me to?"

"No, but to bite him?" Dan said, frowning.

"It made him turn Kate loose."

"And then what were you planning to do?"

"Run, scream for help. Fight."

"And if Walter had had the gun?" Dan posed quietly.

"Who was the other man?" Zack asked.

"We don't know," Kate answered. "We asked, but he said it wasn't important."

"What did he look like? Can you describe him?"

Kate looked at Annie and frowned. "No, I can't. Can you?"

"He was . . . average."

"Tall, short?" Zack prompted.

"Neither."

"Dark?"

"No, but not blond. He was average."

"His clothes?"

"Brown, I think," Annie said. "Gosh, I can't picture him in my head either."

"If you see him again, you are to tell me at once."

"But he helped us."

"I know. But you can't be too careful."

Zack finished breakfast with a frown between his brows, a

frown that lasted all the way to church.

Ted Walter waited at the end of the levee, fingering the bills in his pocket, anxious for the rest of the money he was still owed. He had enjoyed his time with the lovely Mrs. Lawrence, especially listening to her play the piano. But like most of them rich females, she had no time for him. He was happy to see fear in her eyes, though he hadn't much cared for the tall man with the cold stare who had made it clear that Mrs. Lawrence was off limits to the likes of him. That man could be trouble. It was just as well this was a one time deal. He'd take his money and go back to his claim in the morning.

After a week in Reno, where he had lost most of his earnings at the gambling tables or to the various women he used for momentary pleasure, he could feel the pull of attraction to his own woman, his one true love, his mountain. The fever kept him returning to pour his soul and his life's blood into her, to search out her cracks and crevices and glean from her the one thing that gave his life meaning: *gold.*

He looked up and down the levee, impatience stamped on his weathered face and in the tense bunching of muscles in his arms and legs. Surely the bastard wouldn't welsh on a deal? No one did that to him. He waited an hour past their agreed rendezvous time then stormed back to the room he shared with three other men. He pulled his Bowie knife out of his pack and slid it into one of his boots. He went in search of the man who owed him five bucks.

"A bicycle! Oh, Dan, for me?"

Dan rolled his eyes heavenward, but he was pleased with her elated response. "I thought that, since we both avoid horses, perhaps we could still ride together on bicycles."

Annie threw her arms around his neck and kissed him soundly on his cheek. "Thank you. No one's ever given me presents before."

"Well, don't get all mushy on me," he said with asperity, disentangling himself and straightening his vest.

Annie blushed, then snapped back. "I've never been mushy in my life. And if I am mushy, it's over little kittens, never a *man.*"

Zack stepped in before their sniping could turn into warfare. "I put your riding clothes in the bedroom at the top of the stairs, south wing. Why don't you get changed? Dan can teach Annie to ride her bicycle, and you and I, Katie, will try out my new horses."

"You bought more?" Kate asked, excited.

"For riding. Can't ride the thoroughbreds around town. They're too temperamental."

"Wonderful. It's been so long since I've had a good gallop. Oh, come, Annie, let's hurry."

"Do you ride astride or sidesaddle?" he called after them.

"Both, but I prefer astride," she shouted back.

Up the wide staircase they flew, nearly colliding with Martha as they sailed into the guest bedroom.

"I'm so sorry," Kate cried. "I didn't see you."

"How could you, going that fast?" she reproved fondly. "Are you having a nice day?"

"It's been marvelous," Annie enthused. "The church was fantastic. All the beautiful windows, and the pipe organ, and the choir."

"But did you hear the sermon?" Martha asked dryly.

"Sure. He talked about forgiveness. Sometimes that's hard for me."

"Ah, well, it's hard for all of us at times," Martha said, liking the whirlwind of a girl who possessed not a whit of guile. What an odd companion for the austere likes of Mr. Siebert. But that, of course, was because of the other two.

Now them she'd have to watch. She hadn't seen a man look at a woman like Mr. Zack looked at Kate since . . . since Rollins stormed her father's front door and carried her off thirty-two years ago. Oh, yes, she knew what that look meant. And she remembered what followed. That illicit night of passion was one of her most cherished memories, along with her wedding a week later and the birth of her eight children through the years that followed. Perhaps she ought to turn a blind eye and let nature take its course.

"I've laid your clothes out on the bed," Martha told them. "If you need any help, just give me a holler."

"Don't go," Kate implored as she stretched to reach the buttons at her back. "Stay and talk. Have you always lived here?"

"In Sacramento? Goodness, no." Martha turned her around and helped her shed her dress. "We moved here when Rollins couldn't take the mountain winters anymore. Four years now."

"Did you always work here, at this ranch?"

"We've been here since early April when Mr. Standish bought the place. It was a different house then. He had new paper hung, new carpets brought in, new draperies, he had the wood refinished and the ceilings painted. It was our responsibility, my husband's and mine, to see everything got done the way Mr. Zack wanted it."

"It's beautiful."

"It's better now his furniture has arrived. He brought some fine pieces with him."

"I can't imagine living all the time in a place like this," Annie said awesomely. "My home was a shack compared to this. Heck, my home was a shack compared to our room at the hotel."

"But you're different, aren't you, Mrs. Lawrence? This is familiar to you."

"Please, call me Kate. Yes, I—we had a lovely home."

"You miss it?"

"Some of the people I miss. Our servants mostly, Junie in particular. She was my friend, and I worry about her. But, no, I don't wish to return."

"You've no family to miss, only servants?" Martha asked, incredulous. "And you, Miss Annie?"

Annie shook her head. "Don't feel sorry for us, we have each other now," she said brightly. "And I, for one, am going to forget the past and enjoy this gorgeous day."

"Good for you," Martha stated. "Now you be careful on that contraption out there."

"You look very pretty," Kate said, admiring Annie's petite form in her new ruffled yellow blouse and straight dark green split skirt. New, shiny boots peeked out from the bottom of her shortened skirt.

"You'll do indeed," Martha agreed, "but you'll not come back in the same shape if you have as much trouble on that rack of wheels as Rollins did."

"I can't wait to try it."

Martha shook her head, laughing as the girls bounded back down the stairs. The big house had been empty for months. It felt good to have life and laughter in it.

Zack was waiting by the back gate when Kate and Annie returned, two sets of reins in his hand. Annie broke away to join Dan, and Kate slowed and walked toward Zack. His eyes swept the paddocks, the wide expanses of green grass and white fences, the barn, the stables, the orchards, the croplands, the enormous pillared house. His gaze returned to the woman coming down the steps toward him, and he knew that without her, the rest meant nothing. Without her the house would never be a home, the rooms would be forever void of life and love, his black-haired, blue-eyed daughter would never sit at her mother's piano and pick out tunes. His loins filled with heat until he had to turn away.

Kate stopped a few feet from him. He had turned his back to her, but not before she had guessed what was on his mind. He stroked the horse's neck and drew a long breath. His black shirt stretched across the tense muscles of his shoulders and back. She knew those shoulders. She knew those narrow hips, those long legs. She felt her knees go weak with the memory and the desire to belong to him again.

Zack turned and caught the flare of longing in her eyes. "Oh God, you too? We'll never make it through the day without going crazy."

Seized by a reckless streak of bedevilment, she took the few steps that brought her close to him and ran a teasing finger down his chest.

"Will it be terrible for you?"

"Katie," he growled warningly. "Get on the horse."

She flirted provocatively, something she'd never done in her life before. "If that's what you want."

"You teasing little witch, you know exactly what I want."

She laughed and swung herself onto the smaller of the two mares. "Yes, you want to show me your ranch, and I want to see it all."

She sat a horse beautifully, tall, proud, totally at ease. She wore a black riding skirt and a black vest trimmed in silver and red over a billowy sleeved blouse. Her flat brimmed hat was trimmed with a red band and silver conchos. Except for her blue eyes, she looked like Spanish nobility, his princess, his queen, regal, untouchable. But those blue eyes, still laughing when she turned to him, shattered the illusion. She was just Kate. His Katie. He was glad for that.

"Hurry," she cried. "Get up here. You have to see this."

Zack mounted and followed Kate's laughing gaze. There on the lower road was Dan, giving Annie a push on her bicycle and running beside her as she tried valiantly to control the wobbling, careening conveyance.

"Let's give her some moral support," Zack said, reining his mount around. She followed at his side. He watched to see how she handled a horse. She had an easy hand on the reins, and she was perfectly at home in the saddle. She'd been taught well, by her grandfather, he suspected. Zack wished he could have known the man who held such a place of honor in Kate's memories.

Dan and Annie were arguing again when Zack and Kate reached them. Annie swerved into Dan, losing her balance. Over they went, shrieking and yelling at each other. And laughing. They were having fun together, in spite of having fallen into the deep grass along the side of the road. Zack proposed they leave them to it.

"Just keep those horses away from where I'll be falling," Annie threatened as they rode away.

"Does Dan resent entertaining Annie?" she asked. "I know they argue and spat."

"I have a suspicion he enjoys himself. Coming from a family of mechanical people, her liveliness must be a breath of fresh air."

"Mechanical people?"

"Yes. You know, like spring-wound toys that can do only one thing. Wind his mother up and she smiles and throws a perfect dinner party. Wind his father up and he plays king of the hill. The rest are from the same mold. They're all fine people, very correct, very polite, very successful, and very predictable. They can't understand Dan's mentality, his need to move from challenge to challenge so often. They've all been in the same family business for decades. Why tamper with success?"

"I can certainly see how Annie would be a novelty. She has found a woman who is going to help her with her studies. She wants to be able to tell Dan she's read *Jane Eyre.*"

"She's had a rough time of it in the past. Is that why you feel so responsible for her?"

"She helped me when I needed help most. I've always had so much, I want her to have something now."

"She feels responsible for you, too."

"You must think we're two crazy misfits."

Zack laughed. "Who's to say who's crazy? Here's our training ring. Would you like to race?" He led them onto the dirt oval. "Twice around?"

She didn't wait for his signal, but sent her mare into an immediate gallop. Nevertheless, Zack won and gloated disgustingly.

"Your horse is stronger," she claimed.

"Just faster."

"You knew that, you trickster."

"You've raced before," he observed accurately.

"A few times," she admitted.

"On thoroughbreds?"

"Ummm-hmmm."

"Such a mystery woman. Will you ever tell me?"

She looked at him seriously. "Yes. I think for your own safety I'll have to. But not today. Let's not think about it today."

"No. This is a day for more pleasurable pursuits."

She gave him a knowing look. "Are you stalking me again?"

"If I am, you brought it on yourself with that little seductress act back there."

"Me? A seductress?"

"Don't be coy, Katie, my dear. You and I both know you

have me thoroughly bewitched. Whatever I do with you is completely beyond my control."

She snorted. "That will be the day when Zack Standish is helpless."

He grinned boyishly. "Wanna see my orchard?"

"I suppose it has rows and rows of trees."

"Yes."

"And one could get lost in them?"

"Or two."

"You are a scoundrel, Mr. Standish."

"But you want to go with me. I can see it in your eyes."

"You see altogether too much. I am a weak-willed woman." She sighed melodramatically.

Zack threw back his head and let out a bark of laughter. "Such a beautiful liar."

The orchard had been planted in the southeastern corner of the acreage where a lovely stream ran through the property, wending its way from the higher elevations to the Sacramento River. Wildflowers grew in profusion along the banks, a carpet of yellow and blue. They dismounted, letting their reins drop, and walked to the bank of the stream.

"This is lovely, Zack. The entire ranch is beautiful. You must be very pleased with it."

"I am. The minute I set foot on it, I knew I had to have it. Within the week it was mine. I have plans for this place, Katie. I want to return it to its original splendor, I want to fill the paddocks with horses that will be in demand all over the country, I want to plant the half-section to the west in crops, hay, oats, corn, beans, vegetables. With refrigerated cars, fresh produce can be transported great distances without spoiling. This place can be self-supporting."

"Do you know about farming?"

"No. But I'll learn when the time comes. Rollins knows. That man has more practical know-how in his little finger than I have in my whole head even with a college education."

"Different knowledge, perhaps, but not more," she amended, confidently. "I like them, Mr. and Mrs. Rollins. How did you find them?"

"He had a blacksmith shop behind his home in the outskirts

of town. When I was here in April, it caught fire. One of the boys he had working for him had been careless. His shop burned, and before the fire wagons could arrive, the house had gone up with it."

"Were you there?"

He nodded. "I wanted to help, so I joined the volunteers. I already felt that this was my town by then. Martha was distraught. She'd managed to save a few of her cherished possessions, but everything else was gone."

"And you offered them a new start. No wonder they're so devoted to you."

"It was a logical move. The banker gave them a good recommendation. I needed caretakers, they needed a home."

"Are you trying to make yourself sound like a cold-hearted pragmatist?"

"I am a practical man."

"And the sight of Martha weeping over her lost home didn't move you at all?" she asked, a teasing skepticism in her eyes.

"You think I'm governed by sentiment," he asked disparagingly.

"You do seem to have a habit of picking up strays and tucking them into safe havens."

He grinned. "Like you?"

"I am not a stray, but yes. Did I strike a chord of sympathy in you?"

"Sympathy?" he hooted. "Sympathy? No, my dearest. I did not feel pity for you."

"You didn't? What did you feel?" She turned and strolled away, glancing briefly over her shoulder.

Zack watched her, his brows cocked curiously at her capricious behavior. Had she finally stopped running? Was she more comfortable with him, less leery? Was she actually flirting with him, inviting his attentions?

"It's warm, isn't it?" she said, sitting in the shade of a tree. She removed her hat and slid the ribbon from her hair, shaking its thick length free. Her silver trimmed vest followed. And then her knee-length patent leather boots.

"Are you trying to seduce me?" Zack's heart was accelerating, driving his blood hard through his body. Her feet were dainty, high-arched, her ankles thin, her calves gently curved.

She tipped her head back, letting her hair cascade down her back, exposing the slender column of her neck. He followed the line of creamy skin to the exposed vee at her throat where she'd loosened the top of her blouse. Her breasts, full and round, strained at the fabric, the hardened jut of her nipples clearly outlined. His mouth went dry.

"We had a stream like this at the manor," she said dreamily. "I used to go there on very hot days and swim. Then I would stretch out on the grassy bank and let the sun dry me. My mother thought I was horrible, but my grandfather used to laugh. 'Let her alone,' he'd say to my mother. 'She's enjoying life. God knows it's soon over.' I haven't felt like this in years."

"Kate?" Did she know what images she had conjured up in his mind? Did she know what the thought of her lying naked in the hot sun was doing to him?

She opened her eyes slowly, letting her gaze roam from head to toe. Standing in the shade with the sun behind him, he was a black silhouette, but that alone was enough to send her senses reeling. With his broad, square shoulders, his arms akimbo, with his thumbs tucked in the side pockets of his snug black trousers, long legs, slightly parted in a very aggressive stance, he was overpoweringly male. And he wanted her. She felt every inch a woman in that second when their eyes met.

Was she trying to seduce him? "I wouldn't know how to do that," she said, answering his question and her own, but she wished she did. She'd been with him all morning and had been forced by propriety to keep her distance, but she wanted badly to be in his arms again and to feel his lips on her skin, to press her breasts against his chest to ease their taut heaviness. And she was finally alone with him.

"Women are born knowing how to seduce men, and you're doing just fine."

"Who said I was?" she demurred, looking down. "Trying to—to do what you said, that is."

"Come now, you've been a woman of your convictions up until now. Don't disappoint me." He lowered himself to the grass beside her.

"What do you mean?"

"Are you afraid to admit you want me?"

"A lady isn't supposed to be so forward. It's not . . ."

"Don't tell me. Decent, right? Who told you that? Surely not your grandfather. I think he would have told you to be honest above all else. We've gone beyond social facades, Katie. Do you imagine a man wants always to pry such information from his wife?"

"His wife?" she asked, casting him a sidelong look.

He reached into his shirt pocket and pulled something out. She caught a flash of a sparkle before he took her left hand and raised it to his lips.

"My wife," he stated. "Now don't argue with me. I know I said I'd give you time, but your time ran out. You must realize after what happened this morning that you need my protection and the protection of my ring on your finger."

"Zack, no. You promised," she said, trying to withdraw her hand from his.

"Listen to me, sweetheart. Keep the ring, wear it, even if you don't consider us really engaged to be married. Think about it, think about yourself, your safety, your reputation."

"My reputation?"

"You're in the public eye now. People will know you, they will be curious about you. They're going to see us together all the time, because I'm going to be with you. I'm not risking another scene like you described this morning. Soon they'll begin to wonder about us, then they'll begin to talk. Katie, you're not the mistress type, but you could be labelled my mistress if you're not my fiancée. Then every lascivious Walter in the town will descend on you. And that's when the rumors will turn ugly."

She thought to suggest that perhaps she and Zack should not see so much of each other in that case, but she could not utter the words. Not to see Zack?

"Katie, as my fiancée, you can accept my help openly, we can see each other as often as we like, you'll have my protection and the respect due my wife-to-be."

He slid the ring onto her finger. It was a delicate ring, unlike all the rings he'd found in her valise, a simply-cut diamond in a fine filigree setting. "It belonged to my mother, sweetheart. She'd want you to have it. She would have adored you, as I do."

"It's lovely, Zack. I wish . . ." she said, her voice failing her.

"What do you wish?" He pushed back the hair that had fallen forward to hide her sad face and tilted her chin up.

"I wish it could be real," she blurted out the truth then turned away. "I shouldn't have said that. Everything I wish for turns to dust."

She slipped the ring off and handed it to Zack, but Zack put it back on her finger. "I have wishes too, but I make mine come true. One day we will be married, Katie. You can believe that because I believe it."

"Zack," she murmured, looking up. There was a wealth of longing in her eyes. "I want to believe you."

His fingers brushed her forehead and moved down to cover her eyes. "Close your eyes, darling. Can't you see yourself living here, can't you see our children playing in the creek, can't you imagine Christmas morning around the Christmas tree? You'll be playing carols on the piano and we'll all sing, and then will come the presents. Presents for everyone. And on New Year's Eve we'll give a party. And my daughter," he said, caressing the line of her nose, her velvety cheek, "whose eyes will be as blue as yours, whose hair as black, will look eagerly down from the balcony to listen to the music and to watch the dancers, and I'll bring her down for one dance and twirl around the room with her in my arms before we tuck her into bed again."

"My grandfather used to do that," she whispered, opening her eyes to look deeply into his.

"How he must have loved you. How can I do less?"

Her arms went around his neck, and she touched her lips lightly to his. "Zack, I love you so much, and I'm so afraid I'll lose you. I couldn't bear that, I'd want to die."

She held his head and covered his face with kisses between her rushed words. All her suppressed emotions came tumbling out. "I think of you all the time. I dream about you in my sleep. And when I see you, my heart leaps, and I want nothing but to be in your arms. And when I can't be there, I feel as if I'm being tortured. I want to make love with you. Am I a terrible degenerate, do you think me awful?"

He silenced her with a kiss, penetrating and possessive. "You are a miracle. You are everything to me. Show me, my love, how much you want me. Be my seductress."

She scrambled out of his arms and took a few hasty steps away. She turned, blushing. "How do I do that, Zack?"

He came to his feet in one lithe movement and took her face in his hands, touching the hectic color in her cheeks. "Why not do what you want to do? Be brave."

"Truly? You mean I could unbutton your shirt and touch you?" He didn't answer, but she didn't need to hear his response. Her instincts took over, leading her on. She knew a little of what he liked, what could elicit a response from him, but before, when they had been together, he had allowed her no liberty. He had taken control, as if he feared she'd realize what was happening and stop him.

He was unsure of her. The insight came as a delightful shock. Zack, who was always in control, always certain he was right, needed proof of her desire, her need, her love. Their quarrelling and their careless words had undermined them both to that extent.

She unbuttoned his shirt and slid her hands up the hard wall of his chest to his shoulders. As she slid the black cotton over his arms, she pressed her lips to his chest, relishing the feel of the cool curls of hair under her lips. His hands tightened on her shoulders, encouraging her, and she dared to touch her tongue to his hard flat nipples. He groaned and she pressed her mouth closer, using her teeth, sucking gently.

Beneath her lips she felt his heart pounding. She looked up to see his face clenched in tight control. A feline smile curved her lips at his inadvertent challenge. She stepped back, watching in satisfaction as his eyes opened in protest at her absence.

Her fingers went to the buttons of her blouse, and slowly, button by button, she opened it and slid it off her shoulders. Her skirt followed, and she stepped out of it to stand before him in her lacy under clothes. She took her courage in her hands and unlaced the camisole, loosening the confining pressure on her breasts.

"Katie," Zack growled hoarsely. He reached for her, but she stepped away, turning and glancing provocatively over her shoulder.

"God, I thought I could do this," he ground out through his teeth, "but I can't. I'm not strong enough yet to remain passive when you look like that. Maybe next year."

His hands came down gently on her shoulders, caressing the satiny skin under his fingers. He lifted her hair and nuzzled her neck. "I can't keep my hands off you, I have to touch you. I have to taste you."

Sensuous shivers of delight ran through her body. Her eyes closed, her head tipped to the side. His hands came around her waist, pressing her back into his embrace so that she felt cocooned in the heat radiating from his body, imprisoned by his strength.

With her own hands she urged his arms upward until the warmth of his hands cupped the rounded fullness of her breasts. Her head sagged back weakly against his shoulder, her breasts grew heavy and swelled into his possession. A sweet urgency grew within her, filling her with rushing, fluid heat. For having given her body only twice before to Zack's loving, she felt already everlastingly addicted, completely unable to do without him, not even wanting to try. To be with him, to open herself to him and take him into herself, seemed at the moment her only purpose in living.

He slipped the narrow straps from her shoulders and bared her breasts, taking possession roughly, his skin against hers. He kneaded the soft mounds, lifting them, rolling the darker engorged tips between thumbs and fingers.

"Oh Zack," she cried. "You make me feel so wanton, so shamelessly wanton. I know I shouldn't let you do this to me, but I can't make myself care. Whenever I get near you, I crave you. You've become a madness in me."

"A sweet glorious madness," he agreed in deep husky tones as his lips trailed kisses across her shoulder to her neck.

She reached back, pressing her fingers into Zack's powerful flanks, pulling him tight against her buttocks. He groaned into the soft flesh of her neck, and his hands tightened on her breasts. With a boldness she would never have guessed she possessed, she inched her fingers between their bodies until she felt the hard core of his aroused manhood under her palms. Her hands closed tightly over him.

"Witch, witch," he said over and over as if in torment, but he didn't move away when her fingers unfastened his trousers. The touch of her fingers against him, flesh to flesh, was more than he could bear. He swung her around and ravished her mouth, taking her with him to the sweet carpet of grass.

With deliberate masterfulness he kissed and caressed her until she was a writhing mass of nerve ends seeking only the end to her mounting quest. Zack pulled away only seconds to discard the rest of his clothing, but even these were seconds she could not stand to be parted from him. Her hands ran over the broad expanse of his back, the tight muscles of his abdomen, trailing fingers down the dark mat of hair to the proud thrust of his masculinity.

Jerking the last of his clothes from his body, he turned back to her and removed the last barrier from her body. His hands slid the length of her, worshipping her.

His eyes, shimmering with heat, fever-bright, burning with wild possessiveness, devoured her as a starving man. "I will never let you go away from me," he declared fiercely. "You are mine. I'll follow you wherever you go and drag you back to me."

"Yes, yes," she cried, surrendering herself completely, body and soul, into his keeping. "Please, Zack, don't torture me. Take me now."

He stabbed into her swiftly, deeply, burying himself in the wild, silken furnace of her welcoming body. His control vanished, he was a trembling sixteen-year-old again, unable to marshal his responses or rein in his desire.

Passion exploded in them, white hot in its savage need to burn free. Again and again their bodies came together, urgently, ruthlessly, relentlessly, with no thought to temperence, no desire for gentleness, until in a majestic burst of flame they were utterly consumed.

During long moments while their heated bodies cooled and their mad pulse rates slowed, they remained locked together.

Finally Zack rolled to her side. He brushed his fingers gently over her swollen lips.

"Did I frighten you? I don't know what came over me. I—I . . ."

Her lips curled in a beguiling smile and she touched his lips to silence him. "I wasn't frightened. I always feel safe with you. You mustn't be afraid of me. I won't break."

He pulled her into his arms. "Ah, sweetheart, I wish you weren't so stubborn. I was determined not to risk this again. We're playing a dangerous game. I know now that I'm—I'm not going to be able to control this. I can try to protect you, but, Katie, I can't guarantee success, Mother Nature being what she is. I lose my head when I'm with you."

She closed her eyes and sighed. "I know. You're right."

"Then you *will* marry me?"

"I couldn't wear your ring for any other reason. Do you really love me, Zack?" Even after all they'd shared, it was difficult to believe.

He went perfectly still. A quiet watchfulness entered his eyes. "Yes, I love you. Are you saying this is for real?" He took her hand and pressed his lips to the ring on her finger.

"Yes."

"Yes," he shouted, crushing her against his hard body and rolling in the grass with her. "You have made me the happiest man in the world."

"Just one thing."

"Anything. What?"

"Can we take our time about it? We have to talk first. You might change your mind."

"Never," he growled. "I'm not letting you change yours, either. He broke into a broad grin, then laughed out loud. "Let's get dressed. I want the whole world to know you're mine."

"You're asking for a peck of trouble, Zack," she warned.

"I'll take it. I'll take on the whole world for you."

After Zack and Dan returned them to the hotel that night, Kate and Annie, both groaning from all they'd eaten, climbed the stairs to their room. Martha had insisted on cooking a feast to celebrate the good news. She was full of excitement and plans. A wedding at the ranch. It had to be in the rose garden. Rollins would build a trellis for them to be married under.

"Wait," Zack had halted her. "We were thinking in terms of an August wedding."

"August? That's weeks and weeks away," she'd protested.

"But we'll need that time to get the house ready for guests, to finish repairs on the ranch, and don't forget Katie's dress, and Annie's." Martha had relented, already mentally organizing the many chores to be done before August.

"I've never been in a wedding before," Annie said, shoving open their door without thinking.

"Annie, wait," Kate said, grabbing Annie's arm and pulling her back. "I locked the door this morning before we left."

Annie looked at Kate then back at the open door. "Wait here," she said, going to the linen closet. She returned with a broom for each of them. "Now stay behind me. I'm going in first."

"Shouldn't we get Mrs. Williams?"

"I'll take care of this," she replied stonily.

Annie slid into the room, her broom handle at the ready. Kate followed, going immediately to light the lamp beside her bed. She tripped and fell hard against the night table. She managed to right the lamp as it was falling, and to get the wick lit.

She turned and gave a sharp gasp. Annie stood in the middle of what had been their beautiful room, her eyes wide with shock. The whole room had been turned upside down, destroyed.

# Chapter 14

Why couldn't things go his way for once? He knew she was the right woman. He'd watched the hotel for days, he'd even eaten there once. He'd watched her comings and goings from his room across the street. The money and jewels should have been in her room. The hotel didn't have a safe, and she hadn't been to any bank. That left only one place where the stuff could be. Her lover, Zack Standish, had it at his ranch.

He tossed down another scotch and wiped his mouth with the side of his hand. He'd spent too much money on her already to get nothing in return. He had counted on that money, he needed it. But to get it away from Zack Standish. That would be nearly impossible. Nearly.

He felt a sharp jab in the small of his back. He jerked away from the pain and swung around.

"Don't move, pal. I've been lookin' all over town for you. Get up. You're coming with me."

"Walter."

Walter pulled him by the shirt collar out of the saloon. "We have some unfinished business. No one steals from me and gets away with it. Too bad you tried."

"I can explain." He felt frustration choking him, and apprehension. Walter had looked harmless when he'd first approached him. He had later learned that the man could whip almost anybody in town.

"I ain't interested in explanations. I want my money."

"I don't have it. Not on me."

"We had a deal, pal."

"Our deal was for you to bring the girl to me."

"Which I would have done, if you hadn't wanted to play hero. What did you think, she'd fall into your arms with gratitude? You crossed me, and if I don't get my money, I'll break your damn legs and toss you in the river."

"Now wait. This whole deal is bigger than you realize. Where are we going?"

"To the levee where we were supposed to meet. Where no one will see us this time of night."

"Let me explain. Before you do anything we'll both regret, let me tell you who she really is." Cold fear clutched at his gut. How could he have imagined this man could be duped? How could he not have seen the steel beneath the placid exterior?

"You're not listenin' too good, friend," Walter sneered. "I don't give a damn who she is. I want my money."

"We could have thousands. I'll give you thirty percent of whatever I get for her."

"You better talk fast. My patience is running out."

"She's wanted for robbery in Tennessee. There's a reward for her return."

"Mrs. Lawrence? I'm no fool, pal. She ain't no thief."

"Her name isn't Mrs. Lawrence. She's Katrina Montgomery."

"Where's my money?" Ted demanded, ignoring the man's ravings.

"I told you, I don't have it. I was counting on finding the money she stole. I haven't been able to do that yet. That man she's always with, Standish, he has it."

"And you think you can get it from him? I ought to let you try. That man ain't one to fool with."

"You don't have to do anything, just give me a couple more days. I'll find it."

"And thirty per cent is mine?"

The smell of money always worked. "Yeah, I swear it. I'll find that money. Two days. What do you say?"

Walter hesitated. "There's a reward for her return, you say?"

"Yeah, we'll get that, too. But it's not near as much as what she has tucked away. First, we get that, then go for the reward."

"How do I know you won't double cross me on this like you did with the five dollars?"

"I explained that. Well, are you in or not?"

"Yeah, yeah, okay. But I'm warnin ya."

They turned and started back down the levee. Walter tucked his knife under his belt and looked down at the shorter man at his side. He didn't trust him for a minute, but he'd go along with him. Just for two days.

Walter, for all that he'd been living apart from society for years, preferring the company of himself and his two mules, was not a naive person. He'd had second thoughts. The next morning he rose from his bed, dressed, and went to the sheriff's office. He had no fear of reprisal for the way he'd behaved toward the two women the day before. He was certain the wily weasel would have said nothing, and Katrina Montgomery wouldn't draw attention to herself if she was hiding from the law.

"Can I help you?" the deputy on duty asked, putting aside a report he was writing.

"I'm wondering if you have received any notices on a woman wanted for robbery in Tennessee. See, I know where she is."

The week fairly flew for Kate. Mrs. Williams had been correct in her guess that business would increase as word spread that the Hotel deFrance now offered the added attraction of a fine pianist. Throughout the week Kate met a large portion of Sacramento's elite society, gentlemen who held positions of honor, who were numbered among the founders of the city, politicians, councilmen, the mayor, and women whose manner and elegance could be surpassed by none, who placed their own stamp upon the thriving young city.

She was accepted immediately into their circles, recognized and appreciated as a talented young woman who would bring credit to their city.

She received countless offers of work, some from managers of less reputable establishments who offered entertainment, some from rival restaurants. With polite firmness she declined them all. Only a couple offers did she consider accepting, as they wouldn't interfere with her employment. One was from a deacon of the church they attended, who wished her to take over the duties of the organist who was leaving in September, one from the president of the local theatre group, who wished her to work with them on their fall variety show to benefit the new hospital. Both of those offers she had accepted, knowing she would enjoy becoming involved in the community in that way.

Zack had stayed by her side during the evenings since her room had been ransacked. He couldn't have stopped the throng of people who came to speak to Katie and to get acquainted with her, nor would he have wanted to, but he remained always a watchful distance away. And since that dreadful evening when she and Annie had found their safety violated, she had seemed happy for his silent support.

Mrs. Williams had increased security at the hotel, hiring a man to patrol the hotel and to check on all people entering or leaving. She was as upset and angered at the destruction of the room as the girls had been, and concerned for their safety.

"Why don't you marry her now?" she'd said to Zack, seeing Kate's white, strained face the next morning. "Then you can take them to the ranch where they'll be away from this sort of malice. A hotel's no place for two young ladies, anyhow."

Only Zack's sensitivity to Kate's feelings kept him from insisting on the same solution.

"Soon, I promise," he'd said instead. "If you could watch out for them until then, I'd be grateful."

Mrs. Williams had taken her promise seriously, insisting one of the men who worked for her be with them whenever they left the hotel for any reason. And Zack or Dan had been there every evening.

The promised talk between Kate and Zack had never taken place. Both Kate and Annie believed it was because he already knew. During the week, Kate tried on two separate occasions to speak with him privately. With the break-in, she felt as if a sword was dangling over her head on a slowly fraying thread. And if it was over her head, it was over Zack's. She wanted to tell him everything, but he had steered their conversations in a different direction, refusing to be sidetracked to a subject he knew she found upsetting. How could he know her disquiet stemmed from her fear for him?

Saturday morning came none too soon for Kate. "One more night," she said to Annie, "and we can be away from here for two whole days." She and Annie were spending their days off at Zack's.

"Maybe Mrs. Williams is right. Maybe we should go live at the ranch. You haven't been sleeping or eating all week. If you go on like this, you'll get sick."

"No," Kate said perversely. "I won't let a thieving rat order my life. I won't be chased away."

"You're already letting him order your life, by not eating and worrying yourself sick about him."

"That's not fair," she said, at her wits' end. "What am I supposed to do? He's everywhere. In this room, in every strange face, in the eyes of our *guard* whenever we venture beyond these walls. In Zack's presence, or Dan's, every night."

"I know you're afraid, Kate. It's a natural reaction. But that's all the more reason . . ."

"Anne, please."

Annie rarely lost her temper with Kate, but she did then. "Is your stubborn pride worth what you're putting the rest of us through? I never before thought of you as a selfish person. Do you think you're the only one involved? I hate this room as much as you do. Why do you think I sleep with that rolling pin under my pillow? I want to leave, but I can't go and leave you here alone. Don't you suppose Mrs. Williams has better uses for her money than to pay some man to protect you? Don't you think Zack and Dan have better things to do with their evenings than to come down here and sit with you?"

Kate sank on to the edge of her bed, her face as white as her nightdress. All the life seemed to have drained out of her, and Annie feared she'd been too harsh.

"Look, forget I said that," she relented, sitting beside Kate and putting a comforting arm around her shoulders. A shudder ran through Kate's too slender body that made Annie feel all the worse. "I'm sorry, really."

"No. I—I hadn't realized. I've been so wrapped up in my own fears, I didn't see . . ."

"Why don't we try it for a week, until you feel stronger? I'll come back with you then, if it's what you want. Just think, a week of sunshine and fresh air, flowers and grass, Martha's mothering. Horses."

Kate gave a reluctant grin. "Oh, Annie, I admit it sounds heavenly, but what would people say?"

"What's worse, a little gossip or your funeral?" she asked bluntly. "Get your head right, girl. Besides, Martha's there. People know that."

"You certainly have a way of cutting to the heart of the matter," Kate replied dryly, but already she was feeling a great weight lifting from her shoulders. "Very well. We'll go, for a week. And while we're there, I intend to make Zack listen to me."

"I thought we agreed that he already knows."

"The bare facts, maybe. But he has to know Bennett as well as I do. He has to know about Peter Standish. *I* have to know about Peter Standish."

"Then this week is all the more urgent. We'll leave tomorrow morning. No use keeping Martha up tonight."

That night she had a nightmare. It wasn't unlike those she'd had often at the Manor, but this time it was more menacing, more real.

She walked down the broad staircase at the Manor, dreading the party to come, the condescending guests, the snickering behind her back, the blatant propositions because she looked so much like her mother who had been known to have men friends between her two husbands. Another evening to suffer.

Sam Bennett stepped out of the library, blocking her path. "You're wearing that?"

She looked down at him, feeling that sick apprehension begin to crawl around in her network of nerves. "Is it not appropriate?" she asked, her mouth going dry.

Sam looked her up and down, his lips curling in derision. "I don't suppose it makes any real difference to you that we have important guests?"

"Yes, of course it does," she protested. "Shall I change?" She had on her prettiest gown, her only party dress.

"Whatever you think best. I'm not going to make an issue of it. It's what you're hoping I'll do, I realize that, but—"

"That's not true."

"No? Then why did you wear it? You knew I wouldn't approve."

"I didn't."

"And why are you interrupting? You know perfectly well that I will not tolerate a fresh mouth. You do this intentionally every time we have guests, just to cause a disruption. Can you not be satisfied with all I've done for you? Will you find no contentment until you drive every pleasure from this house, until we're all as miserable as you are?"

"That's unfair, and if I'm such a disgrace, why not let me remain in my room as I wished to do?"

"So that's what this is all about? You go too far. You will be at the party whether you wish to be or not, and you may wear that rag or not, as you see fit. I will not have people saying I lock you in your room."

"That was never my intention. I thought I looked nice. You're the one who always starts the arguments."

"Always? Always? Name one time, young lady. Only one."

Her mind was in a muddle, clogged, sloshing in a mire that was sucking her under. She thrashed around in her sinking quagmire and lashed out. "Like tonight."

"Tonight? Are you not the one who presented herself in that disgusting dress?"

She looked down in dismay to see that her lovely rose and gold gown had turned to a shapeless, tattered rag. The mud was up to her knees. She couldn't pull her feet out of it.

"It's the only dress I have," she cried in despair.

"Did I not offer you the chance to go with Corinne to the dressmaker?"

Her heart plummeted, and nausea rose within her. She knew where the argument was leading. "You wouldn't let me go," she heard herself saying, in spite of the inevitable end.

"And you know why. You disobeyed me. I distinctly told you to stay out of the music room."

"I have a lesson tomorrow."

"Are your lessons more important than obeying your father?"

"You're not my father," she argued impetuously. What did she have to lose now.

He smiled satanically. "The judge differs with you. I think until you can learn obedience and self-control, your lessons must be discontinued. I'll speak to the professor tomorrow."

"No, please."

"No, please," he mocked. "You're quite amenable when something you want is at stake, but when it's my party, when it's my reputation at stake . . ."

"Please, I'll go change. I said I would."

"But not until you have driven me to rage. Not until all the enjoyment in the evening ahead has been ruined for me by your stubborn recalcitrance."

How could she tell him she'd had on a perfectly lovely gown?. Where had it gone? Was he the devil? Had he changed it into the rag she now wore? She looked down and saw with rising hope that her pink dress was back.

"See, see," she cried desperately: "See my dress. It is pretty."

His face distorted in disgust. "There is mud on the hem."

She looked down and saw brown fingers crawling upward, staining her gown. Her best gown. "I'll change," she cried, trying to pull her feet free.

"What are you waiting for? The guests are arriving."

The front door opened and in came Corinne, resplendent in a gown of gold, with diamonds, emeralds, and rubies at her throat, her ears, on her wrists and fingers. Her mother's jewels. Corinne looked up and laughed. Others came in then, others dressed as elegantly as she, and they too laughed.

She couldn't move. She strained to get her feet free, but something, someone was holding her down.

"Get moving," Bennett snarled, his eyes glowing red coals in his hateful face.

"I can't," she cried. Mud rose to her thighs, her waist,

sucking at her, devouring her. "I can't get free. Help me. Help me."

"Kate! Kate, wake up." Annie shook her, fighting arms and hands that were flailing in the air, clutching at anything, everything. She lost her balance and fell heavily across Kate's chest.

"Good Lord, girl. Wake up," Annie rasped.

Kate's eyes opened and she stared blankly at Annie, then she sat up and began to shake all over.

"God in Heaven! What's wrong? Are you sick?" Annie laid a hand against Kate's cheek only to find it cold and clammy.

Kate grabbed her hand and held on, though she shivered again and lay back against her pillow. Her teeth chattered against each other. Annie pulled free, drew the covers up, and lit the lamp.

"Nightmare?" she guessed accurately. Kate nodded.

"About Bennett?" She nodded again. "Does this happen often?"

Kate took a deep breath, mentally forcing herself to relax. "They were frequent at the Manor. I haven't had one since I left. I thought they were gone for good."

"Can you tell me about it?"

And for the first time Kate did feel free to talk about her nightmares, the whole dream spilling out in a rush of words. She laughed self-consciously when she finished.

"It doesn't sound so bad now, but I can't explain the suffocating fear that goes with them. I don't think I could make you understand that."

"I've had my share of nightmares," Annie said understandingly. "Do you believe dreams have meaning?"

"My grandfather said dreams were the mind's way of working out a problem, unless you ate something like a dill pickle before you went to bed. Then he said it was indigestion, plain and simple."

"So did you eat a dill pickle?" Annie asked wryly.

"No. But I can see now, from a distance, that Bennett, all of them really, excelled in that sort of sadistic arguing."

"I can't see you falling for that."

"No, that's what's so strange about the dreams. At first,

after Mother died, after Mother was murdered, I was very susceptible to it. The Bennetts were all I had, my only family, and I tried everything to please them, but nothing worked. I was slowly going out of my mind. My maid, Junie, told me one day, after she'd heard one of those arguments that went on and on with no meaning, no purpose, no ending except my devastation, that I could never win. She said that to try would only mean defeat. She said to think of the Bennetts as naughty five-year-olds, since that's what they acted like, and to pretend I was watching them from a long way off where they couldn't reach me. And after that I just kept quiet. I stayed away from them as much as I could. When I was forced to be in their company, I imagined them in short pants and pinafore dresses."

"So that's where that look comes from."

Kate laughed. "It works. Except with Zack." She shook her head. "It never worked with him."

"How did Bennett react?" Annie asked.

"Bennett doesn't like to lose. He soon tired of the effort when he got no response from me. Corinne and Peter were different. By then arguing with me had become a habit. Corinne would end up furious. I don't know about Peter. He wasn't as easy to read as the Bennetts. There were times I was sure he knew what I was doing. He kept up with it just to see how much I could take."

"Testing you?"

"I was a challenge, someone to match wits with. I never liked the man, but I never felt the cold hatred with him that I felt with the Bennetts. Bennett made Peter a partner in a plantation he never rightfully owned. Peter was as much duped as I was."

"You're not feeling sorry for him, are you?"

"No, not after what I overheard. He didn't like the idea of becoming involved in my demise, but he liked less the idea of losing his investment. The fact still remains, however, that I don't know for sure exactly how far involved he let himself become. I didn't wait to find out."

"So you're reserving judgment."

"Yes, I guess that's only fair. Not that I'll ever have

anything more to do with him. But I know how underhanded Bennett can be, and it boils down to how low Peter will stoop to get what he wants."

The next morning, much to the relief of Mrs. Williams, and the delight of Zack, Dan, and Rollins, they loaded their belongings into Zack's carriage and moved to the ranch, where Martha welcomed them with opened arms. Kate relaxed. This was where she needed to be. For the first time in long, dry years, she felt a part of a loving family.

His insides churned and wretched, and he bent over, violently losing the contents of his stomach.

He wiped his eyes and his mouth with his shirt sleeve. His eyes were drawn again to the man who lay a few feet away with his own knife protruding from his back.

He felt nausea rise again, but he subdued it ruthlessly. No time to be weak now. He'd done what needed to be done. Walter had double-crossed him. The bastard had ruined everything. Now not only wouldn't he get the stolen money, he wouldn't get the reward either.

The choking rage he'd felt when he'd gone to the sheriff's office to report on Katrina Montgomery's whereabouts, only to hear the deputy claim that he was too late by several days, that Walter had already notified the authorities in Tennessee, still burned in his gut. He had found Walter, he had made sure Walter never saw a penny of that reward.

So everything was gone. He was stranded in California with no means of support, no money except what he found on Walter, and now he'd killed a man. His whole life had been a series of failures, always moving just beyond his control. And then there were men like Zack Standish who had everything, who, even if his fiancée were guilty, could buy freedom for her. Zack Standish was everything that had always escaped him. He looked again at the dead body by his feet, saw the years of running, dodging the law, saw his life reduced from bright dreams to ashes. He saw his father turn away from him in disgust.

At that moment he hated Zack Standish. He wanted to hurt

him, he wanted to cause him pain, devastating pain. He longed to take something of great value from the man who had it all, take it and destroy it. But even that desire was thwarted, for when he went to the hotel the next morning, he learned that she was gone. She had moved to the home of her fiancée.

He returned to his dingy room and packed his bag. With no reason to remain, and every possibility that he would be associated with the man who was now floating in the waters of the Sacramento River, he prepared to leave town. The money he took from Walter's pockets would get him to San Francisco. Maybe his luck would change there. He could be patient. When he was on his feet again, he'd return for his vengeance.

Fortune smiled on him sooner than he expected, though. He saw them at the train station. They caught his attention immediately, and for a brief second, he thought the man was Zack Standish. But the beautiful woman on his arm addressed him as Peter. He followed them down the boarded platform, through the depot, and out onto Front Street, staying as close as possible, glad now that he wasn't a man people noticed.

"What if this girl isn't Katrina?" the woman asked.

"It has to be. It all fits," said the older man with them. "Zack's investigator turns up with the money and jewels, then we receive word that Katrina is in Sacramento, and curiously, so is Zack. Nah, it's her, all right."

"So how do we go about locating her?" she asked.

"We could start by asking," the man named Peter said, his voice surprisingly condescending, considering how pretty the woman was. "But that might be too simple for you."

"It's been a long and tiring trip," the older man said. "Don't start in on each other again. What we need now is a good hotel. If Katrina is here, she won't escape us."

"You realize, don't you, that your original ideas are now out of the question," Peter said, glancing around the town, keeping his voice low. "Too many people are involved. If anything unfortunate occurs, even accidentally, we will be suspect. She is sure to have confided in Zack for him to have acted in her behalf."

"Well, we have to do something," the girl said. "I don't intend to lose my home because of that snivelling little brat."

"Hmmm. I don't recall her ever snivelling," Peter drawled. "She played us all for fools."

"I still maintain she doesn't know. Even if she heard us, she can't know it all."

"So you keep saying, but you don't believe it any more than I do. There is only one way, *one*, that we can come out of this on top. I have to convince her to marry me. And do keep your voices down."

The girl rounded on him furiously. "You'd like that, wouldn't you? What guarantee do *we* have then that you won't throw *us* out? Papa, don't let him. Can't you see what he's doing?"

"Relax. It's you who must realize how few choices we have here. Peter's right. We can't risk anything else."

"You could marry her, Papa."

The man at her side laughed outrageously.

The girl glared at him. "It's not so funny, Peter. It's just as good a solution as her marrying you. Besides, there's no way you're going to be able to convince her to marry you," she said with satisfaction. "Not when she knows about us."

"In either case," her father interceded, "we're going to have to find a means of forcing her hand. And that's not going to be easy to do."

He'd heard enough. He set his suitcase down and stepped forward. "I may know a way," he said to the backs of the trio.

They returned and looked at him, all three with stunned and wary expressions on their faces.

"Who are you?" the older man asked imperiously.

He smiled crookedly. "I'm the one who notified you that Miss Montgomery is here."

"What do you want?"

"I'd like the reward money, for starters."

"That has been retracted."

"All right. Then I'll tell Miss Montgomery that you're here, and I'll let her know what you are planning."

"How much do you want?" Peter asked.

"I want what was promised. I spent my own money following her here. I've given up a good position to see that she was brought to justice. I don't intend to lose everything for nothing."

"And if we agree?" the old man asked.

"Papa, you can't be serious. We don't need him."

"Shut your mouth, girl."

"If you agree, then I will give you the means to make Katrina Montgomery marry whichever of you wants her, so long as Zack Standish never sees her again. You see, we can work very well together."

"What means?" Peter demanded.

"The money first."

"We don't carry that kind of money with us," the older man said gruffly.

"Then I bid you good day." He turned and walked back to where he'd left his case.

"Wait a minute," Peter said, turning from the stranger back to Bennett. "We have no choice," he said quietly.

"I don't believe this," Corinne shrieked.

"Corinne, do as your father said and *shut up.*"

"You trust him?" Bennett asked.

"I trust that he'll go directly to my brother and sell him the information we just gave him so freely because some people can't keep their voices down."

Peter motioned the man to return. "We have decided to accept your offer. If you could direct us to an acceptable hotel and meet us there in half an hour, we will have your money for you. I hope your advice is worth the price."

The man rocked back on his heels. His luck was indeed changing. Now he would stay for a few more days, just to see Zack Standish get his due.

"I suggest you try the Hotel deFrance. And who shall I ask for at the desk?"

"Come to my room," Peter said. "Peter Russell."

# Chapter 15

On Monday evening a knock at the door interrupted dinner at the Standish Ranch. Zack excused himself to answer the summons.

"Zack Standish?"

"Yes," Zack answered the tall, serious mannered man on the front porch. "I'm Zack Standish."

"I'm Sheriff Merkel. This is my deputy, Ralph Simms. Could we have a moment of your time?"

"Certainly. Please, come in. Martha," he called, "please bring coffee to the sitting room." He offered the sheriff and his deputy a seat.

"This is an official visit, Mr. Standish. Do you know a man by the name of Ted Walter?"

Zack's mouth tightened. "I met him once."

"What is it, Zack?" Dan asked, coming into the room. Kate and Annie followed.

"This is Sheriff Merkel and Deputy Simms. The sheriff just asked if I know Ted Walter."

"That snake," Annie scowled. "What'd he do, complain because I bit his arm?"

"Beg your pardon?" the sheriff asked. "You know this man Walter?"

"He's the one who tried to force Kate to go with him. He's crazy," Annie declared vehemently.

"Perhaps you had better start at the beginning."

Zack related the story of his meeting with Walter at the

hotel, and then Annie told them what happened the following morning.

"So you had cause to wish the man harm?" Merkel asked, directing his attention to Zack again.

"Wish him harm? How would you feel if he tried to drag your woman off against her will?"

"What is this about, Sheriff?" Kate asked, having listened patiently to all of them discussing her as if she weren't there. They were trying to protect her, she knew that, but she had a feeling that this was not about who she really was.

"In a moment, Mrs. Lawrence, if it is Mrs. Lawrence."

Martha arrived with a tray of coffee, and Kate began pouring out cups, ignoring the wildly fluttering nerves in her stomach. She offered the sheriff a cup, but he declined.

"Mrs. Lawrence, the other man, the one your friend—"

"Miss Spooner."

"The one Miss Spooner says came to help you, did you know him?"

"No, sir. We never saw him before that morning. Nor since. Zack asked us to keep an eye out for him, but he never came back."

"Why is that, Mr. Standish?"

"Anything or anyone to do with my fiancée is of concern to me. And frankly, it all sounded too contrived to me."

"How is that?"

"Walter intended to frighten Kate. I don't see how he could have hoped to do anything other, not in broad daylight in the middle of town. The second man, whoever he was, wanted to appear a mystery hero. We may as well tell you that the very evening after Kate and Annie were accosted, their hotel room was broken into."

"Oh? And why did you not report this to me?"

"Because nothing was taken."

"Didn't you find that strange? Strange enough to report?"

"Sheriff, Kate is a beautiful woman. Since she's been in Sacramento, she's had to discourage several men eager to make her acquaintance. We thought, as with Walter, that one of them was striking back at her out of hurt pride, perhaps even Walter himself. I realize that quite a few men in town come down periodically from the mountains where they don't see a woman for months on end, maybe years. Their flirtations are usually harmless, but a few get out of hand. The very reason I insisted she move here was to remove her from that sort of undisciplined behavior."

"Yes, I can understand that if, as it appears, she has no one else to protect her. But I'm afraid that what I've heard this evening only confirms my suspicions."

"And what are they?" Zack asked.

"We're investigating a murder, Mr. Standish."

"Murder?" came the startled exclamation from those in the room aside from the sheriff and the deputy.

"A double murder, actually. Two bodies were found in the river today. One we know is Ted Walter. The other had only one paper on his person with your name on it."

"My name? But . . ."

"Your name and the name Katrina Montgomery." He took his time and searched each of their faces in turn, gauging their reactions. They were a cool lot, that was for sure.

"My doputy remembered the name, curiously enough. It seems Ted Walter was in the office Monday, a week ago, inquiring about a woman wanted for robbery in Tennessee. Sims checked through the notices we've received in the last few months and came up with this." He pulled a paper from his pocket and opened it for Zack to see.

"You understand why I had to come her. Simms didn't make the connection, of course, but he never had the pleasure of dining at the hotel where Mrs. Lawrence plays the piano. I, on the other hand, recognized the similarities between the picture and the person.

"So I asked myself why a man like Ted Walter, who keeps to himself, turns up dead only days after he looks at a picture of your fiancée. And I asked myself why another floating body reveals only your names.

"And now I find you have more cause than I first suspected to wish both men dead. Did you really believe you could get away with murder?"

"Sheriff, we had nothing to do with murder. Apart from that one time, I never saw Walter again. The other man I never saw at all. Who was he?"

"We were hoping you could tell us."

"Sheriff Merkel," Kate implored, "you must believe him. Zack could never have murdered those men. He had no reason."

"No reason except you. Men have been known to kill for love before. I cannot imagine any man wanting to see you sent to prison. I myself am sickened by what I must do. Mr. Standish, I must arrest you for murder on two counts, and Mrs. Lawrence, I must take you into custody for robbery, unless or until you can prove you are who you claim."

"You can't do that, Sheriff," Annie cried. "They haven't done anything wrong. They haven't. Oh, why must all you lawmen be so blind? Any fool can see these two are decent, caring people."

He ignored her. "You will come quietly? I hope I don't have need to restrain you."

Zack gave Dan a slow nod then turned back to the sheriff. "You'll have no trouble from us," he said.

Zack took Kate's hand and pulled her to his side. Her face was paper white, her eyes dark with distress. He placed his arm protectively around her shoulders.

"Sheriff," she said. "I . . ."

"Kate," Zack said softly, "he's only doing what he's paid to do. It will be all right. We'll give you no trouble, Sheriff."

"Well, I will," Annie cried, launching herself toward the sheriff. She landed a blow to his chest before Dan could reach her and restrain her. "Let go of me, you—you . . ."

"Calm down, Annie," Dan said, wrapping his arms round her struggling body. "Please excuse her. She becomes irrational at times, especially if Kate is threatened."

The sheriff cocked a brow, looking at her warily. "I trust you can keep her under control. I assure you, Miss Spooner, no harm will come to your friend." He ushered them toward the door. "Shall we go?"

"You'll pardon me if I don't find that comfortin'. Anyone with no more sense than you can't be trusted to know what harm is and what it ain't."

"Annie, please," Dan groaned, rolling his eyes.

"You're gonna toss her in your stinkin' jail, aren't ya?" Annie railed. "A nice lady like that. A gentlewoman. I know what goes on in jails. I know what men do to women in jail. Is that why you're arresting her? Did you take one look at her and say to yourself, 'Now that one I'm gonna have to arrest.'"

The sheriff turned and walked back to stand in front of Annie, his eyes as gentle as hers were fierce.

"I hope that if the time comes when I'm in trouble, Miss Spooner, I may ask you to fight in my corner. I would consider myself very fortunate. Please don't worry. Mrs. Lawrence will be treated with the utmost respect."

Annie stopped struggling and dropped her head in shame. "I'm sorry. You don't understand. How could you."

"You should contact a lawyer for Mr. Standish," the sheriff suggested.

"I'll do it immediately," Dan said, seeing them out.

"This is what I was afraid would happen," Kate said sadly when she and Zack had been seated in the dusty carriage and the door closed on them. It closed gently, but it resounded in her head as loudly as the doors of an iron cage.

"Don't worry. You won't be in custody long."

"Me? I'm not worried about me. I belong in jail, but you did nothing." Don't worry? Why did everyone say not to worry? Was this not cause for worry?

"They seem to believe two men are dead because of me."

"It's all my fault, all of it," she said, staring into the evening shadows as their carriage took them away from the ranch. Would all Zack's dreams be torn from him just when they'd begun to be realized? It would be better if she had stayed at the Manor and met her own death than to be the cause of Zack's destruction.

"I'll tell them everything," she said. "I'll explain."

"You'll tell them *nothing*, do you understand? Trust me on this, Katie. Promise me you'll say nothing?"

"But, Zack, . . ."

"I want your word. It's important for both our sakes. I can account for my time, they won't be able to make the charges against me stick. It's you I'm concerned about. You must be silent and give me time. I need time. Will you do that?"

"Well, I . . . Yes, all right, if you think that's best."

"Tell them only what's happened since we arrived in Sacramento, and I'll take care of the rest. And take that blank face back out and dust it off. You're going to need it."

"I'm so sorry, Zack. I never meant for any of this to happen."

He turned her into his arms and held her, pressing her head into his shoulder. "Don't lose your courage now. You've done so well up until this moment."

"How much do you know?" she asked quietly.

"I know all I need to know, sweetheart. Now hush and let me hold you for a while. I might not see you in the next several days."

Dan didn't linger after the sheriff took Kate and Zack into custody. He calmed Martha and Rollins as best he could, gave Annie's hand a reassuring pat, then rode into Sacramento to see what he could do for Zack and Kate.

His first stop was at the Western Union office where he sent an urgent message to John Phillips. He found a seat in the corner and made himself comfortable, prepared to wait the night through for the answer he needed.

The next morning Sam Bennett put his scheme into motion. News had spread rapidly through town that "Mrs. Lawrence" was engaged to marry the wealthy and handsome Zack Standish. It had been easy for the Bennetts and Peter to draw information from the talkative townsfolk. Mrs. Williams, the owner of their hotel, added her enthusiastic confirmation to the rumors, singing her praises of both Zack and Kate.

"I knew they were in this together," Corinne said bitterly when they returned to their room. "Didn't I tell you? No one ever listens to me. If you hadn't been so sure you knew best all along, we wouldn't be in this mess."

"We haven't time for your bellyaching now, Corrine," Sam snapped. "We are where we are. This is our last chance to come out of this intact. We have to work together now."

"It's so unfair. If she marries Zack, she'll not only have the Manor, she'll have Zack's wealth as well. I can't bear the thought of it."

"There's another way to look at it, if you can bring yourself to forget your jealousies," Peter drawled spitefully. "If Zack dies, I'll inherit his wealth, if Katrina marries me, I'll get the Manor."

"I like that even less," Corinne spewed.

Peter laughed sardonically. "I thought that might stick in your craw."

"Relax, Corinne," Sam ordered. "Peter and I are partners. What is his is ours as well."

"Which leads me to wonder if I should guard my back around the two of you in the future," Peter said laconically.

"Oh, come now," Sam said, irritated. "A divided camp is easily conquered. We have no time for suspicions."

"Then you shouldn't have swindled me to begin with. I can't forget that, Bennett. I'm not a violent man, but I am now implicated in not one but two murders. Or are there more?"

A knock sounded on the door. Peter answered it and returned with the information they had been awaiting.

"Zack has been arrested for murder. He's in jail now. And 'Mrs. Lawrence,' our dear Katrina, is also in jail, until the sheriff can determine if she's Katrina or not."

"Then the sheriff hasn't received word yet that the charges have been dropped," Sam said, smirking with satisfaction. "Excellent. I think we should progress to step two now. Send the messenger to Zack's ranch and have him deliver this note to Katrina's little friend. Personally. Have him bring her back with him. I want her delivered straight into our hands."

Dan's answer came after an arduous night's vigil. His alarm grew as he read it. "Damn," he muttered, and left the telegraph office. Having learned the name of the finest lawyer in town, he set out to make his acquaintance.

Matthew Meecham was a portly, graying gentleman who seemed to be expecting Dan. He cleared his schedule for the morning and ushered Dan into his office.

"What can I do for you, Mr. Siebert?" he asked, waiting Dan's formal request for his services.

"I'd like you to represent my partner, Zack Standish."

"Ah. I have, of course, heard of his arrest. Very surprising to all of us who have met Mr. Standish."

"And I'd like you to have Mrs. Lawrence released into my custody."

"Ellis," Mr. Meecham called out to his assistant. "Would you bring coffee, please, and see we're not disturbed. Sit down, Mr. Siebert, and tell me what you know."

Dan spent the next hour relating as many details as he could remember of their association with Kate and Annie, and of the men who had been found dead.

"So you suspected all along that she was Katrina Montgomery."

"Suspected, yes, but we had no real proof, not until Zack found the stolen property. If you had met Kate, you'd know, as we did, that she's no criminal. She's an innocent caught up in something she couldn't handle, so she ran away."

"Mr. Standish must love her very much to go to such lengths to keep her safe. He could be considered an accomplice. But since he did return the money and the jewels . . ."

"He loves her. They're engaged to be married."

"Which is all very nice, except it gives him a motive for murder."

"Yes, I realize that, but I received a telegram from our investigator in answer to my own inquiry last night." He handed the reply to Mr. Meecham.

The distinguished lawyer leaned back in his chair and unfolded the telegram. He read aloud, enunciating each word as if within it he might find some clue.

"Katrina Montgomery ward of Sam Bennett who filed charges against her. Property returned and charges dropped. Bennett and Peter Standish partners in plantation inherited from Katrina's dead mother. Peter is Zack's brother. He suspects connection. Have learned Bennett and Standish enroute to Sacramento. Believe Katrina in danger. Full report in post."

Mr. Meecham lowered the telegram to his desk and looked up at Dan, pursing his lips thoughtfully.

"I gather from this that your Kate ran away from a stepfather who owns all that was once in her family. Could it be that what she took she felt she had a right to? Which leads me to another speculation. Could she indeed have a right to it?"

"I'm sorry, I don't follow."

"Ohhh," he said ponderously, "you know the story. Man marries for money, woman dies suddenly, stepchildren left with nothing. Cases have been won on less. Just a thought, mind you. With the money returned and the charges dropped, I see no problem with Miss Montgomery."

"Don't you see, Mr. Meecham, Zack was waiting for this report. He wouldn't have acted precipitately when he knew there was every chance Kate would be cleared of the charges."

"Well, yes. But on the other hand, he had not yet received it."

"Zack is a deliberate man. He has worked tirelessly to get what he wanted, which was that ranch. He wouldn't risk it by murdering two men he didn't even know when it was, as he believed, unnecessary. If Kate had not been cleared, if the return of the stolen property had been refused, he'd have hired you to defend her. He is not a murderer."

"So that leaves us to learn why Zack's name was on the body of the dead man. The coroner has determined that Walter had been dead for three days. The unknown man had been dead only hours when he was pulled from the river. Neither died of drowning. I hate to ask this, Mr. Siebert, but do you think Miss Spooner would be strong enough to view the remains of the unidentified man? If he is the man who interfered when Walter accosted Miss Montgomery, a new possibility opens up."

"You mean the stranger could have killed Walter?"

"They may have argued later."

"Zack thought the whole thing too suspicious to begin with," Dan said musingly. "He said no man would chance that sort of behavior with a lady in broad daylight. He'd be strung up."

"I see. Walter has been prospecting in the mountains for years. He was never a problem before. Did Zack think it was—"

"Contrived. That's the word he used. He was very curious about who this other man was. He wanted to meet him, but the ladies never saw him again."

"But someone knew your Kate was Katrina Montgomery."

"We believe so, yes. We think he was searching for the money when he broke into their room."

"Now answer another question that's been running around in the back of my mind. Your telegram states that Zack's brother is a partner with Kate's guardian. How is it you had to be told this in a telegram?"

"Zack's brother abandoned him and his mother years ago. Zack hasn't seen him since, although he tried about six months ago to find him, at his mother's request. He never received a reply to any of his letters."

"Does Zack know yet that his brother is involved in Kate's past?"

"No. This will come as a shock. But it does explain Kate's fainting spell when she heard his name," he said, grinning. "And her suspicions. She must have thought Zack was in cahoots with Peter." He shook his head, seeing now the reason for much of Kate's erratic behavior.

"You must admit that it's quite a coincidence."

Dan chuckled. "It explains so much. You've no idea."

"Why do you suppose this Bennett and Zack's brother are coming to Sacramento?"

"That I can't answer. They have their precious money and jewelry back."

"Your investigator mentioned danger to Kate. Perhaps the best place for her, at the moment, is right where she is. In the meantime, can you get Miss Spooner in here to identify the body? While you do that, I'll introduce myself to Zack and have a chat with Miss Montgomery. I'll deliver this telegram to your friend. Oh, and you might stop at the post office and see if your report has arrived."

* * *

Annie stared down at the piece of paper the young man had placed in her hand. The words swam before her eyes, and she cursed herself for not paying more attention to her mother's tutelage.

"I—I can't seem to read this," she stammered reluctantly. The young man looked at her incredulously. She lifted her chin and stared him down.

"I can read it to you," he offered.

"Please," she answered haughtily.

He opened the envelope and read. "If you want to help your friends, be at the River Queen at ten o'clock."

"That's it? Who sent it?" she asked, suspicious.

"He said he was a friend, that you'd know. He said he'd helped you once before."

Annie's face cleared. She looked back toward the kitchen. She'd have to tell Martha something.

"Dan sent a message for me to join him in town. I'm going now."

"Wait. I'll get Rollins to take you," Martha insisted.

"No. I don't have time." She looked at the tall clock in the foyer. Twenty minutes. "I can't wait. This man will see me there."

Martha followed her out the front door, saw her being lifted onto the front of the man's horse, saw them ride away. "Wait. Annie, you come back here. Dan wouldn't have expected you to ride a horse. Annie!"

Martha stood as if petrified for a long moment, and then she threw her dish towel down and ran across the back yard to the stables to find Rollins.

Martha and Rollins met Dan on the road leading into town. Martha took one look at his face and knew.

"What's going on?" she cried.

"Where's Annie?" he demanded at the same time.

"A man came to the house with a message that she was to meet you," Martha explained frantically. "I knew it couldn't be true. He took her on his horse. We were coming to find you."

Dan looked back toward town. "They must have taken the

lower road."

"Why would anyone want Annie?" Martha asked, distraught.

"I don't know." He swung his buggy around in the middle of the road. "Come on, let's get back to town quickly. And don't spare the horses."

Even though her bunk was comfortable enough, Kate slept badly. Her nightmare returned in the early hours. After that she didn't care to sleep again.

She wondered how Zack had spent the night. Had he slept peacefully? He had seemed so unconcerned last night, but he didn't know. How could he know?

The sheriff brought in her breakfast and slid the tray through the narrow slot in the door. "Hope your night wasn't too bad," he said apologetically. He noticed her red, swollen eyes, and he felt remorse for having to put her through this.

"Sheriff, I need to talk to Zack."

"I'm sorry, Mrs. Lawrence. I can't allow that. Besides, Mr Standish's lawyer just arrived. I expect they'll be conferring for some time yet."

"Oh. Could I speak to his lawyer then?" She'd made a promise, but Zack would have to forgive her this once for breaking her word. The truth had to be told.

"I'll mention it to him when he's finished with Mr. Standish."

Sheriff Merkel locked the heavy door between the ladies' cells and his office. He was thankful the young lady didn't have to suffer the company of some of the women he occasionally had to lock up. As it was, the scent of their cheap perfume lingered heavily in the cells. That would be offensive enough to a lady like Mrs. Lawrence. Hopefully she'd be gone before the next drunken whore decided to cause trouble. His wife had nearly chewed his ears off when he'd told her what he'd done.

He had just returned to his desk when a tall, austere gentleman walked in. The sheriff turned to face him, wondering what new catastrophe was about to befall him. "May I help you?"

"My name is Sam Bennett. I have here the court order assigning guardianship to me for my stepdaughter Katrina Montgomery. After a very exhaustive search for my daughter, which has led me to Sacramento, I now learn she is being held in your jail. I would appreciate knowing the charges."

Sheriff Markel studied the papers handed to him. The court seal was official, all right. "We have a wanted poster for her that says—"

"Yes, yes. That was a mistake. The money was returned to us shortly after those were released. If you check with the sheriff in Memphis, you'll learn that all those charges have been dropped. I would appreciate a chance to speak with my daughter privately now."

"I must warn you that she is implicated in a murder case."

"Katrina? That's absurd. She's a gentlewoman. What proof have you that she was involved?"

"Her name was found on the body."

"And?"

"Nothing more."

"Just her name? You have subjected her to the humiliation of incarceration because a man had her name in his pocket? It is my understanding that she has become somewhat of a celebrity in town. Is it not possible that this man came to the same conclusions you did about her identity, only earlier? Those posters were distributed throughout the country."

"Which, until you arrived to clear her of the charges, was due cause for us to hold her. You would be just as irate if we had released her and the charges were still standing."

"Well, now that you know she isn't a thief, you may release her."

"There is still the murder."

"For which you have no cause to hold her. Sheriff, I am responsible for that young woman. She is little more than a child and must be protected. And since any trouble she meets with, such as this, reflects badly on my impeccable name, I must insist she be returned to my care. I take my duties seriously and I promised her mother, God rest her soul, that I would protect Katrina and love her as my own. I intend to do that. Now, must I seek out an order from the judge to visit with my own daughter?"

Kate looked up when the heavy iron door opened. Expecting to see Zack's lawyer, she was momentarily stunned to see the tall figure of her stepfather enter the cells.

It was funny, the relief she felt. The dread, the fear, the constant waiting for the inevitable to happen was worse than actually facing it. And perhaps knowing that she had someone in her corner now, perhaps having seen more of the world and the people in it, perhaps having been forced to stand on her own two feet and knowing she could do it, whatever the reason, she didn't see Sam Bennett as so threatening any more.

She faced him stoically. "Hello, Sam."

His nostrils flared at her impudent familiar use of his first name. He didn't care for her lack of fear either.

"So, you are in jail. I should leave you here."

"I don't plan to leave, at least not with you. I'm staying in California."

"I'm afraid I cannot permit that."

"I did not ask for permission. I'm getting married, Sam, and you can't stop me."

"I think I can. I'm still your guardian."

"And why should you want to? You've never enjoyed my presence in your life. I must have been a constant reminder of the woman you murdered."

"Perhaps I've changed my mind," he replied nonchalantly.

"Too late, I'm afraid. I've made a life for myself here, and I'm staying."

"You're going to marry Peter. And if you find that too much to stomach, you can marry me."

Kate laughed in his face. "Sheriff," she called. "I'd rather face a murder charge."

"We have Annie Spooner."

She heard, but by not so much as a blink did she let on it made any difference to her. Sheriff Merkel opened the door and peeked in. "Did you call?"

"Yes, I did. I . . ."

"A few more minutes, if you please, Sheriff," Sam said commandingly.

The sheriff looked at Kate inquiringly. She gave a reluctant nod, although inside she was anxious for those few minutes. Could they really have Annie?

"As I was saying," Bennett went on when Merkel closed the door again, "your wedding will take place immediately upon our return to the Manor."

"Or? Let's get down to the bottom line, Sam. This can only mean one thing. The Manor is mine. How delightful that is to me. The ultimate irony. You must give my grandfather credit. He always did see through your oily veneer to the slime beneath. And how shall I die? As my mother did?"

"So you do know."

"As do a few others. My death will land you in prison for the rest of your life, unless you swing from the gallows. Can you feel the noose tightening, Sam? You surely don't think I'd go to all the trouble of escaping without taking out some form of insurance against just this exigency."

"If it is Zack Standish you told, you've wasted your breath. He won't help you once he learns you're married to his brother."

So she had been right. She hid the shock of that very well, she thought, even when the knowledge brought with it a hundred questions and doubts. Why had Zack lied to her? Had he known all along that Peter was living at the Manor? Did he know about her inheritance?

"And you know Zack Standish so very well? He'll never give me up." She laughed shortly. "No, Sam, it's you who needs help, not me. You see, you must kill me to keep me quiet, but my death is also yours. When I turn twenty, you will be as destitute as you've kept me all these years."

"You've had everything," he retorted thunderously.

She grinned. "I've had nothing but grief. I intend to sell the Manor to the highest bidder now that you and your friends have defiled it beyond acceptance. Zack and I can use the money to build our future."

"Peter may have different ideas," he replied, gaining control of his temper.

"You are in for quite a surprise, Sam, if you imagine Peter is any match for Zack. Oh, yes, quite a surprise. I suggest you go on home to Tennessee and pack your clothes. I'll allow you to keep those."

"No. It will be as I said. You asked what the bottom line was. Here it is. You come with us quietly and you marry Peter, or Annie Spooner will die."

Thoughts of Zack and his lawyer flew from her mind. Thoughts of Dan and Martha and Rollins were dismissed. She saw only Annie, surrounded by these vile people, threatened by their greed and hatred, held hostage to their demands. They had suddenly gone too far. Too far for a Montgomery to tolerate.

For the first time Kate allowed her emotion to show in her eyes, and it was pure hatred that met Sam's surprised gaze. "You'll rue the day you stepped one foot on my grandfather's property. You'll rue the day you heard the name Montgomery. I swear on my mother's grave that I will make you pay until you bleed, and I'll have her help all the way. I will walk out of here with you now, I will go to Annie, but if you lay one putrid finger on my person, if you even breathe in my direction, I'll scream the town down around your ears. We're in my territory now. These people are my friends. And if you've harmed one hair on Annie's head, I'll kill you myself and be very glad to do so."

# Chapter 16

Annie's confidence waned as she neared the docks. Should she have told Martha about the letter? Should she have waited for Rollins to drive her to town? Getting on a horse was bad enough, but to do so with a strange man . . . What if it was a trap? She wished she had Dan's cool logic and unflappable calm. She wished she had Kate's passive face. She had a feeling she would need them all in the next few minutes.

River traffic, both cargo boats and barges and passenger lines, was heavy between Sacramento and San Francisco, not unlike traffic on the Mississippi. The railings of the River Queen stood thick with travellers waiting for the captain to give the orders to pull away from the dock. Annie let herself be lifted from the saddle, glancing warily at the young man beside her. He, she knew instinctively, like the young men who worked the docks back east, would do almost anything for a fast dollar. But this was not the dock at Memphis, and Jake was nowhere around to help her if she met with trouble.

"Where is he?" she asked.

"Who?"

"The man I'm to meet here," she snapped irritably.

"He's on board," the man said as if she were somewhat dimwitted.

"What's going on here?" she demanded, fists planted squarely on her hips. "Who are you?"

"Just a messenger."

"Well, keep your darned message. I'm leaving."

"Feel free, but your friend is waiting on board for you."

"In the first place, he's not my friend. In the second, I don't believe you anymore."

"I think you've misunderstood, Miss Spooner. This friend is with Mrs. Lawrence. He needs your help because Mrs. Lawrence is hurt."

"Kate? Hurt?"

"She's been asking for you. She keeps saying something about Peter being in town."

"Peter? In town?" She knew she was repeating what he said dumbly, but she couldn't seem to control her tongue. Peter? What was going on? Was Kate running away again?

"She's delirious. My friend couldn't make much sense of her rantings when he found her. She mentioned a man named Zack, but when we suggested we find him for her, she became frantic. She wanted only you."

"Where is she? Tell me."

"She's on board. She insisted. We didn't know what else to do with her."

Annie frowned, torn between the urgency to go to Kate, to help her, and the desire to find Dan. Dan could sort this out. He'd know what to do.

The whistle blasted, reverberating through her head. Kate was in jail. She couldn't be here. Unless Peter Standish had found her and demanded her release. Peter? He must be in Sacramento. How else would a stranger know his name? Had Kate struggled and escaped, getting hurt in the process? Why hadn't she gone to Zack? Had she learned something that made that impossible? Was she not only physically hurt but emotionally devastated as well?

The whistle sounded again, and she made her decision. "Take me to her."

She was rushed on board just as the huge red paddle wheel began plowing its way through the water. The gate was closed behind them, and the distance lengthened between the boat and the dock. She felt a moment of uncertainty, but she pushed it aside and thought instead of Kate.

"Where is she?"

"This way." The young man steered her through the crowd

to the stairs and onto the upper deck. They passed door after door before he finally opened one and led her in.

The room was dark after the brightness of the sun reflected off the water and the gleaming white paint on the siding, and her eyes needed a few minutes to adjust themselves. The small cabin held only one bunk, a small chest of drawers, and two chairs. The bunk was empty.

She reeled around as she heard the lock click behind her. "Nooo," she screamed, before his fist connected with her jaw. She had only one thought as pain and blackness engulfed her. Kate.

Sheriff Merkel had little choice in the face of circumstances but to release Miss Montgomery into Mr. Bennett's custody. He had nothing concrete for which to hold her, and she seemed anxious to go with her father. He did think that curious in the light of her earlier demands to talk to Zack's lawyer, but she seemed to have changed her mind. He didn't blame her.

"Sorry to have put you through that," he said as she turned to leave.

"It wasn't so bad," Kate said, glancing once at the door to the men's cells before turning and walking out of his office with her guardian.

"I want to see Annie," Kate demanded curtly.

"All in good time," Sam agreed affably. "She's being held by a friend of ours. She'll be safe enough if you cooperate."

"I have only your word for that, and we both know what your word means."

He clucked his tongue mockingly. "You've grown a sharp tongue."

"I've just grown up."

"Let's hope you haven't grown up too much. Peter will be disappointed."

"Do you expect me to care?"

"No, your feelings are unimportant, actually."

"You're completely amoral. You feel no remorse at all, do you? First my mother, now me."

"Your mother cheated me," he said, his nostrils flaring with renewed hatred. "She should have told me."

"But you swore to her that her wealth meant nothing to you. Another example of your sterling word of honor. Did you kill Mr. Beauchamps, as well?"

She glanced up from beneath her lashes and saw his eyes narrow. "Oh, I've had a long time to think, Sam. Mr. Beauchamps would have known what was in Grandfather's will. He would not have countenanced murder, and he *would* have suspected murder, knowing what he knew."

"Quite a fantasy, my dear," Sam drawled. "Beauchamps died of natural causes."

"You mean he died as a natural result of being poisoned," she said, putting into words her suspicions. "What was it Mrs. Tyree fed him? It could have been any number of slow poisons. Something difficult to detect, I'd imagine. Is she enjoying her home? I wonder how she'll like prison."

"You're wasting your breath if you think I'm going to respond to any of that nonsense."

"Poor Mrs. Tyree. I suppose she'll have an accident now, or she might be convinced to testify against you in exchange for leniency. I will have to name her when I talk to the sheriff."

He chuckled deprecatingly, but just enough unease came through to tell her she was hitting her mark.

"Mr. Beauchamps is gone, rest his soul. I can't do anything for him, but he did leave a widow. I'll sell your flashy carriages and the matched bays you bought last year and give the money to her, even though it came out of my estate to begin with. It's the least I can do since it was my mother's folly which introduced you into this family."

And she couldn't resist one last jab, at a spot she knew would be extremely sensitive. "I don't suppose you found Mr. Beauchamps' third copy of the will. He always did like to make three. But no, you couldn't have destroyed *that* copy, or you'd have no need of me. Mr.—ah, whoever has it, will probably bring it to me on my twentieth birthday."

"Who?"

"Beg your pardon?"

"I said who? Who has it?"

"Who has what?"

He pulled her to a stop and swung her around to face him. "The will, you impudent brat."

She laughed. "But that was pure fantasy," she goaded. "You said so yourself." She sobered and looked pointedly down at the hands holding her upper arms. "You're touching me, Mr. Bennett."

The muscles of his jaw flexed and one corner of his mouth twitched. He looked ready to strangle her. It wasn't wise to tease a man already cornered, and especially not one who had everything to gain by her death, yet some compulsion drove her on, a need to strike back at him for all the misery he'd caused her in the past, a desire to show him he hadn't broken her spirit, that she was a Montgomery through and through, and every bit as strong as any of them.

Now that she had tasted life and love, now that she knew she could exist away from the Manor, now that she realized she had value to herself and to others, the ghosts that had haunted her and kept her silent for so long were exorcised. Her fear of offending Bennett was gone. She couldn't understand why it had ever been there.

"It is unfortunate that you had to overhear that conversation. All of this could have been avoided."

"Oh, I'm sure. Have I caused you a few sleepless nights? I hope so. Poor Corinne, how she must be fretting. Is she impossible to live with these days? She never could bear to be thwarted."

"You can see for yourself shortly."

"She came with you? How cozy. But then she never did trust you to manage anything on your own. I should have guessed she would be here."

His brows drew together in a dark scowl. "That is preposterous. She trusts me implicitly."

"If you say so."

He led her toward the docks instead of to his hotel, one of the finer ones, she suspected, since Corinne was with them. He took her to a shabby place on the edge of town, a place used mostly by the men who worked on the river. Was this where they had brought Annie?

She wasn't surprised to see Peter reclining on the bed, his

back resting against the cracked headboard. He hadn't even taken his shoes off. But of Annie there was not a sign.

"Well, well. I see you are prepared to stoop as low as Bennett, after all, to get what you want. I had wondered, having met your brother. It never ceases to amaze me when two siblings are so completely opposite in character."

Peter didn't appreciate that. Slowly he swung his feet from the bed to the floor and stood, towering over her threateningly. "You think so?"

Her lips twitched into a semblance of a grin. As usual, he was trying to intimidate her with his height. She dusted off a chair and sat down, deliberately exaggerating the distance between their eyes. She looked him up and down and curled her lips as if finding him sadly lacking, returning the disdain he had regularly shown her. She said nothing, just sat quietly and waited for them to make the next move.

"You don't appear to be overly concerned for your friend," he said maliciously.

She chuckled. "I hope you haven't left her with Corinne." She had to stifle a grin which she thought of Corinne trying to keep Annie anywhere against her will.

"Would that upset you?" When she didn't answer, he turned away from her steady scrutiny. "No, she's not with Corinne."

And she wasn't with Peter or Bennett. So where was she, and with whom? Kate would not, however, ask. The less she displayed any of the affection between herself and Annie, the better for both of them.

"Have you nothing to say?" Peter demanded angrily at her continued silence.

She shrugged. "I was told I would be taken to see my friend."

"After the ceremony," he said evenly at the same time a knock sounded at the door.

Sam opened the door and welcomed the slight man who entered. He was dressed formally, and carried a small black book. He smiled kindly at Kate.

"Reverend Johns, this is my daughter, Katrina Montgomery, and her fiancé, Peter Standish. We would like a brief ceremony, please."

Kate smiled warmly at the nervous little preacher. So this was their game. She felt sorry for the minister. He was certain to be embarrassed.

"Katrina," Peter beckoned, holding out a hand to her. "Shall we begin?"

"Peter, darling, I couldn't possibly be married without my maid of honor. We simply must wait for her. She would be devastated if she missed my nuptials."

"She may not be coming at all, Katrina, dear," Bennett said sweetly, but with an underlying menace that she did not fail to hear.

"But you gave me your word she'd be here. No, we will wait for her."

Sam took her arm in a painful grip and steered her to a corner across the room. "You will go through with this or *I will have her killed.*"

"Mr. Bennett, I don't know that you *have* her at all. And I thought I told you *never* to touch me."

She jerked free and returned to Peter's side. "I'm sorry, Reverend Johns, but I've changed my mind. I'm not sure this is the right time to get married. I think when the moon is new. No, a blue moon. Is there a blue moon this month? Then I could wear my blue dress. Blue is more appropriate for a wedding, don't you think? White is such a nothing color. I have such a pretty blue dress, too."

The poor man's brows rose incredulously. "I see. Perhaps more thought is in order. Marriage is a serious commitment, not to be entered into lightly."

"Why don't we all go have a cup of coffee and discuss it further? Maybe Annie will be back by then."

"Now see here, young lady," the reverend reproached, "coffee or a maid of honor, the color of your dress or the moon, should not enter into your decision to marry. I don't believe you appreciate the seriousness of the vows you would be making, and I, in good conscience, cannot say the words to bind you to this man for all time whe you obviously have no concept of what marriage is."

"Katrina, darling," Peter said, pulling her firmly to his side.

"Tell the man you know what you're doing. You're not going to disappoint me now. I've waited too long for you already."

"You are a dear man, Peter," she said, looking up into his stern face and patting his taut cheeks. "But you heard him. He doesn't want to marry us." She fluttered her lashes coquettishly, then turned to the minister. "You are a very wise man, as wise as Reverend Adams. You do your calling credit. I promise I'll think long and hard before I get married. Maybe yellow would be good."

Peter rounded on her as soon as the minister left. "That was a brilliant piece of acting, but it gained you nothing," he snarled. "You don't have a choice in this, Katrina. We are not going to lose the Manor over the likes of you. If you had been reasonable, we could all have had what we want."

"All of us? Or you three? The Manor is mine. I want my inheritance, and I want Zack."

"Zack will never marry you," he spat vindictively. "Leave her to me, Sam. You get back to Corinne and check out of the hotel. I'll take care of Katrina."

"Peter," Sam said uncertainly, seeing the black rage in Peter's eyes.

"Get out of here!" Sam's brows rose, but he left quickly.

"You are living in a dream, my dear," Peter growled maliciously, "if you think you can escape your fate. Zack is my brother. Did you really believe all those lies he told you? Did you think it a coincidence, your meeting him, falling in love with him?" He laughed sardonically. "It's been our plan all along for him to seduce you into trusting him. It prevented you from marrying outside the family. But now that I'm here, Zack's work is finished. He can get on with his own affairs. His fiancée has been waiting, impatiently, I might add, for our business to be concluded so she can join him here."

"I don't believe you," she cried, unaware that, for that one second, she had revealed all the uncertainty she had felt for weeks.

"Yes, you do. You never were very astute when it came to playing games. Did you never wonder about our names? I didn't want Zack to use his real name at first, but he convinced me it was best. He said if he could entice you to trust him as a

Standish, he could get you to do anything."

"And what would that profit you?"

"How do you think we knew where you were? We would have left Zack to arrange the next accident, but unfortunately, we met with unexpected interference. Someone learned who you were."

"You murdered those men," she said in horror, realizing what interference he meant. Had Zack really been involved in murder then? Had the sheriff known what he was doing when he arrested Zack?

"Only one, my dear. He was threatening to tell you everything. We did try to reason with him, but his demands were too high. Time is short, Katrina. We didn't want to chase you down again. We might not have found you in time."

She laughed humorlessly. "And I was reserving judgment of you because I thought there had to be some decency in you."

"Because I'm Zack's brother? Zack and I are alike, my dear. We go after what we want. I want the Manor."

"So does Bennett."

"I can take care of Bennett. You see, Zack and I have always shared a dream. When the opportunity presented itself to take the Manor from Bennett, we set our plan into action. We were duped, of course, because Bennett didn't have clear title to the Manor, and for a while we had to sit back and wait. In the end it was easy. You were very predictable."

"I still don't believe you."

"You were, though. You never suspected a thing, so that night I made certain you heard what you needed to know. Zack took over from there. How delighted he must have been to see how beautiful his quarry was."

She turned away from his cynical mockery. She couldn't let him see how much his cruel words had undercut her confidence and shattered her bravado. Let him think her stupid, but she couldn't bear for him to know that she'd had similar suspicions all along yet had been foolish enough to believe in Zack. A Standish. She still wanted to believe in him. Her heart felt sore, bruised and bleeding. Still she held on. Still she hoped.

She tried to convince herself that what they shared was too

beautiful to be faked, that Zack did love her, that Peter was feeding her a pack of lies. But doubt came fast on the heels of her efforts. Too much of what Peter said made a sick sense when she thought of it in juxtaposition to her own suspicions and to what had actually happened.

The most painfully shameful part was that Zack had accomplished her seduction with infinite ease. She forced the thought away. She was assuming that Zack was guilty. It hadn't been like that, it hadn't. She didn't want to believe Zack could be so calculatingly cruel.

"You're lying," she said woodenly. Even to her ears she sounded unconvinced. Peter heard her doubt, as well.

"When you see Corinne, you'll know I'm telling the truth. She does so enjoy wearing your mother's jewelry. She was delighted when Zack returned it to her."

Peter turned her to face him, and his eyes looked almost gentle. "I'm sorry you have to be sacrificed like this. I always did have a certain fondness for you. Arranged marriages are not so uncommon, and I'd be good to you, Katrina."

"I must be an extremely wealthy woman," she said bitterly, "for all of you to go to such lengths to get my inheritance."

"It's time to face the truth. It doesn't matter if you trusted Zack, or whether or not you were silly enough to fall in love with him. He will never marry you. That's a fact. And if you require further proof, I have several letters from him at the Manor. Our mother died recently. She loved the city, she would never have left, but Zack hated it. He wanted a place in the country. Her death freed Zack to begin a life of his own. I owe him his chance. I'll show you the letters when we get home."

"Zack doesn't need the Manor. He has a ranch here," she said, looking for discrepancies in his story.

"The bank owns the ranch here. Zack is up to his neck in debt. Mother's illness was costly. My brother wants this ranch, but without an infusion of capital, and soon, he'll lose it."

"So if I have to marry someone, it may as well be Zack," she challenged.

"He has a fiancée already."

"Me." She flashed her ring under his nose. "It's your mother's ring."

"Yes, well, he had to do that, although I don't think Mother would have approved of her wedding ring being used in a bogus engagement. Zack's fiancée never liked that ring. Hers is—a bit larger, flashier." He smiled patronizingly.

"Well, I like it," she said with saccharine sweetness.

He lost patience. He pulled out his watch and checked the time. "We will put an end to this nonsense. We cannot ever agree on this, I see that now. But you are one against all of us. Be sensible. Let's get that preacher back here and be done with this."

Her chin rose and she glared at him mutinously. "You may send for the entire Supreme Court, but I'm not marrying anyone until I see Annie. Now, I can't imagine why you would expect me to believe all you've had to say, interesting though it was, when you have done nothing but lie and cheat and murder people.

"I've been brought to this dreary room as if you were afraid to be seen with me. Or are you afraid to be seen at all? Is it Zack you're hiding from? I've been told you have Annie, a means of forcing my hand, however, I have seen no proof of that."

"Oh we have her, be sure of that. And her life is in your hands."

"So you say. But how foolish I would be to believe you when she may be safely tucked away at the ranch. Or already dead." She took a painful breath at that thought.

"She is neither. And whatever happens to her will be on your conscience for the rest of your life."

"I'll take that chance. Annie would want me to."

The steady throb of the engines that sent the blades cutting into the water threatened to lull Annie back into peaceful oblivion, but the throb in her jaw coaxed her awake. The room was in darkness, and no one was stirring, but she felt his presence.

The memory of what had happened returned to her swiftly. She closed her eyes for another minute, gathering her wits about her. She was tied, hands and feet, so even if the door was now unlocked, she couldn't get to it.

She could scream for help, but that, too, seemed unlikely to work. He was too near, she could sense him, she could hear him breathing. He would only render her unconscious again. And what were the chances of anyone hearing, or if they did, of their coming to her aid? Her first scream might alert a few people, but a single scream would be easy enough to explain away. A bad dream, a mouse, a spider; women were skittish creatures. So she would take her own advice, bide her time, get to know her enemy.

She moaned and tried to sit up. Immediately the young man was at her side, sitting on the edge of her bunk.

"If you cry out, I'll have to gag you," was his terse greeting.

He wasn't a bad-looking lad. How had he become involved with Peter Standish? "Who are you?" she asked.

"No names. I'm sorry I had to hit you. I don't go for hitting women."

She tested her jaw. "You couldn't prove that by me. Don't hit me again. Please," she pleaded.

"If you behave, I won't have to."

"I will, I promise. Why are you doing this? What did I ever do to you?"

"I needed the money. I won't hurt you. I'm to keep you out of Sacramento for a few weeks, that's all. Then you'll be free to go."

"A few weeks? Who paid you? This man named Peter?"

"Don't know his name. An older man. He was rich. Look, I do need the money. My ma and my sister . . ., well, I need it, that's all."

"I hope you got paid in advance, because if this man is who I think he is, you'll never see him again."

"I got my money. I ain't stupid. But I get a big bonus if I keep you outta his way for three weeks."

"Why? I'm no threat to anyone."

"He said it was urgent, a matter of protecting the welfare of his family. I reckon you got yourself involved with some rich guy whose pappy objects to you. Am I right?"

She lowered her lashes demurely and played along. "They had no right to interfere. He liked me. We could have been happy."

"Think of it this way. If he still wants you when I bring you back, you'll know he loves you."

"He won't be there. His father will make him return to the East. I'll never seen him again. And you'll never see your bonus."

"Maybe not, but I've been paid to keep you away, and I'm a man of my word."

"What about this woman you mentioned, and the man named Peter? What about Zack?"

"I have no idea. He said to tell you all that because it would get you here."

"You're making a mistake," she said, trying to reason with him. "One you'll be sorry for, if this man gets his way. There really is a woman. Her name is Kate, and she's in terrible danger right now. You aren't protecting anyone, you're being used, just as I am, to force this woman to give up her inheritance to her stepfather."

He shook his head incredulously. "I was told not to listen to you, that you'd concoct some story to get yourself back there. Sorry, miss, but you'll have to stay with me for the three weeks."

She gave up. Peter had planned well in the event that Kate had revealed any of the facts to her. She closed her eyes, wondering where Kate was. Did Peter have her? Or Bennett? Or was she still in jail? What was happening with Dan? He'd been gone all night. Would he be able to piece the facts together when he found Kate and her gone? Did he know enough to be able to do that? Her mouth tightened in determination. Somehow she had to get back there and help Kate.

Adopting one of Kate's passive faces, she turned to her abductor. "I guess I may as well give in gracefully, though the thought of all that lovely money slipping through my fingers makes me sick. Did you see that house?"

"I saw it," he said sourly.

"It ain't fair how some have so much and others have nothing," she said grudgingly. "Do I have to be tied up like a Christmas goose?"

"No, I guess not. But no tricks."

"What match would I be for you? You're ten times as strong as I am." He cut her wrists loose, and she immediately rubbed her sore jaw. "You won't hit me agin, will you?"

"Hey, I said I was sorry. I couldn't take any chances, that's all. I didn't want to hurt you."

She sighed and sat up. "I guess there's always other fish in the sea. I'm not sure I liked living so far from town anyway. I was getting bored, truth to tell. Next time I'll pick a city man." She laughed carelessly. "So what shall we do for three weeks?"

His eyes glinted speculatively. "We might think of a few ways to pass the time."

Her empty stomach growled and she laughed. "How about eating? I didn't eat breakfast. I'm starving."

"I'll go find us some coffee and sandwiches. Do I have to tie you up?"

"I'm not going anywhere. Why bother now?"

"Good girl. I'll only be a minute."

He trusted her, but only so far. He locked the door on his way out. She went immediately to the narrow window and opened the heavy curtains. She gasped. He stood outside looking in at her.

She clutched her chest dramatically. "You scared me," she called out to him. "It's dark in here," she said defensively.

He came back into the room. "I think I'd better tie you to the chair."

"I was only going to ask you to bring back a deck of cards."

"Nevertheless."

She sat down forbearingly and waited until he had finished binding her wrists to the arms of the chair and her shoulders to the back. "Cream and sugar in my coffee, please," she grumbled as he drew the curtains together again.

The minute he left, she set to work trying to get free. She twisted and pulled until her wrists were raw and her upper arms chafed from the rough hemp.

Her temper exploded. "I will get free!" Her body stiffened as she gave a final jerk against her bonds. Her chair tipped to the side under the force of her body weight and crashed to the floor.

"Well, damnation," she cussed, blowing her hair out of

her face.

"This is a fine stew." She gave another violent tug on her arms out of sheer frustration and pulled one of the armrests free.

"Praises be." She set about untying herself, and just managed to get to her feet when the key rattled in the lock. She picked up the broken armrest and stood against the wall by the door.

Her abductor was carrying a tray. He walked thoughtlessly into the room, and straight into Annie Spooner.

# Chapter 17

Corinne strode into the gray room with the splendor and regal bearing of a queen. She was, Kate noticed immediately, wearing the opal brooch. So Zack had returned the jewels. Zack had set her up for her defeat. He had lied about his brother. She felt as if all the blood had drained from her body, leaving her hollow and chilled.

Her legs were shaky. Her skin felt stretched across her cheekbones. Her mind didn't know which way to go. She needed some time to think, she needed to be alone where she didn't have to keep her feelings locked away under a false front, she needed to cry.

"You look absolutely wretched," Corinne said with her usual tact.

Kate didn't respond. She walked sedately to the chair and sat down. Okay, so what if the worst were true and Zack had betrayed her. She still had herself, she still had Annie. And Annie would be impossible to tie down. Annie would come to help her. She had to believe in that.

"Papa is arranging for some tea," she heard Corinne say to Peter. "We don't have much time left. Have you convinced her?"

"No. She's as stubborn as she always was."

"Are you ready now to agree with me that she should be—"

"Not now, Corinne," he barked.

Kate looked up, scrutinizing both the people in front of her. "What?" she asked calmly. "That I should be found dead?

How easily that falls from your tongue. You must have had considerable practice in plotting the demise of people who get in your way. My mother, who became useless when you learned she didn't own the Manor, Mr. Beauchamps, when it became apparent he could upset your plans. Now me. Will Peter be next, because he intends to own the Manor? You must be wary, Peter, because if I do agree to marry you, it will be with the written proviso that Sam and Corinne be expelled from the Manor. In spite of your assurances that you and I could build a comfortable marriage, I refuse to live with the people who murdered my mother."

Corinne's laugh was false and brittle. "Tell her, Peter. Tell her that we're lovers and intend to remain so. Tell her we'll never leave the Manor."

Peter didn't answer. He was grinning at Kate as if seeing in her something that surprised and amused him.

Sam Bennett arrived, carrying a tray with four steaming mugs of coffee. "Sorry, they were out of tea downstairs." He held a cup up to Kate. "How do you take your coffee these days, Katrina, dear?"

"A little sugar, please," she answered politely. She didn't want his solicitousness, but she needed the coffee. She accepted the aromatic brew gratefully, hoping it would fortify her for the coming ordeal. For she was certain it would be just that.

"Now, shall we get down to business?" Sam asked urbanely. "I have here a copy of the deed to the Manor. If you would kindly sign it over to me, along with the power of attorney to manage your trust for the next ten years, you will be free to go."

Kate took the papers and scanned their contents. If she signed them, she would be left with nothing. Sam would have legal rights to everything she owned. Her grandfather would have hated that.

"Have you run the Manor so poorly that you cannot continue without my trust?" she asked. "Perhaps you *should* let Corinne manage your affairs."

He handed her a pen and a small bottle of ink. She ignored them and instead drank her coffee. "Had I still been able to trust Zack, had I married him, I would have had no need for either the Manor or the trust. Had everything been as I was led to believe, I might have signed this. Now I find myself stripped of my fiancé, my love, my charity, my faith in mankind, my future. I find growing in my soul a bitter resentment. I shall have to try very hard not to become as hard and uncaring and vindictive as you three have become.

"I no longer care what your plans for me are. Enough people know the truth to insure you will be brought to justice if I die, for any reason. And if anything happens to Annie Spooner, I will personally see the three of you hang. I will not marry either of you, and I will not sign your ridiculous papers. And when I turn twenty, I will retrieve the last copy of the will, and you will become a distasteful memory in my life."

Their faces began to grow fuzzy, and she felt faint. She drained her cup and reached out to place it on the lamp table. It fell through her numb fingers and bounced on the wood floor. She stared at it as it spun around and around like a top. With deliberate effort she raised her head. Three blurry faces watched her, smirking at her helplessness. She looked back at her empty cup. They had drugged her.

Peter took her elbow and lifted her to her feet. Her knees refused to hold her, and she slumped against him. Bennett had been too polite when he offered her the coffee, she should have suspected.

Peter wrapped his arms around her, molding her softly curved body against his tall form. "Nice," he said, pulling her closer. Her head fell back and she looked at him through dazed and unfocused eyes. Her lips, soft and full, were parted temptingly just inches from his.

He felt a warm stirring of desire in his loins. Was this how she looked, drugged with passion instead of whatever Sam had slipped into her coffee? She felt good in his arms. For a year now he had wanted to possess her, and her coolness toward him had only served to increase that desire. She wasn't cool and distant now. He could almost believe she wanted him to kiss her.

Katrina's body was floating, she felt weightless yet too heavy to move. She stared at the indistinct face above hers. Was that

Zack? Had he come to rescue her? His arms tightened, holding her securely. His lips brushed hers gently then more demandingly. She longed to melt into his embrace, but her mind was screaming a name she wanted to forget. Peter's name. No, it was Corinne screaming. And Peter's arms around her. Zack wasn't here. Zack had not come to help her after all. On that thought she gave in to the potency of the drug.

Dan burst into the sheriff's office and demanded to see Zack. When the sheriff explained that Zack was still with Mr. Meecham, Dan then asked to see Kate.

"Mr. Bennett, her guardian, came for her," the sheriff told him.

"She went with him? Willingly?"

"Yes. She appeared anxious to leave."

"I'll bet. I've got to see Zack and Meecham, and you had better hear what I have to say, as well."

Zack stood when the sheriff opened the door and followed Dan to the cell where he and Meecham had been talking. He knew immediately by the expression on Dan's face that yet another disaster had befallen them.

"What is it?" he asked.

"Did you check the post?" Meecham asked at the same time.

"I got the report," he said, handing the thick envelope through the bars. "But we're too late. Bennett was here and took Kate."

"You released her," Meecham demanded of the sheriff. "I warned you she might be in danger."

"I had to. As you claimed, this Bennett said the charges against her had been dropped. I had no reason to detain her. He showed me the court order giving him guardianship over her and demanded her release."

"And she went?" Zack asked incredulously. "Without seeing me?"

"She was forced to go," Dan explained. "Bennett has Annie. Someone went out to the ranch with a message for her. Martha said it was from me, but I suspect it was about Kate. Annie fell for it. Martha tried to stop her, but you know Annie."

"So Bennett used Annie to get Kate to go with him. What does he want with Kate? That's what I can't understand," Zack fumed in frustration.

"What's going on here?" the sheriff insisted.

Meecham ignored the sheriff. "Read the report."

Zack opened the envelope and read, relaying the information John Phillips had learned.

"As I suspected," Meecham said when Zack finished.

"What? This doesn't say anything we don't already know."

"It says a great deal if you read between the lines. Your Katrina is the granddaughter of a very wealthy man, a very clever, and yet a very just and right-minded man. He watched his son die in the war, he watched his daughter-in-law fall for the wiles of an unscrupulous man. What would you do in that case to protect your fortune for your only living heir?"

"Leave it to Kate," Zack said bleakly.

"Her mother's untimely death would seem to indicate that. With Katrina's mother still alive, Bennett had no hope of getting control of all that money. As Katrina's legal guardian, however, . . ."

"Then the jewels and the money I returned were hers," Zack said regretfully.

"Technically, if what we surmise is indeed fact. Bennett must, however, have hidden that information very well to feel free enough to charge Katrina with theft. What we need is a copy of that will."

"Phillips said there was no will recorded. That's how Bennett inherited the Manor."

"Which doesn't mean there never was a will. In any event, as Montgomery's only living kin, she can contest Bennett's claim to the plantation. Unless . . ."

"Unless what?" Zack demanded. "Unless she marries him, or my brother," he guessed, finally seeing the reason for Kate's sudden flight from her childhood home. "You've got to let me out, sheriff. I have to find her."

"One other possibility exists," Meecham said grimly. "Bennett will have legal claim to the Manor if she dies. I'm surprised she's lived this long."

"Christ," Zack groaned, his knuckles going white as his grip on the bars tightened. "Sheriff," he implored.

"I think, Sheriff," Meecham said authoritatively, "that it is logical to assume, in light of these new disclosures, that my client has been intentionally implicated in these murders in order to remove him from the scene while Bennett retrieved his stepdaughter. It is also fortunate that Bennett did not learn of Mr. Siebert's close association with Zack, or Daniel might now be floating in the river."

"Let me get this straight," the sheriff said, puzzled. "Mrs. Lawrence is Katrina Montgomery, and she ran away from her home because . . ."

"Because she learned that Bennett was planning her marriage to himself or to my brother so they could get title to her inheritance," Zack said impatiently.

"That or the threat of death," Dan added.

"And Annie Spooner? You say she's been kidnapped?"

"She was tricked into going with some man, and neither the Rollinses nor I can locate her," Dan explained again. "The only way Kate would have gone with Bennett is if Bennett had threatened to harm Annie. Kate and Annie are very close friends."

"Yes, I noticed that. I can see how Miss Spooner would jump at the chance to help Kate if such a message were delivered to her."

"Sheriff, we're wasting time," Zack said curtly.

Sheriff Merkel looked at Meecham. "You're willing to accept responsibility for Mr. Standish?"

"I have no choice. The lives of two young women are at stake."

Merkel unlocked the door. He still wasn't certain. "I could lose my badge for this. If you don't come back, Standish, I'll come for you personally. I still have two unsolved murders to deal with."

"I'll be back. And when I return, I'll have my wife with me. No one is going to treat Kate like that and get away with it."

"Nor Annie," Dan declared grinning at his own vehemence. "Though I don't suppose Annie will need much help from me to bring down the wrath of hell on whoever has her."

Zack laughed, lifting some of the forboding of doom that had settled on his shoulders. "Maybe we should stay out of her way, eh?" he offered facetiously.

"What can I do to help?" the sheriff asked.

"Have your men check all the trains and boats leaving town. And contact the sheriff in Memphis. Tell him to watch for their return and stop any marriage. Have him arrest Kate and lock her away from Bennett until I get there, if he has to."

"What can I do?" Meecham asked.

"Who do you know in Tennessee?"

"How about the governor? An old classmate," he explained.

Zack gave a snorting chuckle. "See what he can uncover about Montgomery's will and Kate's rights to the Manor. Tell him to expect to hear from me."

"Send Martha and Rollins back to the ranch and have them pack some clothes for us," Zack said to Dan, his mind working full speed. "I'll go to the bank and get some money. We're travelling again."

"What about Annie?" Dan asked.

Zack paused thoughtfully. "What would they do with Annie?" he asked himself aloud.

"Mr. Standish, Mr. Standish."

Zack turned at his name, irritated at the interruption, especially by the Reverend Adams. The preacher was known for his ability to hold long conversations. Zack didn't have time now.

"You'll have to forgive me, sir, but I have urgent business to attend to."

"I won't detain you then, but I do need a moment of your time."

Summoning his patience, he inclined his head. "Please be brief."

"I may not know you well enough to be this forward, but you have been to my church, and I do feel a responsibility for the moral and spiritual integrity of those I consider my flock."

"Get to the point."

"A friend of mine, the pastor of one of our sister churches, just spoke with me about you. I am concerned that you are trying to pressure your young lady into a hasty marriage. Reverend Johns was quite upset that you were not willing to wait for a wedding at your own church and by your own pastor. Mr. Standish, I have to say that I am appalled that a man of your stature would want a quick ceremony in a seedy hotel room on the riverfront."

Zack turned baffled eyes to Dan. Their gazes locked as their thoughts took the same path. "Could you tell us what Reverend Johns said, exactly? This could be very important."

"Weren't you there?"

"No, I was not. I believe the man your friend met was my errant brother. What was the woman's name?"

"Reverend Johns was very distraught, you understand. He'd never refused to marry anyone until today. He claimed this woman insisted on her maid of honor being present, then changed her mind about the color of her dress, then wanted to discuss it over tea. The two men tried to coerce her into going through with it. That's when Reverend Johns refused. He said the woman thanked him and then mentioned my name. He thought it wise to inform me."

"What was the woman's name?" Zack demanded again.

"Catherine, or Kathleen," he said, "which naturally led me to believe he meant your Mrs. Lawrence, whom you introduced as Kate."

"It's Katrina. And she is *my* wife-to-be. Reverend Adams, you've helped us more than you'll ever know. You can count on me for your new choir robes. Bless you."

Zack took Dan's arm and hurried him away, leaving a bewildered preacher behind.

"Zack," Dan said, urging his friend to slow down. "I don't understand."

"Kate demanded to see Annie before she'd marry Peter. Whatever they threatened, she's not going to be moved until she's certain Annie is safe. Good girl," he said, cheering for Kate.

"So?"

"So, they'll have to produce Annie, who has probably known all along what's been at stake here. Good Lord! It just dawned on me. Kate suspected my relationship with Peter. All those questions about my family."

"Which you denied having."

"What must she be thinking?"

"What you're thinking now."

"Hell! I'm back to the beginning with her. She'll never trust me. She'll never forgive me for lying, for sending that money back."

"Are you giving up on her?"

Zack glared at Dan for allowing such a suggestion to pass his lips. "I'm going to fetch her back here if I have to tie her up and kidnap her myself."

Annie's fist came up, dumping the tray of hot coffee down his front. While the surprise of a nasty scalding was on her side, she yanked him into the room and kicked the door shut. Before he regained his balance, she placed her foot against his thigh and shoved him into the wall. He bounced away, stumbled, and fell heavily against the dresser. She hated to do it, but she hit him over the head with the chair arm.

By the time he regained consciousness, she had hefted him onto the bed and tied his hands and feet to the iron grillwork at the top and bottom of the bed. She sat down beside him and proceeded to tie a gag in his mouth.

He grumbled and grunted at her. She smiled and patted his cheek. "Don't be angry. This is nothing more than you deserve. Tsk, tsk," she clucked, tightening the knot at the side of his head. "Shame on you for kidnapping a poor innocent little girl. And for hitting her. Your mother would be appalled. Now, I'm forced to take a couple dollars from you, but as I see it, you still end up with more than enough for a few hours' work."

She stood up and walked to the door. "Don't try to find me or I'll have you arrested." She grinned impishly as she opened the door. "You're a nice young man, you're just no match for Annie Spooner. Don't pull a foolish stunt like this again. You can't help your mother and sister from prison."

Ignoring the reproving glares of the passengers as she elbowed her way through the crowd, she fairly flew to the the wheelhouse and demanded to speak with the captain.

"I need to get back to Sacramento immediately. It's urgent.

A woman may be killed if I can't get back to help her."

"Calm down," the captain soothed. "It can't be as bad as all that."

"Don't tell me what is or ain't bad. I know what I'm talking about."

"I'm sorry. I can't go back. We have passengers. We'll be stopping in a few miles for . . ."

"I can't wait. What's that town over there?"

"Miss, I can't stop there. The river isn't deep enough."

"I'll swim then."

He grabbed her arm as she spun around to leave. "You're mad. You can't swim that far."

"I can swim back to Sacramento if it's the only way to get there."

"Captain, the *Shenandoah*'s in sight," the navigator said. "We could hail her, come alongside, and transfer the young lady across."

The captain looked at Annie's anxious face. "This better be as serious as you claim.

"It is. I promise. My name is Annie Spooner, and I was tricked on board the *River Queen* by the man tied up in cabin twelve. If not for him, I wouldn't be here at all. Please, Captain."

He nodded. "Contact them, Bailey."

Never had time moved more slowly for Annie than it did on her return to Sacramento. She thanked the captain and dashed from the cargo-laden *Shenandoah* onto the dock. She lifted her skirts and ran toward town, toward the sheriff's office and Zack.

"I need to see Zack right away," she said, bursting into the office, out of breath and gasping for air.

The sheriff came to his feet. "Miss Spooner. I've had men out searching for you close to three hours."

"Not now. I need to see Zack."

"He's gone. I released him. Where have you been? This place has been in an uproar."

"I've been down the river. Sheriff, is Kate still here?"

"No, her stepfather took her."

She slammed her hand onto his desk and slumped into the

chair across from him, dropping her head into her hands. "Damnation. Does Zack know?"

"He's looking for her now. When they thought you'd been kidnapped, they went slightly berserk. If you weren't kidnapped, then Kate isn't—"

"I *was* kidnapped. I got away. I don't stay where I don't wanna be. I hit the poor chap over his head and tied him up for the porter to find later, then I convinced the captain to put me on a boat coming back upriver. I had to get back here. I knew the Bennetts were in town."

Had any other woman told him that story, he wouldn't have believed it. He believed Annie. "We were all too late, but I will go with you to find Zack and Mr. Siebert. They're very concerned about you."

"Did they say where they were going or what they were going to do?"

"If they can't find Kate, they're going back to Tennessee. They missed the train this morning by an hour."

"What time did it leave?"

"Ten thirty. Bennett took Kate at ten."

"They're gone then. When does the next train leave?"

"The express goes through tomorrow. Nothing until then."

"Then Bennett's not on the express?"

"Nope. They'll be stopping in every two-bit town across the line."

"So we could catch up with them. We could reach Memphis before they do."

"We?

"You don't think they're going without me?"

"Somehow I get the impression they aren't going to have much to say about it."

"You are staying here!"

"I am going."

"Be reasonable, Annie. We'll have enough to consider without worrying about you again."

"Then *don't* worry about me. I already proved I can take care of myself. I got away and I got back here, didn't I?

"After you were foolish enough to get caught."

She ignored that. "Besides, I know Memphis. I have friends there, friends who could help us. And I've seen Bennett. I know what he looks like. He questioned me in Memphis when Kate ran away."

"Have you seen my brother?" Zack asked, suddenly alert.

"No. But Kate said you are very like him, only darker and more . . . more . . ."

"More what?" Dan snapped, frustrated.

"More attractive, more irresistable," she threw at Dan. "Nothing you need worry about."

"Well, thank my lucky stars. I wouldn't appreciate you drooling all over me."

"A waste of good spit, I'd say."

"Enough, you two. Annie, try to understand. We could find ourselves in danger."

"Saints preserve us," she groaned. "Zack, I know more about Kate and her life with Bennett and your brother than anyone but Kate herself. And if you *think* you could be in danger, then you definitely need me, because I *know* what you're walking into."

"What do you know?" Zack insisted, taking her by the shoulders, forcing her to look into those piercing blue eyes. She could feel his willpower battling with hers, but hers was just as indomitable.

She smiled grimly. "I'll tell you tomorrow. On the train."

"We know enough," Dan said stubbornly. "You are not going."

"I either go with you, or I'll go on my own, on the very next train. And you don't know me if you think I won't.

She got her way, and the next morning she boarded the *Coastal Express*, though not before another argument from Martha. Zack had warned her that they would have no private car, that the best she could expect was to share a compartment with them. She didn't care.

Kate rolled over, hugging her pillow to her breasts. The sweet smell of lilac filled her senses. She burrowed into the soft warmth of her bed, wrapped in the gentle aftermath of her dream.

"Miss Katrina, I have your tea. Miss Katrina, wake up. Mr. Bennett wants you down to breakfast in half an hour." Junie set the cup on the bedside table and gently shook her mistress.

Kate's eyes snapped open and she sat up. "Junie," she cried, throwing her arms around her friend. "Oh, it's so good to see you. Have you been well? And your mother?"

Junie smoothed her tousled hair. "Fine, fine. I'm not to stay up here with you. You must hurry. Mr. Bennett is in one of his black moods. Oh, Miss Katrina, we never thought we'd see you again. We wondered if you was dead."

"No. And I have the most exciting stories to tell you." She propped herself up and took the tea Junie handed to her.

"Mr. Bennett," Junie reminded her.

"Hmmmph," Katrina snorted. "I shall have a bath before breakfast," she said casually.

"Oh, Miss Katrina, you'll be late. You know how he hates it when . . ."

"Oh, I won't be very late. But bath or no, I will not be on time. I intend for Sam Bennett to know that I will not be slipping meekly under his tyrannical thumb again."

Junie's eyes grew large at Kate's fierceness. She clucked doubtfully. "He can be very cruel when he is disobeyed."

Kate set aside her tea and took Junie's hands in her own. "Listen carefully. I left because I heard them planning to kill me. You can't get meaner than that. I want you to pass the word to all the workers you can trust that Sam had my mother killed. I want them all to know in case something happens to me."

"Your mother? Mrs. Bennett was murdered?"

"Yes. I heard Sam admit it the night I left."

"Why are you back? Why didn't you stay gone?"

"They drugged me and kept me locked in my compartment on the train. They'll do the same here if they think it's necessary to keep me quiet. I have to rely on you and your mama to see they don't poison me or drug me. Junie, I—"

The door burst open and Corinne strode in. "There you are, you wretched girl," she snapped at Junie. "You were to come right back."

"I asked her to stay. You may draw the water for my bath, Junie," Kate said calmly. "And while I bathe, would you select something appropriate for me to wear, please?"

"You can't mean to have a bath now," Corinne scoffed. "Breakfast is nearly served."

Kate shrugged. "Then go eat, for pity's sake. But if you cannot do without me at the table, then you'll have to wait. Go on, Junie."

"She'll be punished, you know," Corinne sneered, looking sidelong at Junie.

"No, she won't. And you'll see that she isn't."

"Me? Why should I? She needs a good thrashing for disobeying Papa."

"Because if he so much as touches her, I'll see that every one of the servants walks out the front gate. Then who will you have to boss around? Peter?" She laughed at Corinne's anger. "Now, if you don't mind, I'd like some privacy. And in the future, remember to knock before you enter my room, or you may find me barging into *your* room at any odd hour of the day. Or night. Or doesn't that concern you? Does Peter no longer visit your bedroom? Have you lost him?"

Kate was not fast enough to avoid the hand that whipped across her face. Kate had expected some form of attack, she'd purposely goaded Corinne into losing her temper. She was stunned, but not too stunned to strike back. Corinne, however, had not anticipated retaliation. She cried out in shock and rage, covering her stinging cheek with her hand.

"You'll pay for that," she wailed, tears gathering in her eyes. "Just wait. You'll pay."

On that parting warning Corinne left Kate to the peace and relaxation of her bath. Kate's cheek smarted too, but she welcomed the discomfort. It helped her gather her emotions and focus her thoughts.

Time. She needed time. Time to give Annie the opportunity to seek help. Time to look for the missing will. Time to learn the truth about Zack. Time to formulate a plan of her own.

# Chapter 18

"She's here," Zack said. "They arrived late last night. The sheriff said he got our message from Merkel in Sacramento, and since then he's had men watching for their return. When he heard they were back at the Manor, he went out there. He asked to see Katrina, but Bennett said she was ill, confined to her bed under doctor's orders."

"What's wrong with her?" Annie asked, alarmed.

"Bennett wouldn't say. Only that she couldn't have visitors."

"He's keeping her a prisoner," Dan surmised.

"The sheriff also said Bennett is within his rights, as Kate's legal guardian, to refuse visitors. There is nothing he can do about it. Bennett and the sheriff had a falling out when our investigator delivered the money and jewels and demanded a release be signed, so Bennett wasn't too happy to see him at all, let alone present him to Kate. To go a step further, Bennett claims that the Manor was burglarized while he was gone. He blames the sheriff, and he has now posted his own guards around the perimeter of the house."

"Against thieves, or to keep us out?" Dan asked disgustedly.

"Oh, I rather think it's to keep Kate in."

"We can't leave her there," Annie cried indignantly. "He'll kill her if she doesn't cooperate."

"She might decide to do just that. I certainly haven't given her reason to trust me," Zack replied, self-deprecatingly. "I lied to her, I led Bennett to her, my name is Standish."

"Well, if you won't do anything, I will."

"Simmer down," Dan placated. "We'll get her back, but we have to do it without threat to Kate. Bennett is desperate. We have to believe that he'll act accordingly. He's facing criminal charges. Right now Kate is his only insurance. As long as he holds her hostage—"

"I'm not leaving her there."

"He won't hurt her if we don't press him," Dan said reasonably. "His options are running out. His only hope is to get her to marry him to prove to everyone else that she believes in him."

"What about Peter? I thought she was to marry him. Now what's going on?"

"That marriage won't help Bennett now," Zack said. "He's in a corner. Kate put him there, Kate's the only one who can get him out."

"As his wife she can't testify against him," Dan explained. "And her marriage to him will guarantee not only his freedom but his fortune."

"I can't bear the thought of her married to that swine," Annie groaned.

"*You* can't?" Zack snapped. "How do you think I feel?"

"Why don't we just go in there and take her?" Annie demanded, frustrated and exasperated.

"The guards, Annie," Dan said dryly.

"The place is a fortress, and the sheriff has no legal reason to remove Kate from the premises. Until we can show him some proof of what we suspect, he can't act. Arranged marriages are not illegal. What Bennett does with his family is strictly Bennett's business. And so far, legal."

"If we could only find that will," Annie said.

"It's probably in the house. Right under their noses," Dan said. "How ironic that would be."

"I have a friend," Annie said, her eyes thoughtful, "who might be able to help us. He was like a father to me when I was here. His name is Jake."

"Jake?" Zack asked. "The Jake Kate mentioned?"

"He helped us escape."

"What could he do in this case?" Dan asked dismissively.

Annie bristled. "So, Mr. Hoity-toity is back. We aren't in Philadelphia. We're in Memphis. Do you know the people here? How they think? The countryside? You might know your way around a big city, but here you're—"

"Okay, I get the message."

"You mean you admit you don't know every damn thing there is to know?"

"What did I tell you about that tongue of yours?"

"Hold it," Zack said, stepping between them. "We don't have time for this. Argue later. Annie's right. Might we see this Jake with you?"

Annie turned a gloating face to Dan. "Of course. I'd be glad to take you there."

"It will have to wait until this evening, though. We have an appointment with Mrs. Beauchamps this afternoon. In the meantime we are searching the records at City Hall."

Kate closed herself in the music room after breakfast. An hour in the company of her erstwhile family was all she could take at one time. Breakfast had been intolerable. Sam had upbraided her for nearly fifteen minutes for disobeying him.

"This is my home," he declared. "My orders are to be obeyed. I will not have you undermining my authority with my servants. As a result of your show of defiance this morning, I am forced to put Junie back in with the other servants. Young Rachel will be taking over the household duties."

"You think to make me suffer by demoting Junie? You've done her a favor, and I daresay the first time Rachel spills the teapot in your lap, your revenge will turn sour in your mouth."

"My daughter says you struck her."

"Sam," Peter interceded, "you can see for yourself that Katrina's cheek is bruised. I know from experience how quick your daughter's hand is. On more than one occasion I have been sorely tempted to return her physical violence, but being a gentleman, I have restrained myself. I see no reason why Katrina should exercise such temperance when she is attacked."

"If you were a gentleman, I would never have struck you," Corinne returned with vitriol.

"Ever blaming others for your own shortcomings," Peter argued back.

"For your information, she struck me first," Corinne claimed.

"From where I was standing, it sounded just the opposite."

"You heard?" she shrieked. "You were eavesdropping?"

"Hardly. Your voices carried quite clearly to the top of the stairs. I did find it an interesting argument."

"An argument she started by insisting on a bath," Corinne said agitatedly.

Kate sat back and watched over the rim of her cup as they bickered back and forth. For the first time she felt nothing but a sense of revulsion and pity for them, pity that they had nothing more constructive to do with their time and energy than engage in empty arguments over trivialities such as a bath. How void their lives must be when her daily movements were their sole interest.

"Judge Barker will come tomorrow. Prepare yourself for your wedding," Bennett ordered, glaring at Kate, letting his words drop like lead weights into the argument between his daughter and his partner.

"You cannot force me to agree, Sam," she replied calmly.

"I say it shall be so!"

"Then bring the judge. I should like a word with him."

"He won't listen. He had no love for your grandfather."

"That's of no importance. You will still be the one to suffer humiliation."

"You will marry me."

"You?" Corinne cried. "Are you serious?"

"She's marrying me," Peter stated.

Katrina laughed at them. "Let me see now. Should I marry Sam, I'd be Corinne's stepmother, and as such, it would be within my rights to discipline her. She's much too spoiled. Perhaps we could send her to college. Women do go to college these days. Of course, if I marry Peter, you'll both be gone," she said directing her comment to Corinne and Sam.

Corinne turned a hateful red. Peter laughed. Sam exploded.

"Don't think we don't know what you're doing, trying to turn us against each other. It won't work."

"I know what I'm doing. I wonder if you do? By now my friends, who know all about you, will be coming for me."

"If you mean Zack, you can forget it," Peter said, irritated.

"The mention of your brother, though I never specified him, seems to annoy you, almost as if you were intensely jealous. I find that odd for two who are reportedly so close, unless you aren't. Maybe you have reason to be uncomfortable at his name. He's a powerful man."

"He won't interfere with me," Peter declared.

"And I say apples are oranges. Truth is truth, Peter. It is yourself you must convince, not me."

"I told you how we planned this—"

"You told me, yes, but telling doesn't make truth. I shall have to wait to know the truth. But you already know it. Is that what scares you?"

"I'm not scared," he flared.

She smiled. "Excuse me. I have finished."

"You are not excused," Sam thundered. "You will sit there until you agree with me."

"Have a nice day," she said, walking serenely from the room. Their voices followed.

"Papa, how can you let her walk out on you? Can't you control her anymore?"

"Corinne, dear, she's not the same girl she was when she left."

"No," Peter said, wolfishly, "she isn't. I see you've noticed that, too, Sam. Has she got your juices flowing? Is that why you want her in your marriage bed?"

"You're disgusting," Corinne spat. "Both of you."

Katrina shut the door and went to the music cabinet that stood beside her grand piano. She was eager to sort through her music, to find works she had learned that would be suitable for playing at the restaurant. She would take them back with her when she returned.

She smiled, realizing what she'd been thinking. She wanted to go back. She would go back. She'd see Zack again and give him a chance to explain. She owed him that much. She owed herself that much. Not a few times she'd told herself that the doubts that crept into her mind served Peter's and Sam's purposes very well.

So why couldn't she find the faith in Zack she wanted so badly? Why did questions still plague her? She trusted Dan. She knew Dan was a good man, a man of honor. Would Dan align himself with a partner who had no integrity? She knew he wouldn't, not knowingly. So that was a mark in Zack's favor.

Annie had trusted Zack. Even when Zack had manipulated them into travelling with him, into staying in Sacramento, even when all the money and jewels had disappeared, Annie had believed in Zack's character. Annie, for all her uneducated ways, was a smart young woman. A worldly-wise woman. She would recognize duplicity when she saw it.

Kate wanted to believe in Zack, too. She loved him, and longed desperately to trust what had grown between them. Zack had said he loved her. He had promised to marry her. They were going to have children together. All those dreams were hers as well. Why then couldn't she shake the doubts? Because he had told her one lie? She'd told more than one herself. But his lie held much more significance.

She made a stack of her favorite music, setting it aside from the rest as she sorted through the cabinet. She came upon an old piece, yellowed with age, a favorite of her grandfather's, Beethoven's "Für Elise." She pulled it out and dusted off the cover. She'd learned it when she was only nine and could barely reach the octaves. She'd played it often for her grandfather until he had died. The pages of music had not been touched in years, since she had long ago committed them to memory.

"You must play with feeling," her professor had said to her frequently. "Yes, that is the way. A little *ritardando* now. Let the music grow at this point, yes." She remembered looking up and seeing the smile of pleasure on her grandfather's face. He had remained with her always during her lessons, and often as she practiced, as if he found in her music a release for a frustrated love of music in his own soul.

"Für Elise." She fingered the name again. Her mastery of that piece had earned her the beautiful piano that replaced the old upright she had begun her lessons with.

She took the music to the piano and sat down. She hadn't played the piece since her grandfather died, wasn't even sure she could play it still. Slowly she opened the timeworn music. A paper fluttered from the music stand, over the keys, and into her lap. She picked it up. Her heart thumped, came to a stop, then began to pound out a frantic rhythm. Her hand shook, making the words difficult to read.

*I, Lawrence B. Montgomery, being of sound mind . . .* She read from the beginning. *And to my granddaughter, and only living heir, I bequeath my land, my home and all its contents, and the remainder of my worldly possessions, which are to be held in trust for her until such time as she marries or reaches the age of twenty years. As executor of her estate, I appoint Mr. Miles Beauchamps, my trusted friend and attorney-at-law.*

There was more, much more, but she didn't want to risk being found with the missing document. Carefully she replaced it and slid the music containing the copy of the will into another collection of Beethoven.

She tried to put it from her mind as she sorted through the remainder of her music, but her thoughts returned to it again and again. "Für Elise." Why hadn't she thought of it? Her music was the only place no one would guess to look. Not even her mother was interested in music, except for what was required at her galas. How like her grandfather to leave a valuable paper in that one special piece of music, almost as a last fond wish and a good-bye to her.

Tears pricked her eyes and ran unheeded down her cheeks. She restored the cabinet to order, then gathered up the music she wanted to keep with her. She dusted off her dress, wiped her face, and walked to the door. She turned to look at her piano. Laying her stack of music on a chair, she walked back and opened the cover. One last time she had to try her grandfather's favorite piece. It came easily to her fingers, even without the printed notes.

Once having begun to play, she found it impossible to stop, using the time to let her music calm her, buoy her spirits, strengthen her resolve. She used the time to think and remember, to sort out truth from fiction, to get in touch with her own instincts.

It wasn't until that afternoon when she attempted to go down to the servants' village, a well-designed and well-built grouping of quarters down by the stream in back of the house, that she learned just how much a prisoner she had been made. Guards stood at every door, forbidding her to leave the house.

"Sorry, miss. Bennett's orders," they said, or words similar. The way they acted toward her made her skin crawl.

She stormed into Bennett's office. "What are those men doing? How dare you forbid me to leave the house? I'll go where I please."

"You may try, but I assure you you will be returned. And I left instructions that you were not to be treated kindly. In fact, I said I didn't care what they might decide to do with you before they returned you to the house."

Which explained the way their eyes ran insultingly over her body.

"You'd like that, wouldn't you?"

"Not particularly, but I won't have you running off again. After we're legally married, you can go wherever you want."

"I'll never marry you."

"You have until tomorrow to change your mind. If you embarrass me in front of Judge Barker, I'll let those men have you. And if that doesn't change your mind, I'll take a whip to your back and toss you in the root cellar until you see sense. You can continue to refuse as long as you want, but each time you do, I'll think up something worse."

"If you can get past Peter to reach me," she said defiantly. "Peter won't permit any of that."

"Peter will have nothing to say about it."

"What won't I have any say in?" came Peter's voice from the doorway.

"It seems I'm to be locked in the cellar, whipped, and given to the guards for their pleasure if I don't agree to marry Sam."

"Here, here, that's no way to treat a lady, Sam. I thought you were a gentleman. Don't fret, Katrina, darling. You'll be quite safe."

"Go to your room, Katrina," Sam ordered, incensed, stalking across the room to the drinks cabinet.

"Shall I obey him, Peter?" she asked submissively.

"Perhaps you had better. It appears you've done enough mischief for now."

She acknowledged his perceptiveness with a slight nod and a sardonic grin, and left them together to battle out the scene she was certain would follow.

Katrina did not go to her room though. She went into the kitchen to see Junie's mother. The kitchen, rebuilt after a fire had destroyed it during the war, was connected to the back of the house, and had above it two bedrooms for the cook and the housekeeper. Those rooms were empty. Bennett didn't want the servants under his roof. The kitchen, alive with pots of fragrant greenery, which were Flora's year-round herb garden, and with the wonderful aromas of cooking and baking, was welcoming, and had always been one of Katrina's favorite places. She'd spent many hours there with Junie as they were growing up. She wanted to go there now.

"How is Junie?" she asked. "She wasn't hurt?"

Flora patted her hand. "No, miss. They didn't lay hand to her. She must talk to you," Flora added on a husky whisper. "She's worried about you, miss. We all are. You should not be here."

"Can she meet me somewhere after dark? Tell her to meet me . . ."

"Those men, they watch everywhere. Mr. Bennett say he tol' them to shoot anyone moving around at night."

"Then how can I talk to her?"

"Do you 'member when you two was little girls, how I'd have to chase you outta that spring house, how you used to like to go there and catch frogs?"

Kate's brows gave an upward twitch. Of course, she remembered. She and Junie had found more places than Flora or Lawrence Montgomery could imagine to explore or get into mischief.

"Your grandpappy bought me when I was a young girl, thirteen. We lived in Mississippi. The man who owned us was a madman. He had my sister whipped because she lay with another man before the massa could take her virginity. He whipped her, then he took her, then he whipped her again. She was with child, and she lost the babe. She died a week later."

"Mr. Montgomery was visitin' at the time. He saw everything. I remember watching his face. I thought he was more evil than the massa. I was scared to move when he bought me. I was shakin' so that Bekka had to hold me to keep me from runnin'.

"We was miles away from that place when Mr. Montgomery stopped the wagon and turned to speak to the slaves he had paid such a high price for.

"'On my plantation,' he said, 'we have no whips for either animal or man.' He needed workers so he bought our papers, but he said he'd hold them for seven years, and after that time, we could be free. All he asked in return was our loyalty and our silence. In those seven years we helped your grandpappy lead hundreds of slaves to freedom."

"He worked for the underground railroad?" Kate asked. "Did he really?"

"He *was* the road to freedom, child. The White Fox. He couldn't right all the wrongs, but he seemed to find the most tormented people and bring them out of hell.

"They almost caught him one night, those fine, upstandin' Southern gentlemen. They would'a hung him, or burned him. My husband, Junie's pa, gave up his life to save Mr. Montgomery."

"I didn't know that, Flora. I never heard any of this before. Poor Junie. Does she know?"

"She does now. I told her when you were gone. I set her to spyin' on them three in there," she said, nodding toward the library. "I wanted to make sure they hadn't killed you like they done your ma."

"You knew that?"

"'Tweren't nothing I could do about it. If I let on I knowed, they'd a done me bad, then you'd a had no one to keep an eye on you."

"Why are you telling me this now?" Kate asked.

"I wanted you to understand why we's doin' what we're gonna do. We're gonna take you out before they kill you."

"Take me out?"

"Like we helped your grandpappy do for those others. Junie

will go with you. She knows the way. Tonight you are to meet with her at midnight. Go down to the wine cellar. She'll meet you there."

"But the guards."

"No one will see her, I promise. She'll explain everything."

Mrs. Lila Beachamps welcomed Zack, Dan, and Annie warmly once she learned of their relationship to Katrina Montgomery.

"They found her, then?" she asked, shaking her head of pure white hair. "That poor child."

Mrs. Beauchamps insisted on performing the proper social niceties. She seated them in her small but pleasant parlor, served coffee, and asked each of them to relay a bit of their background.

Zack wanted to slam his cup down, he wanted to jump up and demand she answer his questions, but he forced himself to be patient. He wouldn't be able to help Kate at all if he alienated all those who could be of assistance.

"Mrs. Beauchamps, could you help us shed some light on Katrina's situation?" Zack asked. "Did you ever see a last will and testament drawn up by your husband for Lawrence Montgomery?"

"How do I know you haven't been sent by Bennett? He's tried several times already to get information from me. He tore my home apart one night looking for something. You are Peter Standish's brother."

"Not because I had a choice, ma'am. But, yes, I am. I am also Katrina's fiance. I love her, Mrs. Beauchamps, and I want a life with her. I don't give one damn, begging your pardon, about that plantation. I want Katie back alive and well. The sheriff won't help until we give him cause to believe Katie's in danger."

"The sheriff won't help, period. Don't count on him. He and Bennett were both involved in the same Klan back in the 'seventies in Nashville. Bennett's responsible for getting the sheriff elected in this county."

"By Klan," Dan asked, "do you mean Ku Klux Klan?"

"In essence. It was the 'Invisible Empire of the South' then, presided over by a grand wizard, with an hierarchy of grand dragons, grand titans, and grand cyclopses. Bennett, a northern man who'd married a girl from Kentucky, joined the club so he wouldn't suffer the fate of most northern carpetbaggers.

"In any event, about that time the Congress put an end to such terrorist organizations, outwardly, at least. The irony is that some of the tangential Klansmen reacted violently to northern congressional interference, and because Bennett was a northerner, they banded together and raided his plantation. They burned it to the ground. Bennett's wife died trying to save their little boy."

"How awful," Annie said sadly.

"Do many people know that story?" Zack asked.

"Uh, yes, those in Nashville. You see, all eight of those Klansmen suffered loss of one kind or another within the year. People don't want to get in Bennett's way. And they are wise not to. My husband never understood how Caroline Montgomery could have married such a vindictive man or brought him to live at the Manor. Or why Lawrence Montgomery permitted it, not that he was well by then. I don't suppose he could manage much of a fight."

"Mrs. Beauchamps," Annie asked gently, "what about your husband? Kate wondered if his death was as deliberate as her mother's."

Mrs. Beauchamps sat straighter and met their questioning eyes squarely. "Your Kate, Lawrence's granddaughter, will be next. Bennett will take from the South what the South took from him. She is all that stands in his way."

"I believe Katie's grandfather left the plantation to her," Annie said. "That's the only reason why Bennett would want her dead."

"You are correct, only Bennett destroyed all proof of that. According to the law, he owns the manor. I did read that will. I bought Miles a typewriter. He couldn't manage it, so I did his typing. Montgomery left everything to Katrina, cutting Bennett out entirely, except for a stipend he was to receive monthly as Caroline's husband. If you knew Lawrence, you'd understand why."

"You mean because Montgomery was an abolitionist," Dan said.

She smiled, surprised. "So you do know. What you don't know is that Lawrence left Katrina a grand sum of money, deposited in a New York bank, which only she can sign for on her twentieth birthday, which was also to be the day my husband relinquished his custody of the Manor to Katrina.

"When Mr. Montgomery died, naturally Bennett learned of the contents of the will. Within the week my husband was dead, his offices were ransacked and burned. A month later Caroline was dead and Sam Bennett had petitioned the court for guardianship of Katrina and ownership of the Manor. It was done expertly. Who would have believed . . ."

"So you don't know of another copy of the will?" Zack asked.

"I made three. Three were signed, witnessed, and affixed with an official seal. My husband retained a copy, which was stolen or burned, Bennett was given a copy, which he has undoubtedly destroyed. I have no idea where the third is. I am so sorry."

"Don't be," Zack said, rising from his chair. "You have confirmed for us that the proof we need does exist. Would you be willing to testify in court to what you've told us?"

She smiled sadly and shook her head. "Yes, I would, but you won't get that far."

"I promise you," Zack said with steely determination. "I *will* get that far."

The tea did not end up in Sam's lap, but in Corinne's, staining her yellow gown. She shrieked and jumped up from her perch on the brocade-covered settee in the parlor.

"Now look what you've done, you stupid girl. You're impossible. Papa, can't you do something about her? Isn't there anyone else out there who can help in the house?"

Kate had gone to Rachel's aid as soon as she saw the heavy silver tray begin to tilt. She'd watched the cups slide across the smooth surface, she'd tried to reach the hot silver pot before it, too, tumbled over and emptied its contents on whomever happened to be near.

"It isn't Rachel's fault," she said evenly, mopping up the tea, collecting shards of broken cups and saucers. "Junie's a strong girl, she can manage the weight of the silver tea service. Rachel cannot."

Flora came bustling in at the crash, clicking her tongue at the mess. "It was bound to happen, giving a child a woman's chore. You get your dress changed, Miss Corinne. Bekka can get that stain out. I'll put another pot of tea to brewin' and I'll serve it in the library in ten minutes. Get up from there now, Miss Katrina, before you cut yourself, and stop your whimpering, Rachel. Go get Muriel to help you clean this room. Go on with you."

"Don't be cross with her," Kate said to Flora.

"Oh, I knows it weren't her fault."

"No, it's Katrina's fault," Corinne said spitefully. "Where is Junie? Get her in here to help me change."

"I'll send Rachel up," Flora said."

"I don't want that clumsy brat."

"Then you shall have to do for yourself. Junie is out in the fields today."

"Get her in here, I said," Corinne screeched.

"Yes, miss," Flora grated furiously. "Very well, miss. Tea will be in an hour then, cause it'll take my bones that long to get out there and back. Supper will be an hour later as well."

"Never mind, Flora," Sam said, finally seeing the unreasonableness of his daughter's request. "You tend to your own duties. Katrina can help my daughter with her dress."

"I don't want her to help. I want Junie."

"Katrina's right, Corinne," Peter drawled from his stance by the window. Until now he hadn't spoken, he'd stood there quietly and watched as if seeing all of them for the first time. "You are a thoroughly spoiled and contrary female. I suggest, Sam, that you forget your daughter's spiteful suggestion of striking back at Katrina through Junie, and get your housemaid back. I also suggest you teach your daughter a little courtesy and restraint. She is becoming intolerably obnoxious. Miss Katrina, while we await our afternoon tea, shall we walk in the gardens?" He smiled genuinely and held out his arm for her to take.

She took it. "A delightful idea." Even Peter was preferable to staying in the midst of the angry occupants of the house. They walked in silence for a while, both thoughtful, both reluctant to speak.

"Peter?"

"Katrina?"

They both laughed. "Go on, Katrina. What is it that's on your mind?"

She took a deep breath and plunged in. "You're not one of them, Peter. Are you? Have you killed anyone?"

"No."

"Get out then. Go. Go while you still can. They are not going to win."

"You don't understand, my dear."

"I'll see that your money is returned to you. As soon as this is all sorted out, I'll repay you every cent Sam took."

"Why so much concern for me?"

"Because you're Zack's brother."

"Zack! It always comes back to Zack. All my life it's been Zack, Zack, Zack."

She frowned questioningly. "In what way?"

"Everything was fine until he was born. Mom, Dad, me, we were a family. When Zack was born, everything changed."

"Peter, babies have a way of changing a household. Babies require attention and caring, and time. As an adult, you can appreciate that."

"It wasn't only the baby. Dad would go away for weeks at a time. He'd found another woman, so he had no time for me either. I blamed my mother for that also. And Zack."

"But surely now you can understand. You're not a child anymore."

"I was sixteen, Katrina, when I realized father meant never to return. Sixteen. I had offers for work. Folks knew the situation, they knew I'd have to find a way to support my ma and my kid brother. But I didn't want to. I left town."

"What did they do?"

"I don't know. But obviously they managed."

"Then what you told me before was a lie."

"Some of it. I did get letters from Zack. I always blamed him for taking what I wanted from me, my mother, my father, my home. It all fell apart when he was born.

"Zack grew to hate me as much as I hated him. When Dad left, Zack suggested I go too. He said he could take care of Mother as well as I could. The kid was only eight, but he sounded twenty."

"Can't you put that behind you now?"

"I've tried to. He wouldn't let me see Mother when she was ill, he saw to it that I received nothing from her when she passed away. Not even a keepsake. I wanted the ring you're wearing. It made me furious when you showed it to me in Sacramento. I had wanted to put it on your finger. But again Zack had come along to rob me of love and happiness.

"Zack means to take you from me. You know I've grown fond of you, Katrina, and I'm very attracted to you." He stopped and pulled her into his arms. He buried his face in the crook of her neck, taking handfuls of her loose hair and pressing kisses in it.

"You asked me why I didn't leave here. It's because of you. Do you think I could have put up with the Bennetts for this long without a very good reason? I've been waiting for you, darling. Zack was very happy to help me find you when I asked him. How he must have laughed when he devised the perfect revenge. I don't intend to let my little brother take you from me."

"Why revenge?"

"Because after all he'd done for Mother, in the end, she asked for me. He must have hated that."

He tilted her chin up and looked into her face. "You are beautiful. More beautiful than your mother."

She remained in his arms, letting him hold her, touch her, though she had to fight her revulsion and her desire to break away and flee. Peter was her safety. If he thought she might come around to wedding him, he would protect her against

Sam. It was urgent that she keep them fighting among themselves, suspecting each other's motives.

A movement at one of the upstairs windows caught her attention. Someone was watching them. She wrapped her arms around Peter's neck and leaned into him. Her whole body, her whole manner was begging him to kiss her. With a deep groan, he tightened his arms and covered her lips with his.

# Chapter 19

Corinne stormed out of the back guestroom, where she had stood watching the two people in the garden below. Down the hall in her own room, she slammed the door and moved to pose in front of her cheval glass, still in just her undergarments after having removed her soiled dress. Her cheeks were flushed, her eyes glittery green with jealousy. She turned this way and that, studying herself in the mirror. She was beautiful. More beautiful than her. How dare he kiss Katrina. How dare he want her.

Intense hatred roiled within her until she grabbed her Wedgwood powder jar and hurled it into the mirror. *Katrina—Katrina—Katrina—* the shattered glass mocked as it cascaded to the floor.

She dissolved into tears of helpless rage, flinging herself onto her bed, her fists pounding out her frustration.

"I want her dead, I want her dead," she sobbed.

From the doorway, Sam watched, but only for a moment before silently closing her door again. He couldn't bear to see her so tormented. He had hoped she was getting better, but just lately he'd caught that haunted look in her eyes again. Bloodlust.

He went to the library and poured himself a whiskey, ignoring the tray of tea and coffee that Flora had replaced. He downed one shot and poured a second.

Shock, insecurity . . . That had been the diagnosis of the doctor he had consulted shortly after the fire that had killed

Corinne's mother. He hadn't told the doctor all of it though. He looked down and rubbed the deep scar that ran the length of his right hand. He hadn't told him that Corinne, then only eight years old, had run out of the flaming house, laughing and wildeyed, that he and his wife had gone back for their son Raymond only to find his door locked. He hadn't told him that Corinne had hated the baby from the moment of his birth. He had only mentioned her deep depression when she learned that her mother had died trying to save the boy.

Nor, in later years when he had found reason to take her back to see the doctor, had he mentioned the woman he'd almost married. Corinne had locked her in the root cellar to punish her for being in his bed. For days she was shut down there before anyone heard her screams.

Nor did he mention the hunting dog he'd brought home one day, a fine English setter. He had loved that dog, and that had been his mistake. The dog disappeared when Corinne had taken him for a walk. She said he ran away from her and never came back, but he'd found the dog's body several days later. He didn't say anything. He was afraid to say anything for fear she would be taken from him and locked away in an asylum.

She got better in the passing years, and he'd begun to believe she was fine. And then he met Caroline Montgomery. He couldn't resist her beauty, and all that southern charm and southern money. Corinne had hated her on sight and had hated worse her daughter Katrina, who had everything a young girl could want.

Caroline's death was inevitable. Beauchamps then had to die. And so it was with the man in California. Katrina would be next. He could prevent it, of course, as he had done in the past year, but he wouldn't this time. Corinne was right. Katrina should have died long ago. If it hadn't been for all that money in New York, he'd have killed her himself. Old Man Montgomery had been clever, all right. If Katrina didn't claim her trust in person within six months of her twentieth birthday, it was to go to medical research. He hated that thought, but if Katrina didn't marry him tomorrow, that's just how it would have to be.

He couldn't lose the Manor. Corinne couldn't survive that.

He knew he couldn't keep covering for her forever, that someday someone would discover the truth. He needed the Manor. It was the perfect place for her, surrounded as it was by an iron fence. She could be let free within the bars to live as normal a life as possible without endangering anyone else. Her doctor would agree to it, he was sure.

"Shall I pour?" Katrina asked, strolling into the room at Peter's side. "I see Corinne has not yet returned."

"She is feeling indisposed. I don't expect her down this afternoon," Sam said crossly. "Do you see now how much of a disruption to the entire household your little fit of defiance has caused? Would it have been so very difficult to wait until after breakfast for your bath?"

"Bath? This has never been about my bath. It's been about power and retaliation. Is it so difficult for you to relinquish some of your iron-fisted control over every movement in this house? Don't mention my bath again. My bath was not unreasonable after days of travelling. Your reaction to it, however, borders on the maniacal."

"I must have discipline!" he shouted, infuriated at her choice of words.

"Why?"

"I won't have you staying in bed till noon."

"And have I ever?"

"No, because I don't permit it."

"I'm sorry to disabuse you, but Junie rarely has to waken me in the morning. Corinne, now that you brought it up, has been known to miss breakfast entirely, and the household was not disrupted by her tardiness. I don't think discipline is the word you mean. Dominance is what you're after. Arbitrary dominance, exerted when, where, however, and with whomever your whimsy demands. I will not be bullied, Sam Bennett. Not ever again."

"Goddamn, you'll do as I say and like it," he thundered, turning deep red.

"Easy, Sam," Peter warned. "You'll have a stroke."

"And wouldn't you love just that!"

"Excuse me. I'll forgo tea today," Katrina said. "Shall I pour your tea before I go, Sam? You really shouldn't become quite so agitated. See if you can calm him down, Peter."

That night Kate waited in her darkened bedroom for the hands of the clock to move around to midnight, when she would meet Junie. She would have lit the lamp and read a book, but she didn't want the others in the house to know she was still awake.

At shortly before eleven the sound of a horse on the lane drew Kate's attention. She watched from behind the drapes as the rider approached. The man strode up the porch steps and rapped on the front door.

Kate snuck out of her room and down the back stairs into the dark kitchen, feeling a sense of déjà vu wash through her. This was how it had all started, standing in the kitchen listening to a conversation she was not intended to hear. The ceiling above her creaked. Kate looked up, imagining Corinne listening from the top of the main staircase.

"Are you sure it's him?" Sam demanded. The night caller answered too quietly for Kate to hear. She opened the door a crack and peered out.

"A girl? How did . . . I thought you paid him . . ." Sam sputtered, glaring at Peter.

"So she got away," he said and shrugged. "It works to our advantage. Take one of the men and bring her back here. As soon as possible. And don't let anyone see you." The rider left hastily at his command.

"I thought you got rid of her. What if she knows? What if she talks?" Sam paced the front hall in a state of nervous anxiety.

"Relax. I did get rid of the girl. I paid to have her disappear, just as you ordered, which was a mistake. When we couldn't produce her, Katrina didn't believe we ever had her. Why are you so upset? Get hold of yourself, Sam. You're coming apart."

"If she talks . . ."

"It won't matter. Katrina wanted her friend to attend her wedding. Well, now she'll have her. She won't be able to delay any longer."

"Yes," Sam sighed, mopping his perspiring brow. "We can make her marry me tomorrow." He grinned, relieved.

"Or me."

Sam blustered again. "Everything's changed, Peter. She has to marry me. She's threatened to expose us. You're in the clear, legally. She could have me thrown in prison. She has to become my wife."

Peter shrugged. "I'll grant you have a problem, but it is me she prefers. I'm sure I can convince her to forget about prosecuting you and Corinne."

"You fools," Corinne spewed, coming down the stairs. "You stupid fools. Dogs fighting over a bone. You're supposed to be intelligent men, and here you are arguing over who gets to marry her. You make me sick. Do you recall what got us into this mess in the first place?"

Kate pressed closer to the door as their voices seemed to fade away. Suddenly the door swung open, forcing her to jump back, and there they were, the three of them, glaring at her.

"So you still like to spy," Corinne sneered.

"Shall I put the kettle on?" Kate asked. "Since we're all up . . ."

Sam pulled a key from his pocket and handed it to Peter. "Lock her in her room."

"No tea?" she asked over her shoulder as Peter took her arm and steered her down the hallway and up the stairs.

"Is there no end to the trouble you will cause?" he asked sardonically, glaring down his imperious nose.

"I did nothing," she said innocently.

"I suppose you heard?"

"That you lost Annie Spooner? Yes. I could have predicted that. So Zack is in town finally. I expected him to arrive ahead of us. He must have run into a problem."

"Why should he be here at all? He has no interest in you."

She smiled, genuinely amused. "Who are you trying to convince?"

He swung her around, pulling her hard against him, forcing the breath from her lungs. She fought against him, turning her face away from his lips.

"It will do no good to fight me. You will be mine."

"Let me go. I hate you," she cried in a harsh guttural whisper.

"You didn't hate me this afternoon in the garden. You'll forget my brother. You'll learn to love me."

"It's too late for that. Two years worth of abuse too late."

"I never abused you," he said, gripping her chin and forcing her to look at him.

"You never helped me either. And in this house, that's the same thing."

"You did well enough on your own. You needed help from no one. Little Snow Princess. Cold, untouched, untouchable. How often I wanted to take you to my bed and melt the ice around you."

"Instead you went to Corinne."

"She was willing enough."

"You're disgusting. Let me go."

"I find I don't want to do that. Tonight I want to see the woman I'm convinced is in there. You aren't ice, are you? That's an act you put on."

"Take your hands off me." She struggled against his strong hold on her waist, pushed against the hand seeking to fondle her breasts. "Stop it, Peter."

"No. Kiss me, Katrina."

His mouth found hers and ground the tender flesh of her lips against the hard edge of her teeth until she was forced to open her mouth to him. He bent her back over his arm, and she was helpless to fight him, she could only grab his shoulders and hang on.

"How touching." Corinne's voice dripped venom.

Peter lifted his head and turned toward the other girl, and Kate struggled, managing to break free and move away. She turned to Corinne, schooling her face to hide her turbulent emotions from both of them.

"Corinne. We didn't expect to see you." She gave a fake laugh. "Don't mind what you just saw. It was—nothing."

Corinne's face twisted in rage. She launched herself at Katrina, her hands extended, her fingers curved into claws. Peter stepped between them, holding Corinne at bay.

Kate patted Peter's arm gratefully. "Thank you. Don't

forget to lock me in. And you'd better keep the key. I wouldn't want to be strangled as I sleep," she said over her shoulder, throwing Corinne a smirk that incensed her all the more.

Kate paced back and forth in her bedroom, annoyed as the hands of her clock now perversely raced their way around the minutes until midnight. She went to the window and watched the guards move about from shadow to shadow below. Would Junie know to stay at home, or would she try to get over the fence to the big house? Would she know that more trouble was afoot?

Kate wanted to stay where she was, where she could watch for Annie, for if Annie was in town, Bennett would try to bring her to the Manor. And yet she needed to see Junie. If Junie knew a way off the property, a way to escape, then now, more than ever, Kate needed to know about it.

With Annie in captivity, Sam and Corinne could force her to do almost anything. All the horrors Sam had threatened her with, though she might be able to endure them, she could never allow to befall Annie. Not when this was a nightmare Annie had no part in.

"Zack, oh Zack, where are you?" she murmured with heartfelt urgency. It seemed hardly possible that only a week ago they had all been dining together at Zack's ranch, she and Zack, Annie and Dan, the Rollinses. Like a house of toy building blocks in the hands of a child, their beautiful world had collapsed, and a careless little foot had kicked the blocks in ten different directions.

She wondered if one of the fates, an older sister perhaps, was sitting back, watching indulgently as a younger sibling wreaked havoc on the painstakingly constructed lives of her mortals. Would she soon put the little one to bed and begin to pick up the scattered parts and fit them back together?

The downstairs clock chimed, dragging Kate from her musings. Midnight. She tried the door. It was locked as she knew it would be. She moved a straight-back chair to the door and braced it under the doorknob, securing her privacy from her own side of the door in case someone came looking for her.

One of the advantages of having lived at the Manor for the whole of her life, was that she knew every corner of the house.

It was to the corner of her large closet that she went, shoving dresses aside to reveal a slender panel. It didn't go to any mysterious passageway, just into the closet of the adjoining room, an escape route in case of fire, her grandfather had explained when he'd shown her the panels.

The door to the next room, an unoccupied room, was not locked. She let herself out into the corridor, and on silent feet, with no rustle of satin and petticoats, she crept to the back stairs. The kitchen was silent and dark, as was the foyer. Voices came from the library, but this night those inside had closed the doors.

Under the main staircase was a door leading down to the cellar. She opened it and stepped down a step so she could turn to close the door behind her. She searched blindly for the shelf on her right, her fingers reaching tentatively to find the matches that were kept there.

She struck a match and lit a candle. Taking several more matches with her, she lifted the candle and made her way down the narrow steps. She couldn't imagine how Junie was planning to get to the wine cellar unless she was thinking of climbing down the coal chute. The outside cellar doors were locked. Even at that, she'd have to get over the fence and cross the backyard first.

"Katrina," she heard whispered.

"Junie, where are you?" she answered.

Junie lit her own candle, directing Kate to the back corner of the wine cellar. "I thought you wasn't comin'."

"They locked me in. I had to go through the closet."

"Why they lock you in?"

"They're afraid I'll try to escape. My friend is in town, and they're going to bring her here and use her to make me marry one or the other of them."

"Oooh, that's why they was lookin' for the iron."

"Iron?"

"One of the guards came to the house for Cyrus. He wanted Cyrus to show him where the irons are kept."

"What irons are you talking about?"

"Your granddaddy never used them. They for brandin' the slaves. Like old Henry got on his chest."

"Oh my God in Heaven. They're planning to use that on Annie to force me into marriage."

"Not on no white woman, surely? They can't do that."

"Junie, they can't do that to *anybody* these days. At least, not legally. And they won't to Annie, if I can do anything to stop them."

"You must leave here."

"That would be wonderful. If the guards outside would go home, I'd give it a try."

"You go the way the slaves went."

"But that . . ." That was secret trails, old barns, supply wagons with false floors, caves . . . "How did you get here? How did you get past the guards?"

"Through the tunnel. Mama showed me. It runs from the spring house into the old cistern. Mr. Montgomery put a door through to here. It ain't used no more for bringin' in water. And it ain't big, but it'll git us outside the guards. Mama says you ought to go tonight."

"I must wait and see if they manage to get Annie. Can you meet me back here at three o'clock? I'll know by then. If they don't get her on the first try, they won't get her at all."

Annie had just dozed off after tossing restlessly in her bed for hours. Her sleep was not peaceful; she was disturbed by sounds, smells, a sense of unease. She rolled over.

At once her mouth and nose were covered by a heavy pad of material saturated with the potent essence of chloroform. She fought to free herself, to scream for Dan and Zack in the next room, but hands held her everywhere, suffocating her until she had to draw deep breaths of chloroform into her nose and mouth, restraining her arms and legs until the feeling and strength in them evaporated. She felt herself being rolled into her blankets, lifted, carried down stairs, and then she felt nothing as she slid into black unconsciousness.

She was confused. She tried to kick at the covers that bound her too tightly, but they only tightened more. It took several minutes for her head to clear, for her to realize someone was holding her, that they were on a horse, that she was bound in her blanket, and gagged.

She moved convulsively, trying to sit up and away from the man's hard chest.

"Easy, girlie. I'm only takin' you for a short ride. You behave now, and I won't have to give you no more of that smelly stuff. It can be dangerous, you know, if you git too much of it."

He was right. She leaned back against him and tried to calm herself, but her heart was racing and she couldn't seem to get enough air. She hated having her mouth covered.

She mumbled to him pleadingly, turning her face up. When he did nothing but look at her curiously, she used his shoulder to try to work the gag down.

"You don't like this?"

"Ung-ung." She continued her guttural muttering.

"Okay, okay, just a second." He slid the binding down and removed the wadding from her mouth.

She gasped for air, filling her lungs again and again. "Please don't put it back. I can't breathe with it. I won't yell. I promise."

"Yeah, all right. No one to hear you now, anyhow."

"Where are we? Was I asleep long?"

"Ten minutes. Fifteen. We're almost there."

"Where? Where am I going?" she asked, but she knew already. She recognized the road.

"To see a friend."

"Is this a special invitation?"

He chuckled. "Yeah, you could say so."

"Bennett's place, right? He must be gettin' desperate if he has to kidnap women. What does he want with me?"

"Hey, I just follow orders. I don't ask questions."

She sighed and relaxed against him. "I guess he'll tell me soon enough. Weren't there two of you?"

"Yeah, but I sent him on ahead. I don't need help to get a mite of a scrap like you back there. Ain't much to ya."

That had been said before, Annie thought. This man, like the others, could probably be duped and dumped, but where would that leave her? If she went willingly, she'd get inside the

Manor. She'd be able to see Kate, to help her escape.

Her only regret was that Zack and Dan had not met Jake. At least they knew who he was and where he lived. If they had any sense, they'd be waiting for Jake when he returned from his trip upriver.

Annie had glimpsed the Manor once or twice while travelling through the area, but she had never seen it at close range, and she was agog at its size and splendor. The house was white brick, gleaming in the silver moonlight, with six tall pillars in front that supported the roof extending over the wide porch. She counted six windows across the second story.

"Holy Jehoshaphat!" she murmured. "It must have thirty rooms."

Her captor snorted. "Yeah. You ain't never been here before?"

"Never." And nothing brought home to her Kate's utter desperation more than the sight of what she was willing to abandon for her freedom.

The guards, alert to their approach, stopped them to check their identities before allowing them access through the high wrought iron gates.

"Is the whole place fenced?" she asked. No wonder the sheriff had called it a fortress.

"Two or three acres around the main house, I guess. Hell of a place."

"Are there other gates than this?"

"Sure," he answered, glancing at her. He chuckled. "But they're guarded around the clock. You won't escape this place, girlie. Might as well forget that idea right now."

"Yes. You're probably right." She sighed resignedly. "I suppose there are worse prisons."

The front door opened, flooding them with golden light. From the cradle of her captor's arms she looked up to see Sam Bennett. She remembered him well, his arrogant posture, his long nose and jutting jaw, his hard, cold eyes. He grabbed her chin and tilted her face to the light.

"You!" He gave a snort of laughter. "I didn't believe she could get away on her own."

"We all need help at one time or another, Mr. Bennett," she answered.

"Put her down and untie her," Sam ordered. "Then get back to your post."

Another man and a woman came through the doorway from a side room as the guard followed his orders, freeing her and taking his leave. Annie turned to study them.

"You must be Peter. I've heard so much about you from Kate. No wonder she was suspicious. You are very much like Zack. A little older, not quite so distinctive, a bit more . . . Well, never mind. And you must be—Corinne?"

"I suppose she told you about me, too," Corinne said importantly, pressing herself against Peter's arm.

"Well, yes, but I got the impression you were about thirteen years old. How could I have made such a mistake?"

Peter laughed outright and turned to tousle Corinne's hair. "Actually . . ."

Corinne jerked away and threw him a poisonous glare. "Go ahead and laugh. I find it equally amusing to hear you described as a pale copy of your brother."

"Peter, please escort this young woman to her accommodations. I shall bring Katrina to see her presently."

Annie pulled her blanket tighter around her and lifted the edge that was dragging on the floor. With her chin bravely elevated, she accompanied Peter to a door beneath the staircase, a door leading downward into darkness.

"All of these empty rooms and I'm to be thrown into a cellar? A dungeon?"

"Sorry, Miss Spooner, but if you are enjoying the full comforts of the manor, what incentive exists for Katrina to cooperate with us?"

"Ah, I'm supposed to suffer, hmm, and you are counting on Kate's gentle heart to put an end to my agony."

"You are very astute. That is precisely what will happen."

"And so I will be taking my comfort at the cost of Kate's suffering? I don't believe either of us will go that far."

"We shall see." He led her into a corner room and lit a candle, placing a glass chimney over the flame. A narrow cot sat against the concrete wall. On the cot was a folded sheet and a couple of blankets and a pillow.

"Hospitality at its best," she said dryly, casting Peter a look of disdain. "Could you find no better life for yourself?"

He gave an indifferent shrug. "It would be to your benefit, as well as Katrina's, to convince her to marry me tomorrow."

"But mostly to yours."

He inclined his head. "And to mine."

Footsteps sounded haltingly on the stairs, and both Annie and Peter turned as Sam led Katrina toward them. Kate stood passively beside Sam when they reached the narrow room, observing the characters in this new scene of the play. She gave Annie a slight smile of recognition.

"Annie, it's nice to see you again. Did you tire of California so soon?"

Annie, as she'd done frequently in the past when she saw that look in Kate's eyes, played along. "I missed my friends here. One in particular. I was hoping to see him tomorrow, but I guess it will wait."

"Well, have you everything you need?"

Annie opened her blanket to reveal her plain nightdress. "I could use some clothes, oh, and shoes. I was snatched from my bed."

"How unmannerly. I shall see you are provided with the necessities in the morning. Sleep well."

"That's enough. I wanted you to face each other. You see, Miss Spooner," Sam explained, "Katrina refused to marry me until you were with her for the ceremony. Now that you are—"

"Oh my, I am confused. Mr. Standish just now told me he was marrying Kate. I must have misunderstood. No, I'm certain, because he agreed that he would have much to gain by marriage to Kate."

"Oh, did he now?"

"Papa, aren't you finished down there yet? Should I come down?"

Sam looked toward the stairs. "No, we're coming directly. Stay up there. It's dirty down here."

"Hurry then. I've made tea."

"That ought to be a delight," Peter drawled under his breath, bringing reluctant grins to the girls' faces.

"Come along, Katrina. Peter can lock your little friend in for the night, I'll lock you in. Tomorrow after the wedding you can move her into the room next to yours. I'll even provide an allowance for a new wardrobe for her as we've separated her from her own."

"How generous of you," she responded without inflection or expression. "Good night, Miss Spooner," Kate added, as Sam steered her away.

Peter closed the bulky wood door between him and Annie. She heard the heavy key turn in the rusted lock, then rattle against a glass jar as Peter replaced it on some high shelf by the door.

With nothing left to do except wait, she made up her bed and crawled under the warming blankets. Cellars were always so cool and damp in the Mississippi Valley. This one was no exception.

Kate was returned to her room, shoved unceremoniously in the door, and made a prisoner again in her own home. Her own home. It was certainly intended to be a prison. She crossed her bedroom and looked out the window across the vast acreage that made up the Manor. Home. Home was Sacramento. Home was Zack.

"I don't belong here anymore, Grandpa," she whispered. "I shall always cherish my memories of you and my childhood home, but the Manor is no longer that place. Do you understand, Grandpa?" How unfortunate that the good always drowned beneath the bad in the mind. That shouldn't be so.

She tiptoed to her closet and took two riding skirts from their hangers, one she had just purchased in the spring, and one she'd outgrown. It should fit Annie. Underclothes, heavy socks, boots, blouses, warm jackets followed, all in pairs, one set for her, one for Annie. She took down from the top shelf a wide carryall, done in delicate needlepoint, and began to fill it with clothes Annie would need. She added candles, matches, threw in a pair of scissors, a few silver-framed photographs. She found she was grabbing all sorts of incidental things she'd never need. She made herself put most of them back. In place of what she left behind she added the selection of music she had taken to her room, including Beethoven's "Für Elise."

She dressed and sat by the window, waiting for the house to settle down for the night. At twenty minutes after two, she slowly inched aside the panel in her closet and climbed through. Carrying her boots and her satchel, she crept to the door.

# *Chapter 20*

The hallway outside Katrina's room was lit by a wall lamp. The door she'd used earlier was still unlocked, but it may as well have been boarded shut, for outside in the hall, across from the door, reading a newspaper by the light of the lamp, sat a guard.

She closed the door. "Damnation," she muttered on a breathless whisper. So now what? Now when escape was so close. Would she be forced to marry Sam or Peter to spare Annie? Because Sam was right. She could never permit Annie to suffer even the least little bit for her sake, for the sake of a piece of property she didn't want. So maybe she should just sign that document handing everything over to Bennett. At least she'd be free. Or would she? Would Bennett let her go, knowing she could accuse him of murder, and probably prove her case, now that she had the will? The thought of being forever locked behind the wrought iron fence was too much to bear. She'd rather face her death.

But not Annie's. She had to get away and take Annie with her. Her eyes fell on the white brick fireplace across the room. She grinned. She could do it. Or at least give it a good try.

The small doors below the bookcases that bracketed the hearth opened to bins for storing wood and coal. Every bedroom at the manor had its own fireplace, each of them across the room from the closet. And as the closets opened into the adjoining rooms, so did the storage bins. If she were very careful and quiet, she needn't go into the hall at all except to take a few steps at the top of the back stairs.

She returned to her own room, straightening the closets as she went to keep her escape route a secret. She opened the wood bin at the other end of her room. It was nearly full. She moved as many logs as she could into the grate of the fireplace, and the last few pieces she shoved under her bed. She squeezed through the opening into the other room, ignoring the snags she put in her clothing. She reached back for her carryall, and when she had tugged it through, she closed the doors to both rooms.

As noiselessly as possible she crossed the room that had once been her mother's boudoir and entered the spacious closet.

Caroline Bennett had moved to the room at the far end of the house shortly after she married Sam, and after Lawrence Montgomery had died. Had Sam begun to mistreat his wife as soon as Lawrence Montgomery was no longer alive to prevent it? Katrina wondered.

The room was kept closed and locked, the furniture covered, drapes drawn. Katrina had once imagined that the Bennetts were afraid of her mother's ghost in the end room. It had been a fanciful idea at the time, but now she could see that they had good reason to avoid any reminder of what they had done to Caroline Montgomery.

Kate found the sliding panel in her mother's closet. Her entrance into the next room, from behind the long row of sheet-covered gowns, was blocked by boxes, which she had to slide to one side. The back room, utilized for storing unused furniture and boxes of odds and ends, was cluttered and so full she had difficulty maneuvering through it without making noise.

She opened the door a crack and peered into the hallway. In passing through her mother's room, she had turned the corner to the north ell of the house, to the rooms over the kitchen which were intended to house the cook and housekeeper. The guard was around the corner from Kate, although she could see his shadow moving now and then on the floor and the walls, and she could smell the smoke from his cigar.

She entered the hall, closing the door behind her and holding her carryall tightly against her breast, lest it bump against something and give her away. Ever so slowly she moved toward the narrow back stairs.

The rest of the house was quiet, and Kate made her way again to the cellar with only a flickering candle for light.

"Junie," she called in a raspy whisper.

The scrape of a match against the stone floor alerted Kate to Junie's presence before the orange glow of the match flared in front of her friend's dark face. Junie lit a lantern and brought it into the main body of the cellar with her.

"Here I am. I was worried you couldn't come."

"They put a guard in the hallway. I had to sneak through our secret doors."

"Landsakes, I ain't thought of them in years."

"Why were you in the dark?"

"I thought maybe you was one of them. Did they get your friend?"

"Yes, she's locked in the back room."

"Down here? Oh." Junie sighed. "Thank goodness. I thought there was ghosts down here. I heard breathing, a voice, someone cussin'. I was ready to run if you didn't come soon."

"Come meet her. Her name is Annie, and she does cuss now and again. She helped me get away the last time." Kate tapped on the heavy oak door. "Annie," she called softly. She tried the door.

"Kate, is that you?"

"Yes, we're getting out of here. Did you see where Peter took the key from when he opened this room?"

"No, it was already open, but I heard him put it in something like a glass dish after he locked me in. To your left, I think, and up high."

"Here it is," Junie said, handing the heavy key to Kate.

Kate dealt with the door in quick order and drew Annie out of her solitary confinement. "Annie, this is Junie. Here, I brought you some clothes. How did you get here? Is Zack here, too? Peter said—"

"No time for this," Junie cut in. "We must get away while the night is still with us. By sunup we must be far into the cave."

"Cave? There's a cave?" Kate asked accusingly. "You never told me about a cave."

"My ma knew. She didn't want us goin' there, so she didn't tell us."

Annie hastily donned the clothes Kate pulled out of the satchel for her. "Ooh, this jacket feels good. It's chilly down here."

"It will be cold in the cave," Junie said. "Take the blankets with you. My ma said to take plenty of candles and matches and a lantern, if you can manage that. I'll look around for some."

"Check the top of the stairs. What about food? Will we need any?" Kate asked.

"Ma will have that at the spring house."

"Here's a lantern," Kate said, "and a tin of kerosene."

"And here are the blankets," Annie said, stuffing them in the carryall. "I'm taking this rope I found. I always like to have rope handy when I'm going into an unknown cave."

"How many have you been in?"

"None."

"We must go," Junie said, leading them to a rack of wine at the end of the cellar. The rack stood slightly away from the wall, and behind it, as the girls could see when Junie moved a light toward it, was a low door. "Crawl through there. I'll follow and move the rack back into place."

"Well, I'll be," Kate said, studying the moving rack, the door that had been painted to look like the rest of the stone walls, and the black hole in the hall. "Grandfather did this?"

"So I'm told. Can you imagine what mischief we'd a got into if we'd know'd this was here?"

Kate shook her head. "I'd hate to think." She lit the lantern and led the way through the crawl space.

"Have I ever mentioned that I hate being in dark tunnels?" Annie said from behind her.

"Have you been in as many tunnels as caves?"

"Exactly. How far do we go in here?"

The tunnel, shored up with rotting fenceposts and broken boards, had seen better days. Twenty years had passed since its original use, Kate reminded herself. She wished she'd been alive then to help those people, people like Raleigh and Jasmine and Davey, from bondage into freedom.

"Annie, did Jasmine tell you about my grandfather? Did she say he helped them get to the North?"

"She mentioned something about it. Hadn't you guessed by then?"

"Not at all. Junie's mother just told me."

"What do you think about it?"

"I think *you* should have told me."

"No, I mean what—"

"I know what you mean. I'd like to have known him then. The White Fox. He would have let me help. I know he would have. You back there, Junie?"

"Right behind you."

"I found my grandfather's will. He left the village and the sixty acres around it to your mother, Henry, old Jedadiah, Millie and Russell."

"What that you say?" Junie squealed.

"It's true. He meant for them to own their homes and their own land. Bennett had to know that. He's been cheating all of us. I'll make it up to you, I promise."

"I see a light up ahead," Annie said, relief paramount in her voice.

Flora helped them out of the tunnel, brushing the dirt from their clothes. "We must be quiet. We are outside the fence, but still close to the guards. Now you listen. You go from here with no light. You follow the creek upstream. Stay to the left. About a mile up you will find a pile of rocks. Go left there, up the side of the ravine. About halfway up you'll find a narrow crack between two rocks. That is the entrance to the cave. It will be grown over, so you must look for it."

The entire creekbed was overgrown on either side with brush. Only a trickle of water wended its way downstream, where in spring the stream ran in torrents. As soon as they rounded the bend that separated them from the lights of the Manor, Kate lit the lantern.

"How did they do it in the dark without killing themselves?" Kate asked.

"They probably had the good sense to stay put when a storm was coming and the moon was hid," Annie said dryly.

"Ouch. That's twice I've turned my ankle."

"Are you all right?" Kate asked. "Let me carry the satchel now. You take the lantern so you can see where you're going."

The small mountain of rocks was not difficult to find. It rose directly out of the creekbed on the inside of a bend where the water wouldn't wash at it so fiercely.

"I'll go up and look for the cave entrance," Junie said. "You stay here and rest a minute."

Kate sat down and helped Annie out of her boot. She probed her slender ankle. "Does it hurt?"

"Nah. I told you, I only twisted it. I do it all the time."

"Annie, what about Zack? I've been going quietly crazy wondering if he betrayed me. Peter said he was involved from the first."

Annie snorted, tugging her boot back on. "Peter said! That should have told you something. Don't worry about Zack. He was beside himself, according to Dan, when he realized you were missing. By the time I got back to Sacramento, they'd put most of the story together. Zack had you investigated."

"What?!"

"He also sent the jewels back so you wouldn't be charged with theft. He did it for you, Kate. Don't be mad at him."

"He had me investigated?"

"It's because he did it that his lawyer was able to see what Bennett was up to."

"When you got back from where? Peter said they had you, but I didn't believe them."

"They did. They hired a boy no older'n me to keep me away till they got done with you."

"Oh-oh. Only one?"

"I found it," Junie cried from up on the bluff. Just then she gave a sharp cry, and Kate and Annie heard her sliding down the loose rocks. They turned at the sound and ran to help her, finding her at the foot of the hill. She was sitting up, holding her right leg. Her dark face was twisted into a grimace of pain.

"Oh, Junie, what have you done?"

"I saved the lantern," she said, and gave a stifled cry of agony when Kate tried to straighten her leg.

"You'll have to leave me," Junie said, wiping back tears she couldn't prevent. "It's broken."

"Don't be ridiculous. We can't leave you here."

"We'll have to straighten your leg," Annie said.

"No, please. Don't touch it."

"Kate, get behind her and hold her hips. And brace yourself. I'm going to have to pull on it."

"Do you know what you're doing?" Kate asked.

"I set one broken bone before. I don't know if I can do it this time, but I have to try. We can't leave it bent like that. It will hurt, Junie. But whether you come with us or stay, you're still gonna have to be able to move."

Kate positioned herself with her legs straddling Junie's. She braced her heels against the rocks and held tight to her lifelong friend. "Scream if you need to, sweetheart."

The first scream, smothered into one of the blankets, came when Annie turned Junie's leg so that it lay straight. The second came when she pulled until the break was realigned.

"Is that it?" Kate asked, blinking back tears for Junie's pain.

Annie ran her hands along Junie's slender leg, probing to test her work. "It feels set. Does it hurt as much?"

"It hurts plenty," Junie said. "Let me get my breath for a minute. Jes' don't touch me, okay?"

"I'm going to find something for a splint and crutches. While I'm gone, could you tear that sheet into strips for me."

Annie took the lantern and went in search of what she needed. Kate gave Junie a hug and leaned her back onto the satchel.

"I'm sorry you got hurt. I never meant for you to be involved in this."

"I was careless. You ain't to blame. Katrina, you have to go on without me. There's climbing' to do in that cave. Everywhere. I can't go with you."

"Can you get back home?"

"If your friend can patch me up and get me a crutch, I can make it. Only I can't do it before daylight. They'll know I helped you and they'll be able to trace my tracks back to the cave. You have to be long gone by then."

She withdrew a folded cloth from her skirt pocket and pressed it into Katrina's hand. "This is an old map of the cave.

The trail is marked in red thread. Be careful you don't go the wrong way. Mama said the cave is full of dead ends and holes. Look where you put your feet."

"Junie," she said gently and wrapped her arms around her. "My dear friend."

Annie returned a few minutes later, two long forked sticks in one hand, a slab of bark in the other. "Got it. This will be perfect," she said, kneeling beside the other two. She tended Junie's leg gently but firmly until the break was supported and wrapped securely. She then padded the forks of the crutches with the leftover material.

"I can't take away the pain, but you'll be able to get around. We should go now. I'll help you up."

"Miss Annie, I'm not going."

"Course you are. We aren't leaving you. Besides, we need you."

"No. I'll hold you back. It's hard goin' in the cave. I can't manage with a broken leg."

Annie looked at Kate, her brow creased with concern. "Talk to her. Tell her."

"Junie's right," Kate said reluctantly. "She'll be safer if she goes home. She can make it in a few easy hours. She'll be in her own bed with her mother's comfort and care. With us she'd be in constant pain, trying to keep up. She could have a worse accident."

"I'll be fine, once I get home," Junie said tearfully. "Please, I want to go home. I hurt too much."

Annie took her hands and squeezed. "I know. I thought you wanted to go with us, that's all. You can go home, of course you can. In fact, I'll help you. We both will."

"No. No. You must go away from here. You must."

"Okay, okay. We will," Kate soothed. "You rest a while now and get your strength back. Take some of this food. When you feel up to it, start back, but take the trip in short distances with rests between. Don't tire yourself."

"And don't let Bennett bully you. You are a free woman. He has no rights over you," Annie said staunchly.

"If he tries, get the other workers behind you and walk away," Kate advised.

"Yes. Go to Jake Denning in Memphis. He'll help you."

"Yes, yes. Please go now. It's almost dawn. The cave is very long; don't give up hope."

Junie watched silently as Kate and her friend packed up their belongings and checked on matches and candles and refuelled their lamp. She had refused to keep the second lantern with her. The other girls would need it, and she intended to remain right where she was until dawn, anyhow.

"Thanks, Annie, for fixin' my leg. Take care of Katrina for me."

"I will, and we'll be back, just as soon as we get this straightened out."

The narrow opening of the cave widened abruptly after a few dozen yards, so that they found themselves in a large cavern with a steeply sloping floor.

"Would you look at this," Annie gaped. "Look, there's writing on the walls."

"Directions. They've marked the way."

"Over here." Kate followed Annie's light. Annie picked up an old rope and tested its strength. "Let's take it, just in case. And look at this. It's a miner's lantern."

"How does it work?"

Annie spit-shined the glass panels and the mirrored reflectors. "This ought to work, it isn't in too bad a shape. Hand me a small candle and a match."

"It would be great if we had extra light."

Annie attached the candle, lit it, and replaced the glass. The reflectors picked up the light and directed it forward. "See. They wore it like a hat. Like this. Hey, look."

Kate laughed. "What else can we find?"

"Nothing. We don't want to carry too much. As it is, we're going to share the load." She took the two blankets out of the satchel, unfolded them, and stuffed them with half of everything.

"Why are you doing that?"

"So that if either of us drops our pack down one of those endless holes, or falls in ourselves, the other pack will be safe." She folded the blanket securely and tied it with a piece of rope so that she could sling it over her shoulders and carry it on her back.

"Can you do that with my satchel? I'd love to have my hands free." She unfolded the map and studied it while Annie attached her satchel to a harness over her shoulders.

"You're not squeamish, are you?" Annie asked. "Afraid of mice or rats, or snakes?"

"Or bats?" Kate asked. "I heard them. No, I'm not squeamish."

"Good. All set?" she asked, adjusting Kate's bag to hang more evenly.

"That's great. So, we follow the arrows, right? They coincide with the marks on the map." She looked around her, reluctant to go on. Suddenly she slapped the map against her thigh and turned to Annie. "What are we doing here? We can't just go meandering off in some cave. I must be crazy. Let's get out of here and walk to town."

"Any minute now Bennett will know we're gone. Did your grandfather never explain to you how the white men used to hunt down the escaped slaves? They called out every able-bodied man and the best bloodhounds in the area. It became a sport. Jasmine and Raleigh were hunted like that. That's exactly how Bennett and his men will hunt us down."

"They can track us in here, too."

"Maybe, but it'll slow 'em down. We can make sure of it."

"We could cover the arrows, rub them out with dirt."

"Send them in the wrong direction." Annie laughed. "One thing I can say for you, knowing you has never been dull."

Zack was restless. He tossed in his narrow bed for nearly an hour, then gave up. He'd slept all he was going to. He pulled on his socks and trousers, slid his feet into his boots, grabbed his shirt and jacket, and let himself out of their room. Knowing that Dan wouldn't thank him for disturbing his sleep, he decided on a predawn walk.

He passed the door to Annie's room, and checked to see that it was still locked. It was. He tucked his shirt into his trousers and slid his arms into his jacket. The door at the end of the hall led onto a narrow set of stairs, an exit in case of fire. He let himself out that door and went quietly down to the street below. He glanced up, not knowing what had drawn his eye to Annie's room. Her window was wide open, her curtains billowing outward on the cool breeze.

He went back up the stairs to the landing of their floor. Her window was only a few feet from the stairs and accessible by way of a brick ledge wide enough to walk on.

What made him decide to walk it he'd never know. A feeling, an intuition. He reached Annie's room and stepped in through the open window, knowing if she were there and she saw him, she'd very likely kill him.

She was not there. Her clothes were hung neatly on hangers and hooks provided, her shoes were placed beside the bed. Her luggage was lying open at the foot of her bed, but Annie was gone. So were all the blankets from the bed.

Zack woke Dan with an urgent shake. "Get up, man. She's gone. They took Annie."

"Who? What? What time is it?"

"It's four o'clock."

"Four?" He groaned then shook himself awake. "How long ago?"

"Who knows? Get dressed. We've played enough games with Bennett. We're going out there and get those girls. Right now!"

"Whoa, now," Dan said, jumping up and snatching up his trousers. "Stop and think this out."

"What's to think? I'm done thinking. Now I'm going to do what I should have done earlier."

"What? Get yourself shot?"

Zack was raging back and forth across the braided rug. Dan was glad their room was above the registration offices, or they'd have irate guests pounding on their door.

"Calm down, Zack. You can't force your way into the Manor. You'll only put them on their guard more than they already are. If they have Annie, then they know we're here. They'll be watching for us."

"I'm going to get them out of there, and don't think I won't."

"All right, all right. I'll even go with you, but first let's go see this Jake fellow."

"It's four in the morning."

Dan closed his eyes and counted to ten. "If he's a friend of Annie's, he won't mind. I didn't."

"What good would that do?"

"I don't know, but Annie wanted his help. I say let's get it."

"Very well. So hurry up."

Jake Denning looked like a wounded bear when he flung open the door to his small cottage. "What the hell is this? Do you know what time it is?"

"Are you Jake Denning?"

"Who's askin'?"

"Mr. Denning, I'm Zack Standish. This is Dan Siebert."

"Standish? Kin to that other varmint? What do you want?"

"No—yes, but . . ."

"Mr. Denning, Annie sent us," Dan blurted.

That was the magic word. His anger disappeared and a quiet wariness crept into his eyes. "Annie?"

"Annie Sp[illegible]r. Short, red hair, mean as a—"

"Wet cat," Jake finished. "Come around back to the gazebo. I don't want to wake my wife."

"This is nice," Dan said, seating himself on the porch swing.

"I built it for Susanna's birthday last year. Annie liked it, too. So what's this about? Have you seen Annie? Is she all right?"

"Sit down, Jake," Zack said. "I have a long story to tell you, and then we need your help."

Jake barely moved a muscle while Zack related the pertinent facts to him. "So Bennett took Annie right outta her bed, eh?" he said when Zack finished.

"He needs her to get Katie to marry him. Him or my brother."

"And you want her for yourself."

"Hell yes, I do. But I don't give a damn about this plantation. I didn't even know she was an heiress until I got tossed in jail for murder."

"Mr. Denning, what can we do to get them away from Bennett?" Dan asked.

"First off, call me Jake. Second, you got some special

interest in my Annie?"

"I . . . well . . . I wouldn't like to see any woman mistreated."

"But you spent many an hour alone with her."

"Only because . . . Look, Mr.—Jake, my relationship with Miss Spooner is not at all . . . like that. And I'd advise you not to suggest that it is in her presence."

Jake laughed. "Yeah, well, she ain't too fond of men. Trust don't come easy to her."

"Jake, she seemed to think you'd be able to help us get Katie. Now we need you to help us get them both back."

"Yeah, right." He rubbed his bristly chin and narrowed his eyes thoughtfully. "It's been a while since I been out there. You got horses?"

"No."

"Let me get dressed. Come on in. I'll get Susanna to make us some breakfast then we'll saddle up and take a ride out there and look the place over."

"Saddle up?" Dan said uneasily.

Zack slapped his shoulder encouragingly. "You're doing it for Annie, my friend."

Dan did it, but it was not with any noble thoughts in his head. When they tied their horses in a small clearing in order to proceed on foot, Dan sent up a disgruntled prayer of thanks.

"Over the ridge is a spot where we can see most of the Manor. It ain't close, but I can't get you much nearer without getting you seen. Except for this ridge running across the edge of their land, most of Montgomery's spread is pretty level. A few hills here and there is all."

Jake pushed his way through underbrush, stepping easily over fallen logs, jumping from rock to rock. Zack was right behind him. Dan glared at them as he struggled to keep up without getting his trousers snagged or his shoes scuffed.

"This is not my idea of a pleasant outing."

Jake looked at Zack and grinned. "You don't care for the outdoors?" he asked over his shoulder to Dan.

"In measured doses and controlled circumstances, like a Sunday stroll in the park," Dan answered.

"He's exaggerating," Zack said. "He's out of sorts because

he had to ride a horse."

"Ah. Stay down now. We won't be far from the main road into the Manor."

The three men watched the sun rise over the hills to the far east and spread its morning hues over the vast croplands and pastures in the valley below their high perch.

"It's a beautiful place."

"Yes. Montgomery loved it. I don't blame him for wanting it to remain in the family."

Zack scanned the plantation with his spyglass. "And I don't blame Kate for wanting to keep it."

"Off to the southwest there, that village below the main house, those are servants' quarters. The foreman lives in the cottage by the stables."

"Is there any way to get inside that fence?" Dan asked.

"We could set up a diversion on one side to draw the guards, then hope to get over before they get back," Jake suggested.

"I don't like it," Zack said. "It's too open around the house, and those guards are apt to shoot at anything that moves. They'd probably get a fat bonus if they shot one of us."

"Zack, something's going on at the main house. Take a look over there."

"It's Bennett, I think, and . . . Well, well, well, my brother, if I'm not mistaken, they're arguing with the guards."

After another twenty minutes the argument had grown to include everyone at the Manor. The servants were lined up and questioned, the guards were sent into the house, the dogs were brought from the kennels.

After twenty more minutes, a small negro girl was brought from the back of the house and shoved to the ground in front of Bennett. Bennett took her by the hair and slapped her face. When the other servants moved to help her, they were held back or threatened at gunpoint.

"What the hell is he doing?" Zack thundered, getting to his feet.

"Shut up, man," Jake warned, pulling him back down. "You think you can help from here? You'd be shot before you got halfway down there. Bennett's outta his mind right now. Can't you guess why?"

"You mean they're gone?"

"That's right."

"But how?"

"And where are they?" Dan asked. "Those dogs will find them in a minute. Can you see them, Zack?"

"You won't see them," Jake said, grinning.

Zack's eyes narrowed. "What do you know that we don't?"

"I know why Annie wanted my help. I know where they are." He threw back his head and laughed.

# Chapter 21

"She didn't come out of her room, I tell ya," the guard insisted. "Not past me."

"Are you sure you were awake the whole time?" Corinne asked.

"She must have gone out the window."

"McLaughlin says no one moved on that side of the house," Sam said. "That's all, Cal, you can go."

"There's only one answer then," Corinne stated, her malicious eyes boring into Peter.

Peter's brows rose quizzically. "Am I being accused of something?"

"You've taken her, haven't you? Where is she? That's it, Papa. It has to be."

"Peter?" Sam Bennett asked seriously.

"Are you asking me whether or not I decided to save two young women from your evil machinations? It really shames me to have to admit that I did not."

"I don't believe you," Corinne spat. "You've been against my father and me ever since you learned about . . ."

"About what? Go on. About being cheated out of my life's savings?"

"Yes," she said baldly. "It would serve you well to see us defeated, reduced to shame and ruin."

"Come now, you're being rather over-dramatic."

"Am I? I saw you kiss her. Not once, but twice. You want her for yourself."

"Well, she is far easier to like than you are of late. Why shouldn't I prefer her company?"

"You won't get away with this," she screeched, flying at Peter with her fingers clenched into curved claws. "I'll kill you, do you hear? You'll never have her. No one will have her."

Peter fended off her attack, taking her wrists and flinging her away from him and into her father's arms, though not before she scratched his neck.

"My God, you're crazy. Keep her away from me," he snarled at Sam. "Take her down to the cellar and lock *her* away."

Sam Bennett went starkly white, then crimson with fury.

"How dare you? How *dare* you! Whatever she does or says, she's my daughter. My daughter."

Peter stood as if turned to stone. "Oh, my God. It's been her. All along she's been doing the killing. The lawyer, Caroline. How many others? The man in California? Katrina was never supposed to survive this, was she? And Annie Spooner?"

"You'll never be able to prove any of that," Corinne said, still furious and fighting to get away from her father.

"No doubt, but that doesn't make you any less ugly. I'm sick to my stomach that I actually . . . slept with you."

"Get out of here," Bennett snarled. "Go on. You've said enough."

"Hey, Mr. Bennett," called one of the guards, bursting into the front foyer. Sam let Corinne go and rushed out to meet him. The guard had Junie by the arm and was yanking her through the door.

Junie hopped on her good leg, using her crutches to try to keep her balance against the guard's shoving. Her eyes were reddened and puffy from crying, and she was clearly in severe pain.

"I found her sneaking back towards her village from out by the ridge."

"The ridge?"

"Thought you'd wanna know, considerin'."

Corinne followed the commotion into the hallway. "Whatever is . . . Junie, what have you done to yourself?"

"She claims she fell and broke her leg," the guard said sourly.

Bennett took Junie's arm. "That will be all, Joe. Good work. Get the dogs and the rest of the men over here. And send word that all the servants are to come to the yard. I want a word with each of them. Someone must know what's going on."

"I suppose this means we'll have to put up with Rachel after all," Corinne grumbled.

Flora came through from the kitchen to announce breakfast. She took one look at her daughter and forgot the morning meal. She physically removed Bennett's hands from Junie, helping her to the sofa in the parlor. In her mother's arms Junie gave way to her tears of pain.

"Rachel," Flora called, bringing the younger girl hustling carelessly into the room. "Go down and bring Cyrus back. I need him."

"Wha . . . yes, ma'am," Rachel said, glancing between Flora and Sam Bennett.

"Never mind," Bennett said. "I've already sent for all the servants."

"What about our breakfast?" Corinne asked. "I'm hungry."

"Your food is staying warm on the stove. You'll have to serve yourself today."

"Just a minute here. You're paid to—"

"Thank you, Flora," Peter said. "I'm quite sure we can manage to lift a spoon or two on our own behalf. Could I assist you in getting Junie to her own bed?"

"Cyrus will take her, sir. Don't let us be a bother to you."

"A bother? Don't you think this whole pathetic scene is a bother?"

"Corinne, just shut your mouth for once," Peter flared. "The poor child is in extreme pain."

"What were you doing out at the ridge?" Sam asked.

"Nothin', sir."

"Nothing?" Corinne sneered. "You broke a leg doing nothing?"

"I went for a walk, and fell down."

"And just happened to have all this lovely material to make a bandage?" Corinne asked, spying the white cotton sheet tied around the splint and padding the crutches.

"Where did this come from?" Sam interrogated.

"I found it."

"That's enough," Flora said, helping Junie to stretch out on the sofa. "Don't fret now, child. I'll help you home and give you something to ease your pain."

"Not so fast. Where are they, Junie?"

Junie didn't even bother to dissemble. "They're gone. They're far away from this evil place by now."

"Where?" he thundered, stepping threateningly close.

"Don't you touch her," Flora warned.

"Papa, you can't mean to take that sass from a servant."

"No, I do not. You will tell me, young lady, exactly where they are."

"She ain't tellin' you nothin'," Flora said, glaring at her employer.

"I'll have her thrown her in jail for kidnapping."

"Then you go right on and git your sheriff and your judge over here."

"You will tell me, or you will find yourself and all your people without homes and without work."

"Ceptin' you can't kick us off land you don't own," Junie shot back. "Our homes is ours and our land is ours. Katrina told me so."

"Papa," Corinne shrieked. "She has it. She has the will."

"Mr. Bennett," the same guard interrupted for the second time. "The servants are outside."

Sam dragged Junie up, giving her only a second to prepare herself to hobble out. Once outside he shoved her so that she fell painfully to the ground in front of all the servants who were assembled.

"I want to know where they are," he ordered them all. "And one of you will tell me."

At their mutinous silence, he ordered the branding iron to be heated in the kitchen stove.

"Slavery is over," Junie said from the ground. "You can't hurt us no more like that. *You'll* go to jail."

Sam took her by the hair and slapped her across the face. "Enough of your impertinence. Where is she?"

"Gone," she spat. "I helped her get away from you, and I'm proud to say it. And I quit."

He raised a hand to strike her again, but Cyrus stopped him. "No more."

"How dare you lay hands on a white man," Sam bellowed. "Bring that iron."

The men clearly didn't want to get involved in anything of the sort and were slow to respond to Sam's orders. The servants gathered around Junie as Cyrus lifted her gently in his arms. "We won't be workin' for you no more, Mr. Bennett. We all quit. We can find work someplace else where they don't hit women."

"Then get off my land."

"Take me home, Cyrus," Junie said. "We don't have to leave the village. Miss Katrina told me that Mr. Montgomery gave us that land when he died. It belongs to us now."

The servants, amused and delighted at the news, turned with Cyrus and Junie to return to their homes. "Mama," Junie said, "get Rachel and bring her home."

Two men arrived as the entire workforce was leaving. "We've found their trail," one of them said. "They're hidin' in a cave."

"What cave?"

"Up on the ridge."

"Well, get 'em out of it."

"We can't do that. The place is honeycombed with passageways. They could be anywhere."

"Then dynamite it. Bring it down on their heads."

"Sir?"

"You heard me."

"But . . ."

"Mr. Bennett wants you to murder his stepdaughter for him, Cal. Isn't that plain enough for you?" Peter drawled.

"Yes sir, but I ain't murderin' no woman. I quit, too."

"Then quit, but you won't get paid," Bennett roared, turning red. His eyes bulged with frustrated fury. "Is there no loyalty left in the world?"

"Papa, don't excite yourself," Corinne said. "I'll take care of everything." She took him by the arm and led him into the house. "Sit down. I'll pour you a brandy."

"It's no good," he said, and wept into his hands. "I wanted it for you, but I've lost it."

Corinne became alarmed. He'd always been so strong, so sure. She'd never seen him broken. She'd never seen his shoulders bent, tears on his face. She was filled with an unholy hatred that Katrina had caused this weakness in him. She detested weakness.

"We haven't lost it yet. You drink this and rest for a while. I have some errands to run."

"Where are you going?"

"I'll be back shortly. Don't worry about a thing now."

Katie's foot slipped. She managed to keep the lantern from breaking, but she fell hard onto her backside and slid down the slippery rock to the mud below.

"Kate, are you okay? Kate?"

"Just winded," she called back to Annie. "Be careful, that's like ice." She lifted the lantern to look at the steep milky incline, its long smooth surface leading up to Annie's light above. "Good heavens, it's like a glass mountain."

"Do you see any markers?"

Kate stood ankle deep in mud and lifted the lantern over her head to look around. She slogged her way forward.

"There's another fork here," she called, "but I can't tell if either branch goes anywhere. I'll check."

"Is it on the map?"

Katie studied the muddied cloth. "No. There's nothing like this. I don't think we're where we hope we are."

"I'm coming down."

"No. Wait. Annie, we've got to face it. We're lost."

"Maybe Junie's ma didn't get the map right. And we're *not* lost. We can always backtrack. You marked the trail."

"Well, what do you think we should do? Go back or go on?"

Annie sighed. "I suppose, if you don't see any markings down there, we should go back and double-check some of the other tunnels. Maybe we simply missed it."

"Let's do that. This place doesn't seem to go anywhere. Toss me down one end of the rope."

They retraced their steps to a point some ways back,

climbing up and down the treacherous paths in the near dark. They arrived at a juncture of three possible paths, none of which was marked, and sat down to rest.

"Let's eat something. It must be near noontime," Annie said. "One of those boiled eggs?"

"I'll bet you're sorry you ever met me," Kate said, tossing her an egg. "Look at us."

Annie laughed. "You're a muddy mess," she said, and they both laughed until they were worn out.

"It's odd in here, isn't it?" Kate mused. "The darkness is so complete, the black so black, that our light seems to get swallowed up in it. How are you doing with candles?"

"I have plenty. I think you ought to turn up your wick though, at least until we're on the right trail again."

"Very well. Do you think we ought to go back?"

Annie chewed at her lower lip. "I don't know. I wouldn't want to fall into Bennett's hands again. Kate, they're insane."

"Yes, they're awful."

"No. I mean insane. At least she is."

"Corinne? She's just a brat."

"No. She's crazy. She has madness in her eyes. True madness."

Kate didn't know how to reply. She'd never thought of Corinne in those terms. Really mad? "She does become irrational at times."

"What puzzles me is why Peter stays with them. He seems . . . well, not so bad."

"Don't be fooled, just because he looks like Zack. I've known him for years, remember?"

"I got the feeling he was disgusted with the both of them."

"He is. They cheated him. I did offer to reimburse him if he got out before he was forced to hurt someone."

"I think he'd like to."

"Now that I'm gone, perhaps he will. He was holding on to the hope that I'd marry him."

"Ah. I see. Greed wins out, eh? Well, that settles it. We don't go back. At least not yet. If nothing more, we can hide out in here."

"Unless they discover it and come looking for us. With

the dogs."

Kate stood up and stretched, lost her balance and fell against the wall of the cave as the rock floor beneath her feet trembled and shifted. A dull roar thundered through the cracks and crevices, echoing round and round through the cave. The glass of their lanterns danced against the metal frames.

"What was that?" Annie cried. "An earthquake?"

"I don't know. I don't think a tremor makes that kind of noise, but then I've never been inside the earth during one."

"You don't suppose . . ."

"No, they wouldn't do a thing . . ."

Their gazes met, both knowing the truth in spite of their denials.

"So, I guess we go on," Annie said resolutely.

"Yes. There is a way out of here. We have only to find it."

"Are you scared?"

"I was more scared when we had the option of going back the way we came. I was afraid we were making a mistake by coming in here. Now that doesn't matter. Now we . . . just get out. Are you afraid?"

"No, I don't think I am, either. Come on, let's find that arrow we missed."

Dan was back in the saddle, and still not liking it. He eyed Zack, sitting comfortably astride his horse, looking at home in his plaid flannel shirt, coarse denim pants, and boots. Zack had always wanted a life in the open spaces, but too much of Mother Nature made Dan uncomfortable. So did his present attire. And his mode of transportation.

"How much farther?" he asked.

"'Bout a mile," Jake replied, grinning. "Gettin' saddle sores?"

"I don't consider the more abused parts of my anatomy a subject for levity."

"Say again?" Jake's brows screwed up quizzically.

"He means don't laugh at his sore backside."

Jake harumphed. "Maybe you better trot on back to town then, boy. This ain't no task for the faint of heart."

"My courage has never been at question. I am on this beast, as you see, I have donned these garments, distasteful though they are, and I am coming with you."

"Fine, fine. No need to get touchy."

"Touchy," Dan mumbled to himself. Just because he preferred the more refined way of life?

"How good is Saul's memory," Zack asked. "Could he have got that map right after all these years?"

"Well, aside from some folks in St. Louis, Saul is the only one I know who's been in there enough to remember. He might look a mite doddery, but he ain't. And some memories don't fade. Saul has scars all over his hide, and no toes on one foot. He ain't gonna forget the way out of hell. If he weren't so stove-up in his old age, he'd be with us now, saving the kin of the man what saved him."

The longer they rode the more concerned Zack became. "We've come too far north surely."

"No. They'll be a couple days comin' through there."

"A couple days? In the center of the earth?"

"That is if they don't get themselves lost."

"What the hell was that?" Zack cried as an explosion rang through the air.

"Hold up here," Jake said, listening intently to the echoing reverberations.

"Well?"

"At a guess, I'd reckon someone was trying' to make certain them girls don't come back out of that cave."

"Christ! They're trying to bury them alive?"

"Relax. That system of caves and tunnels is a secret known only to a very few. Bennett might know of the cave and might know them girls is in there, but he don't know there's a way out. Nobody but nobody's going to tell him that."

"Can we go a little faster?"

"Can your friend take it?"

"I can take it," Dan declared from the rear.

The small corral that had been built decades earlier had fallen apart in places and needed some repairs before the men could safely leave the horses there. Jake had thought of that and had come prepared.

Each of the men was equipped with a light, a pack of supplies, a bedroll, and either a pick or a shovel. Jake wore a gun at his hip, Zack had a coil of rope over his shoulder, and Dan had a wedge of chalk in his pocket.

The entrance to the caves was well-concealed, a small opening at the top of the bluff that slanted down a long narrow chimney into a larger cavern inside.

"Right. Everyone okay?" Jake asked, looking at Dan after they'd all climbed down.

"Yes, fine," Dan replied, gazing around. "Are these Indian markings?"

"Those are, over there. This wall holds the mark of every slave to come through here."

"Fascinating."

"You ain't seen nothin' yet, pal. Ever been in a cave before?"

"No. How about you, Zack?"

"A few, in Texas and New Mexico when I was a kid."

"You got the chalk, Dan?" Jake asked. "You're responsible for marking our way. Always mark on your right side. And mark at every turn. Zack, you got the rope. All the old rope will have to be replaced as we go."

"Got it."

"And stay behind me. There are some treacherous crevices in here. Heard tell they're bottomless. I'll go first."

"Fair enough, only tie this rope around your waist. That way—"

"That way I can take you with me? No. You can't hold me if I fall. If I'm stupid enough to miss a crack big enough for me to fall through, I deserve to fall in it. Just pray those gals have been warned."

The first mile was arduous work, climbing up and down over rocks in cramped spaces, slogging through ankle-deep mire beside crystal clear streams and pools, squeezing between walls of rock.

After that the cave opened up and they made their way through a maze of stalactites and stalagmites in all stages of growth.

"This is astounding, Zack. Do you have any idea of the age of this place? We have to come back here with a photographer."

Dan's natural reserve gave way to excitement and enthusiasm as they trekked farther into the caves. He was all for exploring, and except that the girls needed them, both Zack and Jake would have appreciated more time to look around as well.

"On the way back, after we find Kate and Annie," Zack said. "I sure hope they're in here. I'd hate to think we're wasting this time."

"That dynamite was a dead giveaway. They're here, all right."

"I'm exhausted," Annie said, leaning bonelessly against a boulder. They were in a long, low-ceilinged room, the floor of which, though even, was slick with a thick layer of mud.

"We'll have to go on. We can't stop here." Hours and hours had passed, and they had trudged on, never giving in to the strain on their muscles, to the desire to simply collapse. "How's your water supply?"

"Getting low."

"I hear water up ahead. We'll refill the canteen there."

"Are we still with the map?"

"Yes. Once we found the pipe organ formation, we were in business."

"That really did look like a church organ. Like the one in California. Do you suppose we'll ever get back there?"

"You can do as you please," Kate said determinedly, "but I'm going back."

"Good. I'll go with you."

"I'm not too much excitement for you?"

"Not for me. I'm beginning to love it. What do you think you'll do next?"

"Ha, ha. Just keep moving back there. My feet weigh a ton with all this mud. Okay, now what do we have here?"

"An arrow pointing up?"

"Map says ten feet up." She held up her lantern. "It's too dark. We'll have to go up and take a look."

"I'll go first," Annie said. "You went first the last time."

"Wait. Did you hear something? There it is again."

"Voices. Someone's in here. Are we at the end?"

"No. Only just over halfway."

"Lordy, I thought I was scared being in here alone with just you. The thought of someone else crawling around gives me goosebumps. Who are they?"

"Shh. Get down behind these rocks and put your light out. I want to see them before they see us."

Light flickered from an opening in the rock wall above, casting an eerie orange glow on the ceiling. A shape appeared in that glow. A very large shape.

"I'm through," a deep voice said. "Annie Spooner, you in here, girl? Hey, Red."

"It's Jake. Jake," she called.

Kate struck a match and lit both lanterns, and the girls began the tricky climb up to the ledge where Jake stood—big, strong, utterly comforting Jake.

"I've got 'em," Jake called, cupping his mouth to direct his voice back through the crevice. "Stay there. I'll bring 'em through."

"Jake," Annie cried, being lifted over the rim of the ledge by two burly arms. She wrapped her arms around his neck and gave him a kiss on his bristly cheek. "Jake, you ol' bear. You are a wondrous sight."

Kate got a hug, as well, when she was lifted to join them. "Who's with you?" she asked immediately.

"Two men who are right frantic to find you ladies."

"What about Bennett? Have you seen him?" Annie asked.

"Not since he sent the dogs after you."

Kate's heart was turning flips in her chest. Zack had come to find her. He was tramping through this same muddy cave to reach her.

"I can see you're anxious to go to him. Stay close behind me," Jake said. "They're not far away."

Zack didn't give her a second to breathe before he swept her into his arms. "Katie, Katie," he murmured, pressing kisses to her dirty face. "Are you all right? It's good to have you back in my arms. I couldn't believe you went with him. Why did you go? I'm not letting you out of my sight again. I was so scared for you."

She laughed, and he looked at her, then he kissed her as if his life depended on it.

"Annie," Dan said. "You're both unharmed, I'm happy to see. Weren't you frightened in there?" he asked, indicating the part of the cave the girls had just left.

Annie hadn't been away from Dan for an entire day yet, she realized, but she still felt a warm glow inside her that he'd come along. She imagined she was getting used to him being around.

"It was scary at first, until Kate reminded me of the hundreds and hundreds who had already been through it. We got lost once, but we backtracked until we found another marker."

"At least you stayed out of those deep holes. The old gent who drew us our map said some were endless."

"We found two, but they'd already been marked off with piles of rocks and ropes. It's strange being down here, isn't it?"

"It's incredible."

"Truth to tell, you're probably higher right now than you were at the Manor," Jake said. "If we could walk straight out the walls, we'd be halfway down the hillside. Did you find a decent campsite, Dan? Annie may be excited, but she also looks ready to drop."

"I am tired. Do you have any idea what time it is?" she asked.

"It's almost seven," Dan said, checking his pocket watch. "I found a dry alcove over there."

"Should we tell your friends?" Jake asked.

"Zack'll find us. I think they need to be alone for a while first," Dan said.

Zack led Kate to a corner away from the camp Jake was setting up for the night. "We have to talk, Katie. You have to let me explain. I know you must have a hundred questions."

"No. Just one, really. Why did you lie to me about Peter?"

He leaned against the rock wall and pulled her close within the circle of his arms. "All right. Let's begin there. I lied out of habit. Peter abandoned my mother and me when I was still a small boy. I idolized him, and I was dreadfully hurt when he left us, and I suppose that hurt has turned to bitterness over the years. After a while it was easier to tell people I had no brother. I haven't seen him in nearly twenty years."

"Was it pure coincidence that we met? Peter said you and he had it planned. He said you are engaged to a woman in Philadelphia."

"Lies. All of it. Did you believe him?"

"I had my weak moments, but then I'd remember what was happening and why. Grandfather used to say you could know a man by the company he keeps."

"Why did you keep all of this from me?" Zack asked.

"Because you told me you had no kin, and I couldn't believe you."

"Yes, I've heard my brother and I resemble one another."

"And then you took my money, and Corinne arrived in California wearing that jewelry. Peter said you returned it.'

"I wanted to protect you. I made them drop the charges against you."

"And I was trying to protect you. I've done a poor job of it. You could have been the one found in the river."

"Do you trust me then, Katie?"

"Yes, Zack. I do."

"Then please, will you marry me? You can do whatever you want with the Manor. I don't care. You can keep it, or sell it, or give it away, only be my wife."

"You really don't care?"

"If I have you by my side, my world is complete. I'm not a greedy man."

"Then your ranch isn't mortgaged?"

"No. It's paid for in full. I'm a wealthy man, Katie," he said, frowning curiously. "I thought you knew."

"I'm glad. I mean, not glad that you're wealthy, but glad that you don't need my money."

"I fell in love with a penniless runaway. Your money, my dearest, has been the cause of all our troubles."

"Oh, Zack, everything he said about you was like a knife in my heart. I didn't know what to think. I hated him for saying such awful things, and I didn't want to believe him, but I guess I'm weak. So many doubts and fears. I tried to believe in you, and I hoped, but what he said made so much sense."

Zack smiled sadly with understanding. "It's my fault. If I

hadn't been so prideful, so resentful of Peter, if I'd been honest—"

"Please, let's forget about it. I just want you to hold me."

"Shall we move our bedrolls over here?"

"Zack," she rebuked indignantly. "What would they think?"

"I guess you're right," he said, touching a finger to the wry twist of her lips. "It would be too obvious. All right, but I am going to sleep with you in my arms."

"Yes, I'd like that. I missed you."

"And tomorrow, we'll get out of here and find a preacher. I'm not taking any more chances.

His lips met hers and Katie's world seemed to rock. A low vibrating rumble echoed around them.

Zack lifted his head and straightened, still holding Kate by the shoulders. "What the . . ."

"What is it?" she asked, alert as well to the tremors and the underground thunder. "We heard that earlier. We thought Bennett had dynamited the entrance to the cave."

"Come on." He took her hand and practically dragged her back to the other three. Jake was already stowing gear.

"One of two things," Jake said. "This is a genuine quake, or Bennett's setting off charges on top of the ridge. It wouldn't take much to bring down some of these limestone ceilings. We're getting out before he succeeds."

# Chapter 22

"I told her to stay here," Bennett said, clenching his fingers around his glass of whiskey so tightly he threatened to shatter it in his hand. "If only she had listened."

"If anything can be done for her, Doc Webber will do it," Peter consoled. "Don't blame yourself, Sam. She was always too headstrong. When did she ever listen, especially when she saw a way to get at Katrina? This may be for the best."

"You mean if she dies? You bastard."

"You'd rather everyone know about her? She was ranting for hours upstairs. The doc knows it all."

"I can buy his silence."

"And my brother? Will you be able to buy his? He'll come for Katrina. It's over Sam, at least for me. I'm leaving. I wanted this plantation, but I never wanted it at the expense of Katrina's life. She didn't deserve that kind of death."

"You can't leave me now."

"Your daughter is dying, Sam, because she couldn't wait to kill Katrina. And you were right there with her. Would either of you listen to me?" Blasting sounded again from the distance. Peter looked with disdain at Sam. "We could have found them in that cave, but no, you and Corinne had a better idea. Bury them alive. Katrina was right. You are inhuman. You're as demented as your daughter."

Peter put down his glass and slowly slipped his arms into his coat. "I'll stay in town tonight and send for my things in the morning."

The metallic click of a hammer being cocked sounded behind him. Peter stiffened and turned very slowly to face Sam. "More blood on your hands, Sam?" he asked stonily.

"Peter," Sam said pleadingly, "you have to stay. I won't let you leave. Corinne will need you when she wakes up."

"She's not going to wake up, Sam. The sooner you face that fact, the easier her death will be for you."

"No," he cried in anguish, staggering toward a chair. "It's my fault. I knew we had too much dynamite." His legs crumpled and he sagged against the back of the chair, letting the gun slip from his fingers. He covered his face with his hands and wept. "She wanted to be sure. 'More, more,' she said. 'Blow them up, Papa.' So I used more. I tried to make her get down behind the rocks, to protect herself, but she fought me off. She wanted to watch. She wanted to see them die."

"You couldn't have stopped her. You know it as well as I do." He picked up the gun, amazed that it hadn't discharged.

"I didn't expect so much rock and dirt to reach us. I thought . . ."

"Mr. Bennett," Dr. Webber said from the doorway, drawing Sam's immediate attention.

"Is she going to be all right?"

"She's gone."

"No. No!"

"Sam, her head . . . She would never have been right again. Her injuries were too grave. It's best this way. We both know it."

"Get out. Both of you. Get out of my house." His face turned a mottled red. "Get out, I said. Out."

Sam Bennett waited for the front door to close behind the doctor and Peter. He was alone, all alone. He had no one. Peter had deserted him, the servants had walked away all because he'd slapped Junie, Katrina had betrayed him. His daughter was . . . His daughter was *dead.*

It was her fault. Katrina's. All of it was her fault. Another blast rent the evening air. Sam felt the vibration under his feet, and he smiled a twisted smile. He'd level the entire ridge before he'd allow that little bitch to live. She wouldn't escape him this time. And no abolitionist's tricks would save her. He knew about the tunnel, his men were spread all over the ridge looking for the exit.

Sam stood and walked to the stairs. His shoulders were bent, his head bowed. He felt as if he'd aged ten years. Slowly, he climbed the stairs and went into her room. Lowering the sheet from her colorless face, he sat on the edge of her bed and took her lifeless hand in his.

She looked at peace. He hoped she was. He hoped the demons that drove her were satisfied at last. He arranged her hair around her face, pulling the red locks over the bandage that wound around her battered head.

"My poor baby. You loved me, didn't you? You loved me too much. And I let you down."

His lips trembled and he drew a deep steadying breath and squared his shoulders. "But I won't let you down again. I promise. I'll finish what we started. Can you hear that? They're still blasting. We'll get her. We will. And if somehow she escapes, I'll follow her and kill her myself. I promise you, baby. I promise you."

The blasting was closer. "They must be setting the entire ridge with explosives," Zack said. "They obviously know about this place."

"They don't want me to escape," Kate said, gasping to catch her breath after a particularly strenuous climb. "I found the will, Zack."

"Hmmm. And Bennett knows? That would explain the blasting."

"I didn't tell him. Junie's the only one who knows."

"I think we saw him beating her, Katie. It's possible she had to tell him."

"Beating Junie?"

"When we were watching the Manor. But before we left we also saw one of the workers step forward and take her away from Bennett. Bennett took a swing at the man, but his fist never connected. There was quite a fight for a while, and finally the man picked Junie up and he and the rest of them walked away. They turned their backs on all those guns and left

Bennett standing there in a rage."

"That would have been Cyrus. He's in love with Junie. I don't mind if they told. I didn't expect anyone to have to suffer for me, and poor Junie already has a broken leg."

"I'd say they were pretty brave to defy him like that."

"That was because I told them to quit and walk away if Bennett tried anything with any of them. I told them to go into town to Jake. I also told Junie that my grandfather had willed their homes and their land to them, that it is all legally theirs and has been for years. There's nothing Bennett can do about that."

"Unless he destroys the will."

"And that's why you're all in danger with me."

"Don't start getting maudlin."

"Hey, Zack, hold up a minute," Dan called. "I'm going to pull these ropes back up as we go. Give me a second."

"Good idea," Jake agreed. "No sense leavin' 'em here to rot. Take a break, everybody."

"How much farther?" Annie asked, flopping down beside Kate and Zack.

"Another couple hours, I'd say." Zack took the map from his pocket and studied it. "Maybe less," he surmised. It's easier going from here."

"Put your head down on my lap, Annie," Kate said, tugging her down.

Annie didn't resist. "If I fall asleep, you won't be able to get me awake."

"You close your eyes and rest too, Katie," Zack said, pulling her against the warmth of his chest.

"If we don't get out of here, I'll never forgive myself," she said wearily.

"We'll make it. All those slaves did."

An exceptionally loud blast sounded, too close for comfort, opening a large crevice in the limestone ceiling. Water began to drip through in a steady stream.

"Right," Jake said. "Let's move. Those slaves didn't have a madman after them. Watch your lamps. Don't get them wet. You ain't never seen dark till you've been in a mine or a cave without a light."

They hadn't gone a hundred yards when another deafening blast followed that shook the rocks under their feet. Kate screamed and Zack pulled her between him and the wall, shielding her as the entire cave in front of them collapsed.

Rocks and dirt fell all around them. "Zack," Kate cried as they were being buried under a landslide of dirt.

Long moments passed before anyone dared move. Dirt still continued to fall, but the worst of the cave-in was over. Kate, pressed against Zack's chest, blessed the strong beat of his heart under her ear.

"Sweetheart?" he whispered.

"I'm fine, Zack. You?"

"I'll have a few bruises, but nothing I can't live with. Dan?" he called.

Zack pushed his way out of his little corner, searching for his pack. "Do you have a . . ."

Kate was ahead of him. She lit a match and touched it to a candle, which she secured in the dirt. She lit three more from her satchel before they found a lantern, broken, but functional.

"Dan" Zack called again. "Jake? Annie?"

"Here," came Annie's voice. "Over here."

"I can't see them," Kate said. "They're behind the dirt."

"Zack, I can see stars," Annie said.

Zack frowned. "Annie, don't go to sleep. Stay awake."

"I am awake. Don't start acting like Daniel. Is he with you?"

"I'll look around," Kate said.

"I'll look," Zack said. "You talk to Annie."

Kate nodded, aware of what it was Zack was thinking, hoping to spare her. "Annie, can you move?"

"I'm workin' on it. My legs are buried, but they don't hurt. Give me a minute and I'll be free." And then she screamed.

"Annie," Kate cried. "Annie, what is it?"

"Goddamn you, Dan Siebert." she raged. "Don't you have any more sense than to grab someone in the pitch dark."

"Sorry, I . . ."

The rest Kate couldn't hear. Zack came stumbling back. "Annie, is that Dan?"

"Yeah, it's him."

"Is he okay?"

"He has a broken arm, I think, and a nasty cut on his head. He's bleedin' all over me."

Zack laughed with relief. "Can you find Jake?"

"Dan says he's alive, but he's trapped."

"Annie, can you see a pick or a shovel over there?"

"Zack, I told you, all I see are stars. I don't even have a match on me."

"Okay. Just relax. Dan, is she all right?"

"He's out cold," Annie replied. "I'm free. I'm gonna check Dan's wounds while he can't hit me."

"In his shirt pocket should be a packet of matches."

"Got 'em." She lit a match and surveyed the rubble around her. The instant before the match burned her fingers she found the strap to the miner's lamp. She pulled it free and felt that the candle was still in place. She used another match to light the candle.

"I have light. Dan looks fine. He isn't hurt bad. I'm going to look for Jake."

"We'll be digging our way through. You don't sound too far away."

"Zack," Kate cried. "I found your pack. Your shovel's here, but the handle's broken."

"Annie?"

"I found Jake. Can you hurry? I can't get him out. He's hurt bad."

"Annie, look at the wall on your side. Is there any place you can see where it would be better to tunnel through?"

"Yes. To your left and up about five feet. Hold on, I'll climb up there so you'll know exactly."

"What's the situation with Jake?" Kate asked.

"His legs are pinned under some rocks. He's unconscious. I'm here. Can you tell where I am?"

"I've got you. Stand away now, I'm going to dig through."

It took Kate and Zack twenty minutes to dig through the wall, both working as swiftly as they could. By the time they were through, Annie had Dan's head bandaged with one of his shirt sleeves, and had used the other to fashion a sling for his injured arm.

"I've cleared most of the loose dirt and stones away from Jake, but I can't move those rocks."

"Bring the handle to the shovel, Katie. With that, the three of us ought to be able to free him."

Jake groaned and opened his eyes. "Am I alive?"

"Hey, pal, how are you? Are you in pain?"

"My head hurts. And my right leg. I can't move my legs." He tried to get up, but Zack held him back. "Easy, man. We have to move some rocks. Tell us if we hurt you."

"Jake, we'll get you out. This is all my fault," Kate said, kneeling beside him.

"Shut up, Kate, and get back here and push," Annie barked.

"Okay, you don't have to get so snippy."

"And if I hear you blame yourself one more damn time I'm going to spit up."

"And I'm going to turn you over my knee if you don't stop cussing," Dan threatened feebly.

"Oh-ho, he's awake," Annie chimed. "You couldn't even find your knee, Mr. Siebert."

"All right," Zack said, wedging the handle beneath the top rock. "Ready, push."

The rock gave way and rolled aside. Jake gave a groan and passed out. Two more rocks were moved and Zack was finally able to pull Jake free. Kate looked at the blood soaked pantleg of his trousers and winced.

"Now that the pressure is off, he's beginning to bleed. Annie, toss my satchel over here. I think I still have a pair of scissors in there, and that nightgown you had on."

"Jake had a flask of bourbon," Dan said. "Can you find it?"

Annie brought Kate her satchel then went back to Dan. "Do you need a drink for the pain?" She brushed his hair off his forehead, checking for any sign that his head was bleeding again. "Does your head hurt?"

"Don't get mushy. I meant for Jake—to clean his wound."

"Oh." She pulled her hand back, but Dan caught her wrist and returned her palm to his face.

"On second thought, I can use your care, too. I'm a hurt man. You're quite a girl, Annie Spooner. Have I told you that yet?"

Annie searched his eyes in the shadowy dimness, expecting to find his usual mischievous glint of mockery. It was not there. She felt her cheeks burn, and her stomach did a crazy flip-flop. She scowled and jerked away.

"Now, who's mushy? Pull yourself together."

"Annie, let Zack and Kate take care of Jake. I need you to fix my arm. It hurts like hell. You said you set Junie's leg. Would you give my poor bones a go?"

"You trust me?"

"Sure. Besides, I don't have much choice, do I?"

Annie looked over at Kate and Zack. They seemed to be doing all right. They'd found the scissors and Zack was cutting Jake's pantleg away while Kate was tearing up the nightdress, the nightdress she'd taken off before they had left the Manor. That seemed like a lifetime ago.

She gave Dan a weak grin. "I might hurt you."

"You can't hurt me worse than I'm hurting now."

She untied the sling and examined his arm. "It isn't broken at all. You've dislocated your shoulder. Zack, I could use your help for a second."

"Go ahead," Kate said.

"Put your foot under his arm, and when I tell you to pull, pull hard." She probed Dan's shoulder, ignoring his sharp hissing gasps. "Pull. Hard, Harder! Pull, dammit."

Zack clenched his teeth and did as she said. He could feel the snap when the arm went back into the socket.

Dan was pale and perspiring. "Thanks. That feels better already."

"You look about to keel over. For pity's sake, lay down."

Dan's arm was bound securely to his body and he was much more comfortable. Jake's leg was cleaned and bandaged, and he'd regained consciousness. Not much of the night remained, so they settled down to wait until daybreak to attempt to get out of their hole in the ground, for Zack had found that Annie was not hallucinating. He, too, could see stars through a small opening in the ceiling.

Singing woke Kate in the morning, not the singing of birds, but a male voice, chanting an old familiar tune. She sat up and listened.

"What is it?" Zack asked quietly.

"Shh," she said, motioning him to silence. She stood and moved under the opening that let in the gray morning light. The singing grew louder.

"Get back here, Katie. Someone's coming."

"What's going on?" Annie asked, joining them.

"Quiet, both of you."

The soft melodious singing stopped, and in its place came a clear, sweet whistling. Only one man that she knew could whistle like that. She whistled back, and when he sang the next phrase, she sang it back to him.

"It's Cyrus."

They continued their musical communication until Cyrus stood over the mouth of the hole. "Miss Katrina?"

"Don't come too close, Cyrus. It may not be safe. Cyrus, can you hear me?"

"Yes, miss. I came to look for you. Junie sent me."

"Cyrus, we need help to get out of here. The tunnel on both sides is blocked. Our only way out is up. Jake Denning and two other men are with us, they came to help us. Two are hurt. Can you get some rope and some men to help you pull us out?"

"Yes, miss. I'll go now."

"Cyrus, what about Bennett and his men?"

"Don't know. They just gone. All of 'em gone. Miss Corinne, she's dead now."

Corinne dead? What in the world was happening? Jake moaned as he stirred, and she realized that now was not the time to worry about Corinne. "Hurry back, and Cyrus, we need a wagon to get Jake to town. Go now, before Bennett comes back."

Susanna Denning's arms enveloped Annie in a great hug. "Welcome back," she said, and turned to Kate. "You must be Katrina Montgomery. Jake told me about you."

"Thank you for opening your home to us."

"Nonsense. When Jake sent word from Doc Hart's office, I reckoned he'd want you here. I've put water to heat for baths. And your driver, Cyrus, he brought a trunk of clothes for you.

Said his woman sent them so you wouldn't have to go back there."

"That would be Junie," Kate said. "I'm relieved that she's recovering."

"I have strict orders from Jake," Susanna said. "You're to get cleaned up and have a nice long nap. Your men will be by this afternoon to take you into town to see the judge."

"The judge?" Kate said uncertainly.

"He said you have to register your grandfather's will so your servants have clear title to their land."

"Oh, yes. I do. That's absolutely right," she said, relieved.

"Are you having doubts about Zack again?" Annie asked a little later, as she was rinsing the suds from Kate's hair.

"So much has happened, and so quickly. I feel like Alice in Wonderland, as if I've fallen in a hole, completely out of control and unable to do anything about it. I mean, I love Zack, but . . . what if I'm making a mistake. What if this isn't real?"

"I think I know how you feel—like you've been caught up in a twister and haven't been set down again."

"How can I make him understand?"

"Why worry? Just tell him you want to wait until you feel more rested."

"He won't take it well," she said, and she was proved right that afternoon when Zack and Dan arrived from town.

"I thought we agreed," he argued.

"Zack, I don't disagree, only . . . well . . ."

"Peter got to you. You said you trusted me, but you don't. How could you believe him?" He jumped up, running his fingers through his hair.

"That isn't it at all."

"Then what is it? Every minute we delay puts us at risk. Bennett is still out there somewhere. When he learns you're still alive . . ."

"He won't do anything. He has lost the fight, and he knows it. Besides, he only wanted the Manor for Corinne. With her dead, he doesn't—"

"With her dead, he'll come for you out of revenge."

"A girl only gets married once," Annie said, trying to calm the troubled waters. "Kate wants a pretty wedding."

Thoroughly exasperated, Zack retorted, "I don't think she wants a wedding at all. Every time I suggest it, she retreats."

"That's not fair, Zack," Kate retaliated, truly hurt. "I've tried to explain my reasons." And they were valid reasons. Besides, why the rush?

"Yes, you wanted to protect me, you weren't sure of my motives. I've heard them."

"Why are you being so intractable?"

"Me?"

"Yes, you. It's been push, push, push from the minute we met. Everything has to be your way and right now."

"Now who's being unfair?"

"I never said I didn't want to marry you, only that I wanted to wait until . . ."

"Wait? I've done nothing *but* wait. I think I've been extraordinarily patient."

"When? May I remind you that we've known each other all of one month."

"And that's twenty-nine days too long that I've had to wait. If you've changed your mind again, so be it. But know this. I'm not coming after you again, and I'm not proposing again. A man's pride can take only so much rejection."

"Now you're being melodramatic. When have I ever rejected you?"

"I dropped everything to come after you, to save you from Bennett."

"And I'm supposed to run into your arms with undying—"

"Wait! Stop!" Annie cried. "What are you two doing?"

"They're arguing," Dan said dryly. "Haven't you heard enough of it yet to recognize it?"

"Yes, I've heard it, but it's what I'm hearing now that's bothering me. I think Kate's right. Not one of us is in any state of mind to decide what we want for supper, let alone when to get married."

"I'll decide what I can decide," Zack snapped temperamentally.

"Oh. All right," Annie retorted, hands on hips, glaring up into his stormy blue eyes. "Then go ahead and push her into it. Threaten her. Tell her it's now or never."

"I don't think he said that," Dan interrupted.

"Keep out of this."

"He did say it," Kate stood up for Annie.

"I said I wasn't—"

"I heard what you—"

"Don't tell me to keep out of—"

"I heard what he said, too, even if you—"

The kitchen door slammed as Susanna walked into their argument. All four eyes turned away with varying degrees of embarrassment.

"The coffee is ready," she said calmly. "Please sit down at the table. I have a few words to say."

"I apologize," Kate said. "We had no right to bring our disagreement into your home."

"That's very true, especially since my husband is still laid up at Doc's place because he helped you all. But please, have a seat. I'll get the coffee."

They sat down, Zack glaring at Kate, who then glared back, Annie and Dan waging a silent battle of wills.

"I couldn't help overhearing your argument, if you wish to call it that," Susanna said after placing a mug of coffee in front of each of them and sitting down with her own.

"I knew Lawrence Montgomery," she said quietly. "Most around here did. He wasn't a man to hold himself apart just because he had more money. He used to tote Miss Katrina around with him wherever he went. He was so proud of her. We had a Fourth of July celebration one year. It was the year my Elsie turned fourteen. You would have been ten, Katrina. You wandered over to where the older children were gathered. Your grandfather started to go after you, but I stopped him, because you were so pretty and so unspoiled that I knew the older ones would be kind to you. And they were. I told him he was a lucky man to have so lovely a child in his home. He said something very strange to me then. He said I was the lucky one because I'd live to see my daughter married.

"I argued that he would give you away to your husband, but he only smiled that sad smile he sometimes had. He told me he wanted a church wedding for you, with flowers and candles, and he wanted to be sure you had a good man who would love you, but he doubted that he'd be around to see any of that."

Kate wiped the tears from her cheeks, but they poured back down. Zack handed her his handkerchief.

"I have one more thing to say. You have all been under a great strain these last days. You've neither slept nor eaten as you should. You've been angry, you've been scared to death, you've fought for your very lives. I understand Zack's desire to tuck Katrina under his protective wing. He loves you, child." she said, patting Kate's hand.

"But I also understand Katrina's reluctance to be hurried. She's a woman. Women don't dream of hurried words in a judge's chamber.

"Now, I know Annie has no family to turn to, nor does Katrina. That leaves you gentlemen."

"That leaves me," Dan said. "Zack has no family either. I think I follow you. You want me and my family to arrange Kate's and Zack's wedding."

"Would they object?"

"No. Zack has been like a brother for years. They'll be honored to do that for him."

"With flowers and candles?" Kate asked tearfully, turning to Zack. "Zack?"

His eyes held a telltale sheen. He took a faltering breath. "Ah, Katie, do you expect me to deny you that? I'm sorry. I wasn't thinking."

"You mean you're going to Philadelphia?" Annie asked bleakly.

Kate turned, her brows raised at Annie's lack of enthusiasm. "So are you."

"Not me. I'm no city girl."

"Sacramento's a city," Dan pointed out.

"Annie, you have to go. You have to stand up with me."

"I can't," she said pleadingly.

"Good Lord, woman," Dan barked. "We just get everything settled and you throw a wrench in the works."

"Don't yell at me," she said tremulously. "It's easy for you. They're your family. They won't make fun of you."

"Now that's just plain ridiculous."

"Is it? If they're anything like you . . ."

"I don't make fun of you. Beides I only do it for your own good."

"See, you admit—"

"I'd never say a thing if we didn't have a sort of understanding."

"Understanding? I don't understand anything about you."

"Annie, no one will ridicule you. Why should they?"

"Because I'm not like you. All your sisters, your mother, your grandmother, they'll think I'm . . . I'm . . ."

"They'll think you are delightful, just as we do," Zack said. "I know them. You'll love Dan's grandmother. Truly."

"Don't worry, Annie."

"But, Kate . . ."

"Believe me. No one will ever guess," Kate said, realizing that the very fact that Annie even cared about the reaction of Dan's family meant her feelings for him were far different than she claimed.

"Well, now that that's settled," Susanna said, "I'd like a ride to town. Dan, Annie, would you be so kind? I want to visit Jake, and you two can make your travel arrangements for tomorrow. I agree with Mr. Standish that Bennett poses a threat. You should be on your way as soon as possible."

"Do you want to come along, Kate?" Annie asked.

"No, she doesn't," Dan said firmly. He looked wryly at Zack. "Why don't we meet in town at seven for dinner. We'll treat Mrs. Denning to dinner as thanks for her hospitality."

Zack stood by the window and watched until the buggy was out of sight. He let the curtain drop and turned to Kate. She looked nervous, fiddling with the folds of her dress.

"Mrs. Denning is a perceptive woman. I am afraid of losing you. I want to grab hold of you and never let go. I accused you of not trusting me, but a few minutes ago I realized that I'm guilty, too. I've doubted the strength of your love, and it has scared the hell out of me. I'm really sorry for not understanding."

"This last month . . ." she said, shaking her head. "It's been a nightmare and it's been a beautiful dream, and the wonderful parts are always being interrupted by the terrifying. I find I'm always watching and waiting. I can't relax. I have to relax. Does that make any sense?"

"More than you know. We have to hold tight to one thought, Katie. We love each other. We belong together. Others may threaten to tear us apart, but they won't be able to if we believe in each other."

"Then you don't mind if we go to Philadelphia?"

"Not at all. I think it's a good idea. We'll have time together, we'll have family and friends with us, we'll have a wedding that would have pleased your grandfather. I'm afraid he'll reach out from the grave and haunt me forever if I don't give you that."

She laughed, and her deep blue eyes met his and held. In them he saw a desire that mirrored his own. He held out his arms and she came to him.

"Should we, Zack?" she whispered.

"Damn *shoulds* and *shouldn'ts*. I need you in my arms. I need to make love to you."

He gave her no time to protest, not that she was of a mind to do so. He swept her up into his arms and covered her soft, eager lips with his own. His hunger burned through to the center of her being, setting her aflame, and she met his passion with equal ardor.

"I can't believe this is happening. I was so afraid I'd never get the chance to love you again." He carried her to the only bedroom in the cottage and stood her beside the double bed. With deliberate slowness, he removed each of her garments, worshipping each part of her body as he uncovered it. His own clothes he discarded, and he lay with her on the bed, blanketing her legs with one of his. His hands caressed her, one buried in her hair, holding her head, one sliding over the silken textures of her skin.

"I love you so much, Katie."

"Did you mean what you said about waiting twenty-nine days too long?"

"I've loved you from the minute you dumped us both on the floor in that railroad car and looked up at me through those incredible blue eyes. Why do you think I wouldn't let you go?"

"And you were serious when you wanted me to marry you even then?"

"I thought you'd be blinded by my good looks and my money and say yes before you came to your senses."

"Oh, did you, you conceited—"

"Careful, now."

"Truthfully, I *was* dazzled by you, but your money had nothing to do with it."

"Just my looks?"

She ran a finger along the line of one brow and down his lean, bronzed cheek to his sensuous lower lip. "Well, yes. That and the way you made me feel. Otherwise nothing you threatened would have kept us with you. We'd have gone."

"No you wouldn't. I wouldn't have let you." He captured her finger with his teeth, then drew the tip of it into his mouth.

"Zack, I love you, too. I was so lost without you. Please hold me tight. Don't ever let me go."

Zack embraced her, lifting her up to meet the hard contours of his body. He kissed her nose, her eyelids, trailed hot kisses along the line of her jaw to her mouth. Her waiting lips, already parted invitingly, welcomed him in a kiss that was hungry and deep.

"Sweet, sweet Katie," he groaned, hot blood drumming through his veins and his self-control quickly disintegrating under the enchanting caress of her fingers on his bare skin. Rolling to cover her body with his, he sought and found the sweetness of her lips. His hands molded to the soft contours of her body.

A low moan escaped the depths of her throat as his lips moved down her arched throat to the gentle swell of her breasts. Her flesh shivered and her stomach clenched in sweet agony at the touch of his lips to the burgeoning darker peaks.

"Zack, oh Zack, please."

Every part of her body came instantly alive beneath his caring and coaxing caresses, and her uninhibited response drove Zack over the brink. Their passion broke the bonds of restraint.

In a swift motion and with a groan of need, he parted her thighs and joined his body to hers. His fierce thrusting movements transported them into an elemental storm of wild and mounting sensations over which neither had control, until they were both swept away in convulsive waves of exploding pleasure.

# Chapter 23

The Siebert family butler, who also served as coachman, met them at the depot in Philadelphia with a carriage every bit as big as the one Zack had taken to California. This was fortunate since, not only did Zack, Dan, and Annie have the cases they had brought from California, but Kate also had a trunk of her finest garments.

"Hello, Sandy," Dan said effusively, shaking the older man's hand and slapping him on the shoulder. "It's good to see you looking fit."

"We weren't expecting you back so soon," the tall, thin driver said. "It's a nice surprise. Good to see you, too, Mr. Standish."

"Same here Sandy," Zack said, offering his hand. "Sandy, I'd like you to meet my fiancée, Katie Montgomery, and a good friend, Annie Spooner. This is Mr. Sandusky, ladies. He runs the Siebert household."

"Charmed," he replied, tipping his tall hat, "and take no mind of him. Should you know the truth, it's my wife who runs the place. And me included. And she said not to tarry."

"Well, I guess that's that, then," Dan said dryly. "We had best get moving. I certainly don't want Bea annoyed with me."

"Have you ever been east?" Zack asked Kate, when the luggage had been stowed and the carriage on its way to the Siebert residence.

"I was to Lexington, Kentucky once."

Zack laughed. "I'll show you around. We can visit the

Liberty Bell. Philadelphia has its share of historical sights."

"We planned to go to the Centennial exposition, but grandfather wasn't well, and we were forced to cancel our trip."

"Parts of it are still here. We'll go. And if we're lucky, we'll be able to see a baseball game while we're in town. Would you like that?"

"Yes. Anything. Everything," she answered excitedly.

"Tell me about your family again," Annie asked Dan.

"Again?"

"There are so many. Please," she pleaded nervously.

"All right. From the top down there's Grandmother Siebert, my father's mother, of course. She's been living with us for about seven years. She has arthritis and doesn't get around very well, but she's sharp-witted. Then Dad and Mom. Dad's a bit of a tyrant, so don't let him get to you, and Mom's a busybody who wants to run everyone's life. If you have trouble from anyone, it will be from her. Or maybe Dad, but I doubt it. The rest will be fine."

"Tell me their names again."

"My older brother James, his wife is Jane."

"Jane and James."

"Carl and Madelyn, my sister Ellen and her husband Albert Mendell. Another brother, Tom and his wife Louise, and I've a sister Selina who's away right now."

"I'll never remember."

"When you meet them and put faces to their names, you'll be fine," Zack assured her. "Stop worrying. We want you to enjoy yourself."

"I feel like I'm a phony and I'm imposing myself on you."

"Annie Spooner," Dan rebuked sharply. "You are my personal guest, and if you are not welcome, then neither am I. My family, though they may be stuffy and citified, like me, are not ogres."

She took a deep breath and released it in a whoosh. No matter what was said to her, the longer they drove and the closer to the house they got, the more nervous she became.

When Dan at last pointed out his family home, a beautiful

huge stone structure at the end of a tree-lined street, Annie cracked.

"I'm not going in there. Have Sandy take me back to the depot. I'll go back to Memphis. I mean it, Dan."

Dan looked helplessly at Zack, who looked at Kate, who scowled at Dan for making Annie so insecure about herself.

Dan groaned and turned to Annie, taking her shoulders and giving her a gentle shake. "Now stop this. Pull yourself together."

The carriage stopped in front of the mansion, for that was the only word for it, and Annie paled. "I can't," she squeaked.

Dan's hands tightened on her shoulders and he did the only thing he could think to do. He kissed her. And not in a platonic way. He pulled her into his arms so that her breasts were crushed to his chest and her head cradled in the crook of his elbow. His mouth came down on hers to silence her next protest, but once he met the sweet softness of her lips, he couldn't pull away, and all thoughts of what she might say next vanished.

She was so stunned that for a few seconds she couldn't respond. She remained motionless in his embrace, and then a sweet shock of pleasure coiled its way through her, sending her retreating in surprise and alarm.

The carriage door opened while Annie was still gaping wide-eyed at Dan, and Dan stepped out and pulled her after him, directly into the clutch of chattering folks waiting by the front door.

Kate looked at Zack and Zack looked at Kate, and they both sputtered into laughter.

"That's the first time I've ever seen her at a loss for words," Zack said.

"I'm surprised he didn't get a black eye for his efforts."

"It's not too late yet. I think she's still in shock. When it finally hits her that she's been kissed, and by whom . . ."

"At least she'll have something to think about besides Dan's family. She must be getting sweet on him to care what his family thinks. Ordinarily, if anyone objected to her, she'd turn up her nose or spit in his eye."

"She does seem to be uncharacteristically sensitive. Shall we join them? Dan may yet need our assistance." He helped Kate from the carriage and escorted her up the steps toward the crowd in front of the open door. He stopped in his tracks.

"Oh, good grief. We've got trouble."

"What? Zack?"

"It's Lorraine."

"So who's Lorraine?" she asked, but didn't need much clarification when a curvy blonde threw herself against Dan, wrapping her arms around his neck and kissing him.

"She's one of the reasons he left Philadelphia. She and her mother wanted to become part of the Siebert family."

"I see. And am I likely to find one of your sweethearts in your arms?" she queried, offhand. "Annie isn't enjoying this," she said noticing the fiery glint in Annie's eyes. "Zack, you better do something before she tears Lorraine's hair out."

Zack stepped forward. "Mrs. Siebert, Logan," he greeted Dan's parents. "Daniel, would you be good enough to introduce the ladies?"

Dan extricated himself and stepped aside, reaching for Annie's arm. She didn't protest, but the sparks in her eyes when she looked at Dan promised a reckoning.

Dan pulled himself to his full height and dealt with all the introductions. "That is all of my family, Annie, except for my grandmother."

"She's feeling under the weather today," Mrs. Siebert explained. "Her arthritis."

Lorraine, standing to the side, cleared her throat, and Dan was forced to proceed. "We'll meet grandmother later. This is Lorraine Smythe, a friend of the family. You've met Sandy, this is his wife Bea, our housekeeper and cook. I believe that's everyone."

"I'd like to think I am more than a friend of the family, Daniel." Lorraine pouted prettily.

"I know you would."

They had moved into the foyer and now were directed to make themselves comfortable in the parlor, where tea would be served. Lorraine took a place on the other side of Dan from where Annie sat.

"We have all been dying of curiosity," Mrs. Siebert said. "Your telegram was brief for all that it ordered us to organize a wedding for two weeks hence. You've taken us all quite by surprise, you know."

"We did not have much time ourselves in planning for this, It's all a very long story, which I'll relate another time, but the fact is that Zack and Kate want to be married, and we are the closest to a family that either of them has."

"Then you are not marrying . . . her?" Miss Smythe asked, throwing Annie a sidelong glance.

"Her name is Annie Spooner. No, Annie and I have no immediate plans to be married."

"Well, that's a relief," Mrs. Siebert said.

"Mother!" reprimanded one of the other girls. "That was unkind."

"I only meant that . . . well, we hardly know her. You do understand, Miss Spooner?"

Kate was annoyed at that, and was about to speak up in Annie's behalf when Zack beat her to it.

"You must realize that any woman Dan meets in California will be unknown to you at first. But Annie has been with us for a month now; she is no stranger to us. Perhaps we ought to have a double ceremony. We were in such a hurry to arrange my marriage to Katie that we didn't even consider the possibility that . . ."

"It's out of the question," Mrs. Siebert declared.

Dan's temper had been held in check only by the firmest of control. He had been home less than five minutes, and already his mother was planning his life for him. He had to put a stop to it.

"Only if I say it's out of the question, Mother. I'll marry when and whom I decide. Please understand that." He took Annie's hand and gave it a squeeze, then turned to Zack. "Thank you for suggesting it. Annie and I shall discuss it later."

Annie's mind had begun to function again and she was not finding the discussion at all amusing.

"They're teasing you, Mrs. Siebert. Dan and I are friends.

We've never even talked about this. Behave yourself, Daniel Siebert."

Dan laughed. "I guess my life will forever be a topic for argument. My mother thinks she must select my wife, or I'm doomed to disaster."

"Forgive us, my dear," Mrs. Siebert said. "We meant no embarrassment to you."

"We'll start organizing dinner," Jane said, summoning the rest of her sisters. "I think our guests might need a chance to freshen up and have a rest for a few hours."

"Yes, I would like that," Kate said, setting her teacup aside and standing. "Jane, would you be able to spare some time in the next few days to take Annie and me to look for dresses?"

"Oh-ho," exclaimed James. "You had better watch your wallet, Zack, my friend. Kate sounds serious. And if she's with Jane, she'll visit the most expensive shops in town."

Zack grinned wryly. "I promised her a church wedding and all the trimmings. I can't back out now."

"That's very generous. Does that mean you will pay for a trousseau as well as wedding attire?" Jane asked.

"It means she may have whatever she wants."

Mrs. Siebert showed them to their rooms and returned to oversee the women gathered in the kitchen. Kate and Annie stood in the hallway between their rooms, each waiting for the other's reaction.

"Quite a place, isn't it?" Annie said at last.

"It's beautiful. But so big."

"What did you make of his family?"

"I like them," Kate answered. "What you're asking for is my opinion of Mrs. Siebert."

"All right. Am I wrong, or does she resent me being here? I knew it would happen."

"You're being too sensitive. Dan said they had had that argument often. She will resent anyone who tries to upset her plans for Dan."

"Meaning Miss Smythe."

"Perhaps, but she'll get over it. Don't worry, we'll be across the continent from her in a few weeks."

"And how am I to hold on to my temper for that long?"

"Who said you had to!"

"You mean I can wipe that superior smirk off that chubby blonde's face?"

"Chubby? Lorraine?"

"She's fat."

Kate laughed. "If you say so."

"Are you going to try to catch a nap?" she asked, seeing Kate's smothered yawn. "I'm going to explore while you use the bathroom then."

"I'll see you at dinner."

Annie looked into several rooms as she quietly made her way down the corridor. At the end of the hall she found a small elevator with a brass gate closing it off.

"Would you care to ride in it?"

Annie jumped at the voice, although it was a pleasant voice, made thin by age. She turned to find a slight, white-haired woman standing in her doorway in her dressing gown. Grandmother Siebert. The woman she would love.

"How are you feeling?" Annie asked immediately. "Oh, I'm so sorry. I'm Annie Spooner."

"I imagine you know who I am. Come in and sit with me. My knees are acting up today, and my medicine always puts me to sleep. That is the reason I missed your arrival. You will forgive me, I hope."

Annie followed her into her suite of rooms, taking the comfortable chair facing the older woman.

"So you are the bride?"

"Oh, no. That's Kate. Katrina Montgomery. She's marrying Zack."

"Ah. We had questioned who exactly was to be wed."

"Dan should have made that clear, but we were in a hurry when we left Memphis."

"Memphis? You came from Memphis? I thought California."

"It's a very long story."

"Yes, and you'll want to rest now after your trip," she said understandingly.

"No, I'm fine. I'm too excited to be able to rest."

"Then you must stay and talk to me. I get so little company

up here. Where did you meet my grandson?"

"On the train. I gave him a black eye."

"Now, that must have taken him down a notch. Daniel always was so . . . very proper. Yes, I like you already. So, from the beginning."

And Annie, warming instantly to the bright-eyed old lady, sat with her for the remainder of the afternoon, telling tales and hearing Grandmother Siebert's favorite stories as well.

"So, you see, I was as homeless and poor as you when I met Charles," she said. "He stopped to help me fix my wagon. So proper he was too. Just like Daniel. He was widowed, but he had a daughter with him. He hired me to look after her. She's dead now. Charles never would admit that he was attracted to me. We had a business arrangement. A very stubborn man, my Charles. In the end I had to threaten to leave. Oh, not actually threaten. I told him that my heart was overwhelmed by him and that I was filled with longing, so to protect myself from hurt, I had to find another position."

"What did he do?"

"I wanted him to declare his love for me immediately, but the rascal took weeks to finally realize that he couldn't do without me."

"That's a wonderful story."

"And there were those who wouldn't believe I married for love. Charles was wealthy, you see. You might find you have the same problem with Daniel."

"Except Dan and I are not . . . we barely tolerate each other."

Grandmother Siebert nodded sagely. "So you won't have to worry."

"No. Except I don't like Miss Smythe."

"Her? Is she still here? What a bothersome little twit. She was livid when Dan decided to move to California. She had her cap set for him, you see. Not that she's in love."

"You don't think she is?"

"With herself, yes. With the Siebert name, more than likely. Too bad I don't have another grandson. Well, take no mind of her. Dan cannot stand her. Or that mother of hers, who, if I know my daughter-in-law, will be at dinner this evening."

Annie glanced at the clock on the mantel at the mention of dinner. "Goodness, it's almost time now. I must get dressed."

"Wear something pretty."

"Yes," she replied, knowing she'd need to look her best to face the Siebert clan. And Lorraine Smythe.

Dan sat on Zack's bed while Zack finished dressing. "Is he certain?"

Zack turned and threw him a sardonic look. "As certain as John Phillips is in everything he does. That man doesn't miss much."

"But he couldn't trace him?"

"My brother took a riverboat to New Orleans. Phillips learned that much. But Bennett, after the funeral, just vanished. Phillips talked at length with the sheriff in Memphis. He said Bennett was like the walking dead, wouldn't talk to anyone. He moved out of the Manor and disappeared into thin air."

"You have no idea where he could be?"

"Where would you be if you were half insane and blamed Kate for your daughter's death?"

"You think he'll come here?"

"Phillips has men checking on the depot. If he comes by train."

"I thought we were finished with him. I don't like this."

"Humph," Zack grunted, tying the knot at his throat. "Well, there's not much we can do until he shows himself. Even then, unless he openly threatens to harm Katie, we can't do anything. It's a free country. A man may go where he wishes."

"What about what he did to us?"

"What did he do? How can you prove he knew we were in that cave? Maybe he just wanted to clear some stumps on that ridge." He shook his head.

"Sandy has a nephew who is training to be a policeman. I'll mention to him that the girls will need extra protection."

"That's a good idea. I was wondering how to keep an eye on

Katie without alarming her."

"Why not tell her? She ought to know."

"I don't want a black cloud hanging over her wedding."

Dan saw his grandmother for the first time when she came down the elevator with Annie at her side. Annie helped her out of the narrow cage and into the foyer, and threw Dan a timid smile that did strange things to his mid-section.

"Grandmother," he said, kissing her cheek. "I see you've met Miss Spooner. How are you feeling?"

"Just fine, and your little Annie and I had a nice long chat this afternoon. She reminds me of myself fifty years ago," she added, speaking loudly enough so that her opinion was noted by everyone present. She was still matriarch of the family and wanted it understood that Annie was to be treated respectfully.

"I thought she might," Dan said, grinning crookedly.

"Grandmother Siebert," Zack said, bowing over her hand and bestowing a kiss on her fragile fingers.

"Zack, you rascal. Still trying to sweep me off my feet?"

"Till the day I die, madame."

"Fiddle-faddle. Am I to meet this lovely creature you are in such a hurry to marry?"

Zack pulled Kate to his side, giving her a gentle smile. His eyes, when they rested on her face, radiated his love. "Grandmother, this is my beloved Katie. Katrina Montgomery. Katie, may I introduce Dan's grandmother, Elvira Siebert. We call her Grandmother to avoid confusion in a house full of Mrs. Siebert's."

"I'm pleased to meet you, Grandmother Siebert. You have a wonderful grandson. Annie and I have grown as fond of him as Zack is."

"Well now, it's comforting to know he's cared for, being so far from home. I understand you have no family, Katrina."

"That's right. My father was killed in the war. I lost both my mother and my grandfather almost three years ago."

"Montgomery? From Memphis. That wouldn't be Lawrence?"

"Yes. Did you know him?"

"Only of him. I've been known to bet a horse or two in my day."

"In her nefarious past," Dan intoned.

"You should be so fortunate."

"Well, you'll be happy to know that since I've met Annie and Kate, I've been embroiled in kidnapping, theft, murder, I've been trapped in the bowels of the earth, running for my life. I've even been on the back of a horse."

"My, my. Are you actually becoming human?"

"I came very near to becoming dead."

"Oh, pooh. I think we are being summoned to dinner. Shall we go through to the dining room?"

Mrs. Siebert was standing at the head of the table beside her husband, directing the adult diners to their appointed places and the children to the table in the kitchen. Kate could see that her family had learned over the years to tolerate her self-importance. Perhaps, as with the Bennetts, it was easier to let her have her way than to oppose her.

Mrs. Siebert might not have the power to control Dan's life, but she controlled the seating arrangements, and for the next hour Annie was at one end of the table between Mr. Siebert and Zack, and across from Jane and her husband, and Dan was at the other end, seated beside his mother and Lorraine. Mrs. Smythe was across from him.

Grandmother was across from Annie, at Kate's side, and Kate caught the wink she threw to Annie, which caused Annie to blush.

"You spent the afternoon with Annie?" Kate asked the older lady.

"We had a marvelous talk."

"Good. She was scared to death to come here."

"I understand that. My son and daughter-in-law, though they've been very good to me, are sometimes difficult to live with," she said in a hushed whisper. "Are Daniel and Miss Spooner compatible, do you think?"

"You mean as in . . ."

"Oh course. What else is there?"

"I—ah—they seem to be, though they scrap frequently."

"Do they scrap together, or does Daniel stand there and let her rail at him? I can see where she might have a temper."

"Oh, no. Dan, at least the Dan we've known, has been very

capable of speaking his mind. But then Annie can be provocative. Sometimes I think she likes to fight with him."

"No doubt it's the only time he isn't stuffy."

"Oh, she won't let him be stuffy, and he won't tolerate her riverfront grammar."

"Sounds to me as if they suit each other."

"You would approve?"

"Heartily. Dan needs a woman to set fire to him."

"Then don't, for goodness' sake, suggest it. Right now they love to hate each other. Personally, I'm waiting for Annie to get even with Dan for kissing her in the carriage earlier today."

"Hmm. She didn't mention that."

"Mother," Logan Siebert repeated for the second time, "Mrs. Smythe has asked you a question."

She directed Mrs. Smythe a level gaze. "I do beg your pardon, but I was speaking with our guest of honor. Could you repeat your question?"

"I asked how you felt about having your grandson home again."

"It is a delightful treat, of course," she answered, her twinkling eyes going to Dan's hard-set face.

"Are you going to be able to persuade him to stay in Philadelphia?" Lorraine asked, only half teasing.

"Well now, my dear, if you haven't been able to do that, I see no hope for me."

"We thought that as his grandmother . . ."

"And perhaps Daniel has developed interests in California which call him back."

"Have you found a business to invest your talents in yet?" asked his father.

"I've been looking, but we have barely had time to get settled in. There is no hurry."

"It was a mistake to sell your company here. You could consider returning. We have a vacancy on the board. We've held it open in case you changed your mind."

"Don't do that. We are all returning to Sacramento as soon as the wedding is over."

"I understand Miss Spooner lives in Memphis. I assume she'll be returning there," Mrs. Siebert said.

"No," Zack said firmly. "Annie will be staying with Katie."

"At your house? But Daniel is there. That's unsuitable," Mrs. Siebert said.

"That's enough," Dan warned gently, but he was ignored.

"A newlywed couple are hardly proper chaperones for two single young people, especially when we know nothing about—"

"Mother!" Dan growled. "You will mind your manners."

"Daniel, don't speak to your mother in that tone of voice," Lorraine said, annoyed. "She's only concerned about—"

"Don't tell me what to say or how to say it."

"Dan," Annie said demurely, capturing the attention of everyone around the table. "Could we ask your grandmother to go with us? If she lived with us, we'd be proper. And the climate in California might help her arthritis."

"I'm sorry, that isn't possible," Mr. Siebert said. "My mother is too old for such a trip. It would be much too hard."

"But our trip was marvelous the last time," Annie argued gently. "She'd be very comfortable, truly."

"I think it a splendid idea," Jane said enthusiastically. "She needs to get out more, and we are all guilty of putting our interests before hers. She spends far too much time in those rooms upstairs. What do you say, Grandmother? Would you like to go with Dan?"

"I don't want her going across the country from us. We're her family."

"So is Dan," Zack said. "We'd take the best possible care of her."

"I don't like it," said Mrs. Siebert. "If she goes, then Dan won't be coming back."

"I won't be coming back in any event, except to visit," Dan said. "My home is in Sacramento."

"But you're living at Zack's house," Lorraine argued. "It's hardly the same thing."

"I am having my own house built this fall, on five acres adjoining Zack's land. We'll share the lane."

"We had hoped you'd see reason by now," Mrs. Smythe said, affronted. "Lorraine can't wait forever for you to settle down. She already has several young men interested in her."

If that was meant to bring Dan to heel, it failed miserably. "I'm happy to hear it," Dan said. "I gather these young men are willing to remain in Philadelphia."

"Indeed they are. This is where my daughter wishes to live. How could you even suggest taking her away from the comforts she's grown up with?"

Zack chuckled. "My home has all new plumbing, with hot and cold running water, flush toilets, gas lighting, and central heating throughout its fourteen very large rooms. It is in sparkling condition, and I daresay we'll have electric lighting before very much longer."

"All that is true," Dan said, "but I must remind you that I never once suggested your daughter go with me."

"But your mother . . ."

"My mother had no right."

"Daniel," Logan Siebert barked.

"Logan, the boy is right," Grandmother Siebert said. "He must be permitted the prerogative of arranging his own life."

"But he doesn't have to arrange yours."

"Grandmother," Dan said, "before you decide what you want to do, I must warn you that you will not be permitted to while your days away in bed or sitting in your rooms. We all have work to do."

"Work?" Logan choked out. "My mother will not—"

"What sort of work, Daniel?" Grandmother asked.

"For starters, I'd like your advice in planning my house. Eventually I'd like you to help with decorating. In the meantime, Zack has a garden and orchards that will need your expertise. There will be vegetables to prepare for canning and drying, and in the fall we'll have fruit to put up. And I'd like to enjoy some of your baking again. We have a fine woman who keeps house and cooks for us, but she can't manage everything. We could use another pair of hands."

"And sewing," Annie said. "I'd like to learn to sew." And read, but she didn't dare say that.

"And when the children come along, they'll need a grandmother around," Zack added.

Kate could see what they were doing. In Sacramento Grandmother Siebert would be an integral part of the family, she'd have a contribution to make. She'd have a reason to get up in the morning. She'd feel needed and wanted and productive again.

"What they're saying," Kate explained to the lady at her side, "is that we'd love to have you come live with us."

Her white head nodded. "I think I'd like that, too."

"You can't be serious," Mrs. Siebert exclaimed.

"But I am. You see, Jane is right. I am not yet ready to sit in my rocker and wait to die. Oh yes, I should be delighted to travel again. Do you mind, Daniel, having this old lady under your roof?"

"Why should I mind? We'll have great fun. And you'll like Martha, our housekeeper. She's a darling. Where shall we put her, Zack?"

"I think the north corner. We can install an elevator. Or there is the room—"

"Why don't we let her choose?" Kate suggested, smiling at her new grandmother. "It's not as if we've a shortage of rooms."

"I suppose if you're sure," Logan said uneasily.

"Yes, dear boy, I am. You've been wonderful to give me a home, but . . ."

"You'll always have a home here. You know that."

"Yes, I know. But I don't have many years left. I'd like a few last adventures."

"I can almost guarantee that, if you live with Miss Spooner," Dan said.

"Me? It's Kate who started all this."

In the swing of it again, Dan baited her. "Kate wasn't the one who bit a stranger, attacked the sheriff, and got herself kidnapped."

Grandmother Siebert's eyes widened. "You omitted a few parts of your story this afternoon, I see."

"Well, you know how it is," she said, throwing Dan a glance of daggers.

"Not really," Jane said dryly. "Why don't you enlighten us?"

And so, much to the Smythes' chagrin, Annie and Kate shared center stage for the duration of the meal, telling tales on themselves and on Zack and Dan. By the time coffee was served, the entire Siebert clan, save for Mrs. Siebert, who continued to hold out hope what Dan would come home, had become enamored of both their visitors.

Later that night Dan and Annie helped Grandmother to her room where Bea was waiting to help her into bed. Dan kissed her forehead.

"I'm glad you're coming with us."

"If you have second thoughts, you must let me know."

"Don't worry, we won't." Annie assured her. "Goodnight, Grandmother."

Dan walked Annie toward her room. He very casually draped his arm over her shoulders. Surprisingly she didn't object.

"Are you sleepy yet?"

"I should be, but no. Why?"

"Would you like to get out of the house and go for a walk with me?"

"Just the two of us? You're not going to start that funny business again, are you?"

He grinned and whisked her downstairs and out the front doors. The night was warm, the sky clear and star-studded. They walked toward a park at the end of the street.

"You are happy your grandmother is coming to California? You're not just saying that?"

"Not at all," he said. "I love that old lady. When no one else was in my corner, I could always count on her."

"I think under that stuffy, starchy shirt, there beats a soft heart," she teased.

Dan pulled her to a stop in the shadows of a stand of trees. He took her by the shoulders and turned her to face him.

"Daniel Siebert, if you try to kiss me again, I swear I'll blacken your eye again."

"I shouldn't have done it the first time. I haven't been able to forget it all afternoon or evening. Every time I looked at you at supper, I wanted to kiss you again. And I had to endure Lorraine's inane chatter instead."

"Poor Daniel."

He pulled her against him and locked her in his embrace. "Did no one ever tell you it is unwise to tease the tiger when you are inside his cage?"

"Let me go, Dan. I don't want this," she claimed, but she couldn't take her eyes from his lips.

"I don't believe you." His head lowered to hers.

"I mean it. I'll fight you."

"Wait till afterward." His lips brushed the skin above one eye and down the side of her face.

"Dan, this scares me."

"Hey, it's only me. You aren't afraid of me."

"No, but . . ."

"Relax, Annie. See how good it feels? Is your heart pounding?"

"Oh, Dan," she sighed, giving in to the temptation to taste his kiss again, not yet ready to put a stop to the sweet pleasure coursing through her viens, wanting his lips on her skin for just a little longer. "One, okay? Just one."

"Just one," he agreed, tilting her face up to his. But it was a kiss he intended to claim to the fullest extent.

# Chapter 24

By the end of the week Kate's dress was ready, as was Annie's, and all arrangements for the wedding were finalized. Mrs. Siebert was coming to accept Annie's presence in her home and on what she considered the fringes of Dan's life. Dan, on the other hand, was showing an increasing inclination to seek out Annie and tease her until she was on the verge of a fit of temper.

"They might make a go of it, they might not," Grandmother said to Kate. "But I've not seen this much life in my youngest grandson since he left his teens. I feared he'd die of old age before I did."

"Is that true? Goodness, this is rather normal for them, except that Annie was the one doing the bedevilling before. The worm has turned."

Kate glanced across the room at Zack, who stood staring out the window. His back was rigid, his head held stiffly, as if he feared it might bob if not tightly controlled. His legs were taut, the muscles of his arms flexing as his hands gripped the window frame. Where Dan had relaxed in the past week, Zack had grown more aloof, more distant, more tense.

Kate had tried to talk to him, but he had replied with platitudes that told her nothing of what was troubling him, and made it impossible for her to understand or help.

She knew he missed being alone with her. She could see his frustration in the way his eyes burned into her when he watched her and the way he'd suddenly turn away or leave the room, almost as if he were furious with her and couldn't stand to be near her.

And what could she do about that when she was a guest in a very proper household? She wouldn't for anything offend the people who had been gracious enough to take her to their hearts and give her a wedding she'd always dreamed of.

"Excuse me, Grandmother, but I must see if I can learn what is troubling Zack," she said quietly.

"My dear, he is bothered by time. Too much time. He needs you, but he's too much of a gentleman to come to you in Logan Siebert's home."

"I was just thinking that very thing," she admitted.

"Zachery," Grandmother said from her overstuffed chair in the vast parlor. "Zachery, I have a request to make."

"Yes, of course. How can I be of assistance?"

"I have made arrangements to lease the private car called the Dugan's Palace for our trip to Califronia. I thought it more advisable than travelling in regular first class cars, since I can nap in my compartment when I wish without disturbing the rest of you, and without other passengers disturbing me."

"Yes. That's fine. Dan and I had already begun making inquiries. How did you locate this car? We hadn't yet been able to find one for rent."

"It belongs to an acquaintance. But you see, my dear, I have not seen this car and cannot vouch for its adequacy. I was hoping to get one of the boys to check on its condition, but as they seem to have gone the way of the wind, perhaps you'd be good enough. You might consider taking Miss Montgomery with you. She could use an outing."

"Let's do, Zack," Kate encouraged, seeing him begin to relax already. "We'll make a list of what we need to take for the journey. We may have to buy some games to help pass the time."

If ever there was a mind she could read, it was Zack's at that moment, and his thoughts screamed at her that they would be needing no silly games to occupy their time.

"Zachery Standish, don't think you're going to monopolize this young woman all the way to California."

Kate laughed, and Zack pulled a sheepish grin. Then his eyes began to dance with devilry. He bent down on one knee and kissed the grand old lady's cheek and held her time-worn hand to his heart.

"'Tis you, love of my life, I shall monopolize. We shall watch the stars fill the prairie sky, listen to the wind sing our songs of love, ride up the mountains into the very clouds of rapture."

She swatted him. "Don't be blabberin' out that blarney to me. I know a rake when I see one. Now off you go."

Zack laughed and stood up, grabbing Kate by the waist and lifting her over his head. He swung her in a circle, ignoring her squeals of protest.

"Are you willin', Katie girl, 'cause if you come with me, I intend to ravish you."

She blushed, but at the same time felt a hot thrill course through her, leaving her body aching. Zack stood her on the floor and waited for her response.

"Ravish, hmmm?" She glanced at Grandmother Siebert, who was busy sewing with a knowing grin on her face.

"Well?" Zack shrugged into his coat. "I'm going. Are you coming?"

Grandmother Siebert looked up, glancing from one to the other. "A rake and a rogue," she said, condemning him with a nod of certainty.

"What exactly do you mean by 'ravish'?" Kate asked.

"Yes or no? Decide now."

"Well, I . . . Yes. No, wait."

"Too late," he said, capturing her wrist. "You're mine."

Kate was dragged toward the door. She turned helpless eyes to the older woman. "Am I going to like this?" she cried.

"Depends on how good a rake he is," was her reply as Zack pulled her out the door.

Dugan's Palace was every bit as plush and polished as their previous private car had been, only it was slightly longer, allowing it smaller but more numerous compartments for sleeping. They looked through three standard sleeping rooms, each with an upper and lower bunk, then they found the one Zack had been looking for—a compartment with a double bed. He pulled her into the small quarters and closed and locked the door. He turned toward her and reached up to untie his tie and slip it from around his neck.

His eyes, almost totally black in the darkened compartment, burned into hers, hypnotizing her, paralyzing her as a predator immobolizes its prey.

"Zack," she said, her voice dry and husky.

"Do you know how long it's been? How many agonizing days of watching your body move, remembering what you look like without all those layers of clothes, of the tormenting nights, remembering how you felt in my arms, skin to skin, with my body buried deep within yours. And knowing a thin wall was all that separated you from me. I can't wait three more days until the wedding."

"I thought you were having doubts."

"The only thing I doubted was my ability to conceal from the world how much I wanted you." His coat and shirt came off. "Undress for me, Katie. I'm in no mood to be patient."

Without even touching her, he had turned her into a quivering mass of sensations. Her blood ran hot and thick through her veins, her body turned to warm flowing liquid, in sweet expectation of her lover's possession.

Her fingers trembled as she dealt with the front buttons of her dress. Why did she receive the same devastating jolt of desire every time she looked upon his bare shoulders and chest? Why, when she knew the clean lines of bone and muscle, when she'd run her hands over his firm flesh and felt the tickle of his crisp body hair on the palm of her hand, did the mere sight of him set up such a clamor among her nerve ends? Would it always be so? She felt helpless, she felt caught up and swept away into the depths of his raw passion.

He stood before her in all his naked splendor, tall, dark, gloriously magnificent, and altogether dangerous, and her fingers ceased to work on the delicate laces of her undergarments.

"I can't—Zack . . ."

His hands reached forward and he rent the fine fabric in two, sliding it and the rest of her clothing from her limbs. Her stockings he rolled down her legs with exquisite slowness, following his hands with the softest brush of his lips, until her muscles were trembling and her knees too weak to hold her weight.

When her last garment was removed, he rose to his feet, sliding his hands possessively up the outside of her legs, over the gentle curve of her hips, to the indentation of her slender waist where his grip tightened convulsively.

He had no words of praise or encouragement, love or need. They had been said before, they would be said countless times again, but not now.

He held her away, and with fever bright eyes, he devoured her. His breathing was fast and shallow, his muscles tensed, his nostrils flared, as if in the grip of a fierce tide of emotion.

She didn't fully understand what he was feeling, for in the past his passion had been cloaked in patience and gentleness, but she did know that there would be no concessions this time. She was no longer an innocent girl, she would soon be a wife. The wife of a very virile man. She wanted to be all the woman that he would ever need.

She met his gaze unflinchingly, raising her arms to her hair. His breath hissed sharply inward as her back arched and her firm, full breasts were thrown outward. She smiled a secretive, feline smile and deliberately removed each pin from her hair, letting them fall carelessly to the floor at her feet. With her head thrown back and the pearly white column of her neck submissively exposed, she shook her long mane of raven hair free and tossed it loose with her fingers.

"Witch," he growled.

In a very firm and quick move she found herself pinned to the bed, trapped by his superior weight and strength.

His lips met hers as she crushed her breasts against the hard wall of his chest. Her mouth opened instinctively to allow his bold possession, and he kissed her savagely, drinking from the sweetness of her offering, driven by his pent-up frustrations, his worries, his never-ceasing need to know she was completely and forever his.

Their joining was quick, elemental, and ecstatic, it was an agony of need whose power and demand could and would not be denied.

For Kate it was an experience of wonderment. The

aggression of his desire called forth an answering passion in her that she had never imagined existed. She left her innocence behind, with its hesitation, reluctance, its genteel self-consciousness, and moved into full womanhood where her passion dared to be as demanding as his.

With each kiss, each caress, each sinuous undulation of body against body, their passion grew until its violent culmination tossed them into a world of bliss.

They clung rapturously to each other, their sweat-slicked bodies melding and moving together as their passion receded.

"Katie, my precious Katie," Zack murmured. "You are incredible. God, how I love you."

"I love you, too. I hope I don't have to move for a long time. I have no strength left."

Zack rolled to his side, pulling Kate into his arms. He kissed her closed eyes. "Sleep if you want to. We have all afternoon."

"Have I been thoroughly ravished?"

"Not even close."

The next two days passed uneventfully, although Kate still sensed an inner tension in Zack. He claimed her imagination was overactive and teased her that she wanted him to be tense so she would have an excuse to sneak into his room at night.

"Or are you having second thoughts?" he asked.

"How did I become the subject of this discussion? We were talking about you. You're being deviously evasive, Zack, and I don't like it. If something is bothering you, I want to know about it."

"Don't worry," he said, brushing a wisp of hair from her forehead. "Tomorrow is our wedding day, and neither of us is going to fret about a thing. This is our time, our special moment. Are you looking forward to it, sweetheart?"

"Yes, I am. I just wish . . ."

"What?"

She shrugged and shook her head. "It's silly, but I wish my grandfather could be here."

"I think he'll be watching, and I hope he'd have been

satisfied with your choice of men."

"He would have been, and you know it. It's Bennett, isn't it?"

He gave her a fierce look. "Don't jump to conclusions. Why would I worry about him?"

"Zack Standish, if you think I'm going to marry a man who only considers me an adult in bed, you're crazy."

"I don't want you to worry."

"You'd rather brood by yourself and leave me to wonder why?"

"Well, no, but . . ."

"Is Bennett in Philadelphia?"

"We think so. Phillips traced him to a town south of us. He lost him there."

"What can he do, Zack? We're surrounded by dozens of friends. Besides, with my grandfather's will duly registered, Sam can't hope to gain anything by killing me. And you said, yourself, that the court is reopening the investigation into my mother's death and Miles Beauchamp's. Sam can't afford to show his face."

"Yes. Perhaps you're right, and I'm worrying for nothing."

But he continued to watch the people around them, to eye each vehicle that passed them, to study every face. Zack was alert and waiting. Zack knew he would come. Kate knew Zack was right.

It wasn't until they were all assembled in the church the next day that Zack finally gave a sigh of relief and relaxed. He looked around the group gathered in the bride's room and smiled. For the first time, Kate fully realized how anxious he was to get the wedding done with, not for his own sake, but to insure her safety.

Was Zack assuming that once they were married, Bennett would come after him instead of her? Kate knew Bennett better than that. As she'd said on several occasions, Bennett had lost, and he knew it. If he came for her now, and it looked as if he might have done so, it would be out of hatred and pure revenge. Whether or not she was married made no difference.

"You are beautiful," Zack said, raising her fingers to his lips.

"And you are quite dashing. And suddenly I'm very nervous."

Annie snorted. "It's about time. A bride's supposed to be nervous. Be still now, your veil is crooked."

Grandmother Siebert slipped into the room. "Everyone is seated. Are you ready, my dears?"

"I think so," Kate said. "Are you certain it's all right for us to depart from tradition?"

"Tradition is nothing more than someone's idea of how something should be done. I always did think it silly to keep a man and woman apart until they met at the altar."

"That's good, because I'm not changing my mind about that either," Zack said immovably. "Katie goes down the aisle on my arm. We go together to be married."

"And it will be beautiful. Now I must go. Daniel, as soon as the processional begins, you and Annie lead the way. Don't forget the rings."

"I won't, Grandmother," he said forbearingly, but chuckled, nevertheless, as soon as she was out of sight.

The church was beautiful, done in a profusion of white and blue flowers with rows of tall blue candles behind them. Kate's dress was white with a dash of blue trim, and Annie's was blue, trimmed in white. Zack had selected the colors, and had insisted they be the exact shade of Kate's eyes, and no amount of teasing by the other men over the exorbitant cost could sway him.

The processional began, and Dan held out his arm to Annie. "Maybe we should do this, too, my girl."

"Are you crazy? Daniel Siebert, have you been hittin' the bottle?"

"Now, Annie," he cajoled. "Someone had to test the punch and taste the champagne."

"Champagne? We're having champagne?"

"Naturally. Don't you like it?"

"I've never tasted it."

He led her to the long center aisle of the sanctuary, and they began their slow walk.

"We could do it, Annie," he whispered through still lips. "Think of the time and money we could save."

"Why you—you—"

"Eh, eh, watch your temper. Hundreds of eyes are looking at you."

She smiled straight ahead but gave his arm a sharp pinch. He stiffened and winced slightly, but his own grin remained intact. "Tsk, tsk," he clucked.

"When I get married, it won't be to a miser."

"You think I'm a miser? I'm the one who spent a fortune on your wardrobe."

"That was Zack."

"Huh-uh."

"Really?"

"I've kept the receipts."

"What for? So you can gloat?"

The congregation stood as Zack and Kate started down the aisle, and with their attention directed elsewhere, Annie chanced a look at Dan. He was grinning down at her.

"There's still time."

She threw him a scathing look. "Don't be absurd. I'm not marrying you."

"I think you will."

"And pigs can fly."

Zack's hand tightened over Kate's as they took the last remaining steps to the altar. Their gazes met and held as the organist finished the last phrase.

"I love you," she said simply.

"And I, you."

The church doors slammed behind them, and Zack went rigid. Kate knew without turning who stood at the back of the church.

"Dearly beloved," the minister intoned. Kate didn't hear the rest. The fine hairs on the back of her neck were standing on end. She glanced up at Zack, whose eyes were narrowed and whose jaw was clenched.

"Is there any here who knows just cause why these two should not be joined in marriage? If so, let him—"

"I have cause," bellowed Sam Bennett, and Kate's heart

sank. The perfect revenge. No wonder John Phillips couldn't find him. Sam was waiting to ruin her wedding.

A murmur of curiosity rolled through the church as eyes swivelled from the bride to the intruder.

"That snake," Annie exclaimed, not bothering to hold down her voice. "How dare he."

"Easy, now," Dan warned softly.

"The woman is my ward and does not have my permission to marry this man. I forbid it." With that statement ringing in the sudden silence, he took a long-barreled revolver from beneath his coat and aimed it at the couple at the front of the church. A collective gasp sounded loudly in the sanctuary. Zack stepped forward, pushing Kate behind him.

"She caused my daughter's death," Sam Bennett raved, stepping closer and closer. "She doesn't deserve to live. She must pay so my baby can rest peacefully."

"Bennett," Zack barked. "Put down the gun."

"I want Katrina. No one will get hurt if she comes with me. I'll kill you and as many others as I have to if you try to stop me."

"Okay, Sam, I'm coming. I'll go with you," Kate cried. "Just don't hurt anyone."

"No." Zack vetoed her offer with deadly menace. "You will never come near my wife again."

"Move away from her, or I'll shoot. I'll do it."

"Zack, please. Let me go," Kate pleaded.

"Never," he barked, holding her firmly behind him. "He'll have to kill me first."

A woman stepped into the aisle, a slight and very aged woman. "And you'll have to kill me also," she said.

"Mother, sit down," Logan Siebert hissed.

Annie stared wide-eyed at the nerve of the old lady. Then she grinned. She stepped forward and stood beside Grandmother Siebert. "And me, Mr. Bennett. I kept you from having her twice before. I can do it again."

"You! I should kill you right now."

"God will strike you dead for daring to defile his house," Grandmother decreed.

"Get back where you were," Bennett roared. His hands

shook on the gun. "I'll pull this trigger."

"And when you've killed them, you'll have to go through me," Dan said.

"And me," another said, followed by another, until Kate and Zack were completely cut off from Sam Bennett and his gun.

A loud commotion at the back of the church drew Sam's attention. He swung around and came face to face with Peter Standish.

Sam appeared disoriented. "Peter, you deserted me. You didn't even come for the funeral. You betrayed me when I needed you most."

"Sorry, Sam. I shouldn't have done that. Now let's get out of here and leave these folks to their wedding."

"No. She has to die. She killed Corinne."

"You killed Corinne, Sam. You took her out there, you used too much dynamite, you didn't see that she was protected. Don't blame Katrina for your neglect."

"Shut up. Shut up," he bellowed, going vivid red.

"But it's true. You're to blame for all Corinne's troubles. Her madness came from your loins. You fed it, you let it grow. You didn't love her. If you'd loved her, you would not have let her die."

"No!" Sam cried in anguished denial, then he dropped the gun and grabbed his head. He staggered toward Peter, but he wasn't seeing Peter or anything else. His knees buckled and he crumpled to the floor.

Peter rushed forward and retrieved the gun. He rolled Sam over and checked his pulse. Zack and Kate pushed their way through the crowded aisle, both kneeling beside Bennett's unconscious form.

"Is he . . .?" Kate asked.

"He's alive, but I think he's had a stroke. Don't start taking the blame for this, Katrina. He's been working himself up to it for years now."

"But I . . ."

"You did nothing but fight for your life. He wanted to kill you. I found I couldn't let him do that. I followed him here, hoping I wouldn't be too late."

Zack looked at the stranger who was his brother. He held out his hand, feeling all his resentment drain away.

"Thank you for coming, Peter. Thank you for—caring."

"Long overdue, I'd say. Ah, I hear the police wagon. When I learned about your wedding plans, I knew he'd come. I notified the police. We'll soon be out of your way, and you can go on with your ceremony. I wish you happiness."

"You won't stay?" Zack asked, surprising himself.

"No. Not yet. One day soon I'll come to Sacramento to visit. I need to get my own life in order first. You made me see that, Katrina. I'll say good-bye, then. Oh, and one more thing. What you said—about my investment . . ."

Kate nodded. "Send the documents to Sacramento along with the name of your bank. I'll see that your money is transferred to you."

"Thank you. I know it's insufficient to say that I'm sorry, but I am. And I do wish you well. Both of you."

The police came in and carried Sam Bennett to the wagon. Logan Siebert explained what had happened and directed them to come to the house that evening if they had further questions, but as Peter was intending to go with them, Kate imagined they'd get the entire story.

"Wow. You can't even get married without turning it into another hair-raising adventure," Annie said, coming to Kate's side.

Kate looked at her incredulously, then burst out laughing. "And what possessed you to jump right into the middle of it?"

"I told you. I'm beginning to like adventure."

"Wonderful. We should try getting married, then," Dan said in her ear. "I'll give you an adventure."

"I'm not getting married," she retorted, causing a few heads to turn in her direction.

Dan laughed until Grandmother Siebert brought order to her clan. "All right. We shall start at the beginning. Mrs. Webster, if you'll take your place at the organ, and Pastor, if you please, you may escort me to my pew. All the rest of you, sit back down. We've come for a wedding, a wedding we'll have."

# Chapter 25

Kate sat at her dressing table, brushing out her hair, looking at her reflection in the mirror. Her eyes were bright with anticipation, but she had the look of a woman who'd already been made love to, rather than that of one who was planning to ravish her husband.

A knock sounded at her door. "Come," she said, and watched Annie enter the room with a tray of tea.

"Are you excited?" Annie asked.

"Terribly. You don't think he suspects?"

"No. Mrs. Williams is the only one who knows besides Grandma Vi and me. She's prepared the best room in the hotel for you. And she'll have champagne and an anniversary cake."

"Are you sure you don't want to come?"

"Positive. While you're celebrating your first year of marriage, I'll be telling Dan that we're going to have a baby."

Kate jumped up and hugged her. "Oh, Annie, that's wonderful news."

"I saw the doctor today, but Grandma Vi already told me I was pregnant. And that old lady's always right. But I'm nervous about telling Dan. What if he isn't pleased?"

"Megan will have a playmate. What fun they'll have together."

"We've only been married three months."

"We'll have to put up another swing. And build a playhouse."

"Katie, you aren't listening. Dan may hate the idea."

"Oh, pooh."

Just then Megan, a black-haired, blue-eyed baby of two months, set up a ferocious howl in the next room.

"I'll get her," Annie offered eagerly.

"No, wait. Just listen for a minute."

Presently they heard footsteps coming up the stairs. Kate threw on her robe, and she and Annie tiptoed down the hall to Megan's room.

Dan stood over Megan's crib, playing with her. They watched as he changed her wet diaper, cooing strange sounds to her as he did so.

Kate turned sardonic eyes to Annie. "Any more doubts?" she whispered.

They tiptoed away and returned less quietly. Dan had picked Megan up and was walking her across the room and back. He looked up as they came in.

"I hope you don't mind, but I heard her crying. I think she's hungry."

"I'll take her. She's probably wet, too."

"No, I already changed her."

"You did? That was nice, wasn't it, Megan? Did Uncle Dan stick you with the pins?"

"I most certainly did not, and we can't have the poor scrap lying around in sodden diapers. So if you have everything under control now, I'll go back to my accounts."

Zack came home while Kate was feeding Megan. He came into the nursery to sit with her. He said he liked to watch her feed their child. As soon as Megan had taken her fill, she turned to the sound of her father's voice. It had become a ritual. Zack would spend the hour between the baby's five o'clock feeding and his own supper playing with her, and it was apparent by how she cooed and laughed, patted his face and gave him sloppy wet kisses, that Megan adored her father.

"I'll finish getting dressed. Don't forget we're having dinner at the hotel tonight."

"Oh, I had forgotten. Do we have to?"

Her lips tightened in exasperation. "Yes. This is a night you won't want to miss."

"With whom are we dining?" he asked innocently.

She tried to keep a straight face, but her days of hiding her feelings were long over. She laughed. "You scoundrel. I don't believe for a moment that you don't know."

"Know? Know what?"

"Oooh," she growled. "We're expected at seven-thirty. Don't be late."

"You hear that, Meggie. She's making me leave my little princess and the comfort of my castle. What do you have to say about that?"

Megan's "goo-goo-ga-eee" was almost impossible to interpret. "She wants you to come with me," Kate declared.

"She said that, did she?"

"Didn't you hear her?"

Kate left him to enjoy his daughter and returned to their room. There, she put the finishing touches on her face and hair, and donned her new dress, an elegant gown in Zack's favorite shade of blue. She packed a case for them for the next day and asked Rollins to put it in the back of the buggy, and asked for the third time if Martha and Grandma Vi, Grandmother Elvira Siebert's shortened name, could manage feeding Megan in her absence.

"Now you just go and have a wonderful time, and don't worry about that little angel. If we don't spoil her, Mr. Dan will," Martha said.

At half past seven Zack came down the stairs in his best suit. He looked at Kate and gave a low whistle through his teeth.

"Our dinner guests must be very important," he said.

"Indeed. Shall we go? Rollins already brought the buggy around."

"Why don't we stay home tonight? We'll send Rollins into town with a message for Mrs. Williams. It's a great night for staying home."

Kate plunked her fists on her hips, glaring at him. "I [illegible] going, Zack Standish. Are you coming or not? Before [illegible] answer, be warned that I intend to ravish you."

"What?" he hooted.

"Yes or no? Decide now."

He threw his head back and laughed. "I don't [illegible] You're going to ra . . ."

"Yes or no?"

"Yes."

"Good. We bid you goodnight," she said, encompassing the others in a glance. "Come along, Zack. We mustn't be late."

"You intend to ravish me?" he said incredulously when they were in the buggy and on their way to town.

"You think I can't do it?"

"Well, be reasonable. Ravishment would indicate a certain amount of strength, one over the other."

She laid her hand on his thigh and traced a small pattern with her forefinger. She felt his body's immediate reaction. Slowly she inched her fingers higher.

"Well, my darling," she said provocatively. "There we disagree. I do not need strength when I have—power."

He stopped her hand with his own and gave her a sidelong look from beneath cocked brows.

"So you are in the mood to be reckless tonight. That could land you in trouble." Zack leered at her threateningly, but inside his heart swelled with love.

He knew his young wife well after a year of marriage. Every now and then she'd devise some scheme to seduce him. More often than not, he would turn the tables on her and have her begging to be loved. It was a game, and a game where they both won. But maybe tonight, since she obviously had some extravagant plan in motion, he'd let her win. But not until after he'd given her the present he had tucked in his pocket, a very expensive present, and not until after he'd told her how very much he loved her.